Dealings With The Dead
Vol. I

by

Lucius M. Sargent

Double9
BOOKS

Dealings With The Dead
Vol. I
by Lucius M. Sargent

ISBN: 978-93-61155-39-0

Published by

DOUBLE 9 BOOKS
2/13-B, Ansari Road
Daryaganj, New Delhi – 110002
info@double9books.com
www.double9books.com
Tel. 011-40042856

This book is under public domain

ABOUT THE AUTHOR

Lucius Manlius Sargent was an American novelist, antiquarian, and temperance campaigner who belonged to the well-known Sargent family of Boston. Daniel Sargent Sr. (1730-1806) and Mary Turner (1744-1813), daughter of John Turner of The House of the Seven Gables, had seven children, the youngest of whom was born in Boston. His father was a merchant dealing in fishermen's supplies who had relocated from Gloucester to Boston and profited so greatly from his industry, prudence, and popularity that he occupied what was at the time a conspicuously expensive mansion, despite his reputation for thrift and a dislike of ostentation. He was the brother of businessman-politician Daniel Sargent and artist Henry Sargent (father of Henry Winthrop Sargent), the cousin of Judith Sargent Murray, an early advocate for women's equality, and the nephew of Paul Dudley Sargent, an American Revolutionary War veteran. His paternal grandpa was Epes Sargent, a Massachusetts General Court representative.

CONTENTS

"THE BURIAL SERVICE"

This is a very solemn service, when it is properly performed. When I was a youngster, Grossman was Sexton of Trinity Church, and Parker was Bishop. Never were two men better calculated to give the true effect to this service. The Bishop was a very tall, erect person, with a deep, sonorous voice; and, in the earth-to-earth part, Grossman had no rival. I used to think, then, it would be the height of my ambition to fill Grossman's place, if I should live to be a man. When I was eight years old, I sometimes, though it frightened me half to death, dropped in, as an amateur, when there was a funeral at Trinity.

I am not, on common occasions, in favor of reviving the old way of performing a considerable part of the service, under the church, among the vaults. The women, and feeble, and nervous people will go down, of course; and getting to be buried becomes contagious. It does them no good, if they don't catch their deaths. But, as things are now managed, the most solemn part of the service is made quite ridiculous. In 1796, I was at a funeral, under Trinity Church. I went below with the mourners. The body was carried into a dimly-lighted vault. I was so small and short, that I could see scarcely anything. But the deep, sepulchral voice of Mr. Parker—he was not Bishop then—filled me with a most delightful horror. I listened and shivered. At length he uttered the words, "earth to earth," and Grossman, who did his duty, marvellously well, when he was sober, rattled on the coffin a whole shovelful of coarse gravel—"ashes to ashes"—another shovelful of gravel—"dust to dust"—another: it seemed as if shovel and all were cast upon the coffin lid. I never forgot it. My way home from school was through Summer Street. Returning often, in short days, after dusk, I have run, at the top of my speed, till I had gotten as far beyond Trinity, as Tommy Russell's, opposite what now is Kingston Street.

A great change has taken place, since I became a sexton. I suppose that part of the service is the most solemn, where the body is committed to the ground; and it is clearly a pity, that anything should occur, to lessen the solemnity. As soon as the minister utters the words, "Forasmuch as it hath pleased Almighty God," &c., the coffin being in the broad aisle, the sexton, now-a-days, steps up to the right of it, and makes ready by stooping down, and picking up a little sand, out of a box or saucer—a few more words, and he takes aim—"earth to earth," and he fires an insignificant portion of it on to the coffin—"ashes to ashes," and he fires another volley—"dust to dust," and he throws the balance, commonly wiping his hand on his sleeve. There is something, insufferably awkward, in the performance. I heard a young sexton say, last week, he had rather bury half the congregation, than go through this comic part. There is some grace, in the action of a farmer, sowing barley; but there is a feeling of embarrassment, in this miserable illustration of casting in the clods upon the dead, which characterizes the performance. The sexton commonly tosses the sand on the coffin, turning his head the other way, and rather downward, as if he were sensible, that he was performing an awkward ceremony. For myself, I am about retiring, and it is of little moment to me. But I hope something better will be thought of. What would poor old Grossman say!

A Sexton of the Old School.

No. I

Throw aside whatever I send you, if you do not like it, as we throw aside the old bones, when making a new grave; and preserve only what you think of any value—with a slight difference—you will publish it, and we shouldn't. I was so fond of using the thing, which I have now in my hand, when a boy, that my father thought I should never succeed with the mattock and spade—he often shook his head, and said I should never make a sexton. He was mistaken. He was a shrewd old man, and I got many a valuable hint from him. "Abner," said he to me one day, when he saw me bowing, very obsequiously, to a very old lady, "don't do so, Abner; old folks are never pleased with such attentions, from people of your profession. They consider all personal approaches, from one of your fraternity, as wholly premature. It brings up unpleasant anticipations." Father was right; and, when I meet a very old, or feeble, or nervous gentleman, or lady, I always walk fast, and look the other way.

Sextons have greatly improved within the last half century. In old times, they kept up too close an intimacy with young surgeons; and, to keep up their spirits, in cold vaults, they formed too close an alliance with certain evil spirits, such as gin, rum, and brandy. We have greatly improved, as a class, and are destined, I trust, to still greater elevation. A few of us are thinking of getting incorporated. I have read—I read a great deal—I have carried a book, of some sort, in my pocket for fifty years—no profession loses so much time, in mere waiting, as ours—I have read, that the barbers and surgeons of London were incorporated, as one company, in the time of Henry VIII. There is certainly a much closer relation, between the surgeons and sextons, than between the barbers and surgeons, since we put the finishing hand to their work. And as every body is getting incorporated now-a-days, I see no good reason against our being incorporated, as a society of sextons and surgeons. And then our toils and vexations would, in some measure, be solaced, by pleasant meetings and convivial suppers, at which the surgeons would cut up roast turkeys, and the sextons might bury their sorrows. When sextons have no particular digging to do, out of doors, it seems well enough for them to dig in their closets. There is a great amount of information to be gained from books, particularly adapted to their profession, some of which is practical, and some of which, though not of that description, is of a much more profitable character than police reports of rapes and murders, or the histories of family quarrels, or interminable rumors of battles and bloodshed. There is a learned blacksmith; who knows but there may spring up a learned sexton, some of these days.

The dealings with the dead, since the world began, furnish matter for curious speculation. What has seemed meet and right, in one age or nation, has appeared absurd and even monstrous in another. It is also interesting to contemplate the many strange dispositions, which certain individuals have directed to be made, in regard to their poor remains. Men, who seem not to have paid much attention to their souls, have provided, in the most careful and curious manner, for the preservation of their miserable carcasses. It may also furnish matter for legitimate inquiry, how far it may be wise, and prudent, and in good taste, to carry our love of finery into the place, appropriated for all living. Aristocracy among the dead! What a thought. Sumptuary considerations are here involved. The rivalry of the tomb! The pride—not of life—but of death! How frequently have I seen, especially among the Irish, the practice of a species of pious fraud upon the baker and the milk man, whose bills were never to be paid, while all the scrapings of the defunct were bestowed upon the "birril!" The principle is one and the same, when men, in higher walks, put costly monuments over the ashes of their dead, and their effects into the hands of assignees. And then the pageantry and grandiloquence of the epitaph! In the course of fifty years, what outrageous lies I have seen, done in marble! Perhaps I may say something of these matters—perhaps not.

No. II

Closing the eyes of the dead and composing the mouth were deemed of so much importance, of old, that Agamemnon's ghost made a terrible fuss, because his wife, Clytemnestra, had neglected these matters, as you will see, in your Odyssey, L. V. v. 419. It was usual for the last offices to be performed by the nearest relatives. After washing and anointing the body, the guests covered it with the *pallium*, or common cloak—the Romans used the *toga*—the Hebrews wrapped the body in linen. Virgil tells us, that Misenus was buried, in the clothes he commonly wore.

> Membra toro deffeta reponunt,
> Purpureasque super vestes velamina nota
> Conjiciunt.

This would seem very strange with us; yet it is usual in some other countries, at this day. I have often seen the dead, thus laid out, in Santa Cruz—coat, neckcloth, waistcoat, pantaloons, boots, and gloves. I was never a sexton there, but noted these matters as an amateur. Chaplets and flowers were cast upon the dead, by the Greeks and Romans. The body was exhibited, or laid in state, near the entrance of the house, that all might see there had been no foul play. While thus lying, it was carefully watched. The body of every man, who died in debt, at Athens, was liable to be seized by creditors. Miltiades died in jail. His son, Cimon, could not pay his father's debts; he therefore assumed his debts and fetters, that his father might have funeral rites. Some time before interment, a piece of money, an *obolus*, was put in the mouth of the corpse, as Charon's fee. In the mouth was also placed a cake, made of flour and honey, to appease Cerberus. Instead of crape upon the knocker, some of the hair of the deceased was placed upon the door, to indicate a house of mourning. A vessel of water was placed before the door, until the corpse was removed, that all who touched the dead might wash therein. This is in accordance with the Jewish usage. Achilles was burnt on the eighteenth day after his death. The upper ten thousand were generally burnt on the eighth, and buried on the ninth. Common folks were dealt with more summarily. When ready for the pile, the body was borne forth on a bier. The Lacedemonians bore it on shields. The Athenians celebrated their obsequies before sunrise. Funerals, in some of our cities, are celebrated in the morning. The Greeks and Romans were very extravagant, like the Irish. If baked meats and Chian and Falernian cost less than in more modern times—still sumptuary laws were found necessary. Pittacus made such, at Mytelene. The women crowded so abominably, at the funerals in Athens, that Solon excluded all women, under threescore years, from gadding after such ceremonies. Robes of mourning were sometimes worn; not always. Thousands followed the bodies of Timoleon and Aratus, in white garments, bedecked with garlands, with songs of triumph and dances, rejoicing, that they were received into Elysium.

After the funeral, they abstained from banquets and entertainments. Admetus says they avoided whatever bore an air of mirth or pleasure, for some time. They sequestered themselves from company. It is particularly stated, by Archbishop Potter, that *"wine was too great a friend of cheerfulness to gain admission into so melancholy a society."* If Old Hundred had been known to the Jews, it would, I dare say, have been considered highly appropriate— but their good taste was such, that I much doubt, if, in the short space of eight and forty hours, they would have mingled *sacra profanis*, so very comically, as to bring champagne and Old Hundred together. The Greek mourners often cut off their hair, and cast it upon the funeral pile. This custom was also followed by the Romans. They sometimes threw themselves upon the ground, to express their sorrow. Like some of the Eastern nations, they put ashes upon their heads. They beat their breasts, tore their flesh, and scratched their faces, with their nails. For this, Dionysius says, the women were more remarkable, than the men.

Burning and embalming, the latter of which was a costly business, were practised among the Greeks and Romans; the latter much more frequently, among the Eastern nations. We talk of getting these matters thoroughly discussed, ere long, before the Sextons' board, to see if it may not be well, to bring them into use again. I will send you the result.

In regard to the use of wine and other intoxicating drinks, at funerals, we much more closely resemble the Lacedemonians now, than we did some thirty years ago. When I was a boy, and was at an academy in the country, everybody went to everybody's funeral, in the village. The population was small—funerals rare—the preceptor's absence would have excited remark, and the boys were dismissed, for the funeral. A table with liquors was always provided. Every one, as he entered, took off his hat, with his left hand, smoothed down his hair, with his right, walked up to the coffin, gazed upon the corpse, made a crooked face, passed on to the table, took a glass of his favorite liquor, went forth upon the plat, before the house, and talked politics, or of the new road, or compared crops, or swapped heifers or horses, until it was time to lift. Twelve years ago, a clergyman of Newburyport told me, that, when settled in Concord, N. H., some years before, he officiated at the funeral of a little boy. The body was borne, as is quite common, in a chaise, and six little nominal pall-bearers, the oldest not thirteen, walked by the side of the vehicle. Before they left the house, a sort of master of ceremonies took them to the table, and mixed a tumbler of gin, water and sugar, for each.

There is in this city a worthy man—I shall not name him—the doctor's and the lawyer's callings are not more confidential than ours. He used to attend every funeral, as an amateur. He took his glass invariably, and always had some good thing to say of the defunct. "A great loss," he would say, with a sad shake of his head, as he turned off the heel-tap. I have not seen him at a funeral, for several years. We met about five months ago. "Ah, Mr. Abner," said he, "temperance has done for funerals."

No. III

The board of sextons have met, and we have concluded not to recommend a revival of the ancient custom of burning the dead. It would be very troublesome to do it, out of town, and inconvenient in the city. I have always thought it wrong to bury in the city; and it would be much worse to burn there. The first law of the tenth table of the Romans is in these words—"Let no dead body be interred or burnt within the city." Something may be got to help pay for a church, by selling tombs below. When a church was built here, some years ago, an eminent physician, one of the proprietors, was consulted and gave his sanction. Yet more than one of our board is very sure, that, on a warm, close Sunday, in the spring, he has snuffed up something that wasn't particularly orthodox, in that church. The old Romans were very careful of the rights of their fellows, in this respect: the twelfth law of the tenth table runs thus—"Let no sepulchre be built, or funeral pile raised within sixty feet of any house, without the consent of the owner of that house." They certainly conducted matters with great propriety, avoiding extravagance and intemperance, as appears by the seventh law of the same table—"Let no slaves be embalmed; let there be no drinking round a dead body; nor any perfumed liquors be poured upon it." So also the second law—"Let all costliness and excessive waitings be banished from funerals." The women were so very troublesome upon these occasions, that a special law, the fifth, was made for their government—"Let not the women tear their faces, or disfigure themselves, or make hideous outcries."

It was not unusual for one person to have several funerals: to prevent this, however agreeable to the Roman undertakers, the tenth law of the tenth table was made—"Let no man have more than one funeral, or more than one bed put under him." There was also a very strange practice during the first Decemvirate; the friends often abstracted a finger of the deceased, or some part of the body, and performed fresh obsequies, in some other place; erecting there a *cenotaph* or *empty* sepulchre, in which they fancied the ghost of the departed took occasional refuge, when wandering about—in case of a sudden shower, perhaps; or being caught out too near daylight.

For the correction of this folly, the Decemvirs passed the sixth law of the tenth table—"Let not any part of a dead body be carried away, in order to perform other obsequies for the deceased, unless he died in war, or out of his own country." It was upon such occasions as these, in which an empty form was observed, and no actual inhumation took place, that the practice of throwing three handsful of earth originated. This usage was practised also by the Jews, and has come down to modern times. Baron Rothschild (Nathan Meyer) who died in Frankfort, July 28, 1836, was buried in the ground of the Synagogue, in Duke's Place, London. His sons, Lionel, Anthony, Nathaniel, and Meyer, his brother-in-law, Mr. Montefiore, and his ancient friend, Mr. Samuels, at the age of ninety-six, commenced the service of filling up the grave,—by casting in, each one of them, three handsful of earth. Not satisfied with carrying a bottle of sal volatile to funerals, the women, and even the men, were in the habit of carrying pots of essences, which occasioned the enactment of the eighth law—"Let no crowns, festoons, perfuming pots, or any kind of perfume be carried to funerals."

Burning or interring was adopted, by the ancients, at the will of the relatives. This is manifest from the eleventh law, which prohibits the use of gold in all obsequies, with a single exception—"Let no gold be used in any obsequies, unless the jaw of the deceased has been tied up with a gold thread. In that case the corpse may be *interred* or *burnt*, with the gold thread." A large quantity of silver is annually buried with the dead. It finds its way up again, however, in the course of time.

Common as burning was, among the ancients, it was looked upon, by some, with great abhorrence. The body to be burned was placed upon a pile—if the body of a person of quality, one or more slaves or captives were burned with it. When not forbidden, all sorts of precious ointments and perfumes were poured upon the corpse. The favorite dogs and horses of the defunct were cast upon the pile. Homer tells us, that four horses, two dogs, and twelve Trojan captives were burnt upon the pile, with the dead body of Patroclus. The corpses, that they might consume the sooner, were covered with the fat of beasts. Some near relative lighted the pile, uttering prayers to Boreas and Zephyrus to increase the flame. The relatives stood around, calling on the deceased, and pouring on libations of wine, with which they finally extinguished the flames, when the pile was well burnt down. They then collected the bones and ashes. How they were ever able to discriminate between men, dogs, and horses, it is hard to say. Probably the whole was sanctified, in their opinion, by juxtaposition. The bones might be distinguished, but not the dust. Such bones as could be identified, were washed and anointed *by the nearest relatives*. What an office! How custom changes the complexion of such matters! These relics were then placed in urns of wood, stone, earth, silver, or gold, according to the quality of the parties. Where are these memorials now! these myriads of urns! They were deposited in tombs—of which a very perfect account may be found in the description of the street of tombs, at Pompeii.

No. IV

The Greeks, when interment was preferred to burning, placed the body in the coffin, as is done at present, deeming it safer for the defunct to look upwards. To ridicule this superstition, Diogenes requested, that his body might be placed face downward, "for the world, erelong," said he, "will be turned upside down, and then I shall come right." The feet were placed towards the East. Those, who were closely allied, were buried together. The epitaph of Agathias, on the twin brothers, is still preserved —

> "Two brothers lie interred within this urn,
> They died together, as together born."

"They were lovely and pleasant in their lives," said David, of Saul and Jonathan, "and, in death, they were not divided."

Plato says, that the early Greeks buried their dead, in their own houses. There was a law in Thebes, that no person should build a house, without providing a repository for the dead therein. An inconvenient fashion this. In after-times they buried out of the city, and generally by the way-side. Hence, doubtless, arose the very common appeal, on their tablets—*Siste Viator!* On the road from Cape Ann Harbor to Sandy Bay, now Rockport, are a solitary grave and a monument—the grave of one, who chanced there to die. Our graveyards are usually on the roadside. Sometimes a common *cart-path* is laid out, through an ancient burying-ground. Such is the case in Uxbridge, in this Commonwealth. This is Vandalism. Sextons, who have had long experience, are of opinion, that the rights of the living and the decencies of life are less apt to be maintained, wherever the ashes of the dead are treated with disrespect. Burying, by the road-side, has been said to have been adopted, for the purpose of inspiring travellers with thoughts of mortality—travellers in railway cars, perhaps! The first time I visited St. Peter's, in Philadelphia, I was much impressed with the tablets and their inscriptions, lying level with the floor of the church, and vertical, I supposed, to the relics below—but I soon became familiar, and forgetful.

Every family, among the Greeks, who could afford it, had its own proper burying-ground—as is the case, at the present day, in our own country, among the planters and others, living far apart from any common point. This might be well enough, where the feudal system prevailed, and estates, by the law of descent, continued long in families. If the old usage were now in vogue, in New York, for instance, what a carting about of family urns there would be, on May day! Estates will pass from man to man, and strangers become the custodiers of the dead friends and relatives of the alienors. It is not unusual to find, on such occasions, a special clause, in the conveyance, for their protection, and for the perpetual *tabooing* of the place of sepulture. The first graves of the Greeks were mere caverns or holes; but, in later times, they were capacious rooms, vaulted and paved—so large, indeed, that in some instances, the mourners assembled and remained in them, for days and nights together. Monuments of some sort were of very early date; so were inscriptions, containing the names, ages, virtues, and actions of the deceased, and the emblems of their calling. Diogenes had the figure of a snarling cur engraved upon his tablet. Lycurgus put an end to what he called "talkative gravestones." He even forbade the inscription of the names, unless of men who died in battle, or women in childbed.

Extravagance was, at one time, so notorious, in these matters, that Leon forbade the erection of any mausoleum, which could not be erected by ten men, in three days.

In Greece and Rome, panegyrics were often pronounced at the grave. Games were sometimes instituted in honor of the eminent dead. Homer tells us that Agamemnon's ghost and the ghost of Achilles had a long talk upon this subject, telling over the number they had attended. After the funeral was over, the company met at the house of some near relative, to divert their sorrow; and, notwithstanding the abstemiousness of the Lacedemonians, they had, I am compelled to believe, what is commonly called a good time. The word, used to designate this kind of gathering, *perideipnon*, indicates a very social meeting—Cicero translates this word *circumpotatio*.

Embalming was most in use with the Egyptians, and the process is described by Herodotus and Diodorus. The brain was drawn through the nostrils with an iron scoop, and the void filled with spices. The entrails were removed, and the abdomen filled with myrrh and cassia. The body was next pickled in nitre, for seventy days, and then enveloped in bandages of fine linen and gums. Among the repositories of the curious, are bodies embalmed some thousands of years ago. According to Herodotus, the place for the first incision having been indicated, by the priest, the operator was looked upon, with as much disgust, as we exhibit towards the common hangman,—for, no sooner had he hastily made the incision, than he fled from the house, and was immediately attacked with stones, by the bystanders, as one, who had violated the dead. Rather an undesirable office. After being embalmed, the body was placed in a box of sycamore wood, carved to resemble the human form.

The story of Diogenes, who desired to be buried face downward, reminds me of one, related by old Grossman, as we were coming, many years ago, from the funeral of an old lady, who had been a terrible termagant. She resembled, old Grossman said, a perfect fury of a woman, whose husband insisted upon burying her, face downward; and, being asked the reason, for this strange procedure, replied — "the more she scratches the deeper she goes."

No. V

Nil de mortuis nisi bonum. You will wonder where I got my Latin. If my profession consisted of nothing but digging and filling up—dust to dust, and ashes to ashes—I would not give a fig for it. To a sexton of any sentiment it is a very different affair. I have sometimes doubted, if it might not be ranked among the fine arts. To be sure, it is rather a melancholy craft; and for this very reason I have tried to solace myself, with the literary part of it. There is a great amount, of curious and interesting reading upon these marble pages, which the finger of time is ever turning over. I soon found, that a large part of it was in the Latin tongue, and I resolved to master so much of it, as impeded my progress. I have found, that many superb things are said of the defunct, in Latin, which no person, however partial, would venture to say, in plain English.

The Latin proverb, at the head of this article, I saw, on the gravestone of a poor fellow, who was killed, by a sort of devil incarnate, in the shape of a rumseller, though some persons thought he was worried to death, by moral suasion. *Nothing of the dead but what is good*: Well, I very much doubt the wisdom of this rule. The Egyptians doubted it; and their kings were kept in order, through a fear of the sentence to be passed upon their character and conduct, by an assembly of notables, summoned immediately after their decease. Montaigne says it is an excellent custom, and to be desired by all good princes, who have reason to be offended, that the memories of the wicked should be treated with the same respect, as their own.

In England and our own Commonwealth, we have, legislatively, repudiated this rule, in one instance, at least, until within a few years. I refer to the case of suicide. Instead of considering the account balanced by death, and treating the defunct with particular tenderness, because he was dead, the sheriff was ordered to bury the body of every person, *felo de se*, at the central point where four roads met, and to run a stake through his body. This, to say nothing of its cheating our brotherhood out of burial fees, seems a very awkward proceeding.

There is a pleasant tale, related of Sheriff Bradford, which I may repeat, without marring the course of these remarks. Mr. Bradford was the politest sheriff, that we ever had in Suffolk, not excepting Sheriff Sumner. Sheriff Bradford was a real gentleman, dyed in the wool. It did one's heart good to see him serve an attachment, or levy an execution. Instead of knocking one down, and arresting him afterwards, Mr. Bradford made a pleasant affair of it. It actually seemed, as if he employed a sort of official ether, which took away the pain—he used, while placing his bailiff in a lady's drawing-room, to bow and smile, so respectfully and sympathizingly; and, in a sotto voice, to talk so very clerically, of the instability of human affairs.

An individual, within the sheriff's precinct, cut his own throat. An officious neighbor, who was rather curious to see the stake part performed, brought tidings to Mr. Bradford, while at breakfast. The informant ventured to inquire, at what time the performances would commence. At five o'clock precisely, this afternoon, the sheriff replied. He instantly dispatched a deputy to the son of the defunct, with a note, full of the most respectful expressions of condolence, and informing him, that the law required the sheriff to run a stake through his father's body, *if to be found within his precinct*, and adding that he should call with the stake, at 5 P. M. The body was, of course, speedily removed, and *non est inventus* was the end of the whole matter. Civilization advanced—several of the upper ten thousand cut their throats, or blew their brains out; and it would have been troublesome to carry out the provisions of the law, and cost something for stakes. The law was repealed.

Some sort of ignominious sepulture, for self-murderers, was in vogue, long ago. Plato speaks of it, de legibus lib. ix., p. 660. The attempt to shelter mankind from deserved reproach, by putting complimentary epitaphs upon their gravestones, is very foolish. It commonly produces an opposite effect. One would think these names were intended as a hint, for the Devil, when he comes for his own—a sort of *passover*.

I am inclined to think, if a grand inquest of any county were employed, to discover the last resting places of their neighbors and fellow-citizens, having no other guide, but their respective epitaphs, the names and dates having been previously removed or covered up, that inquest would be very much at a loss, in the midst of such exalted virtues, and supereminent talents, and extraordinary charities, and unbroken friendships, and great public services.

Some inscriptions are, perhaps, too simple. In the burying-ground at the corner of Arch and Sixth streets, Philadelphia, and very near that corner, lies a large flat slab, with these words:

> "Benjamin and Deborah Franklin,
> 1790."

In Exeter, N. H., I once read an epitaph in the graveyard, near the Railroad Depot, in these words:

"Henry's grave."

Pope's epitaph, in the garden of Lord Cobham, at Stow, on his Lordship's Italian friend, was, doubtless, well-deserved, though savoring of panegyric:

To the memory

of

SIGNOR FIDO,

an Italian of good extraction,

who came into England

not to bite us, like most of his countrymen,

but to gain an honest livelihood.

He hunted not after fame,

yet acquired it.

Regardless of the praise of his friends,

But most sensible of their love,

Though he lived among the great,

He neither learned nor flattered any vice.

He was no bigot,

Though he doubted not the 39 articles.

And, if to follow nature,

And to respect the laws of society

Be philosophy,

He was a perfect philosopher,

A faithful friend,

An agreeable companion,

A loving husband,

Distinguished by a numerous offspring,

All which he lived to see take good courses.

In his old age he retired

To the house of a clergyman, in the country,

Where he finished his earthly race,

And died an honor and an example to the whole species.

Reader

This stone is guiltless of flattery;

For he, to whom it is inscribed,

Was not a man

but a

Greyhound.

No. VI

It could not have been particularly desirable to be the cook, or the concubine, or the cup-bearer, or the master of the horse, or the chamberlain, or the gentleman usher of a Scythian king, for Herodotus tells us, book 4, page 280, that every one of these functionaries was strangled, upon the body of the dead monarch.

Castellan, in his account of the Turkish Empire, says, that a dying Turk is laid on his back, with his right side towards Mecca, and is thus interred. A chafing-dish is placed in the chamber of death, and perfumes burnt thereon. The Imam reads the thirty-sixth chapter of the Koran. When death has closed the scene, a sabre is laid upon the abdomen, and the next of kin ties up the jaw. The corpse is washed with camphor, wrapped in a white sheet, and laid upon a bier.

The burial is brief and rapid. The body is never carried to the mosque. Unlike the solemn pace of our own age and nation, four bearers, who are frequently relieved, carry the defunct, almost on a run, to the place of interment. Over the bier is thrown a pall; and, at the head, the turban of the deceased. Women never attend. Mourning, as it is called, is never worn. Christians are not permitted to be present, at the funeral of a Mussulman.

It is not lawful to walk over, or sit upon, a grave. A post mortem examination is never allowed, unless the deceased is so near confinement, that there may be danger of burying the living with the dead. The corpse is laid naked in the ground. The Imam kneels in prayer, and calls the name of the deceased, and the name of his mother, thrice. The cemeteries of the Turks are without the city, and thickly planted with trees, chiefly cypress and evergreens. Near Constantinople there are several cemeteries—the most extensive are at Scutari, on the Asiatic side of the Bosphorus. There, as here, marble columns designate the graves of the eminent and wealthy, but are surmounted with sculptured turbans. The inscriptions are brief and simple. This is quite common: "*This world is transient and perishable—today mine—tomorrow thine.*"

The funeral ceremonies of the Hindoos are minute, trivial, and ridiculous, in the extreme. A curious account may be found, in the Asiatic

Researches, vol. 7, page 264. Formal, or nominal obsequies are performed, says Mr. Colebrooke, not less than ninety-six times, in every year, among the Hindoos.

We do, for the dead, that, which we would have done for ourselves. The desire of making a respectable corpse is quite universal. It has been so, from the days of Greece and Rome, to the present. Such was the sentiment, which caused the Romans to veil those, whose features were distorted in death, as in the case of Scipio Africanus: such obsequies were called *larvata funera*. Such has ever been the feeling, among the civilized and the savage. Such was the opinion of Pope's Narcissa, when she exclaimed—

> One need not sure be ugly, though one's dead;
> And Betty, give this cheek a little red.

The Roman female corpses were painted. So are the corpses of the inhabitants of the Polynesian Islands, and of New Zealand. When a New Zealand chieftain dies, says Mr. Polack, the relatives and friends cut themselves with muscle shells, and let blood profusely, because they believe that ghosts, and especially royal ghosts, are exceedingly partial to this beverage. The body is laid out by the priests. The head is adorned with the most valued feathers of the albatross. The hair is anointed with shark oil, and tied, at the crown, with a riband of *tapa*. The lobes of the ears are ornamented with bunches of white, down, from the sea-fowl's breast, and the cheeks are embellished with red ochre. The brow is encircled with a garland of pink and white flowers of the *kaikatoa*. Mats, wove of the silken flax, are thrown around the body, which is placed upright. Skulls of enemies, slain in battle, are ranged at its feet. The relics of ancestors, dug up for the occasion, are placed on platforms at its head. A number of slaves are slaughtered, to keep the chieftain company. His wives and concubines hang and drown themselves, that they also may be of the party. The body lies in state, three or four days. The priests flourish round it, with wisps of flax, to keep off the devil and all his angels. The *pihe*, or funeral song, is then chanted, which I take to be the Old Hundred of the New Zealanders, very much resembling the *nœnia*, or funereal songs of the Romans. At last, the body is buried, with the favorite mats, muskets, trinkets, &c., of the deceased.

The Mandans, of the Upper Missouri, never inhume or bury their dead, but place their bodies, according to Mr. Catlin, on light scaffolds, out of the reach of the wolves and foxes. There they decay. This place of deposit is without the village. When a Mandan dies, he is painted, oiled, feasted, supplied with bow, arrows, shield, pipe and tobacco, knife, flint, steel, and food, for a few days, and wrapped tightly, in a raw buffalo hide. The corpse is then placed upon the scaffold, with its feet to the rising sun. An additional piece of scarlet cloth is thrown over the remains of a chief or medicine man. This cemetery is called, by the Mandans, the village of the dead. Here the Mandans, especially the women, give daily evidence of their parental, filial, and conjugal devotion. When the scaffold falls, and the bones have generally decayed, the skulls are placed in circles, facing inwards. The women, says Mr. Catlin, are able to recognize the skulls of their respective husbands, by some particular mark; and daily visit them with the best cooked dishes from their wigwams. What a lesson of constancy is here! It is a pity, that so much good victuals should be wasted; but what an example is this, for the imitation of Christian widows, too many of whom, it is feared, resemble Goldsmith's widow with the great fan, who, by the laws of her country, was forbidden to marry again, till the grave of her husband was thoroughly dry; and who was engaged, day and night, in fanning the clods. Some thirty years ago, my business led me frequently to pass a stonecutter's door, a few miles from the city; and, in a very conspicuous position, I noticed a gravestone, sacred to the memory of the most affectionate husband, erected by his devoted and inconsolable widow. It continued thus, before the stonecutter's shop, for several years. I asked the reason. "Why," said the stonecutter, "the inconsolable got married, in four months after, and I have never got my pay. They pass this way, now and then, the inconsolable and her new husband, and, when I see them, I always run out, and brush the dust off."

No. VII

I told that anecdote of the inconsolable widow, related in my last, to old Grossman. He and Smith were helping me at a grave, in the Granary ground. Bless my heart, how things have changed! We were digging near the Park Street side—the old Almshouse fronted on Park Street then—and the Granary stood where Park Street Church now stands, until 1809, and the long building, called the Massachusetts Bank, covered a part of Hamilton Place, and the house, once occupied by Sir Francis Barnard and afterwards by Mr. Andrews, with its fine garden, stood at the corner of Winter Street, on the site of the present granite block; and—but I am burying myself, sexton like, in the grave of my own recollections—I say, I told Grossman that story—the old man, when not translated by liquor, was delightful company, in a graveyard—we were digging the grave of a young widow's third husband. Grossman said she poisoned them. Smith was quite shocked, and told him Mr. Deblois was looking over the Almshouse wall.

Grossman said he didn't mean, that she really gave all three of them ratsbane; but it was clear enough, she was the end of them all; and he had no doubt the widow would be a good customer, and give us two or three jobs yet, before she left off. This led me to tell that story. Smith said there was nothing half so restless, as an Irish widow. He said, that a young Tipperary widow, Nelly McPhee, I think he called her, was courted, and actually had an offer from Tooley O'Shane, on the way to her husband's funeral. "She accepted, of course," said Grossman. "No, she didn't," said Smith— "Tooley, dear," said she, "y'are too late: foor waaks ago it was, I shook hands wi Patty Sweeney upon it, that I would have him, in a dacent time, arter poor McPhee went anunderbood." "Well," said Grossman, "widows of all nations are much alike. There was a Dutch woman, whose husband, Diedrick Van Pronk, kicked the bucket, and left her inconsolable. He was buried on Copp's Hill. Folks said grief would kill that widow. She had a figure of wood carved, that looked very like her late husband, and placed it in her bed, and constantly kept it there, for several months.

In about half a year, she became interested in a young shoemaker, who got the length of her foot, and finally married her. He had visited the widow, not more than a fortnight, when the servants told her they were out of kindling stuff, and asked what should be done. After a pause, the widow replied, in a very quiet way—"Maype it ish vell enough now, to sphlit up old Van Pronk, vat ish up shtair."

Some persons have busied themselves, in a singular way, about their own obsequies, and have left strange provisions, touching their remains. Charles V., according to Robertson and other writers, ordered a rehearsal of his own obsequies—his domestics marched with black tapers—Charles followed in his shroud—he was laid in his coffin—the service for the dead was chanted. This farce was, in a few days, followed by the real tragedy; for the fatigue or exposure brought on fever, which terminated fatally. Yet this story, which has long been believed, is distinctly denied, by Mr. Richard Ford, in his admirable handbook for Spain; and this denial is repeated, in No. 151 of the London Quarterly Review.

Several gentlemen, of the fancy, of the present age, and in this vicinity, have provided their coffins, in their life time. The late Timothy Dexter, commonly called Lord Dexter, of Newburyport; there was also an eminent merchant, of this city. This is truly a Blue Beard business; and, beyond its influence, in frightening children and domestics, it is difficult to imagine the utility of such an arrangement. After a few visitations, these coffins would probably excite just about as much of the *memento mori* sensation, as the same number of meal chests.

Burton, in his Anatomy of Melancholy, states that John Zisca, the general of the Hussites, ordered a drum to be made of his skin, after he was dead, persuaded, that the sound of it would terrify his foes.

When Edward I., of England, was dying, he bound his son, by an oath, to boil his body, and, separating the bones, to carry them always before him in battle, against the Scots; as though he believed victory to be chained to his joints.

The bodies of persons, executed for crime, have, in different ages, and among different nations, been delivered to surgeons, for dissection. It seems meet and right, that those, who have been worse than useless, in their lives, should contribute, in some small degree, to the common weal, by such an appropriation of their carcasses. In some cases, these miserable creatures have been permitted to make their own bargains, with particular surgeons, beforehand; who have, occasionally, been taken in, by paying a guinea to an unscrupulous fellow, who knew, though the surgeons did not, that he was sentenced to be hung in chains, or, as it is commonly called, gibbeted. The difficulty of obtaining subjects, for anatomical purposes, has led to outrages upon the dead. Various remedies have been proposed—none effectual.

Surgical students, will not be deterred, by the "Requiescat in pace," and the judges, between the demands of science and of sympathy, have been in the predicament of asses, between two bundles of straw. A poor vagabond, *nullius filius vel ignoti*, was snatched, by some of these young medical dogs, some years ago, and Judge Parsons, who tried the indictment, with a leaning to science, imposed a fine of five dollars. Not many years after, a worthy judge, a reverencer of Parsons, and a devotee to precedent, imposed a fine of five dollars, upon a young sloven, who but half completed his job, and left a respectable citizen of Maine, half drawn out from his grave, with a rope about his neck.

It seems scarcely conceivable, that a pittance should tempt a man to take his fellow's life, that he might sell the body to a surgeon. In 1809, Burke was executed in Edinburgh, for this species of murder. It was his trade. Victims were lured, by this vampyre, to "the chambers of death," strangled or suffocated, without any visible mark of murder, and then sold to the surgeons.

This trade has been attempted in London, at a much later day. Dec. 5, 1831, a wretch, named Bishop, and his accomplice, Williams, were hung, for the murder of an Italian boy, Carlo Ferrari, poor and friendless, whose body they sold to the surgeons. They confessed the murder of Ferrari and several others, whose bodies were disposed of, in a similar manner.

From a desire to promote the cause of science, individuals have, now and then, bequeathed their bodies to particular surgeons. These bequests have been rarely insisted upon, by the legatees, and the intentions of the testator have seldom been carried out, by the executors; a remarkable exception, however, occurred, in the case of the celebrated Jeremy Bentham, an account of which I must defer for the present, for funerals are not the only things, which may be of unreasonable length.

No. VIII

That eminent friend of science and of man, Jeremy Bentham, held the prejudice against dissection, in profound contempt, and bequeathed his body, for that object, to Dr. Fordyce, in 1769. Dr. Fordyce died, in 1792, and Mr. Bentham, who survived him, and seems to have set his heart upon being dissected, aware of the difficulties, that might obstruct his purpose, chose three friends, from whom he exacted a solemn promise, to fulfil his wishes. Accordingly, Mr. Bentham's body was carried to the Webb Street School of Anatomy and Surgery, and publicly dissected, June 9, 1832, by Dr. Southwood Smith, who delivered an admirable lecture, upon that occasion. I wholly object to such a practice, not, upon my honor, from selfish motives, though it would spoil our business; but because the moral injury, which would result, from such a disposition of mortal remains, would be so much greater, than the surgical good. Mr. Bentham's example is not likely to be commonly adopted.

A great amount of needless care is sometimes taken, by the living, in regard to their relics, and their obsequies, which care belongs, manifestly, to survivors. Akin to the preparation of one's coffin, and storing it in one's domicil, for years perhaps, is the preparation of one's shroud, and death cap, and all the et cætera of laying out. In ninety and nine cases, in every one hundred, these things are done, for the gratification of personal vanity, to attract attention, and to procure a small sample of that lamentation, which the desolate widower and orphans will pour forth, *one of these days*. It is observed, by one of the daughters, that the mother is engaged in some mysterious piece of needle work. "What is it, dear mother?" "Ah, my child, you should not inquire. We all must die—it is your poor mother's winding sheet." The daughter is convulsed, and pours forth a profluvium of tears. The judicious parent soothes, and moralizes, and is delighted. The daughter flies to her sisters; and, gathering in some private chamber, their tears are poured forth, as the fact is announced. The husband returns—the eyes of his household are like beet roots. They gather round their miserable meal. The husband has been informed. The sweet-breads go down, untasted. How grateful these evidences of sympathy to the wife and mother! A case occurred in my practice, of this very description, where the lady survived, married again, and the shroud, sallowed by thirty years' *non user*, was given, in an hour of need, to a poor family.

Montaigne, vol. 1, page 17, Lond., 1811, says, "I was by no means pleased with a story, told me of a relation of mine, that, being arrived at a very old age and tormented with the stone, he spent the last hours of his life in an extraordinary solicitude, about ordering the pomp and ceremony of his funeral, pressing all the men of condition, who came to see him, to promise their attendance at his grave."

Sophia Charlotte, the sister of George I., of England, a woman of excellent understanding, was the wife of Frederic I. of Prussia. When dying, one of her attendants observed how sadly the king would be afflicted by her death. "With respect to him," she replied, "I am perfectly at ease. His mind will be completely occupied in arranging the ceremonial of my funeral; and, if nothing goes wrong in the procession, he will be quite consoled for my loss."

Man goeth to his long home, as of yore, but the mourners do not go about the streets, as they did, when I was young. The afternoons were given to the tolling of bells, and funeral processions. This was about the period, when the citizens began to feel their privations, as cow-yards grew scarce; and, when our old friend, Ben Russell, told the public, in his Centinel, that it was no wonder they were abominably crowded, and pinched for gardens, for Boston actually contained seventeen thousand inhabitants. I have seen a funeral procession, of great length, going south, by the Old South Church, passing another, of equal length, going north, and delaying the progress of a third, coming down School Street. The dead were not left to bury the dead, in those days. Invitations to funerals were sent round, as they are at present, to balls and parties. Othello Pollard and Domingo Williams had full employment then. I have heard it stated of Othello, that, having in hand two bundles of invitations, one for a fandango, of some sort, and the other for a funeral, and being in an evil condition, he made sad work in the delivery. Printed invitations are quite common, in some countries.

I have seen one, in handbill form, for the funeral of a Madame Barbut, an old widow, in Martinique, closing with these words, "*un de profundis, si vous,*" etc. Roman funerals were distinguished as *indictiva* and *tacita*: to the former, persons were invited, by a crier; the others were private. The calling out, according to a prearranged list, which always gave offence to somebody, was of old the common practice here. Such was the usage in Rome, where the director was styled *dominus funeris* or *designator*. I doubt, if martinets are more tenacious of their rank, in the army, than mourners, at a funeral.

There was a practice, in Rome, which would appear very grotesque, at the present time. Pipers, *tibicines,* preceded the corpse, with players and buffoons, who danced and sang, some of whom imitated the voice, manner and gestures of the defunct. Of these, Suetonius gives some account, in his lives of Tiberius, Vespasian, and Cæsar.

The practice of watching a corpse, until the time of burying or burning, was very ancient, and in use with the Greeks and Romans. The bodies of eminent men were borne to the grave, by the most distinguished citizens, not acting merely as pall bearers, but sustaining the body on their shoulders. Suetonius states, that Julius Cæsar was borne by the magistrates; Augustus by the senators. Tacitus, Ann. iii. 2, informs us, that Germanicus was supported, on the shoulders of the tribunes and centurions. Children, who died, before they were weaned, were carried to the pile by their mothers. This must have been a painful office.

No. IX

When I first undertook, there was scarcely any variety, either in the inscriptions, or devices, upon gravestones: death's heads and crossbones; scythes and hour glasses; angels, with rather a diabolical expression; all-seeing eyes, with an ominous squint; squares and compasses; such were the common devices; and every third or fourth tablet was inscribed:

> Thou traveller that passest by,
> As thou art now, so once was I;
> As I am now, thou soon shalt be,
> Prepare for death and follow me.

No wonder people were wearied to death, or within an inch of it, by reading this lugubrious quatrain, for the hundredth time. We had not then learned, from that vivacious people, who have neither taste nor talent for being sad, to convert our graveyards into pleasure grounds.

To be sure, even in my early days, and long before, an audacious spirit, now and then, would burst the bonds of this mortuary sameness, and take a bolder flight. We have an example of this, on the tablet of the Rev. Joseph Moody, in the graveyard at York, Maine.

> Although this stone may moulder into dust,
> Yet Joseph Moody's name continue must.

And another in Dorchester:

> Here lies our Captain and Mayor of Suffolk,
> Was withall,
> A godly magistrate was he, and major general.
> Two troops of hors with him here came, such
> Worth his love did crave.
> Ten companyes also mourning marcht
> To his grave.
> Let all that read be sure to keep the faith as
> He has don;
> With Christ he lives now crowned, his name
> Was Humphrey Atherton,
> He dyed the 16 of September, 1661.

The following, also, in the graveyard at Attleborough, upon the tablet of the Rev. Peter Thacher, who died in 1785, is no common effort, and in the style of Tate and Brady:

> Whom Papists not
> With superstitious fire,
> Would dare to adore,
> We justly may admire.

And another, in the same graveyard, upon the slave, Cæsar, is very clever. The two last lines seem by another hand:

> Here lies the best of slaves,
> Now turning into dust,
> Cæsar, the Ethiopian, craves
> A place, among the just.
> His faithful soul is fled
> To realms of Heavenly light,
> And by the blood that Jesus shed,
> Is changed from black to white.
> January 15, he quitted the stage,
> In the 77 year of his age.

An erratum, ever to be regretted, is certainly quite unexpected, on a gravestone. In the graveyard at Norfolk, Va., there is a handsome marble monument, sacred to the memory of Mrs. Margaret, &c., wife of, &c., who died, &c.: "*Erratum, for Margaret read Martha.*"

In olden time, there was a provost of bonny Dundee, and his name was Dickson. He was a right jolly provost, and seemed resolved to have one good joke beyond the grave. He bequeathed ten pounds, apiece, to three men, remarkable above their fellows, for avarice, and dulness, on condition, that they should join in the composition of his epitaph, in rhyme and metre. They met—the task was terrible—but, Dr. Johnson would have said, what will not a Scotchman undertake, for ten pounds! It need not be long, said one—a line apiece, said the second—shall I begin? said the third. This was objected to, of course; for whoever commenced was relieved from the onus of the rhyme. They drew lots for this vantage ground, and he, who won, after a copious perspiration, produced the following line—

> Here lies Dickson, Provost of Dundee.

This was very much admired—brief and sententious—his name, his official station, his death, and the place of his burial were happily compressed in a single line. After severe exertion, the second line was produced:

> Here lies Dickson, here lies he.

It was objected, that this was tautological; and that it did not even go so far as the first, which set forth the official character of the deceased. It was said, in reply, by one of the executors, who happened to be present, and who acted as *amicus poetæ*, that the second line would have been tautological, if it *had* set forth the official station, which it did not; and that as there had once been a female provost, the last word effectually established the sex of Dickson, which was very important. The third legatee, though he had leave of absence for an hour, and refreshed his spirit, by a ramble on the Frith of Tay, was utterly unable to complete the epitaph. At an adjourned meeting, however, he produced the following line,

Hallelujah! Hallelujee!

There are some beautiful epitaphs in our language—there are half a dozen, perhaps, which are exquisitely so, and I believe there are not many more. I dare not present them here, in juxtaposition with such light matter. Swift's clever epitaph, on a miser, may more appropriately close this article:

Beneath this verdant hillock lies
Demer, the wealthy and the wise.
His heirs, that he might safely rest,
Have put his carcass in a chest—
The very chest, in which, they say,
His other self, his money, lay.
And if his heirs continue kind
To that dear self he left behind,
I dare believe that four in five
Will think his better half alive.

No. X

Catacombs, hollows or cavities, according to the etymological import of the word, are, as every one knows, receptacles for the dead. They are found in many countries; the most ancient are those of Egypt and Thebes, which were visited in 1813 and 1818, by Belzoni. Psamatticus was a famous fellow, in his time: he was the founder of the kingdom of Egypt; and, after a siege of nearly three times the length of that at Troy, he captured the city of Azotus. The flight of the house of our lady of Loretto from Jerusalem, in a single night, would have seemed less miraculous to the Egyptians, than the transportation of the sarcophagus of Psamatticus, by a travelling gentleman, from Egypt to London. So it fell out, nevertheless. Belzoni penetrated into one of the pyramids of Ghizeh; he obtained free access to the tombs of the Egyptian kings, at Beban-el-Malook; and brought to England the sarcophagus of Psamatticus, exquisitely wrought of the finest Oriental alabaster. Verily kings have a slender chance, between the worms and the lovers of *vertu*. "Here lie the remains of G. Belzoni"—these brief words mark the grave of Belzoni himself, at Gato, near Benin in Africa, where he died, in December, 1823, safer in his traveller's robes, than if surrounded with aught to tempt the hand of avarice or curiosity. The best account of the Egyptian catacombs may be found in Belzoni's narrative, published in 1820.

The catacombs of Italy are vast caverns, in the via Appia, about three miles from Rome. They were supposed to be the sepulchres of martyrs, and have furnished more capital to priestcraft, for the traffic in relics, than would have accrued, for the purposes of agriculture, to the fortunate discoverer of a whole island of guano. The common opinion is, that they were heathen sepulchres—the *puticuli* of the ancients. The catacombs of Naples, according to Bishop Burnet, are more magnificent than those of Rome. Catacombs have been found in Syracuse and Catanea, in Sicily, and in Malta.

Jahn, in his Archæologia, sec. 206, speaks of extensive sepulchres, among the Hebrews, otherwise called the *everlasting houses*; a term of peculiar inapplicability, if we may judge from Maundrell's account of the shattered and untenantable state, in which they are found. They are all located beyond the cities and villages, to which they belong, that is, beyond their more inhabited parts. The sepulchres of the Hebrew kings were upon

Mount Zion. Extensive caverns, natural or artificial, were the common burying-places or catacombs. Gardens and the shade of spreading trees were preferred, by some; these are objectionable, on the ground, suggested in a former number: to alienate the estate and leave the dead, without the right of removal, reserved, is, virtually, a transfer of one's ancestors—and to remove them may be unpleasant. For this contingency the Greeks and Romans provided, by reducing them to such a portable compass, that a man might carry his grandfather in a quart bottle, and ten generations, in the right line, in a wheelbarrow. Numerous catacombs are to be found in Syria and Palestine. The most beautiful are on the north part of Jerusalem. The entrance into these was down many steps. Some of them consisted of seven apartments, with niches in the walls, for the reception of the dead.

Maundrell, in his travels, page 76, writing of the "grots," as they were styled, which have been considered the sepulchres of kings, denies that any of the kings of Israel or Judah were buried there. He describes these catacombs, as having necessarily cost an immense amount of money and labor. The approach is through the solid rock, into an area forty paces wide, cut down square, with exquisite precision, out of the solid mass. On the south is a portico, nine paces long, and four broad, also cut from the solid rock. This has an architrave, sculptured in the stone, of fruits and flowers, running along its front. At the end of the portico, on the left, you descend into the passage to the sepulchres. After creeping through stones and rubbish, Maundrell arrived at a large room, seven or eight yards square, cut also from the natural rock. His words are these:—"Its sides and ceiling are so exactly square, and its angles so just, that no architect, with levels and plummets, could build a room more regular." From this room you pass into six more, of the same fabric; the two innermost being deepest. All these apartments, excepting the first, are filled around with stone coffins. They had been covered with handsome lids, and carved with garlands; but, at the period of this visit, the covers were mostly broken to pieces, by sacrilegious hands. Here is a specimen of the "everlasting houses," and a solemn satire upon the best of all human efforts—impotent and vain—to perpetuate that, which God Almighty has destined to perish. But of this I shall have more to say, when I come to sum up; and endeavor, from these dry bones, to extract such wisdom as I can, touching the best mode, in which the living may dispose of the dead, whose *memories* they are bound to embalm, and whose *bodies* are entitled to a decent burial.

The catacombs of the Hottentots are the wildest clefts and caverns of their mountains. The Greenlanders, after wrapping the dead, in the skins of wild animals, bear them to some far distant Golgotha. In Siberia and Kamtschatka, they are deposited in remote caverns, with mantles of snow, for their winding sheets. It is the valued privilege of the civilized and refined to snuff up corruption, and swear it is a rose—to bury their dead, in the very midst of the living—in the very tenements, in which they breathe, the larger part of every seventh day—in the vaults of churches, into which the mourners are expected to descend, and poke their noses into the tombs, to prove the full measure of their respect for the defunct. But the tombs are faithfully sealed; and, when again opened, after several months, perhaps, the olfactory nerves are not absolutely staggered—possibly a dull smeller may honestly aver, that he perceives nothing—what then? The work of corruption has gone forward—the gases have escaped—how and whither? Subtle as the lightning, they have percolated, through the meshes of brick and mortar; and the passages or gashes, purposely left open in the walls, have given them free egress to the outward air.

Very probably neither the eye nor the nose gave notice of their escape. Doubtless, it was gradual. The yellow fever, I believe, has never been seen nor smelt, during its most terrible ravages. I do remember—not an apothecary—but a greenhorn, who, in 1795, heard old Dr. Lloyd say the yellow fever was in the air, and who went upon the house top, next morning early, to look for it—but he saw it not; and, ever after, said he did not think much of Dr. Lloyd. I have something more to say of burials under churches, and in the midst of a dense population.

No. XI

A few more words on the subject of burying the dead under churches, and in the midst of a dense population. If men would adopt the language of the prologue to Addison's Cato—"*dare to have sense yourselves*"—the folly and madness of this practice would be sufficiently apparent. Upon some simple subjects, one grain of common sense is better, than any quantity of the uncommon kind. But it is hard to make men think so. They prefer walking by faith—they must consult the savans—the doctors. Now I think very well of a good, old-fashioned doctor—one doctor I mean—but, when they get to be gregarious, my observation tells me, no good can possibly come of it. At post mortems, and upon other occasions, I have, in my vocation, seen them assembled, by half dozens and dozens, and I have come to the conclusion, that no body of men ever look half so wise, or feel half so foolish.

Some of the faculty were consulted, in this city, about thirty years ago, upon the question of burying under churches; and, on the strength of the opinion given, a large church, not then finished, was provided with tombs, and the dead have been buried therein, ever since. Now I think the public good would have been advanced, had those doctors set their faces against the selfish proposition. That it is a nuisance, I entertain not the slightest doubt. The practice of burying in their own houses, among the ancients, gave place to burying without the city, or to cremation. The unhealthiness, consequent upon such congregations of the dead, was experienced at Rome. The inconvenience was so severely felt, in a certain quarter, that Augustus gave a large part of one of the cemeteries to Mæcenas, who so completely purified it, and changed its character, that it became one of the healthiest sites in Rome, and there he built a splendid villa, to which Augustus frequently resorted, for fresh air and repose. Horace alludes to this transformation, Sat. 8, lib. 1, v. 10, and the passage reminds one of the change, which occurred in Philadelphia, when the Potter's field was beautifully planted, and transformed into Washington Square.

> Hoc miseræ plebi stabat commune sepulchrum,
> Pantolabo scurræ; Nomentanoque nepoti.
> Mille pedes in fronte, trecentos cippus in agrum
> Hic dabat, heredes monumentum ne sequeretur.

Nunc licet Esquiliis habitare salubribus, atque
Aggere in apprico spatiari, quâ modo tristes
Albis informem spectabant ossibus agrum.

Millingen, in his work on Medical jurisprudence, page 54, remarks—"From time immemorial medical men have pointed out to municipal authorities the dangers, that arise from burying the dead, within the precincts of cities, or populous towns."

The early Christians buried their martyrs, and afterwards eminent citizens, in their temples. Theodosius, in his celebrated code, forbade the practice, because of the infectious diseases.

Theodolphus, the Bishop of Orleans, complained to Charlemagne, that vanity and the love of lucre had turned churches into charnel houses, disgraceful to the church, and dangerous to man.

Cuthbert, Archbishop of Canterbury, first sanctioned the use of churches, for charnel houses, in 758—though Augustine had previously forbidden the practice. As Sterne said, in another connection, "they manage these matters much better, in France;" there Maret, in 1773, and Vicq d'Azyr, in 1778, pointed out the terrible consequences, so effectually, that none, but dignitaries, were suffered to be buried in churches. In 1804, inhumation, in the cities of France, was wholly forbidden, without any exception. The arguments produced, at that time, are not uninteresting, at this, or any other. In Saulien, about 140 miles from Paris, in the year 1773, the corpse of a corpulent person was buried, March 3, under the church of St Saturnin. April 20, following, a woman was buried near it. Both had died of a prevailing fever, which had nearly passed away. At the last interment a foul odor filled the church, and out of 170 persons present, 149 were attacked with the disease. In 1774 at Nantes, several coffins were removed, to make room for a person of note; and fifteen of the bystanders died of the emanation, shortly after. In the same year, one third of the inhabitants of Lectouse died of malignant fever, which appeared, immediately after the removal of the dead from a burial-ground, to give place to a public structure.

The public mind is getting to be deeply impressed, upon this subject. Cities, and the larger towns are, in many instances, building homes for the dead, beyond the busy haunts of the living. The city of London has, until within a few years, been backward, in this sanatory movement. At present, however, there are six public cemeteries, in the suburbs of that city, of no inconsiderable area: the Kensall Green Cemetery, established by act 2 and 3 of William IV., in 1832, containing 53 acres—the South Metropolitan, by act 6 and 7 William IV., 1836, containing 40 acres—the Highgate and Kentish Town, by act 7 and 8 William IV., containing 22 acres—the Abney

Park, at Stoke Newington, containing 30 acres, 1840—the Westminster, at Earlscourt, Kensington road, 1840—and the Nunhead, containing 40 acres, 1840. Paris has its beautiful Père La Chaise, covering the site of the house and extensive grounds, once belonging to the Jesuit of that name, the confessor of Louis XIV., who died in 1709. New York has its Greenwood; Philadelphia its Laurel Hill; Albany its Rural Cemetery; Baltimore its Green Mount; Rochester its Mount Hope; we our Mount Auburn; and our neighboring city of Roxbury has already selected—and well selected—a local habitation for the dead, and wants nothing but a name, which will not long be wanting, nor a graceful arrangement of the grounds, from the hands of one, to whom Mount Auburn is indebted, for so much of all that is admirable there. I shall rejoice, if the governors of this cemetery should decree, that no *tomb* should ever be erected therein—but that the dead should be laid in their *graves*.

My experience has supplied me with good and sufficient reasons—one thousand and one—against the employment of tombs, some of which reasons I may hereafter produce, though the honor of our craft may constrain me to keep silence, in regard to others. Some very bitter family squabbles have arisen, about tombs. Two deacons, who were half brothers, had a serious and lasting dispute, respecting a family tomb. They became almost furious; one of them solemnly protesting, that he would never consent to be buried there, while he had his reason, and the other declaring, that he would never be put into that tomb, while God spared his life. This, however, is not one of those one thousand and one reasons, against tombs.

No. XII

The origin of the catacombs of Paris is very interesting, and not known to many. The stone, of which the ancient buildings of Paris were constructed, was procured from quarries, on the banks of the river Bièore. No system had been adopted in the excavation; and, for hundreds of years, the material had been withdrawn, until the danger became manifest. There was a vague impression, that these quarries extended under a large part of the city. In 1774 the notice of the authorities was called to some accidents, connected with the subject. The quarries were then carefully examined, by skilful engineers; and the startling fact clearly established, that the southern parts of Paris were actually undermined, and in danger of destruction. In 1777 a special commission was appointed, to direct such works, as might be necessary. On the very day of its appointment, the necessity became manifest—a house, in the Rue d'Enfer, sunk ninety-two feet. The alarm— the fear of a sudden engulphment—was terrible. Operatives were set at work, to prop the streets, roads, palaces, and churches. The supports, left by the quarriers, without any method or judgment, were insufficient—in some instances, they had given way, and the roof had settled. Great fear was felt for the aqueduct of Arcueil, which supplied the fountains of Paris, and which passed over this ground, for it had already suffered some severe shocks; and it was apprehended, not simply that the fountains would be cut off, but that the torrent would pour itself into these immense caverns. And now the reader will inquire, what relation has this statement to the catacombs? Let us reply.

For hundreds of years, Paris had but one place of interment, the Cemetery des Innocens. This was once a part of the royal domains; it lay without the walls of Paris; and was given, by one of the earlier kings, to the citizens, for a burying-place. It is well known, that this gift to the people was intended to prevent the continuance of the practice, then common in Paris, of burying the dead, in cellars, courts, gardens, streets, and public fields, within the city proper. In 1186 this cemetery was surrounded with a high wall, by Philip Augustus, the forty second king of France. It was soon found insufficient for its purpose; and, in 1218, it was enlarged, by Pierre de Nemours, Bishop of Paris. Generation after generation was deposited there, stratum super stratum, until the surrounding parishes, in the fifteenth century, began to complain of the evil, as an insufferable nuisance. Such a colossal mass of putrescence produced discomfort and disease. Hichnesse speaks of several holes about Paris, of great size and depth, in which dead bodies were deposited, and left uncovered, till one tier was filled, and then covered with a layer of earth, and so on, to the top. He says these holes were cleared, once in thirty or forty years, and the bones deposited, in what was called *"le grand charnier des Innocens;"* this was an arched gallery, surrounding the great cemetery.

With what affectionate respect we cherish the venerated name of François Pontraci! *Magnum et venerabile nomen!* He was the last—the last of the grave-diggers of *le grand charnier des Innocens!* In the days of my novitiate, I believed in the mathematical dictum, which teaches, that two things cannot occupy the same place, at the same time. But that dictum appears incredible, while contemplating the operations of Pontraci. He was a most accomplished stevedore in his department—the Napoleon of the charnel house, the very king of spades. All difficulties vanished, before his magic power. Nothing roused his indignation so much, as the suggestion, that a cemetery was *full*—*c'est impossible!* was his eternal reply. To use the terms of another of the fine arts, the touch of Pontraci was irresistible—his *handling* masterly—his *grouping* unsurpassed—and his *fore-shortening* altogether his own. *Condense!* that word alone explained the mystery of his great success. Knapsacks are often thrown aside, *en route*, in the execution of rapid movements. In the grand march of death, Pontraci considered coffins an encumbrance. Those wooden surtouts he thought well enough for parade, but worse than useless, on a march. He had a poor opinion of an artist, who could not find room, for twenty citizens, heads and heels, in one common grave. Madame Pontraci now and then complained, that the fuel communicated a problematical flavor to the meat, while roasting—*"c'est odeur, qui a rapport à une profession particulière, madame,"* was the reply of Pontraci. The register, kept by this eminent man, shows, that, in thirty years, he had deposited, in this cemetery, ninety thousand bodies. It was calculated, that twelve hundred thousand had been buried there, since the time of Philip Augustus. In 1805, the Archbishop of Paris, under a resolve of the Council of State, issued a decree, that the great cemetery should be suppressed and evacuated. It was resolved to convert it into a market place. The happy thought of converting the quarries into catacombs fortunately occurred, at that period, to M. Lenoie, lieutenant general of police. Thus a receptacle was, at once, provided for the immense mass of human remains, to be removed from the Cemetery des Innocens. A portion of the quarries, lying under the *Plaine de Mont Souris*, was assigned, for this purpose. A house was purchased with the ground adjoining, on the old road to Orleans.

It had, at one time, belonged to Isouard, a robber, who had infested that neighborhood. A flight of seventy-seven steps was made, from the house down into the quarries; and a well sunk to the bottom, down which the bones were to be thrown. Workmen were employed, in constructing pillars to sustain the roof, and in walling round the part, designed for *le charnier*. The catacombs were then consecrated, with all imaginable pomp.

In the meantime, the vast work of removing the remains went forward, night and day, suspended, only, when the hot weather rendered it unsafe to proceed. The nocturnal scenes were very impressive. A strange resurrection, to be sure! Bonfires burnt brightly amid the gloom. Torches threw an unearthly glare around, and illuminated these dealings with the dead. The operatives, moving about in silence, bearing broken crosses, and coffins, and the bones of the long buried, resembled the agents of an infernal master. All concerned had been publicly admonished, to reclaim the crosses, tombstones, and monuments of their respective dead. Such, as were not reclaimed, were placed in the field, belonging to the house of Isouard. Many leaden coffins were buried there, one containing the remains of Madame de Pompadour. During *the* revolution, the house and grounds of Isouard were sold as national domain, the coffins melted, and the monuments destroyed. The catacombs received the dead from other cemeteries; and those, who fell, in periods of commotion, were cast there. When convents were suppressed, the dead, found therein, were transferred to this vast omnibus.

During the revolution, the works were neglected—the soil fell in; water found its way to the interior; the roof began to crumble; and the bones lay, in immense heaps, mixed with the rubbish, and impeding the way. And there, for the present, we shall leave them, intending to resume this account of the catacombs of Paris, in a future number.

No. XIII

In 1810, the disgusting confusion, in the catacombs of Paris, was so much a subject of indignant remark, that orders were issued to put things in better condition. A plan was adopted, for piling up the bones. In some places, these bones were thirty yards in thickness; and it became necessary to cut galleries through the masses, to effect the object proposed.

There were two entrances to the catacombs—one near the barrier d'Enfer, for visitors—the other, near the old road to Orleans, for the workmen. The staircase consisted of ninety steps, which, after several windings, conducted to the western gallery, from which others branched off, in different directions. A long gallery, extending beneath the aqueduct of Arcueil, leads to the gallery of Port Mahon, as it is called. About a hundred yards from this gallery, the visitor comes again to the passage to the catacombs; and, after walking one hundred yards further, he arrives at the vestibule, which is of an octagonal form. This vestibule opens into a long gallery, lined with bones, from top to bottom. The arm, leg, and thigh bones are in front, compactly and regularly piled together. The monotony of all this is tastefully relieved, by three rows of skulls, at equal distances, and the smaller bones are stowed behind. How very French! This gallery leads to other apartments, lined with bones, variously and fancifully arranged. In these rooms are imitation vases and altars, constructed of bones, and surmounted with skulls, fantastically arranged. This really seems to be the work of some hybrid animal—a cross, perhaps, between the Frenchman and the monkey.

These crypts, as they are called, are designated by names, strangely dissimilar. There is the Crypte de Job, and the Crypte d'Anacreon—the Crypte de La Fontaine, and the Crypte d'Ezekiel—the Crypte d'Hervey, and the Crypte de Rousseau. An album, kept here, is filled with mawkish sentimentality, impertinent witticism, religious fervor, and infidel bravado.

The calculations vary, as to the number of bodies, whose bones are collected here. At the lowest estimate, the catacombs are admitted to contain the remains of three millions of human beings.

While contemplating the fantastical disposition of these human relics, one recalls the words of Sir Thomas Browne, in his Hydriotaphia—

"Antiquity held too light thoughts from objects of mortality, while some drew provocatives of mirth from anatomies, and jugglers showed tricks with skeletons."

Here then, like *"broken tea-cups, wisely kept for show,"* are the broken skeletons of more than three millions of human beings, paraded for public exhibition! Most of them, doubtless, received Christian burial, and were followed to their graves, and interred, with more or less of the forms and ceremonies of the Catholic church, and deposited in the earth, there to repose in peace, till the resurrection! How applicable here the language of the learned man, whom we just quoted—"When the funeral pyre was out, and the last valediction over, men took a lasting adieu of their interred friends, little expecting the curiosity of future ages should comment upon their ashes; and having no old experience of the duration of their relics, held no opinion of such after-considerations. But who knows the fate of his bones, or how often he is to be buried! Who hath the oracle of his ashes, or whither they are to be scattered?" How little did the gay and guilty Jeane Antoinette Poisson, Marquise de Pompadour, imagine this rude handling of her mortal remains! She was buried in the Cemetery des Innocens, in 1764— and shared the common exhumation and removal in 1805.

It seems to have been the desire of mankind, in every age and nation, to repose in peace, after death. In conformity with this desire, the cemeteries of civilized nations, the morais of the Polynesian isles, and the cities of the dead, throughout the world, have been, from time immemorial, consecrated and tabooed. So deep and profound has been the sentiment of respect, for the feelings of individuals, upon this subject, that great public improvements have been abandoned, rather than give offence to a single citizen.

Near forty years ago, a meeting was held in Faneuil Hall, to consider a proposition for some change, in the Granary burying-ground, which proposition, was rejected, by acclamation. During the Mayoralty, of the elder Mr. Quincy, it was the wish of very many to continue the mall, through the burial-ground, in the Common. The consent of all, but two or three, was obtained. They were offered new tombs, and the removal of their deceased relatives, under their own supervision, at the charge of the city. These two or three still objected, and this great public improvement was abandoned; and with manifest propriety. The basis of this sentiment is a deep laid and tender respect for the ashes of the dead, and an earnest desire, that they may rest, undisturbed, till the resurrection; and this is the very last thing, which is likely to befall the tenant of a tomb; for the owner—and tombs, like other tenements, will change owners—in the common phraseology of leases, has a right to enter, "to view, and expel the lessee"—if no survivor is at hand to prevent, and the new proprietor has other tenants, whom he prefers for the dark and gloomy mansion. And they, in process of time, shall be served, in a similar manner, by another generation. This is no exception; it is the general rule, the common course of dealing with the dead. A tomb, containing the remains of several generations, may become, by marriage, the property of a stranger. His wife dies. He marries anew. New connections beget new interests. The tomb is *useless*, to him, because it is *full*. A general clearance is decreed. A hole is dug in the bottom of the tomb; the coffins, with an honorable exception, in respect to his late beloved, are broken to pieces; and the remains cast into the pit, and covered up. The tablet, overhead, perpetuates the lie—"Sacred to the memory," &c. However, the tomb is white-washed, and swept out, and a nice place he has made of it! All this, have I seen, again and again.

When a tomb is opened, for a new interment, dilapidated coffins are often found lying about, and bones, mud, and water, on the bottom. We always make the best of it, and stow matters away, as decently as we can. We are often blamed for time's slovenly work. Grossman said, that a young spendthrift, who really cared for nothing but his pleasures, was, upon such an occasion, seized with a sudden fit of reverence for his great grandfather, and threatened to shoot Grossman, unless he produced him, immediately. He was finally pacified by a plain statement, and an exhibition of the old gentleman's bones behind the other coffins. We could not be looked upon, more suspiciously, by certain inconsiderate persons, if we were the very worms that did the mischief. As a class, we are as honorable as any other. There are bad men, in every calling. There is no crime, in the decalogue, or out of it, which has not been committed, by some apostle, in holy orders. Doctors and even apothecaries are, occasionally, scoundrels. And, in a very old book, now entirely out of print, I have read, that there was, in the olden time, a lawyer, *rara avis*, who was suspected of not adhering, upon all occasions, to the precise truth. Tombs are nuisances. I will tell you why.

No. XIV

Tombs are obviously more liable to invasion, with and without assistance, from the undertaker and his subalterns, than graves. There may be a few exceptions, where the sexton does not cooperate. If a grave be dug, in a suitable soil, of a proper depth, which is some feet lower than the usual measure, the body will, in all probability, remain undisturbed, for ages, and until corruption and the worm shall have done their work, upon flesh and blood, and decomposition is complete. An intelligent sexton, who keeps an accurate chart of his diggings, will eschew that spot. On the other hand, every coffin is exposed to view, when a tomb is opened for a new comer. On such occasions, we have, sometimes, full employment, in driving away idlers, who gather to the spot, to gratify a sickly curiosity, or to steal whatever may be available, however "sacred to the memory," &c. The tomb is left open, for many hours, and, not unfrequently, over night, the mouth perhaps slightly closed, but not secured against intruders. During such intervals, the dead are far less protected from insult, and the espionage of idle curiosity, than the contents of an ordinary toy-shop, by day or night. Fifty years ago, curiosity led me to walk down into a vault, thus left exposed. No person was near. I lifted the lid of a coffin—the bones had nearly all crumbled to pieces—the skull remained entire—I took it out, and, covering it with my handkerchief, carried it home. I have, at this moment, a clear recollection of the horror, produced in the mind of our old family nurse, by the exhibition of the skull, and my account of the manner, in which I obtained it. "What an awful thing it would be," the dear, good soul exclaimed, "if the resurrection should come this very night, and the poor man should find his skull gone!" My mother was informed; and I was ordered to take it back immediately: it was then dark; and when I arrived at the tomb, in company with our old negro, Hannibal, to whom the office was in no wise agreeable, the vault was closed. I deposited the skull on the tomb, and walked home in double quick time, with my head over my shoulder, the whole way. I relate this occurrence, to show how motiveless such trespasses may be.

There is a morbid desire, especially in women, which is rather difficult of analysis, to descend into the damp and dreary tomb—to lift the coffin lid—and look upon the changing, softening, corrupting features of a parent or child—to gaze upon the mouldering bones; and thus to gather materials, for fearful thoughts, and painful conversations, and frightful dreams!

A lady lost her child. It died of a disease, not perfectly intelligible to the doctor, who desired a post mortem examination, which the mother declined. He urged. She peremptorily refused. The child was buried in the Granary ground. A few months after, another member of the same family was buried in the same vault. The mother, notwithstanding the remonstrances of her husband, descended, to look upon the remains of her only daughter; and, after a careful search, returned, in the condition of Rachel, who would not be comforted, because it was not. In a twofold sense, it was *not*. The coffin and its contents had been removed. The inference was irresistible. The distress was very great, and fresh, upon the slightest allusion, to the end of life. Cases of premature sepulture are, doubtless, extremely rare. That such, however, have sometimes occurred, no doubt has been left upon the mind, upon the opening of tombs. These are a few only of many matters, which are destined, from time to time, to be brought to light, upon the opening of *tombs*, and which are not likely to disturb the feelings of those whose deceased relatives and friends are committed to well-made *graves*. On all these occasions, ignorance is bliss.

Tombs, not only such as are constructed under churches, but in common cemeteries, are frequently highly offensive, on the score of emanation. They are liable to be opened, for the admission of the dead, at all times; and, of course, when the worms are riotous, and corruption is rankest, and the pungent gases are eminently dangerous, and disgusting. Even when closed, the intelligible odor, arising from the dissolving processes, which are going on within, is more than living flesh and blood can well endure. Again and again, visitors at Mount Auburn have been annoyed, by this effluvium from the tombs. By the universal adoption of well-made graves, this also may be entirely avoided.

When a family becomes, or is supposed to be, extinct, or has quitted the country, their dead kindred are usually permitted to lie in peace, in their *graves*. It is not always thus, if they have had the misfortune to be buried in *tombs*. To cast forth a dead tenant, from a solitary *grave*, that room might be found for a new comer, would scarcely be thought of; but the temptation to seize five or six *tombs*, at once, for town's account, on the pretext, that they were the tombs of extinct families, has, once, at least, proved irresistible, and led to an outrage, so gross and revolting, in this Commonwealth, that the whole history of cemeteries in our country cannot produce a parallel. In April, 1835, the board of health, in a town of this Commonwealth, gave notice, in a *single* paper, that certain tombs were dilapidated; that no representative of former owners could be found; and that, if not claimed and repaired, within sixty days, those tombs would be sold, to pay expenses, &c. In fulfilment of this notice, in September following, the entire contents of five tombs were broken to pieces, and shovelled out. In one of these tombs there were thirty coffins, the greater part of which were so sound, as to be split with an axe. A portion of the silver plate, stolen by the operatives employed by the board of health, was afterwards recovered, bearing date, as recently as 1819. The board of health then advertised these tombs for sale, in *two* newspapers. Nothing of these brutal proceedings was known to the relatives, until the deed of barbarity was done. Now it can scarcely be credited, that, in that very town, a few miles from it, and in this city, there were then living numerous descendants, and relatives of those, whose tombs had thus been violated. Some of the dead, thus insulted, had been the greatest benefactors of that town, so much so, that a narrative of their donations has been published, in pamphlet form. Among the direct descendants were some of the oldest and most distinguished families of this city, whose feelings were severely tried by this outrage. The ashes of the dead are common property. The whole community bestirs itself in their defence. The public indignation brought those stupid and ignorant officials to confession and atonement, if not to repentance. They passed votes of regret; replaced the ashes in proper receptacles within the tombs; and put them in order, at the public charge. A meagre and miserable atonement, for an injury of this peculiar nature; and, though gracelessly accorded, —extorted by the stringency of public sentiment, and the fear of legal process, —yet, on the whole, the only satisfaction, for a wrong of this revolting and peculiar character. The insecurity of tombs is sufficiently apparent. An empty tomb may be attached by creditors; but, by statute of Mass., 1822, chap. 93, sec. 8, it cannot be, while in use, as a cemetery. But no law, of man or nature, can prevent the disgusting effects, and mortifying casualties, and misconstructions of power, which have arisen, and will forever continue to arise, from the miserable practice of burying the dead, in *tombs*.

No. XV

There is, doubtless, something not altogether agreeable, in the thought of being buried alive. Testamentary injunctions are not uncommon, for the prevention of such a calamity. As far, as my long experience goes, the percentage is exceedingly small. About twenty-five years ago, some old woman was certain, that a person, lately buried, was not exactly dead. She gave utterance to this certainty—there was no *evidence*, and ample room therefore for *faith*. The defunct had a little property—it was a clear case, of course—his relatives had buried him alive, to get possession! A mob gathered, in King's Chapel yard; and, to appease their righteous indignation, the grave was opened, the body exposed, doctors examined, and the mob was respectfully assured, that the man was dead—dead as a door nail. A proposition to bury the old woman, in revenge, was rejected immediately. But she did not give up the point—they never do. She admitted, that the party was dead, but persisted, that his death was caused, by being buried alive.

Some are, doubtless, still living, who remember the affair in the Granary yard. Groans had been heard there, at night. Some person had been buried alive, beyond all doubt. A committee was appointed to visit the spot. Upon drawing near, subdued laughter and the sounds of vulgar merriment arose, from one of the tombs—a light was seen glimmering from below—the strong odor, not of corruption, but of mutton chops, filled the air. Some vagabonds had cleared the tomb, and taken possession, and, with broken coffins for fuel, had found an appetite, among the dead. The occupation of tombs, by the outcasts of society, was common, long before the Christian era.

That the living have been buried, unintentionally, now and then, is undoubtedly true. Such has probably been the case, sometimes, under catalepsy or trance, the common duration of which is from a few hours, to two or three days; but of which Bonet, *Medic., Septentrion, lib. 1, sec. 16, chap. 6*, gives an example, which lasted twenty days. Bodies have been found, says Millingen, in his Curiosities of Medical Experience, page 63, where the miserable victims have devoured the flesh of their arms; and he cites John Scott and the Emperor Zeno, as examples. Plato recites the case of a warrior, who was left ten days, as dead, upon the field of battle, and came to life, on his way to the sepulchre. In Chalmers' Memoir of the Abbe Prevôt, it is related, that he was found, by a peasant, having fallen in an apoplectic fit. The body was cold, and carried to a surgeon, who proceeded to open it. During the process, the Abbe revived, only, however, to die of the wound, inflicted by the operator.

The danger of burying alive has been noticed by Pineau, *Sur le danger des Inhumations precipitées, Paris, 1776*. Dr. John Mason Good, vol. 4, page 613, remarks, that catalepsy has been mistaken for real death; and, in countries where burial takes place speedily, it is much to be feared, that, in a few instances, the patient has been buried alive. A case of asphyxy, of a singular kind, is stated, by Mr. Pew, and recited by Dr. Good, of a female, whose interment was postponed, for a post mortem examination— most fortunately—for the first touch of the scalpel brought her to life. Diemerbroeck, *Tractat de Peste, Lib. 4, Hist. 8*, relates the case of a rustic, who was laid out for interment. Three days passed before the funeral. He was supposed to have died of the plague. When in the act of being buried, he showed signs of life, recovered, and lived many years. Dr. Good observes, that a critical examination of the region of the heart, and a clear mirror, applied to the mouth and nostrils, will commonly settle the question of life or death; but that even these signs will sometimes fail. What then shall be done? Matthæus Hildanus and others, who give many stories of this kind, say—wait for the infallible signs of putrefaction. It may be absurd to wait too long; it is indecorous to inhume too soon.

The case, recited by Mr. Pew, reminds me of Pliny's account of persons who came to life, on the funeral pile. "Aviola in rogo revixit: et, quoniam subveniri non potuerat, prævalente flamma, vivus crematus est. Similis causa in L. Lamia, prætorio viro, traditur."—Lib. 7, sec. 53.

Old Grossman's stories, in this connection, were curious enough. He gave a remarkable account of a good old deacon, who had a scolding wife. She fell sick and died, as was supposed, and was put in her coffin, and screwed down, and lifted. Everything, as Grossman said, went on very pleasantly, till they began to descend into the tomb, when the sexton, at the foot, slipped, and the coffin went by the run, and struck violently against the wall of the tomb. One instant of awful silence was followed, by a shrill shriek from the corpse—"*Let me out—let me out!*" The poor old deacon wrung his hands, and looked, as Grossman expressed it, "real melancholy." The lid was unscrewed, as soon as possible, and the lady, less in sorrow, than in anger, insisted on immediate emancipation. All attempts to persuade her to be still, and go home as she came, for the decency of the thing, were unavailing. The top of the coffin was removed. The deacon offered to help her out. She refused his proffered hand; and, doubling her fist in his face, told him he was a monster, and should pay for it, and insisted on walking back, in her death clothes. About six months after, she died, in good earnest. "The poor deacon," said Grossman, "called us into a private room, and reminding us of the sad turn things took, last time, begged us to be careful; and told us, if all things went right, he would treat us at his store, the next day. He retailed spirit, as all the deacons did, being the very persons, pointed at, by the finger of the law, as men of sober lives and conversations."

Grossman told another story. We could scarcely credit it. He offered to swear to it; but we begged he wouldn't. It was of a woman, who was a cider sot. Her husband had tried all sorts of preventive experiments, in vain. His patience was exhausted. He tapped a barrel, and let her drink her fill. She and the barrel gave out together. She was buried. The coldness of the tomb brought her to life. She felt around the narrow domicil, in which she lay. Her consciousness, that she was in her coffin, and that she had been buried, was clear enough; but her other impressions were rather cloudy. It never occurred to her, that she had been buried alive. She imagined herself, in another world, and, knocking, as hard as possible, against the lid and sides of her coffin, she exclaimed, "Good people of the upper world, if ye have got any good cider, do let us have a mug of it." Luckily, the mouth of the tomb had not been closed, and, when the sexton came to close it, he was scandalized, of course, to hear a thirsty corpse, crying for cider; but the woman was soon relieved from her predicament. The Mandans, whose custom of never burying their dead, I have alluded to, may possibly be influenced, by a consideration of this very contingency. In some places, bodies have been placed in a lighted room, near the charnel house, there to remain, till the signs of corruption could no longer be mistaken. The tops of the coffins being loose; and a bell so connected with the body, as to ring on the slightest movement.

No. XVI

My profession is very dear to me; and nothing would gratify me more, than to see my brother artists restored to their original dignity. It is quite common to look upon a sexton, as a mere grave-digger, and upon his calling, as a cold, underground employment, divested of everything like sentiment or solemnity.

In the olden time, the sexton bore the title of sacristan. He had charge of the sacristy, or vestry, and all the sacred vessels and vestments of the church. At funerals, his office corresponded with that of the Roman *dominus funeris* or *designator*, referred to by Horace, Ep. i., 7, 6—and by Cicero to Atticus, iv., 2. He was, in point of law, considered as having a freehold, in his office, and therefore he could not be deprived, by ecclesiastical censure. It was his duty to attend upon the rector, and to take no unimportant part, in all those inestimable forms, and ceremonies, and circumgyrations, and genuflections, which render the worship of the high church so exceedingly picturesque. The sexton of the Pope's chapel was selected, from the order of the hermits of St. Augustine, and was commonly a bishop. His title was *prefect of the Pope's sacristy*. When the Pope said mass, the sexton always tasted the bread and wine first. And, when the Pope was desperately sick, the sexton gave him extreme unction. I recite these facts, that the original dignity of our office may be understood.

The employment of sextons has been rather singular, in some countries. M. Outhier states, that, when he visited the church of St. Clara, at Stockholm, he observed the sexton, during the sermon, with a long rod, waking those, who had fallen asleep.

I fully believe, that the sextons of this city are all honorable men; and yet it cannot be denied, that the solemn occasion, upon which their services are required, is one, upon which pride and sensibility forbid all higgling, on the part of the customer. However oppressively the charge of consigning a relative to the ground may bear, upon one of slender means, the tongue of complaint is effectually tied. The consciousness of this furnishes a strong temptation to imposition. The same desire to promote the public good, which induced Mr. Bentham to give his body for dissection, has led distinguished individuals, now and then, to prescribe simple and inexpensive obsequies, for themselves.

Livy says, book 48, sec. 10, that Marcus Emilius Lepidus directed his sons to bury him without parade, and at a very small charge. As he was the Pontifex Maximus, possessed of wealth, and of a generous spirit, the promotion of the public good was the only motive. Cheating at funerals was as common at Athens, as at Rome. Demades, as Seneca relates, book 6, ch. 33, *de beneficiis*, condemned an unprincipled Athenian sexton, for extortion, in furnishing out funerals. The friends and relatives are so busy with their sorrow, that they have neither time nor taste, for the examination of accounts, and, least of all, such as concern the obsequies of near friends. I was never more forcibly impressed with the truth, that, where the carcass is, there the vultures will be gathered together, than in the little island of St. Croix, during the winter of 1840. I was there with a friend, a clergyman, who visited that island, for the restoration of his wife's health. She died. Her remains were never buried there, but brought to this city, and here interred. In that island there is a tribunal, called the *Dealing Court*, analogous to the court of probate, or orphan's court, in this country. In less than forty-eight hours, a bill was presented, from this court, for "*dealing*" with the estate of the deceased. She had no estate; no act had been done. "True, but such is the custom of our island—such is the law of Denmark." After taking counsel, the bill was paid. The Danish Lutheran is the established religion of the island. The Episcopal lives, by sufferance. A few days after this lady's decease, a bill was presented, from the officers of the *Danish Lutheran* church, for granting permission to dig her grave, in the *Episcopal* ground. It was objected, that no permission had been asked, that no burial had been intended, that the body had been placed in spirits, for its removal to the United States. It was replied, "Such is the usage of the island; the permission is granted, and may be used or not; such is the law of Denmark."

Shortly after this, a bill was presented, for digging the grave. It was in vain to protest, as before, and to assert, that no grave had been dug. The answer was the same; "the grave must be paid for; it will be dug or not, as you wish; such is the usage of the island; such is the law of Denmark." In due time, another demand was made, for carrying round invitations, and attendance upon the funeral. It was useless to say, that no invitations were sent—no funeral was had. "Such is the custom of the island; such is the law of Denmark." The reader, by this time, will be satisfied, that something is rotten in Denmark; this narrative appears so very improbable, that I deem it right to assure the reader the circumstances are stated faithfully, and that the clergyman referred to, is still living.

In commending a respectable frugality, in our dealings with the dead, not only with regard to their obsequies, but in relation to sepulchral and monumental expenditure, I oppose the interest of our profession, and cannot be accused of any selfish motive. A chaste simplicity is due to the occasion; for surely no more illy chosen hour can be given to the gratification of pride, than that, in which the very pride of man is humbled in the dust. How often have my thoughts descended from the costly, sculptured obelisk, to the carnival of worms below!

A well-set example of comely modesty, in these matters, would be productive of much advantage to the community. The man of common means, if he happen to be also a man of common sense, will not imitate the man of opulence, in the splendor of his equipage or furniture. But he will too readily enter into what he deems a righteous rivalry of funereal parade, and leave his debts unpaid, rather than abate one cubit, in the height of his monument, or obelisk. It is not now the custom to bury with the dead, or deposit with their ashes, as in urn burial, articles of use and value to the living. We have been taught, that those graves are the least likely to be violated, in which are deposited little else than mortal remains. But, in a certain sense, the dead can no longer be said to carry nothing with them. The silver and its workmanship alone, which are annually buried, furnish no inconsiderable item.

The outer coffin of Nathan Meyer Rothschild "was of fine oak, and so handsomely carved and decorated with massive silver handles, at both sides and ends, that it appeared more like a cabinet, or splendid piece of furniture, than a receptacle of the dead. A raised tablet of oak, on the breast, was carved with the arms of the deceased." The arms of the deceased! Very edifying to the worms, those cunning operatives, who work so skilfully, in silence and darkness! The arms of the deceased! Matthew Prior had some shrewd notions of heraldry. He wrote his own epitaph—

> Heralds and nobles, by your leave,
> Here lie the bones of Matthew Prior;
> The son of Adam and of Eve;
> Let Bourbon and Nassau go higher.

No. XVII

My attention has been called, by a young disciple of the great Pontraci, "a sexton of the new school," to an interesting anecdote, which I have heard related, in days by-gone, and which has, more than once, appeared in print. It is, by many, believed, that the remains of Major Pitcairn, which were supposed to have been sent home to England, are still in this country, and that those of Lieutenant Shea were transmitted, by mistake. Whether *he* or *Shea* will ever remain doubtful. Major Pitcairn was killed, as is well known, at the battle of Bunker's Hill. Shea died of inflammation on the brain. They were alike in size. On the top of the head of the body, selected by the sexton of Christ Church, as the remains of Major Pitcairn, it is stated, there was a blistering plaster; and, from this circumstance, the impression has arisen, that the monument in Westminster Abbey, however sacred to the memory of Pitcairn, stands over the remains of Lieutenant Shea. There is not more uncertainty, in relation to the remains of Major Pitcairn, than has existed, in regard to the individual, by whose hands he fell; though it is now agreed, that he was shot by a black soldier, named Salem. Fifty men, at the lowest estimate, have died in the faith, that they killed Pitcairn. He was a man of large stature, fearless, and ever in the van, as he is represented by Marshall, at the battle of Lexington.

He was a palpable mark, for the muskets and rifles of the sharp-shooters. It is not improbable, that fifty barrels were levelled at his person, when he fell; and hence fifty claimants, for the merit of Pitcairn's destruction. Upon precisely similar grounds, rest the claims of Col. Johnson, for the killing of Tecumseh.

When the flesh has gone and nothing but the bones remain, it is almost impossible, to recognize the remains of any particular individual, buried hastily, as the fallen commonly are, after a battle, in one common grave; unless we are directed, by certain external indicia. In April, 1815, I officiated at the funeral of Dr. John Warren, brother of the patriot and soldier, who fell so gloriously, at Bunker's Hill, and whose death was said, by the British General, Howe, to be an offset, for five hundred men. Dr. James Jackson delivered the eulogy, on Dr. John Warren, in King's Chapel. General Warren was buried in the trenches, where he so bravely fell; and, when disinterred, in 1776, for removal to Boston, the remains were identified, by an inspection of the teeth, upon which an operation had been performed, the evidence of which remained. This testimony was doubtless corroborated, by the mark of the bullet on his forehead; for he was not a man to be wounded in the back. "The bullet which terminated his life," says Mr. A. H. Everett in his memoir, "was taken from the body, by Mr. Savage, an officer in the Custom House, and was carried by him to England. Several years afterwards, it was given by him at London, to the Rev. Mr. Montague of Dedham, Massachusetts, and is now in possession of his family."

These translations of the dead, from place to place, are full of uncertainty; and hence has arisen a marvellous and successful system of jugglery and priestcraft. The first translation of this kind, stated by Brady, in his Clavis, is that of Edward, king of the West Saxons. He was removed with great pomp from Wareham to the minster of Salisbury. Three years only had passed since his burial, and no error is imputed, in the relation. In the year 359, the Emperor Constantius was moved, by the spirit, to do something in this line; and he caused the remains of St. Andrew and St. Luke to be translated, from their original resting-places, to the temple of the twelve apostles, at Constantinople. Some little doubt might be supposed to hang over the question of identity, after such a lapse of years, in this latter case. From this eminent example, arose that eager search for the remains of saints, martyrs, and relics of various descriptions, which, for many centuries, filled the pockets of imposters, with gold, and the world, with idolatry. So great was the success of those, engaged in this lucrative employment, that John the Baptist became a perfect hydra. Heads of this great pioneer were discovered, in every direction. Some of the apostles were found, upon careful search, to be centipedes; and others to have had as many hands as Briareus. These monstrosities were too vast to be swallowed, without a miracle. Father John Freand, of Anecy, assured the faithful, that God was pleased to multiply these remains for their devotion. Consecration has been refused to churches, unprovided with relics. Their production therefore became indispensable. All the wines, produced in *Oporto* and *Zeres de la Frontera*, furnish not a fourth part of the liquor, drunken, in London alone, under the names of Port and Sherry; and the bones of all the martyrs, were it possible to collect them, would not supply the occasions of the numerous churches, in Catholic countries. Misson says eleven holy lances are shown, in different places, for the true lance, that pierced the side of Christ.

Many egregious sinners have undoubtedly been dug up, and their bones worshipped, as the relics of genuine saints. Though not precisely to our purpose, it may not be uninteresting to the reader, to contemplate a catalogue of some few of the relics, exhibited to the faithful, as they are enumerated, by Bayle, Butler, Misson, Brady and others;—the lance—a piece of the cross—one of Christ's nails—five thorns of the crown—St. Peter's chain—a piece of the manger—a tooth of John the Baptist—one of St. Anne's arms—the towel, with which Christ wiped the feet of the apostles— one of his teeth—his seamless coat—the hem of his garment, which cured the diseased woman—a tear, which he shed over Lazarus, preserved by an angel, who gave it, in a vial, to Mary Magdalene—a piece of St. John the Evangelist's gown—a piece of the table cloth, used at the last supper—a finger of St. Andrew—a finger of John the Baptist—a rib of our Lord—the thumb of St. Thomas—a lock of Mary Magdalene's hair—two handkerchiefs, bearing impressions of Christ's face; one sent by our Lord, as a present to Aquarus, prince of Edessa; and the other given by him, at the foot of the cross, to a holy woman, named Veronica—the hem of Joseph's garment—a feather of the Holy Ghost—a finger of the Holy Ghost—a feather of the angel Gabriel—the waterpots, used at the marriage in Galilee—Enoch's slippers—a vial of the sweat of St. Michael, at the time of his set-to with the Devil. This short list furnishes a meagre show-box of that immense mass of merchandise, which formed the staple of priestcraft. These pretended relics were not only procured, at vast expense, but were occasionally given, and received, as collateral security for debts. Baldwin II. sent the point of the holy lance to Venice, as a pledge for a loan. It was redeemed by St. Lewis, King of France, who caused it to be placed in the holy chapel at Paris. The importation of this species of trumpery, into England, was forbidden, by many statutes; and, by 3. Jac. i., cap. 26, justices were empowered to search houses for such things, and to burn them.

It is pleasant to turn from these shadowy records to matters of reality and truth. There was an exhumation, some years ago, of the remains of a highly honorable and truly gallant man, for the purpose of returning them to his native land. Suspicions of a painful nature arose, in connection with that exhumation. Those suspicions were cleared away, most happily, by a venerable friend of mine, with whom I have conversed upon that interesting topic. I will give some account of the removal of Major André's remains, in my next.

No. XVIII

Major John André, aid-de-camp to General Clinton, and adjutant general of the British army, was, as every well-read school-boy knows, hanged as a spy, October 2, 1780, at Tappan, a town of New York, about five miles from the north bank of the Hudson.

In June, 1818, by a vote of the Legislature of New York, the remains of that gallant Irishman, Major General Richard Montgomery, were removed from Quebec. Col. L. Livingston, his nephew, superintended the exhumation and removal. An old soldier, who had attended the funeral, forty-two years before, pointed out the grave. These relics were committed to the ground, once more, in St. Paul's church-yard in New York; and, by direction of the Congress of the United States, a costly marble monument was erected there, executed by M. Cassieres, at Paris. Nothing was omitted of pomp and pageantry, in honor of the gallant dead.

Still the remains of André, whose fate was deeply deplored, however just the punishment—still they continued, in that resting place, humble and obscure, to which they had been consigned, when taken from the gallows. The lofty honors, bestowed upon Montgomery, operated as a stimulus and a rebuke. Mr. James Buchanan, the British consul, admits their influence, in his memorable letter. He addressed a communication to the Duke of York, then commander-in-chief of the British army, suggesting the propriety of exhumating the remains of André, and returning them to England. The necessary orders were promptly issued, and Mr. Buchanan made his arrangements for the exhumation.

Mr. Demarat, a Baptist clergyman, at Tappan, was the proprietor of the little field, where the remains of André had been buried, and where they had reposed, for forty-one years, when, in the autumn of 1821, Mr. Buchanan requested permission to remove them. His intentions had become known—some human brute—some Christian dog, had sought to purchase, or to rent, the field of Mr. Demarat, for the purpose of extorting money, for permission to remove these relics. But the good man and true rejected the base proposal, and afforded every facility in his power.

A narrow pathway led to the eminence, where André had suffered— the grave was there, covered with a few loose stones and briars. There was nothing beside, to mark the spot—I am wrong—woman, who was last at the cross, and first at the tomb, had been there—there was a peach tree, which a lady had planted at the head, and whose roots had penetrated to the very bottom of the shallow grave, and entered the frail shell, and enveloped the skull with its fibres. Dr. Thacher, in a note to page 225 of his military journal, says, that the roots of two cedar trees "had wrapped themselves round the skull bone, like a fine netting." This is an error. Two cedars grew near the grave, which were sent to England, with the remains.

The point, where these relics lay, commanded a view of the surrounding country, and of the head-quarters of Washington, about a mile and a half distant. The field, which contained about ten acres, was cultivated—a small part only, around the consecrated spot, remained untilled. Upon the day of the exhumation, a multitude had gathered to the spot. After digging three feet from the surface, the operative paused, and announced, that his spade had touched the top of the coffin. The excitement was so great, at this moment, that it became necessary to form a cordon, around the grave. Mr. Buchanan proceeded carefully to remove the remaining earth, with his hands—a portion of the cover had been decomposed. When, at last, the entire top had been removed, the remains of this brave and unfortunate young man were exposed to view. The skeleton was in perfect order. "There," says Mr. Buchanan, "for the first time, I discovered that he had been a small man."

One by one, the assembled crowd passed round, and gazed upon the remains of André, whose fate had excited such intense and universal sensibility. These relics were then carefully transferred to a sarcophagus, prepared for their reception, and conveyed to England. They now repose beneath the sixth window, in the south aisle of Westminster Abbey. The monument near which they lie, was designed by Robert Adam, and executed by Van Gelder. Britannia reclines on a sarcophagus, and upon the pedestal is inscribed—"Sacred to the memory of Major André, who, raised by his merit, at an early period of life, to the rank of Adjutant General of the British forces in America, and, employed in an important but hazardous enterprise, fell a sacrifice to his zeal for his king and country, on 2d of October, 1780, aged twenty-nine, universally beloved and esteemed by the army, in which he served, and lamented even by his foes. His generous sovereign, King George III., has caused this monument to be erected." Nothing could have been prepared, in better taste. Here is not the slightest allusion to that great question, which posterity, having attained full age, has already, definitively, settled—the justice of his fate. A box, wrought from one of the cedar trees, and lined with gold, was transmitted to Mr. Demarat, by the Duke of York; and a silver inkstand was presented to Mr. James Buchanan, by the surviving sisters of Major André.

Thus far, all things were in admirable keeping. It was, therefore, a matter of deep regret, that Mr. James Buchanan should have thought proper to disturb their harmony, by suggestions, painfully offensive to every American heart. Those suggestions, it is true, have been acknowledged to be entirely groundless. But that gentleman's original letter, extensively circulated here, and transmitted to England, has, undoubtedly, conveyed these offensive insinuations, where the subsequent admission of his error is not likely to follow. Mr. Buchanan, on the strength of some loose suggestions, at Tappan, and elsewhere, corroborated by an examination of the contents of the coffin, had assumed it to be true, or highly probable, that the body of André had been stripped, after the execution, from mercenary, or other equally unworthy, motives. This impression he hastily conveyed to the world. I will endeavor to present this matter, in its true light, in my next communication.

No. XIX

After having removed the entire cover of André's coffin, "I descended," says Mr. Buchanan, "and, with my own hands, raked the dust together, to ascertain whether he had been buried in his regimentals, or not, as it was rumored, among the assemblage, that he was stripped: for, if buried in his regimentals, I expected to find the buttons of his clothes, which would have disproved the rumor; but I did not find a single button, nor any article, save a string of leather, that had tied his hair." Mr. Buchanan had evidently arrived at the conclusion, that André had been stripped. In this conclusion he was perfectly right. He had also inferred, that this act had been done, with base motives. In this inference, he was perfectly wrong. "Those," continues he, "who permitted the outrage, or who knew of it, had no idea, that the unfeeling act they then performed would be blazoned to the world, near half a century, after the event." All this is entirely gratuitous and something worse. General Washington's head-quarters were near at hand. Every circumstance was sure to be reported, for the excitement was intense; and the knowledge of such an act, committed for any unworthy purpose, would have been instantly conveyed to Sir Henry Clinton, and blazoned to the world, some forty years before the period of Mr. Buchanan's discovery.

Dr. James Thacher, in his military journal, states, that André was executed "in his royal regimentals, and buried in the same." Dr. Thacher was mistaken, and when he saw the letter of Mr. Buchanan, and the offensive imputation it contained, he investigated the subject anew, and addressed a letter to that gentleman, which was received by him, in a becoming spirit, and which entirely dissipated his former impressions. In that letter, Dr. Thacher stated, that he was within a few yards of André, at the time of his execution, and that he suffered in his regimentals. Supposing, as a matter of course, that André would be buried in them, Dr. Thacher had stated that, also, as a fact, though he did not remain, to witness the interment. He then refers to a letter, which he has discovered in the Continental Journal and Weekly Advertiser, of October 26, 1780, printed in Boston, by John Gill. This letter bears date, Tappan, October 2, the day of the execution, and details all the particulars, and in it are these words—"*He was dressed in full uniform; and, after the execution, his servant demanded the uniform, which he received. His body was buried near the gallows.*" "This," says Dr. Thacher, "confirms the correctness of my assertion, that he suffered in his regimentals, but not that they were buried with the body. I had retired from the scene, before the body was placed in the coffin; but I have a perfect recollection of seeing him hand his hat to the weeping servant, while standing in the cart."

Mr. Buchanan observes, that an aged widow, who kept the toll-gate, on hearing the object stated, was so much gratified, that she suffered all carriages to pass free. "It marks strongly," he continues, "the sentiments of the American people at large, as to a transaction, which a great part of the British public have forgotten." This passage is susceptible of a twofold construction. It may mean, that this aged widow and the American people at large were unanimous, in lamenting the fate of Major André—that they most truly believed him to have been brave and unfortunate. It may also mean, that they considered the fate of André to have been unwarranted. Posterity has adjusted this matter very differently. Nearly sixty-eight years have passed. All excitement has long been buried, in a deeper grave than André's. A silent admission has gone forth, far and wide, of the perfect justice of André's execution. A board of general officers was appointed, to prepare a statement of his case. Greene, Steuben, and Lafayette were of that board. They were perfectly unanimous in their opinion. Prodigious efforts were made on his behalf. He himself addressed several letters to Washington, and one, the day before his death, in which he says: "Sympathy towards a soldier will surely induce your excellency and a military tribunal to adapt the mode of my death to the feelings of a man of honor." The board of officers, as Gordon states, were induced to gratify this wish, with the exception of Greene. He contended, that the laws of war required, that a spy should be hung; the adoption of any less rigorous mode of punishment would excite the belief, that palliatory circumstances existed in the case of André, and that the decision might thereby be brought into question. His arguments were sound, and they prevailed.

Major André received every attention, which his condition permitted. He wrote to Sir Henry Clinton, Sept. 29, 1780, three days before his execution—"I receive the greatest attention from his excellency, General Washington, and from every person, under whose charge I happen to be placed." Captain Hale, like Major André, was young, brave, amiable, and accomplished. He entered upon the same perilous service, that conducted André to his melancholy fate. Hale was hanged, as a spy, at Long Island. Thank God, the brutal treatment he received was not retaliated upon André. "The provost martial," says Mr. Sparks, "was a refugee, to whose charge he was consigned, and treated him, in the most unfeeling manner, refusing the attendance of a clergyman, and the use of a bible; and destroying the letters he had written, to his mother and friends."

The execution of Major André was in perfect conformity with the laws of war. Had Sir Henry Clinton considered his fate unwarranted, under any just construction of those laws, he would undoubtedly have expressed that opinion, in the general orders, to the British army, announcing Major André's death. These orders, bearing date Oct. 8, 1780, refer only to his *unfortunate fate*. They contain not the slightest allusion to any supposed injustice, or unaccustomed severity, in the execution, or the manner of it.

The fate of André might have been averted, in two ways—by a steady resistance of Arnold's senseless importunity, to bring him within the American lines—and by a frank and immediate presentation of Arnold's pass, when stopped by Paulding, Williams, and Van Wart. His loss of self-possession, at that critical moment, is remarkable, for, as Americans, they would, in all human probability, have suffered him to pass, without further examination; and, had they been of the opposite party, they would certainly have conducted him to some British post—the very haven where he would be.

No. XX

How shall *we* deal with the dead? We have considered the usages of many nations, in different ages of the world. Some of these usages appear sufficiently revolting; especially such as relate to secondary burial, or the transfer of the dead, from their primary resting-places, to vast, miscellaneous receptacles. The desire is almost universal, that, when summoned to lie down in the grave, the dead may never be disturbed, by the hand of man—that our remains may return quietly to dust—unobserved by mortal eye. There is no part of this humiliating process, that is not painful and revolting to the beholder. Of this the ancients had the same impression. Cremation and embalming set corruption and the worm at defiance. Other motives, I am aware, have been assigned for the former. The execution of popular vengeance upon the poor remains of those, whose memory has become odious, during a revolution, is not uncommon. A ludicrous example of this occurred, when Santa Anna became unpopular, and the furious mob seized his leg, which had been amputated, embalmed, and deposited among the public treasures, and cooled their savage anger, by kicking the miserable member all over the city of Montezuma.

In the time of Sylla, cremation was not so common as interment; but Sylla, remembering the indignity he had offered to the body of Marius, enjoined, that his own body should be burnt. There was, doubtless, another motive for this practice among the ancients. The custom prevailed extensively, at one time, of burying the dead, in the cellars of houses. I have already referred to the Theban law, which required the construction of a suitable receptacle for the dead, in every house. Interment certainly preceded cremation. Cicero De Legibus, lib. 2, asserts, that interment prevailed among the Athenians, in the time of Cecrops, their first king. In the earlier days of Rome, both were employed. Numa was *buried* in conformity with a special clause in his will. Remus, as Ovid, Fast. iv. 356, asserts, was *burnt*. The accumulation of dead bodies in cellars, or subcellars, must have become intolerable. This practice undoubtedly gave rise to the whole system of household gods,

Lares, Lemures, Larvæ, and Manes. Such an accumulation of ancestors, it may well be supposed, left precious little room for the amphoræ of Chian, Lesbian, and Falernian.

Young aspirants sometimes inwardly opine, that their living ancestors take up too much room. Such was very naturally the opinion of the ancients, in relation to the dead. Like François Pontraci, they began to feel the necessity of condensation; and cremation came to be more commonly adopted. The bones of a human being, reduced to ashes, require but little room; and not much more, though the decomposition by fire be not quite perfect. Let me say to those, who think I prefer cremation, as a substitute for interment, that I do not. It has found little favor for many centuries. It seems to have been employed, in the case of Shelley, the poet. However desirable, when the remains of the dead were to be deposited in the dwelling-houses of the living, cremation and urn burial are quite unnecessary, wherever there is no want of ground for cemeteries, in proper locations. The funereal urns of the ancients were of different sizes and forms, and of materials, more or less costly, according to the ability and taste of the surviving friends. Ammianus Marcellinus relates, that Gumbrates, king of Chionia, near Persia, burnt the body of his son, and placed the ashes in a *silver* urn.

Mr. Wedgewood had the celebrated Portland vase in his possession, for a year, and made casts of it. This was the vase, which had been in possession of the Barberini family, for nearly two centuries, and for which the Duke of Portland gave Mr. Hamilton one thousand guineas. In the minds of very many, the idea of considerable size has been associated with this vase. Yet, in fact, it is about ten inches high, and six broad. The Wedgewood casts may be seen, in many of our glass and china shops. This vase was discovered, about the middle of the sixteenth century, two and a half miles from Rome, on the Frescati road, in a marble sarcophagus, within a sepulchral chamber. This, doubtless, was a funereal urn. The urns, dug up, in Old Walsingham, in 1658, were quite similar, in form, to the Portland vase, excepting that they were without ears. Some fifty were found in a sandy soil, about three feet deep, a short distance from an old Roman garrison, and only five miles from Brancaster, the ancient Branodunum. Four of these vases are figured, in Browne's Hydriotaphia; some of them contained about two pounds of bones; several were of the capacity of a gallon, and some of half that size. It may seem surprising, that a human body can be reduced to such a compass. "How the bulk of a man should sink into so few pounds of bones and ashes may seem strange unto any, who consider not its constitution, and how slender a mass will remain upon an open and urging fire, of the carnal composition. Even bones themselves, reduced into ashes, do abate a notable proportion." Such are the words of good old Sir Thomas.

It was an adage of old, "He that lies in a golden urn, will find no quiet for his bones." If the costliness of the material offered no temptation to the avarice of man, still, after centuries have given them the stamp of antiquity, these urns and their contents become precious, in the eyes of the lovers of *vertu*. There is no security from impertinent meddling with our remains, so certain, as a speedy conversion into undistinguishable dust. Sir Thomas Browne manifestly inclined to cremation. "To be gnawed," says he, "out of our graves, to have our skulls made drinking bowls, and our bones turned into pipes, to delight and sport our enemies, are tragical abominations, escaped in burning burials." Such anticipations are certainly unpleasant. An ingenious device was adopted by Alaricus—he appointed the spot for his grave, and directed, that the course of a river should be so changed, as to flow over it.

It has been said, that certain soils possess a preserving quality. I am inclined to think the secret commonly lies, in some peculiar, constitutional quality, in the dead subject; for, wherever cases of remarkable preservation have occurred, corruption has been found generally to have done its full day's work, on all around. If such quality really exist in the soil, it is certainly undesirable. Those who were opposed to the evacuation of the Cemetery des Innocens, in the sixteenth century, attempted to set up in its favor the improbable pretension, that it consumed bodies in nine days. Burton, in his description of Leicestershire, states, that the body of Thomas, Marquis of Dorset, "was found perfect, and nothing corrupted, the flesh not hardened, but in color, proportion and softness, like an ordinary corpse, newly to be interred," after seventy-eight years' burial.

A remarkable case of posthumous preservation occurred, in a village near Boston. The very exalted character of the professional gentleman, who examined the corpse, after it had been entombed, for forty years, gives the interest of authenticity to the statement. Justice Fuller, the father-in-law of that political victim, General William Hull, *who was neither a coward nor a traitor*, was buried in a family tomb, in Newton Centre. It was ascertained, and, from time to time, reported, that the body remained uncorrupted and entire. Mr. Fuller was about 80, when he died, and very corpulent. About forty years after his burial, Dr. John C. Warren, by permission of the family, with the physician of the village, and other gentlemen, examined the body of Mr. Fuller. The coffin was somewhat decomposed. So were the burial clothes. The body presented, everywhere, a natural skin, excepting on one leg, on which there had been an ulcer. There decomposition had taken place. The skin was generally of a dark brown color, and hard like dried leather; and so well preserved, about the face, that persons, present with Dr. Warren, said they should have recognized the features of Justice Fuller. My business lies not with the physiology, however curious the speculation may be. Were it possible, by any means, to perpetuate the dead, in a similar manner, it would be wholly undesirable. Dust we are, and unto dust must we return. The question is still before us,—How shall *we* deal with the dead?

No. XXI

It is commonly supposed, that the burial of articles of value with the dead, is a practice confined to the Indian tribes, and the inhabitants of unenlightened regions; who fancied, that the defunct were gone upon some far journey, during which such accompaniments would be useful. Such is not the fact. Chilperic, the fourth king of France, came to the throne A. D. 456. In 1655 the tomb of Chilperic was accidentally discovered, in Tournay, "restoring unto the world," saith Sir Thomas Browne, vol. 3, p. 466, "much gold adorning his sword, two hundred rubies, many hundred imperial coins, three hundred golden bees, the bones and horse-shoes of his horse, interred with him, according to the barbarous magnificence of those days, in their sepulchral obsequies." Stow relates, in his survey of London, that, in many of the funeral urns, found in Spitalfields, there were, mingled with the relics, coins of Claudius, Vespasian, Commodus, and Antoninus, with lachrymatories, lamps, bottles of liquor, &c.

As an old sexton, I have a right to give my advice; and the public have a right to reject it. If I were the owner of a lot, in some well-governed cemetery, I would place around it a neat, substantial, iron fence, and paint it black. In the centre I would have a simple monument, of white marble, and of liberal dimensions; not pyramidal, but with four rectangular faces, to receive a goodly number of memoranda, not one of which should exceed a single line. I would have no other monument, slab, or tablet, to indicate particular graves. I would have a plan of this lot, and preserve it, as carefully, as I preserved my title papers. Probably I should keep a duplicate, in some safe place. When a body came to be buried, in that lot, I would indicate the precise location, on my plan, and engrave the name and the date of birth, and death, and nothing more, upon the monument. If the dryness and elevation of the soil allowed, I would dig the graves so deep, that the remains of three persons could repose in one grave, the uppermost, five or six feet below the surface. After the burial of the first, the grave would be filled up, and an even, sodded surface presented, as before, until re-opened. Thus, of course, those, who had been lovely and pleasant, in their lives, like Jonathan and Saul, would, in death, be not divided. This, so far from being objectionable, is a delightful idea, embalmed in the classical precedents of antiquity. It is a well-known fact, that urns of a very large size were, occasionally, in use, in Greece and Rome, for the reception and commingling of the ashes of whole families. The ashes of Achilles were mingled with those of his friend, Patroclus. The ashes of Domitian, the last, and almost the worst, of the twelve Cæsars, were inurned, as Suetonius reports, ch. 17, with those of Julia.

With the Chinese, it is very common to bury a comb, a pair of scissors to pare the nails, and four little purses, containing the nail parings of the defunct. Jewels and coins of gold are sometimes inserted in the mouths of the wealthy. This resembles the practice of the Greeks and Romans, of placing an obolus, Charon's fee, in the mouth of the deceased. This arrangement, in regard to the nail parings, seems well enough, as they are clearly part and parcel, of the defunct. Rings, coins, and costly chalices have been found, with the ashes of the dead.

Avarice, curiosity, and revenge, personal or political, have prompted mankind, in every age, to desecrate the receptacles of the dead. The latter motive has operated more fiercely, upon the people of France, than upon almost any other. No nation has ever surpassed them, in that intense ardor, nor in the parade and magnificence, with which they *canonize*— no people upon earth can rival the bitterness and fury, with which they *curse*. Lamartine, in his history of the Girondists, states, that "dragoons of the Republic spread themselves over the public places, brandishing their swords, and singing national airs. Thence they went to the church of Val de Grace, where, enclosed in silver urns, were the hearts of several kings and queens of France. These funeral vases they broke, trampling under foot those relics of royalty, and then flung them into the common sewer." And how shall *we* deal with the dead?

With a reasonable economy of space, a lot of the common area, at Mount Auburn, or Forest Hills, will suffice, for the occasion of a family of ordinary size, for several generations. In re-opening one of these graves, for a second or third interment, the operative should never approach nearer than one foot to the coffin beneath. The careless manner, in which bones are sometimes spaded up, by grave-diggers, results from their want of precise knowledge of previous inhumations. Common sense indicates the propriety of keeping a regular, topographical account of every interment.

But it is quite time to bring these lucubrations to a close. To some they may have proved interesting, and, doubtless, wearisome to others. The account is therefore balanced. Most heartily do I wish for every one of my readers a decent funeral, and a peaceful grave. I have tolled my last knell, turned down my last sod, and am no longer a Sexton of the Old School.

No. XXII

Some commendatory passages, in your own and other journals, my dear Mr. Transcript, seem very much to me like a theatrical *encore*—they half persuade me to reappear. There are other considerations, which I cannot resist. Twenty devils, saith the Spanish proverb, employ that man, who employeth not himself. I am quite sensible of my error, in quitting an old vocation prematurely. You have no conception of the severe depression of spirits, produced in the mind of an old sexton, who, in an evil hour, has cast his spade aside, and set up for a man of leisure. It may answer for a short time—a very short time. I can honestly declare, that I have led a wearisome life, since I gave up undertaking. Many have been the expedients I have adopted, to relieve the oppressive tedium of my miserable days. The funeral bell has aroused me, as the trumpet rouses an old war horse. How many processions I have followed, as an amateur! One or two young men of the craft have been exceedingly kind to me, and have given me notice, whenever they have been employed upon a new grave, and have permitted me to amuse myself, by performing a portion of the work.

My own condition, since I left off business, and tried the terrible experiment of living on my income, and doing nothing, has frequently and forcibly reminded me of a similar passage, in the history of my excellent old friend, Simon Allwick, the tallow-chandler, with whom I had the happiness of living, in the closest intimacy, and whom I had the pleasure of burying, about twenty years ago.

Mr. Allwick was a thrifty man; and, having acquired a handsome property, his ambitious partner persuaded him to abandon his greasy occupation, and set up for a gentleman. This was by no means, the work of a day. Mr. Allwick loved his wife—she was an affectionate creature; and, next to the small matter of having her own way in everything, she certainly loved Allwick, as her prime minister, in bringing that matter about. She was what is commonly called a devoted wife. Man is, marvellously, the creature of habit. So completely had Allwick become that creature, that, when his partner, upon the occasion of an excursion, as far as Jamaica Pond, for which Allwick literally tore himself away from the chandlery, could not restrain her admiration of that pretty, pet lake, he candidly confessed, that he felt nothing of the sort. And, when Mrs. Allwick exclaimed, with uplifted hands and tears in her eyes, that, in a cottage, on the borders of such a lake, she should be the happiest of the happy—"So should I, my dear," said her husband, with a sigh, so heavily drawn, that it seemed four to the pound—"so should I, my dear, if the lake were a vat of clear melted tallow, and I had a plenty of sticks and wicks."

Suffice it to say, Mrs. Allwick had set her heart upon the measure. She had a confidential friend or two, to whom she had communicated the *projét*: her pride had therefore become enlisted; for she had given them to understand, that she meant to have her own way. She commenced an uncompromising crusade, against grease, in every form. She complained, that grease spots were upon everything. She engaged the services of a young physician, who gave it, as his deliberate opinion, that Mr. Allwick's headaches arose from the deleterious influence of the fumes of hot grease, acting through the olfactory nerves, upon the pineal gland.

He even expressed a fear, that insanity might supervene, and he furnished an account of an eminent tallow-chandler in London, who went raving mad, and leaping into his own vat of boiling grease, was drawn out, no better than a great candle. It was a perfect *coup de grace*, when Mrs. Allwick drove candles from her dwelling, and substituted oil. The chandlery adjoined their residence, in Scrap Court; and it must be admitted, that, with the wind at south, the odor was not particularly savory. Mrs. Allwick was what the world would style a smart woman, and she was in the habit of calling her husband a very *wicked* man and their mansion the most unclassical villa, though in the very midst of *grease*!

It is quite superfluous to say, the point was finally carried—the chandlery was sold—a country house was purchased, not on the lake, but in a sweet spot. There was some little embarrassment about the name, but two wild gooseberry bushes having been discovered, within half a mile, it was resolved, in council, to call it Mount Gooseberry. Since the going forth of Adam from Eden, in misery and shame, never was there such an exodus, as that of poor Allwick from the chandlery. I have not time to describe it. I am glad I have not. It was too much. Even Mrs. Allwick began to doubt the perfect wisdom of her plan. But the die was cast. On they went to their El Dorado. It was a pleasant spot. It was "a bonnie day in June." The birds were in ecstacies—so was Mrs. Allwick—so were the children—the sun shone—the stream ran beautifully by—the leaves still glistened in the morning dew—there was a sprinkling of lambs on the hills—old Cato was at the door, to welcome them, and Carlo most affectionately covered the white frocks of the children with mud. "Was there ever anything like this?" exclaimed the delighted wife. "Isn't it a perfect pink, papa?" cried the children. In answer to all this, the *jecur ulcerosum* of poor Allwick sent forth a deep groan, that shook the very walls of his tabernacle.

The mind of man is a mill, and will grind chaff if nothing more substantial be supplied; and, peradventure, the upper will grind the nether millstone to destruction. For a brief space, Mr. Allwick found employment. Fences were to be completed—trees and bushes were to be set out—the furniture was to be arranged—but all this was soon over, and there was my good old friend, Simon Allwick, the busiest man alive, with nothing to do! Never was there a heart, in the bosom of a tallow-chandler, so perfectly "untravelled." Poor fellow, he went "up stairs and down stairs, and in my lady's chamber," but all to no other purpose, than to confirm him, in a sentiment of profound respect, for that homely proverb, *it is hard for an old dog to learn new tricks.*

"Where is your father?" said Mrs. Allwick to the children, after breakfast, one awful hot morning, near the end of June. The children went in pursuit—there he was—he had sought to occupy his thoughts, by watching the gambols of some half a dozen Byfield cokies—there he was—he had rested his arms upon the rail of the fence, and had been looking into the sty—his chin had dropped upon his hands—he had fallen asleep! He was mortified and nettled, at being found thus, and continued in a moody condition, through the day. On the following morning, he went to the city, and remained till night. His spirits were greatly improved, on his return; and to some felicitations from his wife and family, he replied—"My dear, I feel better, certainly; and I have made an arrangement, which, I think, will enable me to get along pretty comfortably—I have seen Mr. Smith, to whom I sold the chandlery, and have extended the term of payment. He still dips on Mondays, Wednesdays, and Fridays, and has agreed to set a kettle of fat and some sticks for me, in the little closet, near the back door, that I may slip in, and amuse myself, on dipping days."

I ought to have been warned, by this example; but I had quite forgotten it. It is very agreeable to be thus welcomed back to the performance of my former duties. No one, but he, who is deprived of some long-cherished occupation, can truly comprehend the pleasure of occasionally handling a corpse.

No. XXIII

Few things can be imagined, more thoroughly revolting and absurd, than the vengeance of the living, rioting among the ashes of the dead — rudely rolling the stone away from the door of the sepulchre — entering the narrow houses of the unresisting, *vi et armis*, with the pickaxe and the crowbar — and scattering to the winds the poor senseless remains of those, who were consigned to their resting-places, with all the honors of a former age. This, were it not awful, would be eminently ridiculous. For the execution of such posthumous revenge the French nation has the precedence of every other, civilized and savage. Frenchmen, if not, through all time, from the days of Pharamond to the present, remarkably zealous of good works, are clearly a peculiar people.

The history of the world furnishes no parallel to that preposterous crusade, carried on by that people, in 1794, against the dead bodies of kings and princes, saints and martyrs. This war, upon dead men's bones, was not projected and executed, by the rabble, on the impulse of the moment. A formal, deliberate decree of the Convention commanded, that the tombs should be destroyed, and they were destroyed, and their contents scattered to the winds, accordingly. Talk not of all that is furious and fantastical, in the conduct of monkeys and maniacs — a nation of chimpanzees would have acted with more dignity and discretion. A colony of grinning baboons, as Shakspeare calls them, bent upon liberty, equality, and fraternity, might have dethroned some tyrannical ourang outang, who had carried matters with too high a hand, and extorted too many cocoa nuts, for the support of his civil list; but, after having cut off his head, it is not to be believed, that they would have gone about, scratching up the ashes of his ancestors, and wreaking their vengeance upon those unoffending relics.

This miserable onslaught upon the dead began, immediately after December 20, 1794. The new worship commenced on that day, and the goddess of reason then, for the first time, presented herself to the people, in the person of the celebrated actress, Mademoiselle Maillard. St.

Genevieve, the patroness of the city of Paris, died in 512, and her remains were subsequently transferred to the church, which bears her name, and which was erected, by Clovis, in 517. The executive agents of the National Convention commenced their legalized fooleries, upon the ashes of this poor old saint. These French gentlemen—the politest nation upon earth—without the slightest regard for decency, or sanctification, or common sense, dug up Madame Genevieve's coffin, and, to aggravate the indignity, dragged the old lady's remains to the place of public execution, the *Place de Grève*; and, having burnt them there, scattered the ashes to the winds. The gates of bronze, presented by Charlemagne to the church of St. Denis, were broken to pieces. Pepin, the sire of Charlemagne and son of Charles Martel, was buried there, in 768. Nothing remained of Pepin but a handful of dust, which was served in a similar manner. It is stated by Lamartine, that the heads of Marshal Turenne, Duguesclin, Louis XII., and Francis I., were rolled about the pavement; sceptres, crowns, and crosiers were trampled under foot; and the shouts of the operatives were heard, when the blows of the axe broke through some regal coffin, and the royal bones were thrown out, to be treated with senseless insult.

Hugh Capet, Philip the bold, and Philip, the handsome, were buried beneath the choir. The ruthless hands of these modern vandals tore from the corpses those garments of the grave, in which they had reposed for centuries, and threw the relics upon beds of quicklime.

Henry IV. fell by the hands of Ravaillac, the assassin, May 14, 1610. His body, was carefully embalmed, by Italians. When taken from the coffin, the lineaments of the face fully corresponded with the numerous representations, transmitted by the hands of painters and statuaries. That cherished and perfumed beard expanded, as if it had just then received the last manipulation of the friseur. The marks were perfectly visible, upon the breast, indicating the first and second thrust of Ravaillac's stilletto. The popularity of this monarch protected his remains, though for a brief space. He was frank, brave, and humane. For two days, all that remained of this idol of the people—was exhibited to public view.

The exhumed king was placed at the foot of the altar, and a countless multitude passed, in mute procession, around these favored relics. This gave umbrage to Javogues, a member of the Convention. He denounced this partiality, and railed against the memory of Henri le Grand. The multitude, impressible by the slightest impulse, hurled the dead monarch into the common fosse of quicklime and corruption; execrating, under the influence of a few feverish words, from the lips of a republican savage, the memory and the remains of one, cherished by their predecessors, for nearly three hundred years. A similar fate awaited his son and grandson, Louis XIII. and XIV. The vault of the Bourbons was thoroughly ransacked, in the same spirit of desolation. Queens, dauphinesses, and princesses, says the historian of the Girondists, were carried away, in armsful, by the laborers, to be cast into the trench, and consumed by quicklime. In the vault of Charles V., surnamed the wise, besides the corpse were found, a hand of justice and a golden crown. In the coffin of his wife, Jeanne of Bourbon, were her spindles and marriage rings. These relics were thrown into the ditch—the corpses—not the articles of gold, however debased by their juxtaposition. Of the French gentlemen it may be affirmed, as of Madame Gilpin—

"Though on pleasure she was bent,
She had a frugal mind."

An economy, perfectly grotesque, mingled with an unmanly desecration. Even the lead was scraped together from these coffins, and converted into balls. In the vault of the Valois no bodies were discovered. The people were very desirous of showing some tokens of their wrath, upon the poor carcass of Louis XI., but it could not be found. Abbés, heroes, ministers of state were indiscriminately cast into the fosse. Upon the exhumation of Dagobert I., and his queen, Matilde, who had been buried twelve hundred years, her skeleton was found without a head. Such is said to have been the case with several other skeletons of the queens of France.

In one of the upper lofts of the cabinet of Natural History of the Jardin des Plantes, among stuffed beasts and birds, surrounded by mixed and manifold rubbish, and covered with dust, there lay a case or package, unexamined and unnoticed, for nine long years. This envelope contained the mortal remains of a Marechal of France, the hero of an hundred battles,—of no other than Henry de la Tour, Viscount de Turenne. He was killed by a cannon ball, July 27, 1675, at the age of 64. All France lamented the death of this great man. The admiration of all Europe followed him to the grave. Courage, modesty, generosity, science have embalmed his memory. The king, Louis le Grand, ordered a solemn service to be performed, for the Marechal de Turenne, in the Cathedral church at Paris, as for the first prince of the blood, and that his remains should be interred in the abbey of St. Denis, the burial-place of the royal personages of France, where the cardinal, his nephew, raised a splendid mausoleum to his memory. So much for glory—and what then? In 1794, the remains of this great man were upon the point of being cast into the common fosse, by the agents of the Convention, when some, less rabid than the rest, smuggled them away; and, for security, conveyed them to the lumber room of the cabinet of Natural History of the Jardin des Plantes. Having reposed, nine years in state, peradventure between a dilapidated kangaroo and a cast-off opossum—these remains of the great Turenne were, at length, committed, in a quiet way, to the military tomb of the Invalids.

No. XXIV

Burning dead saints, is a more pardonable matter, than burning living martyrs—the combustion of St. Genevieve's dry bones, than the fiery trial of Latimer and Ridley—the fantastical decree of the French Convention, than the cruel discipline of bloody Mary. Dark days were they, and full of evil, those years of bitterness and blood, from 1553 to Nov. 17, 1558, when, by a strange coincidence, this hybrid queen, whose sire was a British tyrant, and whose dam a Spanish bigot, expired on the same day with the Cardinal, Reginald Pole. From the remarkable proximity of the events arose a suspicion of poison, of which the public mind has long since been disabused.

In this age of greater intelligence and religious freedom, the outrages, perpetrated, in the very city of London, within five brief years, are credible, only on the strength of well authenticated history. According to Bishop Burnet, two hundred and eighty-four persons were burnt at the stake, during four years of this merciless and miserable reign. Lord Burleigh makes the number of those, who died, in that reign, by imprisonment, torments, famine, and fire, to be near four hundred. Weever, in his Funeral Monuments, page 116, quotes the historian Speed, as saying, "In the heat of those flames, were burnt to ashes five bishops, one-and-twenty divines, eight gentlemen, eighty-four artificers, an hundred husbandmen, servants, and laborers, twenty-six wives, twenty widows, nine virgins, two boys, and two infants; one of them whipped to death by Bonner, and the other, springing out of the mother's womb from the stake, as she burned, thrown again into the fire." Here, in passing, suffer me to express my deep reverence for John Weever. I know of no book, so interesting to the craft, as his Funeral Monuments, a work of infinite labor and research. Weever died in 1632, and lies in St. James, Clerkenwell. His epitaph may be found in Strype's Survey:

> Lancashire gave me birth,
> And Cambridge education;
> Middlesex gave me death,
> And this church my humation;
> And Christ to me hath given
> A place with him in heaven.

The structure of these lines will remind the classical reader of Virgil's epitaph:

Mantua me genuit: Calabri rapuere; tenet nunc
Parthenope; cecini pascua, rura, duces.

The short and sharp reign of Mary Tudor was remarkable for burning Protestant Christians and wax candles. That fountain of fun, pure and undefiled, that prince of wags, Theodore Hook, was offered, very young, for admission at the University; and, when the chancellor opened the book, and gravely inquired if he was ready to sign the thirty-nine articles, "Yes, sir," replied the young puppy, "forty, if you please." Now, in contemplation of the enormous consumption of wax, especially upon the occasion of funeral obsequies, during Mary's reign, it would seem that a belief, in its vital importance, might have formed an additional article, in the Romish creed.

I have never thought well of grafting religion upon the selfishness of man's nature. Nominal converts, it is true, are readily made, in that way. In Catholic countries, wax chandlers are Romanists, to a man. I always considered the attempt, a few years since, to convert the inhabitants of Nantucket to Puseyism, by a practical appeal to their self interest, however ingeniously contrived, a very wicked thing. And I greatly lauded the good old bishop of this diocese, for rebuking those very silly priests, who promoted a senseless and extravagant consumption of one of the great staples of that island, by burning candles in the day time. He made good use of his mitre as an extinguisher.

On a somewhat similar principle, I have always objected to every attempt to augment the revenues of a state by taxing corpses—not upon the acknowledged principle, that taxation without representation is inadmissible—but because the whole system is a most miserable mingling of *sacra profanis*. I may not be understood by all, in this remark: I refer to those acts of Parliament, which, for the purposes of levying a tax, or promoting some particular branch of industry, have attempted to regulate a man's apparel, and the fitting up of his narrow house, after he is dead. The compulsory employment of flannel, by British statute, is an example of this legislative interference.

Nothing is more common, in Strype's Ecclesiastical Memorials, than entries, such as these: "1557, May 3. The Lord Shandois was buried with heralds, an herse of wax, four banners of images, and other appendages of funeral honor." "On the 5th, the Lady Chamberlain was buried with a fair herse of wax." "May 28, in the forenoon, was buried Mrs. Gates, widow, late wife, as it seems, to Sir John Gates, executed the first year of this queen's reign. She gave seventeen fine black gowns, and fourteen of broad russet for poor men. There were carried two white branches, ten staff torches, and four great tapers." "July 10th the Lady Tresham was buried at Peterborough, with four banners, and an herse of wax, and torches." "1558, September 14th, was buried Sir Andrew Judd, skinner, merchant of Muscovy, and late Mayor of London, with ten dozen of escutcheons, garnished with angels, and an herse of wax." What is an herse of wax? This will be quite unintelligible to those, who have supposed that word to import nothing else than the vehicle, in which the dead are carried to the grave. Herse also signifies a temporary monument, erected upon, or near, the place of sepulture, and on which the corpse was laid, for a time, in state; and a herse of wax was a structure of this kind, surrounded with wax tapers. This will be made manifest, by some additional extracts from the same author: "1557. The 16th day of July, died the lady Anne, of Cleves, at Chelsey, sometime wife and queen unto King Henry VIII., but never crowned. Her corpse was cered the night following." "On the 29th began the herse at Westminster, for the Lady Anne of Cleves, consisting of carpenters' work of seven principals, being as goodly an herse as had been seen." "On the 3d of August the body of the Lady Anne of Cleves was brought from Chelsey, where her house was, unto Westminster, to be buried—men bore her, under a canopy of black velvet, with four black staves, and so brought her into the herse, and there tarried *Dirge*, remaining there all night, with lights burning." "On the 16th day of August the herse of the King of Denmark was begun to be set up, in a four-square house. August 18, was the King of Denmark's herse in St. Paul's finished with wax, the like to which was never seen in England, in regard to the fashion of square tapers." And on the 23d, also was the King of Denmark's herse, at St. Paul's, "taken down by the wax chandlers and carpenters, to whom this work pertained, by order of Mr. Garter, and certain of the Lord Treasurer's servants." These herses were, doubtless, very attractive in their way. "Aug. 31, 1557. The young Dutchess of Norfolk being lately deceased, her herse began to be set up on the 28th, in St. Clements, without Temple bar, and was this day finished with banners, pensils, wax, and escutcheons."

The office of an undertaker, in those days, was no sinecure. He was an *arbiter elegantiarum*. A funeral was a festival then. Eat, drink, and be merry, for tomorrow you die, was the common phylactery.

> "The funeral baked meats
> Did coldly furnish forth the marriage tables."

Baked meats shall be the subject of my next.

No. XXV

Pliny, xviii. 30, refers to a practice among the Romans, very similar to that, in use among certain unenlightened nations, of depositing articles of diet upon tombs and graves, such as beans, lettuces, eggs, bread, and the like, for the use of ghosts. The stomachs of Roman ghosts were not supposed to be strong enough for flesh meat. Hence the lines of Juvenal, v. 85:

> Sed tibi dimidio constrictus cammarus ovo
> Ponitur, exigua feralis cæna patella.

The *silicernium* or *cæna funebris* was a very different, and more solid affair. At first blush—to use a common and sensible expression—there seems no respectable keeping, between the art of burying the dead, and that of feasting the living. Depositing those, whom we love, in their graves, is certainly the very last relish for an appetite. Something of this was undoubtedly done, of old, under the promptings of Epicurean philosophy— upon the *dum vivimus vivamus* principle—and, in that spirit which teaches the soldier, when he turns from the grave, to change the mournful, for the merry strain. The desire of equalling or excelling others, in the magnificence of funereal parade, has ever been a powerful motive. The eyes of others destroy us, said Franklin, and not our own. Grief for the departed, and sympathy with the bereaved, were not deemed sufficient, to insure an imposing parade. Games and festivals were therefore provided, for the people. Among other attractions, masses of uncooked meat were bestowed upon all comers. This was the *visceratio* of the Romans. This word seems to have a different import; *viscera*, however, signifies all beneath the skin, as may be seen by consulting Serv. in Virg., Æn. i., 211. Suetonius Cæs. 39, and Cicero de Officiis ii. 16, refer to this practice. It was by no means very common, but frequently adopted by those, who could afford the expense, and were desirous of the display.

Marcus Flavius had committed an infamous crime. He was popular, and the ædiles of the people had fixed a day for his absolution. Under pretence of celebrating his mother's funeral, he gave a *visceratio* to the people: Populo visceratio data, a M. Flavio, in funere matris. Erant, qui, per speciem honorandæ parentis, meritam mercedem populo solutam interpretarentur;

quod eum, die dicta ab ædilibus, crimine stupratæ matris familæ absolvisset. Liv. viii. 22. A note upon this passage, in Lemaire's edition, fully explains the nature of this practice.

This was a very different affair from the *silicernium*, or feast for the friends, after the funeral. Upon such occasions, the Falernian flowed, and boars were roasted whole. The reader, by opening his Livy, xxxix. 46, will find an account of the funeral of P. Licinius: a *visceratio* was given to the people; one hundred and twenty gladiators fought in the arena; the funeral games lasted three days; and then followed a splendid entertainment. On that occasion, a tempest drove the company into the forum; this occurred, in the year U. C. 569. Through all time, the practice has prevailed, more or less, of providing entertainments, for those, who gather on such occasions. In villages, especially, and within my own recollection, the funeral has been delayed, to enable distant friends to arrive in season; and the interval has been employed, in the preparation of creature comforts, not only for such as attended, and observed the ceremonial of an hour, but for such, as came to the bereaved, like the comforters of the man of Uz, "every one from his place, and sat down with him, seven days and seven nights." Animal provision must surely be required, to sustain such protracted lamentation.

In the age, when Shakspeare wrote, and for several ages before and after, "baked meats," at funerals, were very common. So far, from contenting themselves with the preparation of some simple aliment, for such as were an hungered, the appetites of all were solicited, by a parade of the rarest liquors and the choicest viands. Tables were spread, in the most ample manner, and the transition was immediate from the tomb to the festal board. The *requiescat in pace* was scarcely uttered, before the blessing was craved, on the baked meats. It matters little, from what period of history we select our illustrations of this truth. Suppose we take our examples from the reign, preceding that, in which Shakspeare was born; comprehend some other incidents in our collection; and rely, for our authority, on good old John Strype, who was himself born in 1643. There is no higher authority. I will present a few specimens from his Ecclesiastical Memorials: "1557, May 5. Was the Lady Chamberlain buried. At the mass preached Dr. Chadsey. A great dole of money given at the church, and after, a great dinner. May 29, was buried Mrs. Gates; after mass a great dinner. June 7, began a stage play at the Grey Friars of the passion of Christ. June 10.—This day Sir John, a chantry priest, hung himself with his own girdle. The same day was the storehouse in Portsmouth burnt, much beer and victual destroyed. A judgment, perhaps, for burning so many innocent persons. June 29.— This same day was the second year's mind (i. e. yearly *obit*) of good master Lewyn, ironmonger; at his dirge were all the livery. After, they retired to the widow's place, where they had a cake and wine; and besides the parish, all comers treated." Aug. 3.—After giving a long account of the funeral of Ann of Cleves, Strype adds, "and so they went in order to dinner." After reciting the particulars of the King of Denmark's funeral, in London, Aug. 18, 1557, he adds: "After the dirge, all the heralds and all the Lords went into the Bishop of London's place, and drank. The next day was the morrow-mass, and a goodly sermon preached, and after, to my Lord of London's to dinner."

The account of the funeral of Thomas Halley is entitled to be presented entire: "On the 24th of this month, August, Mr. Thomas Halley, clarentieux, king-at-arms, was buried, in St. Giles's parish, without Cripplegate, with coat, armor, and pennon of arms, and scutcheons of his arms, and two white branches, twelve staff torches, and four great tapers, and a crown. And, after dirge, the heralds repaired unto Greenhill, the waxchandler, a man of note (being waxchandler to Cardinal Pole) living hard by; where they had spice-bread and cheese, and wine, great plenty. The morrow-mass was also celebrated, and sermon preached; and after followed a great dinner, whereat were all the heralds, together with the parishioners. There was a supper also, as well as a dinner." After a long account of the funeral of the Countess of Arundel, Oct. 5, 1557, follow the customary words—"and, after, all departed to my Lord's place to dinner." "Nov. 12, Mr. Maynard, merchant, was buried; and after, the company departed to his house, at Poplar, to a great dinner." "Oct. 19, died the Lord Bray; and so he went by water to Chelsea to be buried, &c. &c. Many priests and clerks attended. They all came back to this Lord's place, at Blackfriars, to dinner." At the funeral of Richard Capet, Feb. 1, "All return to dinner." "On the 16th, Mr. Pynohe, fishmonger, and a brother of Jesus, was buried. All being performed at the church, the company retired to his house to drink." On the 24th, "a great dinner," after the funeral of Sir George Bowers. This testimony is inexhaustible. After the funeral of Lady White, March 2, Strype says "there was as great a dinner as had been seen." I will close with two examples. "Aug. 3, 1588. The Lady Rowlet was buried; and after mass, the company retreated to the place to dinner, which was plentifully furnished with venison, fresh salmon, fresh sturgeon, and many other fine dishes. On the 12th, died Mr. Machyl, alderman and clothesworker." After a sermon by a grey friar, "the Lord Mayor and Aldermen, and all the mourners and ladies went to dinner, which was very splendid, lacking no good meat, both flesh and fish, and an hundred marchpanes."

It is certain, that all this appears to us now to have been in very bad taste; and it is not easy to comprehend the principle, which conducted to the perpetration of such sensual absurdities; unless we suppose it to have been the design of all concerned, to felicitate the heir, upon his coming to possession; the widow, upon the fruition of an ample dower and abundant leisure; or the widower, upon the recovery of his liberty. This is not the only occasion, upon which man's features are required, from the extreme suddenness of the change, to undergo a process of moral distortion, amounting to grimace. Thus, grief, for the death of one monarch, is rudely expressed, by turbulent joy at the succession of another. Suffer me to conclude, in the words of father Strype—"The same day queen Mary deceased, in the morning between 11 and 12, the Lady Elizabeth was proclaimed queen: in the afternoon all the churches in London rang their bells; and at night were bonfires made, and tables set in the streets, and the people did eat, and drink, and make merry."

No. XXVI

Among the dead—the mighty dead—there is one, in regard to whom, our national dealings may be fairly set forth, in the words of Desdemona—

> In faith, 'twas strange, 'twas passing strange;
> 'Twas pitiful, 'twas wondrous pitiful:
> She wish'd she had not heard it.

Forty-nine years have passed, since the interment of George Washington. Forty-nine years ago, "the joint committee," says Chief Justice Marshall, "which had been appointed to devise the mode, by which the nation should express its feelings, on this melancholy occasion, reported" a series of resolutions, among which was the following: "That a marble monument be erected, by the United States, at the city of Washington, and that the family of General Washington be requested to permit his body to be deposited under it; and that the monument be so designed, as to commemorate the great events of his military and political life." To the letter, transmitting the resolutions to Mrs. Washington, she replied, as follows: "Taught by the great example, which I have so long had before me, never to oppose my private wishes to the public will, I must consent to the request made by Congress, which you have had the goodness to transmit to me; and, in doing this, I need not, I cannot, say what a sacrifice of individual feeling I make, to a sense of public duty."

All this is very fine. The nation requested permission to remove the remains—Mrs. Washington consented—but that monument! The remains have slumbered quietly, where they first were interred, for nine and forty years—and the monument is like Rachel's first born—it is not! There is something better in prospect. Such, however, is the record thus far. It is very true he needs no monument. No immortal can say more justly, from his elevated sphere, to every inhabitant of this vast empire, *si monumentum quæris, circumspice!*

This fact, however, so far from taking the tithe of a hair from the balance of this account, illustrates the national delinquency. It may be matter of amusing speculation, to contrast the zeal, which prevails, especially in England, in relation to the most trifling memorials of Shakspeare, and the popular indifference, in regard to certain relics, known to have been the property of Washington, and to have been personally used by him.

All are familiar with the recent excitement, on the subject of Shakspeare's house—that mulberry tree—a hair of him, for memory.

Washington's library has lately been sold, for just about the price of four shares in one of the cotton mills at Lowell. A few years since, the cabinet of medals, struck at different times, in honor of the Father of his country, and which had become the property of one of his representatives, was sold by him, for five hundred dollars, and purchased by an individual citizen of Massachusetts. There are some things, seemingly so vast—so very—very national—that one can scarcely believe it possible for any private cabinet to contain them gracefully.

Soon after the destruction of the Bastile, July 14, 1789, La Fayette sent its massive key to Washington—his political father—as the first fruits of those principles of liberty, which were then supposed to be bourgeoning forth, in a *free* French soil. This colossal key was suspended, in the front entry, at Mount Vernon. A short time ago, an aged friend, residing in a neighboring town, and once intimate in the family of Washington, told me he had often seen that famous key, in its well known position. This also became the property of Washington's representatives. A few years since, I saw it stated, in the public journals, that, among other effects, this key of the Bastile was sold at auction, and purchased for seventy-five cents, by a gentleman, who had the good taste to return it to some member of the family.

Eminent men, as they arise, are occasionally compared to Washington. Points of resemblance, now and then, may assuredly be found; but there never breathed a man, whose mental and moral properties combined, could endure a rigid comparison with his. Whoever attempts to run this parallel, between him and any other, will readily acknowledge the truth of the proverb, *nullum simile quatuor pedibus currit*. Select the example from the present, or the past, from our own or from other lands, and inquire, to which of them all would Erskine, so chary of his praise, so slow of faith in his fellow, have applied those memorable words, inscribed, in the presentation copy of his work, transmitted to Washington—*You, sir, are the only individual, for whom I ever felt an awful reverence*. Of whom else would Lord Brougham have pronounced this remarkable passage—"It will be the duty of the historian and the sage, in all ages, to omit no occasion of commemorating this illustrious man; and, until time shall be no more, will a test of the progress, which our race has made in wisdom and virtue, be derived, from the veneration paid to the immortal name of Washington."

I have not yet met with any gentleman of our calling, who is not decidedly in favor of the election of General Taylor, or who would not gratuitously attend, in a professional way, upon Messieurs Cass and Van Buren. We perceive a resemblance between the first president and the present candidate, in their willingness to draw long bills on posterity for fame, in preference to numerous drafts, at sight, without grace, for daily applause. But we behold, in Washington, the image and superscription, not of Cæsar, but of a peerless mortal—of one, created, verily, a little lower than the angels—

> "A combination, and a form, indeed,
> Where every god did seem to set his seal,
> To give the world assurance of a man."

No men have done more to bedim the reputation of Washington, than Jefferson and Randolph. Verily they have their reward. In no portion of our country has the memory of that great man been more universally cherished and beloved, than in New England. A sentiment, not only of reverence for his character, but of affection for his person, was very general, in this quarter; and manifested itself, in a remarkable manner, upon the occasion of his death. Nothing could have been more unexpected, than the announcement of that event, in Boston. I will close this article, with a simple illustration of the popular feeling, when the sad tidings arrived. At the close of that year, 1799—I was a small boy then—I was returning from a ride on horseback, to Dorchester Point—there was no bridge, and it was quite a journey. As I approached the town, I was very much surprised, at the tolling of the bells. Upon reaching home, I saw my old father, at an unusual hour for him, the busiest man alive, to be at home, sitting alone in our parlor, with his bandanna before his eyes. I ran towards him, with the thoughtless gayety of youth, and asked what the bells were tolling for. He withdrew the handkerchief from his face—the tears were rolling down his fine old features—"Go away child," said he, "don't disturb me; do you not know, that Washington is dead?"

The reader has surmised, that the worthy old man had sipped at the fountain of executive patronage. Not at all. He had never seen Washington, and never held an office civil or military, saving under Hancock's commission, as justice of the peace, which was accounted a very pretty compliment, in those days. No. He was nothing but an American, and he shed those American tears, upon the death of one, whose character and conduct had filled his heart with sentiments of pride, and love, and "awful reverence."

No. XXVII

I am rather inclined to suspect, that man is a selfish animal. A few days ago, I administered a merited rebuke to a group of young sextons, who had gathered together, after a funeral, and were seated upon a barrow bier, before an unclosed tomb. They had been discussing the subject of capital punishment, and were opposed to it unanimously. They frankly admitted, that they were not influenced, by any consideration of humanity, but looked simply to the fact, that, as the bodies of executed criminals went, commonly, to the surgeons, every execution deprived us of a job. One observed, that Boston was dreadfully healthy—another remarked, that homœopathy had proved a considerable help to us. Several compliments were paid to Thompson, Brandreth, and Mrs. Kidder. But they appeared to anticipate emolument from no source, so certainly, as from the approaching cholera.

I was greatly shocked, and expressed my opinion very freely. I reminded them of the primitive dignity of the sacristan's office. I should deeply regret, to see our calling reduced to the level of a mere trade, with its tariff— shrouds all rising—coffins looking up! We have a fair share of funerals, and the members of our profession have no just cause for complaint. Steam has helped us prodigiously. It has been said, that, comparing the amount of steam travel with the amount of ante-steam travel, i. e., the present with the past, the relative amount of deaths, from accident, is about the same. Suppose it to be so; the cheapness and facility of locomotion, at present, stimulate a much larger number to move—there is a vast increase of frivolous and pleasure travel—cars are filled with women, crates with bandboxes, and death is to be averaged over the integer—I therefore repeat, that steam has helped our profession. If steam had been known, in ancient Rome, it would have been reckoned a deity, whose diet, like the sacrifice of Juggernaut, would have been flesh and blood.

There is a very natural sensibility, on the part of steamboat and railroad proprietors, to the announcement of disasters, by steam. There is a wonderful eagerness to persuade the public to contemplate these catastrophes, with the larger end of the telescope toward the eye. This also is a great help to our profession. There is really no lack of business, and it is quite abominable, for thoughtless young sextons to pray for the advent of the cholera.

We dwell in a region of the earth, seldom touched by this besom of destruction. Pestilence and famine have rarely come nigh unto us. It would be impious to envy the denizens of milder climes.

"With gold and gems if Chilian mountains glow,
If bleak and barren Scotia's hills arise;
There plague and poison, lust and rapine grow,
Here peaceful are the vales and pure the skies."

I thank heaven, I was not an undertaker, in London, in 1665, when there were scarcely enough of the living to bury the dead. When I used to wrap myself up, in the pages of Robinson Crusoe, how little I suspected, that Daniel Defoe was the writer of some twenty volumes beside. His inimitable history of the plague, of 1665, is admirable reading, for the members of our craft.

At irregular periods, plague, yellow fever, sweating sickness, and cholera have visited the earth, with terrible effect. Let us take a cursory view of these awful visitations. A. D. 78, 10,000 perished daily at Rome. The plague returned there A. D. 167. Terrible plague in Britain A. D. 430. A dreadful plague spread over Europe, Asia and Africa, A. D. 558, and continued, for several years. 200,000 died of the plague in Constantinople, A. D. 746. This plague raged for three years, and extended to Calabria, Sicily and Greece. William of Malmsbury states, that A. D. 772, an epidemic disease carried off 34,000 in Chichester, England. 40,000 died of pestilence in Scotland, A. D. 954. Hollingshed gives an account of a terrible plague among cattle, A. D. 1111, and in Ireland A. D. 1204. In this year a general plague raged in Europe. In London 200 persons were buried daily, in the Charterhouse yard. A dreadful mortality prevailed in London and Paris, A. D. 1362 and '7. Great pestilence in Ireland A. D. 1383. Endemic destroyed 30,000 in London A. D. 1407. Great numbers died of plague in Ireland, following famine, A. D. 1466. Dublin was severely visited with plague A. D. 1470. Rapin and Salmon give an account of the plague at Oxford, A. D. 1471, and throughout England A. D. 1478.

The sweating sickness, *sudor Anglicus*, first appeared, in England, in 1483, in the army of Henry VII., on his landing at Milfordhaven. A year or two after, it travelled to London, and remained there, with intermissions, for forty years. It then passed over to the continent, and overran Holland, Germany, Flanders, France, Denmark, and Norway. It continued in those countries, from 1525 to 1530; it then returned to England; and was last known there, in 1551. It was a malignant fever, accompanied with very great thirst, delirium, and excessive sweat. Dr. Caius called it "a contagious, pestilential fever of one day, prevailing with a mighty slaughter, as tremendous as the plague of Athens." Dr. Willis says, "Its malignity was so extreme, that as soon as it entered a city, it made a daily attack, on five or six hundred persons, of whom scarcely one in a hundred recovered." Strype says, "The plague of sweat this summer, 1551, was very severe, and carried away multitudes of people, rich and poor, especially in London, where, in one day, July 10th, died an hundred people, and the next, one hundred and twenty. From the 8th of this month to the 19th, there died in London, of this sweat, 872."

Stowe says that, in the 9th year of Henry VII., 1517, half the population, in the capital towns of England, died of the sweating sickness: and that it proved fatal, in three hours. In the year 1500, Stowe also says, that the plague was so terrible in London, that Henry VII. and his court went over to Calais. The plague prevailed in England and Ireland, in 1603, and in London 30,000 persons died. In 1611, 200,000 died of pestilence, in Constantinople; 35,000 persons died of an epidemic in London, in 1625. In 1632 a general mortality prevailed in France; 60,000 died in Lyons. The plague was brought from Sardinia to Naples, in 1656, and 400,000 of the Neapolitans died, in six months. In the great plague of London, of 1665, described by De Foe, 68,596 persons died. In 1720, 60,000 perished of the plague at Marseilles.

An account is given, by the Abbe Mariti, of one of the most awful plagues ever known, which prevailed in Syria, in 1760. In Persia, 80,000 inhabitants of Bassorah, died of the plague, in 1773. In 1792, the plague destroyed 800,000 persons in Egypt. In 1799, 247,000 died of the plague at Fez; and in Barbary, 3000 daily, for several days. In 1804 and '5, an immense number were destroyed, by the plague, in Gibraltar. At the same place, in 1828, many were swept away, by an epidemic fever, scarce distinguishable from the plague. Verily the vocation of an undertaker is anything but a sinecure! But, in such terrible emergencies, as were hourly occurring, during the prevalence of the great plague of London, such an operator as Pontraci would have cast aside all thoughts of shrouds and coffins. In one single night 4000 died. The hearses were common dead carts; and the continued cry, *bring out your dead*, rang through every heart. Defoe rates the victims of the plague of 1665, at 100,000.

At present, we have a deeper interest in the pestilence of modern times, though by some accounted of great antiquity. The Indian or Asiatic cholera traversed the north, east and south of Europe, and the countries of Asia, and, in two years, prostrated 900,000 victims. It subsequently appeared in England, at Sunderland, Oct. 26, 1831; in Scotland, at Edinburgh, Feb. 6, 1832; in Ireland, at Dublin, March 3, 1832. The mortality was great, but much less than upon the continent. Between March and August, 1832, 18,000 died of cholera, in Paris. In July and August, 1837, it reappeared in

Rome, the Two Sicilies, Genoa, Berlin, and some other cities. Its ravages, in this country, were far less notable, than in many others. It is very wise to cast about us, and determine what we will do, if it should come again, and it is very likely to take us in its progress. But let us not forget, that it will most easily approach us, through our fears; and probably, in no disease, are fear and grief more fatal *avant couriers*, than in affections of the abdominal viscera.

I am half inclined to the opinion of a charming old lady of my acquaintance, who, after listening to a learned discussion, as to the seat of the soul—the fountain of sensibility,—and whether or not it was seated in the conarion—the pineal gland—gave her decided opinion, that it was seated in the bowels.

No. XXVIII

The dead speak from their coffins—from their very graves—and verily the heart of the true mourner hath ears to hear. Gloves and rings are the valedictories of the dead—their *vales*, or parting tokens, received by the mourners, at the hand of some surviving friend. This appropriated word, *vale*, as almost every one knows, is the leave-taking expression of the mourners; and, when anglicised, and used in the plural number, as one syllable, signifies those *vales* or vails, tokens, in various forms, from shillings to crown pieces, bestowed by parting visitors, on domestics, from the head waiter to the scullion. They are intended as leave tokens. Every servant, in the families of the nobility, from the highest to the lowest, expects a *vale*, not in the classical sense of Menalcas—*Longum, formose, vale, vale*, but in lawful money, intelligible coin. This practice had become so oppressive to visitors, in the early part of the reign of George III., that Sir Jonas Hanway, remarkable, among other things, for his controversy with Dr. Johnson, on the subject of tea drinking, wrote and published eight letters to the Duke of Newcastle, against the custom of giving vails, in which he relates some very amusing anecdotes. Mr. Hanway, being quietly reproached, by a friend, in high station, for not accepting his invitations to dinner, more frequently, frankly replied, "Indeed, my Lord, I cannot afford it." He recites the manner of leaving a gentleman's house, where he had dined; the servants, as usual, flocked around him—"your great coat, Sir Jonas"—a shilling—"your hat, sir:" a shilling—"stick, sir:" a shilling—"umbrella, sir:" a shilling—"sir, your gloves"—"well, keep the gloves, they are not worth the shilling." A remarkable example of the insolence of a pampered menial was related to Mr. Hanway, by Sir Timothy Waldo. He had dined with the Duke of Newcastle: as he was departing, and handing over his coin to the train of servants, that lined the hall, he put a crown into the hand of the chief cook, who returned it, saying, "I never take silver, sir." "Indeed"—Sir Timothy replied, returning the piece to his pocket, "I never give gold."

Sir Jonas was an excellent man; and, whatever objections he may have had to the practice of giving extravagant vails to servants, I think he would have little or nothing to say, against the practice of giving such vails, as the dead may be supposed, vicariously, to bestow upon the living, in the form of rings and gloves. The dead, it must be conceded, seem not so much disposed to give vails, at present, as they were, one hundred years ago. In such dispensations, in the olden time, the good man, the clergyman, was seldom forgotten. Gloves and rings were showered down, upon the Lord's anointed, at weddings, christenings, and funerals. When a child, I was very much puzzled, upon two points; first, what became of all the old moons, and, secondly, what the minister did with his gloves and rings. If he had had the hands of Briareus, he could not have worn them all.

An interesting little volume is now lying upon my table, which explains the mystery, not at all, in relation to the moons, but most happily, in respect to rings and gloves. It is the Astronomical Diary or Almanac of Nathaniel Ames, Boston, New England, printed by J. Draper, for the booksellers, 1748. This little book is interleaved; and the blank leaves are written over, in the hand-writing of good old Andrew Eliot, who, April 14, 1742, was ordained pastor of the new North Church, in Boston, as colleague with Mr. Webb, where, possessing very little of the locomotive or migratory spirit of the moderns, this excellent man remained, till his death, Sept. 13, 1778. If gall and wormwood are essential to the perfection of Christian theology, Dr. Eliot was singularly deficient, as a teacher of religion. His sermons were very full of practical godliness, and singularly free from brimstone and fire. He was elected President of Harvard University, but his attachment to his people caused him to decline the appointment. After this passing tribute, let us return to the little Almanac of 1748. On the inside of the marble cover the first entry commences thus: "Gloves, 1748, January." The gloves, received by Dr. Eliot, are set against particular names, and under every month, in the year. Certain names are marked with asterisks, doubtless denoting, that the parties were dead, or *stelligeri*, after the fashion of the College catalogue; and thus the good doctor discriminated, between funerals, and weddings and christenings. Although a goodly number of rings are enrolled, together with the gloves, yet a page is devoted to rings, exclusively, in the middle of the book. This is not arranged, under months, but years; and commences, in 1741, the year before he was ordained, as colleague with Mr. Webb. At the bottom of the record, the good man states how many pairs were kid; how many were lambswool; and how many were long or women's gloves, intended, of course, for the parson's lady.

These rings and gloves were sold, by the worthy doctor, with the exception of such, as were distributed, in his own household, not a small one, for he left eleven children. A prejudice might have prevailed, an hundred years ago, against dead men's gloves, similar to that, recorded in the proverb, against dead men's shoes; certain it is, these gloves did not meet with a very ready market. It appears by the record, in the doctor's own hand, that Mrs. Avis was entrusted with fifteen pairs of women's and three dozen of men's; and returned, unsold, eight pairs of women's, and one dozen and ten pairs of men's. A dozen pairs of men's were committed to Mrs. Langstaff; half a dozen women's to Mr. Langdon, and seventeen pairs to Captain Millens. What a glove and ring market the dear Doctor's study must have been. In thirty-two years, he appears to have received two thousand nine hundred and forty pairs of gloves, at funerals, weddings, and baptisms. Of these he sold to the amount of fourteen hundred and forty one pounds, eighteen shillings, and one penny, old tenor, equal to about six hundred and forty dollars. He also sold a goodly number of his rings. From all this, the conclusion is irresistible, that this truly good man and faithful minister must have been, if I may use the common expression, hand and glove with his parishioners. The little volume before me contains the record of other matters, highly interesting, doubtless, in their day but of precious little moment, at the present hour. Of what importance can it be, I beg leave to inquire, for any one to know, on what precise day, one hundred years ago, the worthy pastor borrowed a box of candles of Deacon Langdon, or a loaf of sugar of his own father, or ten shillings, old tenor, of Deacon Grant! Who, of the present generation, cares, on what day, one hundred years ago, he repaid those three pounds to Deacon Barrett! Of what consequence to any living mortal can it be, that, on the thirteenth day of April, one hundred years ago, Betty Bouvè came to live at the manse, as a maid! It is past. The last of that box of candles has burnt down into the socket, long ago. That sugar has dissolved, and lost its sweetness. And Betty Bouvè! The places that knew her know her no more. Her sweeping days are over; for time, with its irresistible broom, hath swept her from the face of the earth, and given her the grave for a dustpan.

The good old man himself has been called to the account of his stewardship. "It was a pleasant day," saith Father Gannett, on the fly-leaf of his almanac, "Sept. 15, 1778, when near four hundred couples and thirty-two carriages followed the remains of Dr. Andrew Eliot from his house, before the south side of his meeting-house, into Fore Street, up Cross Street, through Black Horse Lane, to Corpse Hill." I adopt Mr. Gannett's orthography, though rather less accurate than applicable.

No. XXIX

The true value of an enlightened conscience may be duly estimated by him, who has enjoyed the luxury of travelling in the dark, with the assistance of a lantern, without a candle. A man, who has a very strong sense of duty, and very little common sense, is apt to be a very troublesome fellow; for he is likely to unite the stupidity of an ass with the obstinacy of a mule. Yet such there are; and, however inconvenient, individually, the evil is immeasurably increased, when they become gregarious, and form a party, for any purpose whatever. Such conscience parties have existed, in every age and nation. A few individuals, of higher intelligence, dissatisfied with their civil, political, military, religious, or literary importance, and fatally bent upon distinction, are necessary to elevate some enormous green cheese high in the firmament, and persuade their followers, that it is neither more nor less than the moon, at full. Herod was the great director of that conscience party, that believed it to be their bounden duty, to murder all the little children in Judea, under a certain age. The terrible sacrifice, on St. Bartholomew's eve, was conducted by a conscience party. The burnings and starvings, in bloody Mary's reign, were planned and executed, by a conscience party. In no country has conscience been so very rampant, as in Ireland, from the days of Heremon and King Olam Fodla, to the present hour. Almost every reader is aware how conscientiously Archbishop Sharp was murdered, in presence of his daughter, in Scotland.

The widows of Hindostan, when they attempt to escape from the funeral pile, on which their late husbands are burning, are driven back into the flames, by a conscience party. It is well known, that certain inhabitants of India deposit their aged and decrepit parents, upon the very margin of the river, that the rising waters may bear them away. This is not the act of a few individuals; but the common practice, clearly indicating the existence of a conscience party, who undoubtedly believe they are acting, in a most filial and dutiful manner, and doing the very best thing in the world, for all parties. Infanticide is tolerated in China. Very little account is made of female babies there. This has been doubted and denied. Doubt and denial are of no use. There is a conscience party there, who believe it to be their duty to their male babies, to drown the females, unless they are pretty, and then they have a chance for life, in being sold for concubines. Among the numerous and best modern authorities, on this point, is Gutzlaff, whose voyages, along the coast of China, were published, in London, 1834. "At the beach of Amoy," says he, "we were shocked, at the spectacle of a pretty, new-born babe, which, shortly before, had been killed. We asked some of the bystanders what this meant; they answered with indifference, 'it is only a girl.'" Gutzlaff remarks, "It is a general custom among them to drown a large proportion of their new-born female children. This unnatural crime is so common, that it is perpetrated, without any feeling, and even in a laughing mood; and, to ask a man of distinction, whether he has daughters, is a mark of great rudeness." Earle, in his narrative of New Zealand, London, 1832, states that the practice existed there.

The insurrection of Shays, in this Commonwealth, in 1787, was a matter of conscience, beyond all doubt. He and many of his associates believed themselves a conscience party. After General Lincoln had suppressed the rebellion, great lenity was shown to the prisoners—not an individual was executed—and Shays, who died in 1825, at the age of 85, was even pensioned, in his old age, for his prior services in the revolution.

The revolt of the Pennsylvania line, in 1781, was, I admit, less an affair of the conscience, than of the stomach and bowels; for the poor fellows were nearly starved to death. The insurrection under Fries, commonly called the whiskey rebellion, in Western Pennsylvania, in 1792, was a different affair. A conscience party resolved to drink nothing but untaxed whiskey—they conscientiously believed the flavor to be utterly ruined, by the excise. It is certain, that, when General Washington moved against the rebels, there was conscience enough, among them, to make cowards of them all, for they scattered, in all directions.

A conscience party existed, in the early settlement of our country, when our pious ancestors, having fled to the howling wilderness, that they might enjoy liberty of thought, on religious subjects, began to hang the poor Quakers, for the glory of God.

Never before had there been such a conscience party in Massachusetts, as from 1689 to 1693. It was then Cotton Mather exclaimed from the pulpit, that witchcraft was the "most nefandous high treason against the Majesty on high." It was then, that he satisfied himself, by repeated trials, that devils were skilled in Latin, Greek and Hebrew. It was then, that they hanged old women, for riding on broomsticks through the air; a mode of conveyance, which Lord Mansfield declared, long after, to be perfectly lawful, for all who preferred that mode of equitation.

A conscience party has recently appeared, in this country, which it is not easy to describe. Every other party seems to have contributed to its formation. It is a sort of political mosaic, made up of tag, rag, and bobtail. Some of the prominent members of this party were whigs, but yesterday; and yet they have put forth all their energies, to elect, as president, a man, whom they and all other whigs have hitherto opposed, and denounced, and who, it was manifest, from the beginning, could not possibly be elected. This man has been accounted, by the whigs, a political charlatan; and all that he has done, to obtain the support of this conscience party, such of them at least, as were once whigs, is to avow certain sentiments, on the subject of slavery, the very contrary of those, which he has hitherto maintained, most openly and zealously. No grave and reflecting whig puts any more confidence, in the promises of this political spin-button, than he would put, in the words of Nicholas Machiavelli. Nor could this candidate do more to check the progress of slavery, than every honest whig believes will be done, by the candidate of their party, who certainly resembles Washington, in three particulars; he is himself a slaveholder—he is an honest man—and he wears the same political phylactery, "*I will be the president of the people, not of a party.*"

In consideration of the limit of power, neither of these candidates can do more than the other, for the object in view, if they were equally honest, which nobody dreams of, unless he dreams in Sleepy Hollow. If there had been an anti-cholera party, Van Buren might have commanded suffrages, as sensibly, by pledging himself to do all in his power, to prevent its extension. The remaining candidate, it is agreed, would, if elected, have turned the hopes, one and all, of both whig and conscience parties topsy-turvy. His election, it is clear, was made more probable, by every vote, given by a whig to that candidate, whose election was clearly impossible. These irregular whigs, have, therefore, spent their ammunition, as profitably, as the old covenanter spent his, who fired a horse pistol against the walls of Sterling Castle. Such is the conscience party.

When I refer to the universal consent of the whigs, during the former canvass for Martin Van Buren, that he was, politically, the very devil incarnate; and, in making a selection of those, who were the loudest, and longest, and the most vehement of his antagonists, find them to be the very leaders of the present movement, in his favor; I am reminded of Peter Pindar's pleasant story of the chambermaid and the spider; and, not having my copy of Peter at hand, I will endeavor to relate the tale in prose, as well as I am able.

A chambermaid, in going her rounds, observed an enormous spider, black and bloated, so far from his hole of refuge, that, lifting her broom, she exclaimed, "Now, you ugly brute, I have you! You are such a sly, cunning knave, and have such a happy non-committal way with you, that I never have been able to catch you before; for, the moment I raised my broom, you were out of sight, forsooth, and perfectly safe, in that Kinderhook of a hole of yours—but, now prepare yourself, for your hour has come." The spider turned every one of his eight eyes down upon the chambermaid, and, extending his two forelegs in a beseeching manner, calmly replied, "Strike, peerless maid, but hear me! I have given you infinite trouble, and have been a very bad fellow, I admit. Crafty and cruel, I have been an unmitigated oppressor of flies, and all inferior insects. I have sucked their blood, and lived upon their marrow. But now my conscience has awakened, and I am in favor of letting flies go free. It is not in quest of flies, that I am here, sweet maid; (and then he seemed perfectly convulsed;) I am changed at heart, and become a new spider. Pardon me for speaking the truth; my only object, in being here, is, from this elevated spot, to survey your incomparable charms." The chambermaid lowered her broom; and gently said, as she walked away, "Well, a spider is not such a horrid creature, after all."

I may be thought, in these remarks, to have offended against the dictum—*ne sutor ultra crepidam*. Surely I am not guilty—my dealings are with *the dead*. Perhaps I am mistaken. The conscience party may not be dead, but cataleptic—destined to rise again—to fall more feebly than before.

No. XXX

Funerals, in the earlier days of Rome, must have been very showy affairs. They were torch-light processions, by night. You will gather some information, on this subject, by consulting a note of Servius, on Virg. Æn. xi. 143. Cicero, de legibus, ii. 26, says, that Demetrius ordered nocturnal funerals, to check the taste for extravagance, in these matters: "Iste igitur sumptum minuit, non solum pœna, sed etiam tempore; ante lucem enim jussit efferri." A more ancient law, of similar import, will be found recited, in the oration of Demosthenes, against Macartatus, viii., 82, Dove's London ed. Orat. Attici. *Funes* or *funiculi* were small ropes or cords, covered with wax or tallow; such were the torches, used on such occasions; hence the word *funus* or funeral. A confirmation of this may be found in the note of Servius, Æn. i. 727. In a later age, funerals were celebrated in the forenoon.

There were some things done, at ancient funerals, which would be accounted very extraordinary at the present day. What should we say to a stuffed effigy of the defunct, composed entirely of cinnamon, and paraded in the procession! Plutarch says; "Such was the quantity of spices brought in by the women, at Sylla's funeral, that, exclusive of those carried in two hundred and ten great baskets, a figure of Sylla at full length, and of a lictor besides, was made entirely of cinnamon, and the choicest frankincense."

At the head of Roman funerals, came the *tibicines,* pipers, and trumpeters, immediately following the *designator,* or undertaker, and the lictors, dressed in black. Next came the "præficæ, quæ dabant cæteris modum plangendi." These were women hired to mourn, and sing the funeral song, who are popularly termed *howlers.* To this practice Horace alludes, in his Art of Poetry:

> Ut, qui conducti plorant in funere, dicunt,
> Et faciunt prope plura dolentibus ex animo—

which Francis well translates:

> As hirelings, paid for the funereal tear,
> Outweep the sorrows of a friend sincere.

I once witnessed an exhibition of this kind, in one of the West India Islands. A planter's funeral occurred, at Christianstadt, the west end of Santa

Cruz. After the corpse had been lowered into the grave, a wild ululation arose, from the mouths of some hundred slaves, who had followed from the plantation—"Oh, what good massa he was—good, dear, old massa gone—no poor slave eber hab such kind massa—no more any such good, kind massa come agin." I noticed one hard-favored fellow, who made a terrible noise, and upon whose features, as he turned the whites of his big eyes up toward heaven, there was a sinister, and, now and then, rather a comical expression, and who, when called to assist in filling up, appeared to throw on the earth, as if he did it from the heart.

After the work was done, I called him aside. "You have lost an excellent master," said I. The fellow looked warily round, and, perceiving that he was not overheard, replied, in an undertone—"No massa, he bad mule—big old villain—me glad the debble got him." Having thus relieved himself of his feelings, he hastened to join the gang, and I soon saw him, as they filed off, on their way back to the plantation, throwing his brawny arms aloft, and joining in the cry—"Oh, what kind, good massa he was!" Upon inquiry, I learned, that this planter was a very bad mule indeed, a merciless old taskmaster.

Not more than ten flute players were allowed, at a funeral, by the Twelve Tables. The flutes and trumpets were large and of lugubrious tones; thus Ovid, Fast. vi. 660: Cantabat mœstis tibia funeribus; and Am. ii. 66: Pro longa resonent carmina vestra tuba.

Nothing appears more incomprehensible, in connection with this subject, than the employment of players and buffoons, by the ancients, at their funerals. This practice is referred to, by Suetonius, in his Life of Tiberius, sec. 57. We are told by Dyonisius, vii. 72, that these Ludii, Histriones, and Scurræ danced and sang. One of this class of performers was a professed mimic, and was styled *Archimimus*. Strange as such a proceeding may appear to us, it was his business, to imitate the voice, manner, and gestures of the defunct; he supported the dead man's character, and repeated his words and sayings. In the Life of Vespasian, sec. 19, Suetonius thus describes the proceeding: In funere, Favor, archimimus, personam ejus ferens, imitansque, ut est mos, facta ac dicta vivi, etc. This Favor must have been a comical fellow, and is as free with the dead, as Killigrew, Charles the Second's jester, was, with the living; as the reader will perceive, if he will refer to the passage in Suetonius: for the fellow openly cracks his jokes, on the absurd expense of the funeral. This, we should suppose, was no subject for joking, if we may believe the statement of Pliny, xxxiii. 47, that one C. Cæcillius Claudius, a private citizen, left rather more than nine thousand pounds sterling, by his will, for his funeral expenses.

After the archimimus, came the freemen of the deceased, *pileati*; that is, wearing their caps of liberty. Men, not unfrequently, as a last act, to swell their funeral train, freed their slaves. Before the corpse, were carried the images of the defunct and of his ancestors, but not of such, as had been found guilty of any heinous crime. Thus Tacitus, ii. 32, relates, that the image of Libo was not permitted to accompany the obsequies of any of his posterity.

The origin of the common practice of marching at military funerals, with arms reversed, is of high antiquity. Thus Virgil xi. 93, at the funeral of Pallas—*versis Arcades armis*: and upon another occasion, *versi fasces* occur in Tacitus iii. 2, referring to the lictors.

In our cities and large towns, the corpse is commonly borne to the grave, in a hearse, or on the shoulders of paid bearers. Originally it was otherwise. The office of supporting the body to the grave was supposed to belong, of right, and duty, to relatives and friends; or, in the case of eminent persons, to public functionaries. Thus, in Tacitus, iii. 2, we find the expression, *tribunorum centurionumque humeris cineres portabantur*: and, upon the death of Augustus, Tac. i. 8, it was carried by acclamation, as we moderns say, *corpus ad rogum humeris senatorum ferendum.*

The conduct of both sexes, at funerals, was, in some respects, rather ridiculous, in those days. Virgil says of King Latinus, when he lost his wife,

————it, scissa veste, Latinus,
Canitiem immundo perfusam pulvere turpans;

which means, in plain English, that the old monarch went about, with his coat torn, defiling his white hair with filthy dust.

Cicero, in his Tusculan Questions, iii. 26, is entirely of this opinion: detestabilia genera lugendi, pædores, muliebres lacerationes genarum, pectoris, feminum, capitis percussiones—detestable kinds of mourning, covering the body with filth, women tearing their cheeks, bosoms, and limbs, and knocking their heads. Tibullus, in the concluding lines of his charming elegy to Delia, the first of his first book, though he evidently derives much happiness, from the conviction, that she will mourn for him, and weep over his funeral pile, implores her to spare her lovely cheeks and flowing hair. No classical reader will censure me, for transcribing this very fine passage:

Te spectem, suprema mihi quum venerit hora,
Te teneam moriens, deficiente manu.
Flebis et arsuro positum me, Delia, lecto.
Tristibus et lacrymis oscula mixta dabis.
Flebis; non tua sunt duro præcordia ferro,

Vincta, nec in tenero stat tibi corde silex.
Illo non juvenis poterit de funere quisquam
Lumina, non virgo, sicca referre domum.
Tu manes ne læde meos: sed parce solutis
Crinibus, et teneris, Delia, parce genis.

The *suttee*, or sacrifice of the widows of Hindostan, on the funeral pile of their husbands, was not more a matter of course, than the laceration of the hair and cheeks, among Roman women. It was undoubtedly accounted disreputable, for a widow to appear in public, after the recent funeral of her husband, with locks unpulled and cheeks unscratched. To such extremity had this absurd practice proceeded, that the fifth law of the tenth of the Twelve Tables, to which reference has been made, in a former number, was enacted to prevent it—*mulieres genas ne radunto.*

No discreet matron perpetrates any such absurdity, in modern times. The hair and cheeks of the departed have, occasionally, given evidence of considerable laceration, from some cause unknown; but neither the law of the Tables, nor the pathos of a Tibullus is commonly required, to prevent a Christian widow, from laying violent hands, upon her cheeks or her hair.

No. XXXI

The cholera seems to be forgotten—but without reason—for the yellowest and most malignant of all yellow fevers is down upon us, proving fatal to the peace of many families, and sweeping away our citizens, by hundreds. The distemper appears to have originated in California, and to have been brought hither, in letters from Governor Mason and others. It is deeply to be deplored, that these letters, which are producing all this mischief, had not been subjected to the process of smoking and sprinkling with vinegar; for the disease is highly contagious. This fever differs entirely from the *febris flava*—the *typhus icteroides* of *Sauvages*. The symptoms are somewhat peculiar. The pulse is quick and fluttering—the head hot—the patient neglects his business, bolts his food, and wanders about—sometimes apparently delirious, and, during the paroxysms, calls furiously for a pickaxe and a tin pan. But the most certain indication, that the disease has entered into the system, is, not that the patient himself becomes yellow, but that everything, upon which he turns his eyes, assumes the yellow appearance of gold. The nature of this distemper will, however, be much better understood, by the presentation of a few cases of actual occurrence.

I. Jeduthan Smink—a carpenter, having a wife and two children, residing at No. 9 Loafer's Lane. This is a strongly marked case. Mr. Smink, who is about five and twenty years of age, has always entertained the opinion, that work did him harm, and that drink did him good—labors—the only way in which he will labor—under the delusion, that all is gold that glistens—packed up his warming pan and brass kettle, to send them to the mint.

II. Laban Larkin, a farmer—caught the fever of a barber, while being shaved—persuaded that the unusual yellowness of his squashes and carrots can only be accounted for, by the presence of gold dust—turned a field of winter rye topsy turvy, in search of it—believes finally, in the sliding qualities of subterraneous treasure—thinks his gold has slipped over into his neighbor's field of winter rye—offers to dig it all up, at the halves—excited and abusive, because his neighbor declines the offer—told him he was a superannuated ass, and behind the times.

III. Molly Murphy resides, when at home, which is seldom, in Shelaly Court, near the corner, easily found by any one, who will follow his nose;

has a husband and one child, a dutiful boy, who vends matches and penny papers, on week days, and steals, on Sundays, for the support of the family. Molly can read; has read what Gov. Mason writes about pigs rooting up gold, by mistake, for groundnuts—her brain much disturbed—has an impression, that gold may be found almost anywhere—with a tin pan, and no other assistance but her son, Tooley Murphy, she has actually dug over and washed a pile of filth, in front of her dwelling, which the city scavengers have never been able materially to diminish—urges her husband to be "aff wid the family for Killyfarny, where the very wheelbarries is made out of goold." Dreams of nothing but gold dust, and firmly believes it to be the very dust we shall all return to—while asleep, seized her husband by the ears, and could scarcely be sufficiently awakened, to comprehend that she had not captured the golden calf.

Let us be grave. I shall not inquire, if Bishop Archelaus was right in the opinion, that the original golden calf was made, not by the Israelites, but by Egyptians, who were the companions of their flight; nor if the modern idol be a descendant in the right line. It is somewhat likely, that the golden calf of 1848, will grow up to be a terrible bull, for some of the adventurers.

That there is gold in California, no one doubts. Governor Mason's standard of quantity is rather alarming—there is gold enough, says he, in the country, drained by the Sacramento and Joaquin rivers, and more than enough, "*to pay the cost of the present war with Mexico, a hundred times over.*" This is encouraging, and may lead us to look upon the prospect of another, with more complacency; though the whole of this treasure will not buy back a single slaughtered victim—not one husband to the widow—nor one parent to an orphan child—nor one stay and staff, the joy and the pride of her life, to the lone mother. *N'importe*—we have gold and glory! "The people," says Mr. Mason, "before engaged in cultivating their small patches of ground, and guarding their herds of cattle and horses, have all gone to the mines. Laborers of every trade have left their work benches, and tradesmen their shops. Sailors desert their ships, as fast as they arrive on the coast."

There is a marvellous fascination in all this, no doubt; and as fast and as far as the knowledge radiates, thousands upon thousands will be rushing to the spot. The shilling here, however, which procures a given amount of meat, fire and clothes, is equal to the sum, whatever it may be, which, there procures the same amount and quality. Loafers and the lovers of ease and indolence, who are tobacco chewers, to a man, are desirous of flying to this El Dorado. Let them have a care: an ounce of gold dust, valued at $12 there, though worth $18 here, is said to have been paid, for a plug of tobacco. A traveller in Caffraria, having paid five cowries, (shells, the money of the country) for some article, complained, that forty were demanded, for a like article, in a village, not far off; and inquired if the article was scarce; "no," was the reply, "but cowries are very plenty."

Our adventurers intend to remain, perhaps, only till they obtain a competency. Even that is not the work of a day; and will be longer, or shorter, in the ratio of the consumption of means, for daily support, during the operation. There will, doubtless, be some difference also, as to the meaning of the word competency. An intelligent merchant, of this city, once defined it to mean a little more, in every individual's opinion, than he hath. Like the lock of hay, which Miss Edgeworth says is attached to the extremity of the pole, and which is ever just so far in advance of the hungry horses, in an Irish jaunting car, so competency seems to be forever leading us onward, yet is never fairly within our grasp.

John Graunt, of whom a good account may be found in Bayle, says, that, if the art of making gold were known, and put extensively in practice, it would raise the value of silver. Of course it would, and of everything else, so far as the quantity of gold, given in exchange for any article, is the representative of value. As gold becomes plenty, it will be employed for other uses, sauce-pans perhaps, as well as for the increase of the circulating medium. The amount of gold, which has passed through the British mint, from the accession of Elizabeth, 1558, to 1840, is, according to Professor Farraday, 3,353,561 pounds weight troy; and nearly one half of this was coined during the reign of George III.

Gold is a good thing, in charitable fingers; but it too frequently constructs for itself a chancel in our hearts. It then becomes the golden calf, and man an idolater. How dearly we get to love the chink and the glitter of our gold! How much like death it does seem, to go off 'change, before the last watch!

Three score years and ten, devoted to the turning of pennies! How many of us, after we have had our three warnings, still hobble up and down, day after day, infinitely more anxious about pennies, than we were, fifty years ago, about pounds! An angel, the spirit, for example, of Michael de Montaigne, perched upon the City Hall—the eastern end of the ridge pole—must be tempted to laugh heartily. Without any angelic pretensions, I have done so myself, when, upon certain emergencies, the kegs, boxes, and bags of gold and silver, hand-carted and hand borne, have gone from bank to bank, backward and forward, often, in a morning, like the slipper, in the *jeu de pantoufle*! What an interest is upon the faces of the crowd, who gaze upon the very kegs and boxes; feasting upon the bald idea—the unprofitable consciousness—that gold and silver are within; and reminding one of old George Herbert's lines,—

"Wise men with pity do behold
Fools worship mules, that carry gold."

"Verily," saith an ancient writer, "traffickers and the getters of gain, upon the mart, are like unto pismires, each struggling to bear off the largest mouthful."

I am glad to see that the moderns are collecting the remains of good old George Herbert, and giving them an elegant *surtout*. His address to money is a jewel, and none the worse for its antique setting:

"Money! Thou bane of bliss, and source of wo!
Whence com'st thou, that thou art so fresh and fine?
I know thy parentage is base and low;
Man found thee, poor and dirty, in a mine.

"Surely thou didst so little contribute
To this great kingdom, which thou now hast got,
That he was fain, when thou wert destitute,
To dig thee out of thy dark cave and grot.

"Then, forcing thee by fire, he made thee bright;
Nay, thou hast got the face of man, for we
Have, with our stamp and seal, transferred our right;
Thou art the man, and we but dross to thee!

"Man calleth thee his wealth, who made thee rich,
And, while he digs out thee, falls in the ditch."

The mere selfish getters of gain, who dispense it not, are, *civiliter et humaniter mortui*—dead as a door nail—dead dogs in the manger! I come not to bury them, at present; but, if possible, to awaken some of them with my penny trumpet; otherwise they may die in good earnest in their sins; their last breath giving evidence of their ruling passion—muttering not the *tête d'armée* of Napoleon, but the last words of that accomplished Israelite, who caused his gold to be counted out, before his failing eyes—*per shent*.

No. XXXII

Making mourning, as an abstract phrase, is about as intelligible, as *making fish*. These arbitrary modes of expression have ever been well enough understood, nevertheless, by those employed in the respective operations. *Making mourning*, in ancient times, was assigned to that class of hired women, termed *præficæ*, to whom I have had occasion to refer. They are thus described, by Stephans—adhiberi solebant funeri, mercede conductæ, ut flerent, et fortia facta laudarent—they were called to funerals, and paid, to shed tears, and relate the famous actions of the defunct. Doubtless, by practice, and continual exercise of the will over the lachrymary organs, they acquired the power of forcing mechanical tears. We have a specimen of this power, in the case of Miss Sophy Streatfield, so often referred to, by Madame D'Arblay, in her account of those happy days at Mrs. Thrale's. *Making mourning*, in modern times, is, with a few touching exceptions, confined to that important class, the dress-makers.

The time allowed, for mourning, was determined, by the laws of Numa. Plutarch informs us, that no mourning was allowed, for a child, that died under three years, and for all others, a month, for every year it had lived, but never to exceed ten, which was the longest term, allowed for any mourning. We often meet with the term, *luctus annus*, the year of mourning; but the year of Romulus contained but ten months; and, though Numa added two, to the calendar, the term of mourning remained unchanged. The howlers, or wailing women, were employed also in Greece, and in Judea. Thus in Jeremiah ix. 17, *call for the mourning women, &c., and let them make haste and take up a wailing for us, that our eyes may run down with tears, &c.*

By the laws of Numa, widows were required to mourn ten months or during the year of Romulus. Thus Ovid, Fast. i. 35:

Per totidem menses a funere conjugis uxor
Sustinet in vidua tristia signa domo.

Numa was rather severe upon widows. The *tristia signa*, spoken of by Ovid, were sufficiently mournful. According to Kirchmaun de Fun. iv. 11, they were not to stir abroad in public—to abstain entirely from all entertainments—to lay aside every kind of ornament—to dress in black—and not even to kindle a fire, in their houses. Not content with stinting and freezing these poor, lone creatures, to death, Numa forbade them to repeat the matrimonial experiment, for ten months. Indeed, it was accounted infamous, for a widow to marry, within that period. As though he were resolved to add insult to injury, he, according to Plutarch, permitted those to violate this law, who would make up their minds, to sacrifice a cow with calf. This unnatural sacrifice was intended, by Numa, to frighten the widows. Doubtless, in many instances, the legislative bugbear was effectual; but it is quite probable there were some courageous women, in those days, as there are, at present, who would have slaughtered a whole drove, rather than yield the tender point.

The Jews expressed their grief, for the death of their near friends, by weeping, and crying aloud, beating their breasts, rending their clothes, tearing their flesh, pulling their hair, and starving themselves. They neither dressed, nor made their beds, nor washed, nor saw visitors, nor shaved, nor cut their nails, and made their toilets with sackcloth and ashes. The mourning of the Jews lasted commonly seven days, and never more than thirty—quite long enough, we should think, for such an exhibition of filth and folly. The Greeks also did much of all this—they covered themselves with dust and dirt, and rolled in the mire, and beat their breasts, and tore their faces.

The color of the mourning garb, among the Romans, was originally black—from the time of Domitian, white. At present, the color of the mourning dress, in Europe is black—in China white—in Turkey blue or violet—in Egypt yellow—in Ethiopia brown. There have come down to us two admirable letters from Seneca, 63, and 99, on the subject of lamentation for the dead; the first to Lucilius, after the death of his friend, Flaccus— the second to Lucilius, communicating the letter Seneca had written to Murullus, on the death of his son. These letters must be read, *cum grano salis*, on account of the stoical philosophy of the writer. He admits the propriety of decent sorrow, but is opposed to violent and unmeasured lamentations— *nec sicci sint occuli, amisso amico, nec fluant*—shed tears, if you have lost your friend, but do not cry your eyes out—*lacrimandum est, non plorandum*—let there be weeping, but not wailing. He cites, for the advantage of Lucilius, the counsel of Ulysses to Achilles, whose grief, for the death of Patroclus, had become inordinate, to give one whole day to his sorrow, and have done with it. He considers it not honorable, for men, to exhibit their grief, beyond the term of two or three days. Such, upon the authority of Tacitus De Mor. Germ. 27, was the practice of the ancient Germans. Funerum nulla ambitio: ... struem rogi nec vestibus, nec odoribus, cumulant: ... lamenta ac lacrimas cito, dolorem et tristitiam tarde, ponunt; feminis lugere honestum est; viris meminisse: there was no pride of funereal parade; they heaped no garments, no odors, upon the pile; they speedily laid aside their tears and laments; not so their grief and sorrow. It was becoming, for *women* to mourn; for *men* to cherish in their memories.

In his letter to Lucilius, Seneca enters upon an investigation, as to the real origin of all this apparent sorrow, so freely and generally manifested, for the dead; and his sober conviction breaks forth, in the words—Nemo tristis sibi est. O infelicem stultitiam! est aliqua et doloris ambitio! No one mourns for himself alone. Oh miserable folly! There is ambition, even in our sorrow! This passage recalls Martial's epigram, 34, De Gellia:

> Amissum non flet, quum sola est Gellia, patrem;
> Si quis adest, jussæ prosiliunt lacrymæ.
> Non dolet hic, quisquis landari, Gellia, quærit;
> Ille dolet vere, qui sine teste dolet.

Arthur Murphy, in his edition of Dr. Johnson's works, ascribes to that great man the following extraordinary lines:

> If the man, who turnips cries,
> Cry not, when his father dies,
> 'Tis a proof, that he had rather
> Have a turnip than his father.

Under the doctor's sanction, for a bagatelle, I may offer a translation of Martial's epigram:

> When no living soul is nigh,
> Gellia's filial grief is dry;
> Call, some morning, and I'll warrant
> Gellia'l shed a perfect torrent.
> Tears unforc'd true sorrow draws:
> Gellia weeps for mere applause.

It is our fortune to witness not a little of this, in our line. We are compelled to drop in, at odd, disjointed moments, when the not altogether disagreeable occupations of the survivors contrast, rather oddly, to be sure, with the graver duties to the dead. A rich widow, like Dr. Johnson's *protègè*, in his letter to Chesterfield, is commonly overburdened with help. It is quite surprising, to observe the solicitude about her health, and how very fervent the hope of her neighbors becomes, that she may not have taken cold. The most prominent personages, after the widow and the next of kin, are the coffin-maker and the dress-maker—both are solicitous of making an excellent fit. Those, who, like myself, have had long practice in families, are often admitted to familiar interviews with the chief mourners, which are likely to take place, in the midst of dress-makers and artists of all sorts. How many acres of black crape I have witnessed, in half a century! "Mr. Abner—good Mr. Abner," said Mrs. ——, "dear Mr. Abner," said she, "I shall not forget your kindness—how pleasant it is, on these occasions, to see a face one knows. You buried my first husband—I thought there was nothing like that: and you buried my second husband—and, oh dear me, I thought there was nothing like that—and now, oh dear, dear me, you are going to bury my third! How I am supported, it is hard to tell—but the widow's God will carry me through this, and other trials, for aught I know—Miss Buddikin, don't you think that dress should be fuller behind?" "Oh dear ma'am, your fine shape, you know," said Miss Buddikin. "There now, Miss Buddikin, at any other time I dare say I should be pleased with your flattery, but grief has brought down my flesh and spirits terribly. Good morning, dear Mr. Abner—remember there will be no postponement, on account of the weather."

No. XXXIII

I am sad. It is my duty to record an event of deep and universal interest. On Sunday night, precisely as the clock of the Old South Church struck the very first stroke of twelve, departed this life, of no particular malady, but from a sort of constitutional decay, to which the family has ever been periodically liable, and at the same age, at which his ancestors have died, for many generations, A. Millesimus Octingentesimus Quadragesimus Octavus.

It has been a custom in France, and in other countries, to send printed invitations to friends and relatives, inviting them to funerals. I have heard of a thriving widow—*la veuve Berthier*—who added a short postscript—*Madame Berthier will be happy to furnish soap and candles, at the old stand, as heretofore*. I trust I shall not be deemed guilty of a like indiscretion, if I add, for general information, that the business will be conducted hereafter, in the name of A. M. O. Q. Nonus.

I did intend to be facetious, but, for the soul of me, I cannot. It is enough for me to know that the old year is dead and gone, and that the hopes and fears of millions are now lying in its capacious grave. Between the old year and the new, the space is so incalculably narrow, that, if those ancient philosophers were in the right, who contended, that an angel could not live in a vacuum, no angel, in the flesh, or out of it, could possibly get between the two: the partition is thin as tissue paper—thin as that between wit and madness, which is so exceedingly thin, as to be often undistinguishable, leaving us in doubt, on which side our neighbors may be found,—when at home.

I see, clearly, in the close of another year, another milestone, upon Time's highway, from chaos to eternity. Is it not wise, and natural, and profitable, for the pilgrim to pause, and mark his lessening way? He cannot possibly know the precise number of milestones, that lie between the present and his journey's end; but he may sometimes shrewdly guess from the number he has passed already. There is precious little certainty, however, in the very best of man's arithmetic, on a subject like this: for, at every milestone, from the very first, and at countless intermediate points, he will observe innumerable tablets, recording the fact, that myriads of travellers have stopped here and there, not for the want of willingness to go forward, but for the want of breath—not for the night, to be awakened at the morning watch, by the attentive host, or the railway whistle,—but for a long, long while, to be summoned, at last, by the piercing notes of a clarion, loud and clear, which, as the bow of Ulysses could be bent only by the master's hand, can be raised, only by the lips and the lungs of an archangel.

Well, Quadragesimus Octavus hath gone to his long home, and the mourners go about the streets—a motley group it is, that band of melancholy followers! Upon this, as upon all other occasions of the same sort, true tears, from the very well-spring of the heart, fall, together with showers of hypocritical salt water. Little children, who must ever refer their orphanage to the year that is past, are in the van; and with them, a few widowers and widows, who have not been married quite long enough, to be reconciled to their bereavement. There are others, who also have been divorced from their partners by death, and who submit, with admirable grace; and wear their weeds—of the very best make and fashion, by the way—with infinite propriety.

It is quite amazing to see the great number of mourners, who, though, doubtless, natives, have a very Israelitish expression, and wear phylacteries, upon which are written three or four words whose import is intelligible, only to the initiated, but which, being interpreted, signify—*three per cent. a month*. None seem to wear an expression of more heartfelt sorrow, for the departure of Quadragesimus Octavus, during whose existence, being less greedy of honors than of gain, they were singularly favored, converting the necessities of other men into an abundance of bread and butter, for themselves.

In the melancholy train, we behold a goodly number of maiden ladies, dressed in yellow, which is the mourning color of the Egyptians, and some of these disconsolate damsels are really beginning to acquire the mummy complexion: it happened that, as the old year expired, they were just turned of thirty.

There are others, who have sufficient reason to mourn, and whose numerous writings have brought them into serious trouble. Their works, commencing with a favorite expression—*for value received I promise to pay*, owing to something rather pointed in the phraseology, were liable to be severely criticised, so soon as the old year expired.

The lovers of parade, and show, and water celebrations, and torch-light processions, trumpeting and piping merrymakings, and huzzaings, the brayings of stump orators, and the intolerable noise and farrago of electioneering; the laudings and vituperatings of Taylor, Cass, and Van

Buren; the ferocious lyings and vilifyings of partisans, politically drunk or crazy—the lovers of all or any of these things are one and all, attendants at the funeral of Quadragesimus Octavus.

The good old year is gone—and, in the words of a celebrated clergyman, to a bereaved mother, who would not be comforted, but wailed the louder, the more he pressed upon her the duty of submission—*"what do you propose to do about it?"* I cannot answer for you, my gentle reader, but I am ready to answer for myself. As an old sexton, I believe it to be my duty to pay immediate attention to the very significant command—whatsoever thy hand findeth to do, do it with thy might; for there is no work, nor device, nor knowledge, nor wisdom in the grave, whither thou goest. If good old Samuel had been an undertaker, he could not have said, more confidently than I do, at this moment, whose corpse have I taken, or whose shroud have I taken, or whom have I defrauded, or whom have I buried east for west, or wrong end foremost? Of what surgeon have I received a fee, for a skeleton, to blind mine eyes withal? I have neither the head nor the heart for mystical theology. I believe in the doctrine of election, as established by the constitution and laws of the United States, and of the States respectively, so far as regards the President, Vice President, and all town, county and state officers: and I respect the Egyptians, for one trait, recorded of them, by an eminent historian, who states, that those, who worship an ape, never quarrel with those, who worship an ox. A very fine verse, the thirteenth of the last chapter of Ecclesiastes—"Let us hear the conclusion of the whole matter: fear God, and keep his commandments: for this is the whole duty of man."

Let us try, during the year, upon whose threshold we are now standing, to do as much good, and as little harm, as possible. I respectfully recommend to all old men and women, who are as grey and grizzly as I am, to make themselves as agreeable as they can; and remember, that old age is proverbially peevish and exacting. In the presence of children, do not forget the wise sayings of Parson Primrose, who candidly confessed, when solicited to join in some childish pastime, that he complied, for he was tired of being always wise. Pray allow all you can for the vivacity and waywardness of youth. Nine young ladies, in ten, may find a clever fit, in Pope's shrewd line—

"Brisk as a flea, and ignorant as dirt."

All, that can be said about it, lies in a filbert shell, *ita lex scripta est, ita rerum natura.* You will not mend the matter, by scowling and growling, from morning to night. Can you not remember, that you yourself, when a boy, were saluted now and then, with the title of "proper plague"—"devil's bird"—or "little Pickle?" I can. Some years ago, my very worthy friend, the Rev. John S. C. Abbott, did me the kindness to give me one of his excellent works, the Path of Peace. The preface contains a very short and clever incident, of whose applicability, you can judge for yourself.

"Mother," said a little boy, "I do not wish to go to Heaven."

"And why not, my son?"

"Why, grandfather will be there, will he not?"

"Yes, my son, I hope he will."

"Well, as soon as he sees us, he will come, scolding along, and say, 'Whew, whew, whew! what are these boys here for?' I am sure I do not wish to go to Heaven, if grandfather is to be there."

This is a short tale of a grandfather, but it is a very significant story, for its length; and calculated, I fear, for many meridians.

Well, here we are, in the very midst of bells and bonfires, screaming for joy, in honor of the new year, with our spandy new weepers on, for the old one.

No. XXXIV

Viewed in every possible relation, the most melancholy and distressing funerals, of which I have any knowledge, were a series of interments, which occurred in Charleston, South Carolina, not very many years ago, and of which, in 1840, I received, while sojourning there, a particular account, from an inhabitant of that hospitable city. These funerals were among the blacks; and, as there was no epidemic at the time, their frequency, at length, attracted observation. Every day or two, the colored population were seen, bearing, apparently, one of their number to the place, appointed for all living. Suspicion was, at last, awakened—a post mortem examination was resolved on—the graves, which proved to be uncommonly shallow, were opened—the coffins lifted out, and examined—and found to be filled, not with corpses, but with muskets, swords, pistols, pikes, knives, hatchets, and such other weapons, as might be necessary, for the perfection of a deadly work, which had been long projected, and was then not far from its consummation.

These, I say, were the most melancholy funerals, of which I have any knowledge. This was burying the hatchet, in a novel sense. In 1840, the tumult of mind, resulting from immediate apprehension, had, in a great degree, subsided; yet a rigorous system of espionage continued, in full operation—the spirit of vigilance was still on tiptoe—the arsenal was in excellent working order, and capable, at any moment, of turning its iron shower, in every direction—the separate gathering of the blacks, for religious worship, had been, and still was, prohibited; for it was believed, that the little tabernacle, in which, before this alarming discovery, the colored people were in the habit of assembling, had been used, in some sort, for the purpose of holding insurrectionary conclaves; perhaps for the purpose also of muttering prayers, between their teeth, to the bondman's God, to give him strength to break his fetters.

At the time, to which I refer, the slaves, who attended religious services, on the Sabbath, entered the same temples with their masters, who paid their vows, on cushions, while many of the slaves worshipped, squatting in the aisles. At this time, slaves, *ex cautela*, were forbidden, under penalty of imprisonment and the lash, from being present at any conflagration. Under a like penalty, they were commanded to retire instantly, upon the very first stroke of the curfew bell, to their homes and cabins. At every quarter of an hour, through the whole night, the cry of *all's well* was sent forth by the armed sentinel, from the top of St. Michael's tower. Such was the state of things, in 1840, in the city of Charleston.

Melancholy as were these funerals, the undertakers were quite as ingenious, as those cunning Greeks, who contrived the Trojan horse, *divinâ Palladis arte*. Melancholy and ominous funerals were they—for they were incidents of slavery, the curse colossal—that huge, unsightly cicatrice, upon the very face of our heritage. Well may we say to the most favored nation of the earth, in Paul's proud words,—*would to God ye were not only almost, but altogether such as we are, saving these bonds.*

After taking a mental and moral *coup d'œil* of these matters, I remember that I lay long, upon my pillow, not consigning my Southern friends and brethren, votively, to the devil; but thanking God, for that blessed suggestion, which led good, old Massachusetts, and the other states of the North, to abolish slavery, within their own domains.

Slavery is a curse, not only to the long-suffering slave, but to the mortified master. This chivalry of the South—what is it? Every man of the South, or the North, who comes to the blessed conclusion, that, while others own *jackasses, horses, and horned cattle*, he actually *owns men*—what a thought!—will soon become filled with this very chivalry. It is the lordly consciousness of dominion over one's fellow-man—a sort of Satrap-like feeling of power—a sentiment extremely oriental, which begets that important and consequential air of superiority, that marks the Southern man and the Southern boy,—Mr. Calhoun, diving, like one of Pope's heroes, after first principles, and fetching up, for a fact, the pleasant fancy, that *man is not born of a woman*—or the young, travelling gentleman, full of "Suth Cralina," who comes hither, to sojourn awhile, and carries in every look, that almost incomprehensible mixture of pride and sensitiveness, which is equally repulsive and ridiculous.

The bitterness of sectional feeling is a necessary incident of slavery. Civil and servile wars are among its terrible contingencies. Slavery cannot endure in our land, though the end be not yet. I had rather the cholera should spread, than this moral scourge, over our new domains—not, upon my honor, because the former would be a help to our profession, but because a dead is more bearable, than a living curse.

Of all the sciolists, who have offered their services, to remedy this evil, the conscience party is the most remarkable. A self-consecrated party, with their phlogistic system, would deal with the whole South, which, on this topic, is a perfect hornet's nest already, precisely as an intelligent farmer, in Vermont, dealt with a hornet's nest, under the eaves of his dwelling—he applied the actual cautery; his practice was successful—he destroyed the nest, and with it his entire mansion. There are men, of this party, to whom the constitution and laws of the Union are objects of infinite contempt; who despise the Bible; who would overthrow the civil magistrate; and unfrock the clergy. But there are many others, who abjure such doctrines—a species of conscience comeouters—who intend, after they have unkennelled the whirlwind, to appoint a committee of three, from every county, to hold it by the tail, *ne quid detrimenti respublica caperet*. These are to be selected from the most careful and judicious, who, when the firebrand is thrown into the barrel of gunpowder, will have a care, that not more than a moderate quantity shall be ignited.

The constitution is a contract, made by our fathers, and binding on their children. Who shall presume to say that contract is void, for want of consideration, or because the subject is *malum in se*? Who shall decide the question of *nudum pactum* or not? Not one of the parties, nor two, nor any number, short of the whole, can annul this solemn contract; nor can a decision of the question of constitutionality come from any other tribunal, than the Supreme Judicial Court of the United States.

Lord Mansfield's celebrated dictum—*fiat justitia, ruat Cælum*, has been often absurdly applied, and in connection with this very question of slavery and its removal. *Justitia* is a broad word, and refers not solely to the rights of the slave, but to those of the freeman. The proposition of the full-bottomed abolitionist—immediate emancipation, or dissolution of the Union, and civil and servile war to boot, if it must be so—is fit to be taught, only to the tenants of a madhouse. But there is a spirit abroad, whose tendency cannot be mistaken. Slavery is becoming daily more and more odious, in the east, in the west, in the north, ay, and in the south. Individually, many slaveholders are becoming less attached to their *property*. There may be too much even of *this good thing*. Slavery would continue longer, in the present slave states, if it were extended to the new territories; for it would be rendered more bearable in the former, by the power of sloughing off the redundancy, on profitable terms. The spirit of emancipation is striding over the main land, walking upon the waters, and planting its foot, upon one dark island after another. *Let us hope*—better to do that, than mischief. Let us rejoice, that, as the Scotch say, *there is a God aboon a'*—better to do that, than spit upon our Bibles, and scoff at law and order. It is always better to stand still, than move rudely and rashly, in the dark. Such was the decided opinion of my old friend and fellow-sexton, Grossman, when he fell, head first, into an unclosed tomb, and broke his enormous nose.

No. XXXV

In looking up a topic, for my dealings with the dead, this afternoon, I can think of nothing more interesting, at the present time, than *Lot's wife and the Dead Sea*. I consider Lieutenant Lynch the most fortunate of modern discoverers. He has discovered the long lost lady of Lot—the veritable pillar of salt! There are some incredulous persons, I am aware, who are of opinion, that the account of this discovery should be received, *cum grano salis*; but my own mind is entirely made up. I should have been better pleased, I admit, if he had verified the suggestion, which led to the discovery, by bringing home a leg, or an arm. Possibly, it may be thought proper to send a Government vessel, for the entire pillar, to ornament the Rotunda at Washington. The identification of Lot's wife is rendered exceedingly simple, by the fact, that seventeen of her fingers, and not less than fourteen of her toes, broken off from time to time, by the faithful, as relics, are exhibited in various churches and monasteries.

Models of these, in plaster, could readily be obtained, I presume; and an application of their fractured parts to the salt corpse, discovered by Lieutenant Lynch, would settle the question, in the manner, employed to test the authenticity of ancient indentures. Besides, every one knows, that salt is a self preserver, and lasting in its character, especially the Attic. The very elements of preservation abound in the Dead Sea, and the region round about. Its very name establishes the fact—*Asphaltites*—so called from the immense quantity of *asphaltum* or bitumen, with which it abounds. This is called *Jews' Pitch*, and was used of old, for embalming; and the corpse of Mrs. Lot, after the salt had thoroughly penetrated, rolled up, as it probably was found by Lieutenant Lynch, in a winding sheet of bitumen, which readily envelopes everything it touches, would last forever. This pitch is often sold by the druggists, under the name of mummy.

In Judea, with the territory of Moab, on the East, and the wilderness of Judah, on the West, and having the lands of Reuben and Edom, or Idumea, on the North and South, lies that sheet of mysterious and unfrequented water, which has been called the East Sea—the Salt Sea—the Sea of the Desert—the Sea of the Plain—the Sea of Sodom—and, more commonly, the Dead Sea. To this I beg leave to add another title, the Legendary lake, or Humbug water. More marvel has been marked, learned, and inwardly digested, by Christians, on the subject of this sheet of water, than the broad ocean has ever supplied, to stir the landman's heart. Its dimensions, in the first place, have been set down, with remarkable discrepancy. Pliny, lib. v. 15, says, Longitudine excedit centum M. passuum, latitudine maxima xxv., implet, minima sex, making the length one hundred miles, and the breadth, from twenty-five miles, to six. Josephus estimates its length at five hundred and eighty furlongs, from the mouth of the Jordan, to the town of Segor, at the opposite end; and its greatest breadth one hundred and fifty furlongs. The Rev. Dr. William Jenks, of whose learning and labors a sexton of the old school may be permitted to speak, with great respect, sets down the length, in his New Gazetteer of the Bible, appended to his Explanatory Bible Atlas, of 1847, at thirty-nine miles, and its greatest breadth at nine. Carne, in his Letters from the East, says the length is sixty miles, and the breadth from eight to ten. Stephens states the length to be thirty miles, in his Incidents of Travel.

The origin of this lake was ascribed to the submersion of the valley of Siddim, where the cities stood, which were destroyed, in the conflagration of Sodom and Gomorrah. This tremendous gallimaufry or hotch potch, produced, as some suppose, an intolerable stench, and impregnated the waters with salt, sulphur, and bitumen.

Pliny, in the passage quoted above,—observes—Nullum corpus animalium recipit—no animal can live in it. Speaking of these waters, Dr. Jenks remarks—"no animals exist in them." On the other hand, Dr. Pococke, on the authority of a monk, tells us, that fish have been caught in the Dead Sea. Per contra again, Mr. Volney affirms, that it contains neither animal nor vegetable life. M. Chateaubriand, on the other hand, who visited the Dead Sea, in 1807, remarks—"About midnight, I heard a noise upon the lake, and was told by the Bethlehemites, who accompanied me, that it proceeded from legions of small fish, which come out, and leap upon the shore." The monks of St. Saba assured Dr. Shaw, as he states in his travels, that they had seen fish caught there.

In the passage quoted from Pliny, he says—Tauri camelique fluitant. Inde fama nihil in eo mergi—bulls and camels float upon this lake: hence the notion, that nothing will sink in it. It is true, that the water of the Dead Sea is specifically heavier than any other, owing to the great quantity of salt, sulphur, and bitumen; but Dr. Pococke found not the slightest difficulty, in swimming and diving in the lake. Sir Thomas Browne, treating of this, in his Pseudodoxia, vol. iii., p. 341, London, 1835, observes—"As for the story, men deliver it variously. Some, I fear too largely, as Pliny, who affirmeth that bricks will swim therein. Mandevil goeth further, that iron swimmeth and feathers sink." "But," continueth Sir Thomas, "Andrew Thevet, in his Cosmography, doth ocularly overthrow it, for he affirmeth he saw an ass with his saddle cast therein and drowned."

Another legend is equally absurd, that birds, attempting to fly over the lake, fall, stifled by its horrible vapors. "It is very common," says Volney, "to see swallows skimming its surface, and dipping for the water, necessary to build their nests." Mr. Stephens, in his Incidents of Travel, vol. ii. chap. 15, gives an interesting account of the Dead Sea, and says—"I saw a flock of gulls floating quietly on its bosom."

It has been roundly asserted, that, in very clear weather, the ruins of the cities, destroyed by the conflagration, are visible beneath the waters. Josephus soberly avers, that a smoke constantly arose from the lake, whose waters changed their color three times daily.

The waters of Jordan and of the brooks Kishon, Jabbok, and Arnon, flow into the Dead Sea, yet produce no perceptible rise of its surface. The influx from these mountain streams is considerable. Hence another legend, to account for this mystery—a subterraneous communication with the Mediterranean—which would surely make the matter worse, for Dr. Jenks and other writers state, that "the waters lie in a deep caldron, many hundred feet *below* the Mediterranean." Evaporation, which is said to be very great, explains the mystery entirely. At the rising of the sun, dense fogs cover the lake.

Chateaubriand says—"The first thing I did, on alighting, was to walk into the lake, up to my knees, and taste the water. I found it impossible to keep it in my mouth. It far exceeds that of the sea, in saltness, and produces, upon the lips, the effect of a strong solution of alum. Before my boots were completely dry, they were covered with salt; our clothes, our hats, our hands were, in less than three hours, impregnated with this mineral." "The origin of this mineral," says Volney, "is easy to be discovered, for, on the southwest shore, are mines of fossil salt. They are situated, in the sides of the mountains, which extend along the border; and, for time immemorial, have supplied the neighboring Arabs, and even the city of Jerusalem."

"Whoever," says Mr. Carne, in his Letters from the East, "has seen the Dead Sea, will have its aspect impressed upon his memory. It is, in truth, a gloomy and fearful spectacle. The precipices, in general, descend abruptly to the lake, and, on account of their height, it is seldom agitated by the winds. Its shores are not visited, by any footstep, save that of the wild Arab, and he holds it in superstitious dread. On some parts of the rocks, there is a thick, sulphureous incrustation, and, in their steep descents, there are several deep caverns, where the benighted Bedouin sometimes finds a home. The sadness of the grave was on it and around it, and the silence also. However vivid the feelings are, on arriving on its shores, they subside, after a time, into languor and uneasiness; and you long, if it were possible, to see a tempest wake on its bosom, to give sound and life to the scene."

"If we adopt," says Chateaubriand, "the idea of Professor Michaelis, and the learned Busching, in his memoir on the Dead Sea, physics may be admitted, to explain the catastrophe of the guilty cities, without offence to religion. Sodom was built upon a mine of bitumen, as we know from the testimony of Moses and Josephus, who speak concerning wells of bitumen, in the valley of Siddim. Lightning kindled the combustible mass, and the cities sank in the subterranean conflagration." In Calmet's Dictionary of the Bible, vol. iii., article Lot, it is stated, that the Mahometans have added many circumstances to his history. They assert, that the angel Gabriel pried up the devoted cities so near to Heaven, that the angels actually heard the sound of the trumpets and horns, and even the yelping of puppies, in Sodom and Gomorrah: and that Gabriel then let the whole concern go with a terrible crash. Upon this, Calmet remarks,—"Romantic as this account appears, it preserves traces of an earthquake and a volcano, which were, in all probability, the *natural secondary cause* of the overthrow of Sodom, and of the formation of the Dead Sea." Lot's wife in my next.

No. XXXVI

The conversion of Lot's wife into a pillar of salt has given rise to as much learned discussion, as the question, so zealously agitated, between Barcephas and others, whether the forbidden fruit were an *apple* or a *fig*. *But his wife looked back from behind him, and she became a pillar of salt.* Gen. xix. 26. Very little account seems to have been made of this matter, at the time. The whole story, and without note or comment, is told in these fifteen words. It would have seemed friendly, and natural, and proper, for Abraham to have said a few words of comfort to Lot, on this sudden and singular bereavement; but, instead of this, we are told, in the following verse, that Abraham got up, next morning, and looked, very philosophically, at the smoke, which went up from the cities of the plain, like the smoke of a furnace. This neglect of Lot's wife is, too frequently, a wife's lot. Some of the learned have been sorely perplexed, to understand, why this unfortunate lady has not long since melted away, under the influence of the rains; for a considerable quantity of water has fallen, since the destruction of Sodom. But they seem to forget, that there is no measure of limitation, for a miracle; and that the salt might have been purposely designed, like *caoutchouc*, to resist the action of water. The departure from Sodom was sudden, to be sure; but the lady was clothed, in some sort, doubtless; yet nothing has been said, by travellers, about her drapery, and whether that also was converted into salt, or cast off, by the mere energy of the miracle, is unknown.

This pillar of salt Josephus says he has seen; and, though he does not name the time, it is of little consequence, as, in such a matter, we can well afford to throw in a century or two; but it must have been between A. D. 37, and a point, not long after the 13th year of Domitian. Such being the term of the existence of Josephus, as nearly as can be ascertained. The cities of the plain were destroyed, according to Calmet's reckoning, 1893 years before Christ; therefore, *the pillar*, which Josephus saw, must have then been standing more than nineteen centuries. These are the words of Josephus: "*But Lot's wife, continually turning back, to view the city, as she went from it, and being too nicely inquisitive what would become of it, although God had forbidden her so to do, was changed into a pillar of salt, for I have seen it, and it remains at this day."* Antiq., vol. i. p. 32, Whiston's translation, Lond. 1825. The editor, in a note states, that Clement of Rome, a cotemporary of Josephus, also saw it, and that Irenæus saw it, in the next century. Mr. Whiston prudently declines being responsible for the statements of modern travellers, who say they have seen it. And what did they see?—a pillar of salt. This is quite probable. Volney remarks, "At intervals we met with misshapen blocks, which prejudiced eyes mistake for mutilated statues, and which pass, with ignorant and superstitious pilgrims, for monuments of the adventure of Lot's wife; though it is nowhere said that she was metamorphosed into stone, like Niobe, but into salt, which must have melted the ensuing winter." Volney forgets, that the salt itself was miraculous, and, doubtless, water proof.

Mr. Stephens, in his Incidents of Travel, though he gives a description of the Dead Sea, in whose waters he bathed, says not a syllable of Lot's wife, or the pillar of salt.

Some of the learned have opined, that Lot's wife, like Pliny, during the eruption of Vesuvius, was overwhelmed, by the burning and flying masses of sulphur and bitumen; this is suggested, under the article, Lot's Wife, in Calmet. "Some travellers in Palestine," says he, "relate that Lot's wife was shown to them, i. e. the rock, into which she was metamorphosed. But what renders their testimony very suspicious is, that they do not agree, about the place, where it stands; some saying westward, others eastward, some northward, others southward of the Dead Sea; others in the midst of the waters; others in Zoar; others at a great distance from the city." In 1582, Prince Nicholas Radziville took a vast deal of pains to discover this remarkable pillar of salt, but all his inquiries were fruitless. Dr. Adam Clarke suggests, that Lot's wife, by lingering in the plain, may have been struck dead with lightning, and enveloped in the bituminous and sulphureous matter, that descended. He refers to a number of stories, that have been told, and among them, that this pillar possessed a miraculous, reproductive energy, whereby the fingers and toes of the unfortunate lady were regenerated, instanter, as fast as they were broken off, by the hands of pilgrims. Irenæus, one of the fathers, asserts, that this pillar of salt was *actually alive in his time!* Some of those fathers, I am grieved to say it, were insufferable story-tellers. This tale is also told, by the author of a poem, *De Sodoma,* appended to the life of Tertullian. Some learned men understand the Hebrew to mean simply, that *"she became fixed in the salsuginous soil"* —anglice, *stuck in the mud.* If this be the real meaning of the passage, it must have been some other lady, that was seen by Josephus, Clement, Irenæus, and Lieut. Lynch.

Sir Thomas Browne, credulous though he was, had, probably, no great confidence in the *literal* construction of the passage in Genesis. In vol. iii. page 327, of his works, London, 1835, he says—"We will not question the metamorphosis of Lot's wife, or whether she were transformed into a real statue of salt; though some conceive that expression metaphorical, and no more thereby than a lasting and durable column, according to the nature of salt, which admitteth no corruption." This is evidently the opinion of Dr. Adam Clarke. In other words, God, by her destruction, while her husband and daughters were saved, made her a *pillar or lasting memorial* to the disobedient. In this sense a pillar of *salt* means neither more nor less than an *everlasting memorial*. Salt is the symbol of perpetuity; thus Numbers xviii. 19. *It is a covenant of salt forever*: and 2 Chron. xvii. 5, the kingdom is given to David and his sons forever, *by a covenant of salt*. If this be the true construction, those four gentlemen, to whom I have referred, have been entirely misled, in supposing that any one of those masses of salt, which Volney says may be mistaken, for the remains of mutilated statues, has ever, at any period of the world, been the object of Lot's devotion, or the partner of his joys and sorrows.

In vol. ii. page 212, of his Incidents of Travel, New York, 1848, Mr. Stephens, referring to an account, received by him, respecting what he supposed to be an island in the Dead Sea, writes thus—"*It comes from one who ought to know, from the only man, who ever made the tour of that sea, and lived to tell of it.*" If Mr. Stephens will look at Chateaubriand's Travels, and his fine description of the Dead Sea, he will find there the following passage: "*No person has yet made the tour of it but Daniel, abbot of St. Saba. Nau has preserved in his travels the narrative of that recluse. From his account we learn,*" &c.

"The celebrated lake," says Chateaubriand, "which occupies the site of Sodom, is called in Scripture the Dead or Salt Sea." Not so: it is no where called the Dead Sea, in the sacred writings. By the Turks, it is called Ula Deguisi, and by the Arabs, Bahar Loth and Almotanah.

It is quite desirable for travellers to be well apprized of all, that is previously known, in regard to the field of their peregrination. Goldsmith once projected a plan of visiting the East, for the purpose of bringing to England such inventions and models, as might be useful. Johnson laughed at the idea, and denounced Goldsmith, as entirely incompetent, from his ignorance of what already existed—"he will bring home a wheelbarrow," said Johnson, "and think he had made a great addition to our stock." Mr. Stephens has preserved a respectable silence, on the subject of Lot's wife.

The island, which is above referred to, turned out, like Sancho's in Barrataria, to be an optical illusion. The Maltese sailor, who said he had rowed about the lake with his employer, a Mr. Costigan, who died on its shores, was disposed, after fingering his fee, to enlarge and improve his former narrative. Mr. Stephens does not give the date of Costigan's visit to the Dead Sea. He, however, furnishes a linear map of its form. This also is drawn by the Maltese sailor, from memory. All that can be said of it is, that it corresponds with other plans, in one particular,—the Jordan enters the sea, at its northern extremity. Probably, no very accurate plan is to be found, such have been the impediments in the way of any deliberate examination— unless Lieutenant Lynch has succeeded in the work. The figure of the Dead Sea, in the Atlas of Lucas, has no resemblance to the figure, in the late Bible Atlas by Dr. Jenks.

No. XXXVII

Dr. Johnson said, if an atheist came into his house, he would lock up his spoons. I have always distrusted a sexton, who did not cherish a sentiment of profound and cordial affection, for his bell. It did my heart good, when a boy, to mark the proud satisfaction, with which Lutton, the sexton of the Old Brick, used to ring for fire. I have no confidence in a fellow, who can toll his bell, for a funeral, and listen to its deep, and solemn vibrations, without a gentle subduing of the spirit. I never had a great affection for Clafflin, the sexton of Berry Street Church; but I always respected the deep feeling of indignation he manifested, if anybody meddled with his bellrope.

Bells were treated more honorably in the olden time, and ringing was an art—an accomplishment—then. Holden tells us some fine stories of the societies of ringers. In his youth, Sir Matthew Hale was a member of one of those societies. In 1687, Nell Gwinne—and it may be lawful to take the devil's water, as Dr. Worcester said, to turn the Lord's mill—Nell Gwinne left the ringers of the church bells of St. Martin's-in-the-Fields, where there is a peal of twelve, a sum of money, for a weekly entertainment. I never shall get the chime of the North Church bells out of my ears—I hope I never shall—more than half an hundred years ago, my mother used to open the window, of a Christmas eve, that we might hear their music!

In the olden time, bells were baptized—*rantized* I presume—and wore *posies* on their collars. They were first cast in England, in the reign of Edmund I., and the first tunable set, or peal, for Croyland Abbey, was cast A. D. 960. Weever tells us, in his Funeral Monuments, that, in 1501, the bells of the Priory of Little Dunmow, in Essex, were baptized, by the names of St. Michael, St. John, Virgin Mary, &c. As late as 1816, the great bell of Notre Dame, in Paris, was baptized, by the name of the Duke of Angouleme. Bells were supposed to be invested with extraordinary powers. They were employed, not only to call the congregation together, to give notice of conflagrations, civil commotions, and the approach of an enemy, and to ring forth the merry holiday peal—but to quell tempests, pacify the restless dead, and arrest the very lightning. Bells often bore inscriptions like these:

Laudo Deum verum, plebem voco, conjugo clerum,
Defunctos ploro, pestem fugo, festa decoro.

Funera plango; Fulgura frango; Sabbata pango;
Excito lentos; Dissipo ventos; Paco cruentos.

The *passing bell* was the bell, which announced to the people, according to Mabillon, that a spirit was taking its flight, or *passing away*, and demanding their prayers. Bells were also used to frighten away evil spirits, that were supposed to be on the watch, for their customers. The learned Durandus affirms, that all sorts of devils have a terror of bells. This, of course, can only be true of bells, that have been received into the flock, that is, baptized. Such was the Popish belief, and that the very devil, himself, cared not a fig, for an unbaptized bell. De Worde, in his Golden Legend, sayeth "it is said the evill spirytes that ben in the regyon of the ayre doubte moche, when they here the belles rongen, and this is the cause why the belles ben rongen, whan it thondreth, and when grate tempests and outrages of wether happen, to the ende that the feinds and wycked spirytes should be abashed and flee, and cease of the movinge of tempests."

Compared with the big bells of the earth—ours—the very largest—are cowbells, at best. The great bell of St. Paul's weighs 8400 pounds—a small affair; Great Tom of Lincoln, 9894—Great Tom of Oxford, 17,000. This is precisely the weight of the bell of the Palazzo, at Florence;—St. Peter's at Rome, 18,607—the great bell at Erfurth, 28,224—St. Joan's bell, at Moscow, 127,836—the bell of the Kremlin, 443,772. The last is the marvel of travellers, and its metal, at a low estimate, is valued at £66,565. During the fusion of this bell, considerable quantities of gold and silver were cast in, the pious contribution of the people. This enormous mass has never been suspended.

There was a bell—*parvis componere magna*—a very little bell indeed—very—a perfect *tintinabulum*. It made a most ridiculous noise. An account of this bell may be found, in a pamphlet, entitled Historical Notices, &c., of the New North Religious Society, in the town of Boston, 1822. It weighed, says the writer, "*between three and four hundred.*" Twelve or thirteen hundred such bells, therefore, would just about counterpoise the bell of the Kremlin. "Its tone," says the writer, "*was unpleasant.*" The preposterous clatter of this bell was, nevertheless, the gathering cry of the worshippers, at the New North Church, for the term of eighty-three years, from 1719 to 1802, when it was purchased by the town of Charlton, in the county of Worcester; probably to frighten the *evyll spirytes*, in the shape of wolves and foxes, abounding there, that would be likely to *doubte moche*, when this bell was *ben rongen*. Not to look a gift horse in the mouth is a proverb—not to criticise the tone of a gift bell may be another. This bell, which a stout South Down wether might almost have carried off, was the gift of *Mr. John Frizzell*, a merchant of Boston, to the New North Church, *on the island of North Boston*, as all that portion of the town was then called, lying North of Mill Creek. On the principle which gave the title of Bell the Cat to the famous Archibald, Frizzell should have borne the name of Bell the Church. Let it pass: Frizzell and his little bell are both translated. The tongue of the former is still; that of the latter still waggeth, I believe, in the town of Charlton.

The authenticity of the statements in the pamphlet to which I have referred, admits not of a doubt. The name of its highly respectable author, though not upon the title-page, appears in the certificate of copyright; and, in the range of my limited reading, I have met with nothing, more curious and grotesque, than his account of the installation of the Rev. Peter Thacher, over the New North Church, Jan. 27, 1720. Upon no less respectable evidence, would I have believed, that our amiable ancestors could have acted so much like *evil spirytes*, upon such an occasion. I have not elbow room for the farce entire—one or two touches must suffice. After agreeing upon a mode of choosing a colleague, for the Rev. Mr. Webb, and pitching upon Mr. Thacher, a quarrel arose, among the people. The council met, on the day of installation, at the house of the Rev. Mr. Webb, at the corner of North Bennet and Salem Streets. The aggrieved assembled, at the house of Thomas Lee, in Bennet Street, next to the Universal meeting-house. A knowledge of these points is necessary, for a correct understanding of the subsequent strategy. If the Council attempted to go to the New North Church, through the street, in the usual way, they must necessarily pass Lee's house. The aggrieved waited on the Council, by a committee, requesting them not to proceed with the installation of Mr. Thacher; and assuring them, that, if they persisted, force would be used, to prevent their occupation of the church.

Instead, therefore, of proceeding through the street, the Rev. Mr. Webb led the Council, by his back gate, through Love Lane, and a little alley, leading to the meeting-house, and thus got possession of the pulpit. Thus, by a knowledge of by-ways, so important in the *petite guerre*, the worthy clergyman outwitted the malcontents. A mob, to whom an installation, in such sort, was highly acceptable, had already gathered. The party at Lee's house, being apprised of the ruse, and perceiving they were *in danger of the council*, flew to the rescue. They rushed into the church; vociferously forbade the proceedings, and were "*indecent*," says the writer, "*almost beyond credibility.*" "However incredible," continues the narrator, "it is a fact, that some of the most unruly did sprinkle a liquor, which shall be nameless, from the galleries, upon the people below." The wife of Josiah Langdon used to tell, with great asperity, of her being a sufferer by it. This good lady retained her resentment to old age—the filthy creatures entirely spoiled a new velvet hood, which she had made for the occasion, and she could not wear it again.

In the midst of this uproar, Mr. Thacher was installed. "The malcontents," says the writer, "went off in a bad humor. They proceeded to the gathering of another church. In the plenitude of their zeal, they first thought of denominating it the *Revenge* Church of Christ; but they thought better of it, and called it the New Brick Church. However, the first name was retained, for many years, among the common people. Their zeal was great, indeed, and descended to puerility. They placed the figure of a cock, as a vane, upon the steeple, out of derision of Mr. Thacher, whose Christian name was Peter. Taking advantage of a wind, which turned the head of the cock towards the New North Meeting-house, when it was placed upon the spindle, a merry fellow straddled over it, and crowed three times, to complete the ceremony." The solemn, if not the sublime, and the ridiculous, seem, not unfrequently, to have met together at ordinations, in the olden time. "I could mention an ordination," says the Rev. Leonard Woods, of Andover, in a letter, written and published, a few years since, "that took place about twenty years ago, at which I, myself, was ashamed and grieved, to see two aged ministers literally drunk; and a third indecently excited with strong drink. These disgusting and appalling facts I should wish might be concealed. But they were made public, by the guilty persons; and I have thought it just and proper to mention them, in order to show how much we owe to a compassionate God, for the great deliverance he has wrought." Legitimate occasion for a Te Deum this, most certainly.

No. XXXVIII

The *præficæ*, or mourning women, were not confined to Greece, Rome, and Judea. In 1810, Colonel Keatinge published the history of his travels. His account of Moorish funerals, is, probably, the best on record. The dead are dressed in their best attire. The ears, nostrils, and eyelids are filled with costly spices. Virgins are ornamented with bracelets, on their wrists and ankles. The body is enfolded in sanctified linen. If a male, a turban is placed at the head of the coffin; if a female, a large bouquet. Before a virgin is buried, the *loo loo loo* is sung, by hired women, that she may have the benefit of the wedding song. "When a person," says Mr. Keatinge, "is thought to be dying, he is immediately surrounded by his friends, who begin to scream, in the most hideous manner, to convince him that there is no more hope, and that he is already reckoned among the dead."

Premature burial is said to be very common, among the Moors. For this, Mr. Keatinge accounts, in this manner: "As, according to their religion, they cannot think the departed happy, till they are under ground, they are washed instantly, while yet warm; and the greatest consolation the sick man's friends can have, is to see him smile, while this operation is performing; not supposing such an appearance to be a convulsion, occasioned by washing and exposing the unfortunate person to the cold air, before life has taken its final departure."

When a death occurs, the relations immediately set up the *wooliah woo*; or death scream. This cry is caught up, from house to house, and hundreds of women are instantly gathered to the spot. They come to scream and mourn with the bereaved. This species of condolence is very happily described by Colonel Keatinge. "They," the howlers, "take her," the mother, widow or daughter, "in their arms, lay her head on their shoulders, and scream without intermission for several minutes, till the afflicted object, stunned with the constant howling and a repetition of her misfortune, sinks senseless on the floor. They likewise hire a number of women, who make this horrid noise round the bier, over which they scratch their faces, to such a degree, that they appear to have been bled with a lancet. These women are hired at burials, weddings and feasts. Their voices are heard at the distance of half a mile. It is the custom of those, who can afford it, to give, on the evening of the day the corpse is buried, a quantity of hot-dressed victuals to the poor. This, they call "the supper of the grave."

Dr. E. D. Clarke observes, in his Travels in Egypt, Lond., 1817, that he recognized, among the Egyptians, the same notes, and the repetition of the same syllables, in their funeral cries, that had become familiar to his ear, on like occasions, among the Russians and the Irish.

Dr. Martin, in his account of the Tonga Islands, in the South Pacific, compiled from Mariner's papers, in his narrative of the funeral of a chief, states, that the women mourned over the corpse, through the whole night, sitting as near as possible, singing their dismal death song, and beating their breasts and faces.

The desire, to magnify one's apostleship, is, doubtless, at the bottom of all extravagant demonstrations of sorrow, at funerals, in the form of screaming, howling, yelling, personal laceration, and disfigurement. In the highly interesting account of the missionary enterprise, upon which the Duff was employed, in 1796, it was stated, that, at the funeral of a chief of Tongataboo, the people of both sexes continued, during two days, to mangle and hack themselves, in a shocking manner;—some thrust spears, through their thighs, arms, and cheeks; others beat their heads, till the blood gushed forth in streams; one man, having oiled his hair, set it on fire, and ran about the area, with his head in a blaze. This was a burning shame, beyond all doubt. I never forget old Tasman's bowl, when I think of this island. Tasman discovered Tongataboo, in 1643. At parting, he gave the chief a wooden bowl. Cook found this bowl, on the island, one hundred and thirty years afterwards. It had been used as a divining bowl, to ascertain the guilt or innocence of persons, charged with crimes. When the chief was absent, at some other of the Friendly Islands, the bowl was considered as his representative, and honored accordingly. Captain Cook presented the reigning chief with a pewter platter, and the bowl became immediately *functus officio*, the platter taking its place, for the purposes of divination.

In 1818, Captain Tuckey published the account of his expedition, to explore the Zaire, or Congo river. He describes a funeral, at Embomma, the chief mart, on that river. In returning to their vessel, after a visit to the chief, Chenoo, the party observed a hut, in which the corpse of a female was deposited, dressed as when alive. On the inside were four women howling lustily, to whom two men, outside, responded; the concert closely resembling the yell, at an Irish funeral. Captain Tuckey should not have spoken so thoughtlessly of the *keena*, the funeral cry of the wild Irish, the most unearthly sound, that ever came from the agonized lungs of mortal. For the most perfect description of this peculiar scream, this inimitable hellabaloo, the reader may turn to Mrs. Hall's incomparable account of an Irish funeral. In close connection with this incident, Captain Tuckey, remarks, that, in passing through the burying ground, at Embomma, they saw two graves, recently prepared, of monstrous size, being not less than nine feet by five.

This he explains as follows:—"Simmons (a native, returned from England to his native country) requested a piece of cloth to envelop his aunt, who had been dead seven years, and was to be buried in two months. The manner of preserving corpses, for so long a time, is by enveloping them in the cloth of the country, or in European cotton. The wrappers are successively multiplied, as they can be procured by the relations of the deceased, or according to the rank of the person; in the case of a rich and very great man, the bulk being only limited, by the power of conveyance to the grave." When the Spaniards entered the Province of Popayan, they found a similar practice there, with this difference, that the corpse was partially roasted, before it was enveloped. When a chief dies, among the Caribs of Guyana, his wives, the whole flock of them, watch the corpse for thirty days, to keep off the flies,—a task which becomes daily more burdensome, as the attraction becomes greater. At the expiration of thirty days, it is buried, and one of the ladies, probably the best beloved, with it.

Some of the Orinoco tribes were in the practice of tying a rope to the corpse, and sinking it in the river; in twenty-four hours, it was picked clean to the bones, by the fishes, and the skeleton became a very convenient and tidy memorial. This is decidedly preferable to the mode, adopted by the Parsees. Their sacred books enjoin them not to pollute *earth, water*, or *fire,* with their dead. They therefore feel authorized to pollute the air. They bury not; but place the corpses at a distance, and leave them to their fate. It was the opinion of Menu, that the body was a tenement, scarcely worth inhabiting; "a mansion," says he, "with bones for beams and rafters,— nerves and tendons for cords; muscles and blood for mortar; skin for its outward covering; a mansion, infested by age and sorrow, the seat of many maladies, harassed with pains, haunted with darkness, and utterly incapable of standing long—such a mansion let the vital soul, its tenant, always quit cheerfully."

This contempt for the tabernacle—the carcass—the outer man—strangely contrasts with that deep regard for it, evinced by the Egyptians, and such of the Jews, Greeks, and Romans, as were in the practice of embalming. When that extraordinary man, Sir Thomas Browne, exclaimed, in his Hydriotaphia, "who knows the fate of his bones or how oft he shall be buried? Who hath the oracle of his ashes, or whither they are to be scattered?" he, doubtless, was thinking of Egyptian mummies, transported to Europe, forming a part of the materia medica, and being actually swallowed as physic. A writer, in the London Quarterly, vol. 21, p. 363, states, that, when the old traveller, John Sanderson, returned to England, six hundred pounds of mummies were brought home, for the Turkey Company. I am aware, that it has been denied, by some, that the Egyptian mummies were broken up, and sent to Europe, for medicinal uses. By them it is asserted, that what the druggists have been supplied with is the flesh of executed criminals, or such others, as the Jews can obtain, filled with bitumen, aloes and other things, and baked, till the juices are exhaled, and the embalming matter has fitted the body for transportation. The Lord deliver us from such *"doctors' stuff"* as this.

No. XXXIX

Non sumito, nisi vocatus: let no man presume to be an undertaker, unless he have a *vocation*—unless he be *called*. If these are not the words of Puddifant, to whom I shall presently refer, I have no other conjecture to offer. Though, when a boy, I had a sort of hankering after dead men's bones, as I have already related, I never felt myself truly called to be a sexton, until June, 1799. It was in that month and year, that Governor Sumner was buried. The parade was very great, not only because he had been a Governor, but because he had been a very good man. All the sextons were on duty, but Lutton, as we called him—his real name was Lemuel Ludden. He was the sexton of the Old Brick, where my parents had worshipped, under dear parson Clarke, who died, the year before. He had the cleverest way, that man ever had, of winning little boys' hearts—he really seemed to have the key to their little souls. Lutton was sick—he was not able to officiate, on that memorable day; and no recently appointed ensign ever felt such a privation more keenly, on the very day of battle. He was a whole-souled sexton, that Lutton. He, most obligingly, took me into the Old Brick Church, where Joy's buildings now stand, to see the show. There was a half-crazy simpleton, whom it was difficult to prevent from capering before the corpse—a perfect Davie Gelatly. An awkward boy, whose name was Reuben Rankin, came from Salem, with a small cart-load of pies, which his mother had baked, and sent to Boston, hoping for a ready sale, upon the occasion of such an assemblage there. Like Grouchy, at Waterloo, he lost his *tète*; followed the procession, through every street; and returned to Salem, with all his wares.

It was, while contemplating the high satisfaction, beaming forth, upon the features of the chief undertaker, that I first felt my *vocation*. I ventured, timidly, to ask old Lutton, if he thought I had talents for the office. He said, he thought I might succeed, clapped me on the shoulder, and gave me a smile of encouragement, which I never shall forget, till my poor old arm can wield a spade no more, and the sod, which I have so frequently turned upon others, shall be turned upon me.

Old Grossman said, in my hearing, the following morning, that it had been the proudest day of his life. It is very pardonable, for an undertaker, on such occasions, to imagine himself the observed of all observers. This fancy is, by no means, confined to undertakers. Chief mourners of both sexes are very liable to the same impression. An over-estimate of one's own importance is pretty universal, especially in a republic. I never did go the length of believing the tale, related, by Peter, in his letter to his kinsfolk, who says he knew a Scotch weaver, who sat upon his stoop, and read the Edinburgh Review, till he actually thought he wrote it. I see nothing to smile at, in any man's belief, that he is the object of public attention, on occasions of parade and pageantry. It rather indicates the deep interest of the individual—a solemn sense of responsibility. At the late water celebration, I noticed many examples of this species of personal enthusiasm. The drivers of the Oak Hall and Sarsaparilla expresses were no mean illustrations; and when three cheers were given to the elephant, near the Museum, in Tremont Street, I was pleased to see several of the officials, and one, at least, of the water commissioners, touch their hats, and smile most graciously, in return.

Puddifant, to whom I have alluded, officiated as sexton, at the funeral of Charles I. What a broad field, for painful contemplation, lies here! It is a curious fact, that, while preparations were being made, for depositing the body of King Charles in St. George's Chapel, at Windsor, a common foot soldier is supposed to have stolen a bone from the coffin of Henry VIII., for the purpose of making a knife-handle. This account is so curious, that I give it entire from Wood's Athenæ Oxonienses, folio edit. vol. ii., p. 703. "Those gentlemen, therefore, Herbert and Mildmay, thinking fit to submit, and leave the choice of the place of burial to those great persons, (the Duke of Richmond, Marquis of Hertford, and Earl of Lindsey) they, in like manner, viewed the tomb house and the choir; and one of the Lords, beating gently upon the pavement with his staff, perceived a hollow sound; and, thereupon ordering the stones to be removed, they discovered a descent into a vault, where two coffins were laid, near one another, the one very large, of an antique form, and the other little. These they supposed to be the bodies of Henry VIII., and his third wife, Queen Jane Seymour, as indeed they were. The velvet palls, that covered their coffins, seemed fresh, though they had lain there, above one hundred years. The Lords agreeing, that the King's body should be in the same vault interred, being about the middle of the choir, over against the eleventh stall, upon the sovereign's side, they gave orders to have the King's name, and year he died, cut in lead; which, whilst the workmen were about, the Lords went out, and gave Puddifant, the sexton, order to lock the chapel door, and not suffer any to stay therein, till further notice."

"The sexton did his best to clear the chapel; nevertheless, Isaac, the sexton's man, said that a foot soldier had hid himself so as he was not discovered; and, being greedy of prey, crept into the vault, and cut so much of the velvet pall, that covered the great body, as he judged would hardly be missed, and wimbled a hole through the said coffin that was largest, probably fancying that there was something well worth his adventure. The sexton, at his opening the door, espied the sacrilegious person; who, being searched, a bone was found about him, with which he said he would haft a knife. The girdle or circumscription of capital letters of lead put upon the King's coffin had only these words—King Charles, 1648." This statement perfectly agrees with Sir Henry Halford's account of the examination, April 1, 1813, in presence of the Prince Regent.

Cromwell had a splendid funeral: good old John Evelyn saw it all, and describes it in his diary—the waxen effigy, lying in royal robes, upon a velvet bed of state, with crown, sceptre and globe—in less than two years suspended with a rope round the neck, from a window at Whitehall. Evelyn says, the "funeral was the joyfullest ever seen: none cried but the dogs, which the soldiers hooted away with a barbarous noise, drinking and taking tobacco in the streets as they went." Some have said that Cromwell's body was privately buried, by his own request, in the field of Naseby: others, that it was sunk in the Thames, to prevent insult. It was not so. When, upon the restoration, it was decided, to reverse the popular sentiment, Oliver's body was sought, in the middle aisle of Henry VII's chapel, and there it was found. A thin case of lead lay upon the breast, containing a copper plate, finely gilt, and thus inscribed—Oliverius, Protector reipublicæ Angliæ, Scotiæ, et Hiberniæ, natus 25 April, 1599—inauguratus 16 Decembris 1653—mortuus 3 Septembris ann—1658. Hic situs est. This plate, in 1773, was in possession of the Hon George Hobart of Nocton in Lincolnshire. By a vote of the House of Commons, Cromwell's and Ireton's bodies were taken up, Jan. 26, 1660—and, on the Monday night following, they were drawn, on two carts, to the Red Lion Inn, Holborn, where they remained all night; and, with Bradshaw's, which was not exhumed, till the day after, conveyed, on sledges, to Tyburn, and hanged on the gallows, till sunset. They were then beheaded—the trunks were buried in a hole, near the gallows, and their heads set on poles, on the top of Westminster Hall, where Cromwell's long remained.

The treatment of Oliver's character has been in perfect keeping, with the treatment of his carcass. The extremes of censure and of praise have been showered upon his name. He has been canonized, and cursed. The most judicious writers have expressed their views of his character, in well-balanced phrases. Cardinal Mazarin styled him *a fortunate mad-man*; and, by Father Orleans, he was called a *judicious villain*. The opinion of impartial men will probably vary very little from that of Clarendon, through all time: he says of Cromwell—"he was one of those men, *quos vituperare ne inimici quidem possunt, nisi ut simul laudent;"* and again, vol. vii. 301, Oxford ed. 1826: "In a word, as he was guilty of many crimes, against which damnation is denounced, and for which hell-fire is prepared, so he had some good qualities, which have caused the memory of some men, in all ages, to be celebrated; and he will be looked upon by posterity as *a brave wicked man."* Oliver had the nerve to do what most men could not: he went to look upon the corpse of the beheaded king—opened the coffin with his own hand— and put his finger to the neck, where it had been severed. *He could not then doubt that Charles was dead.*

At the same time, when the authorized absurdities were perpetrated upon Oliver's body, every effort was ineffectually made to discover that of King Charles, for the purpose of paying to it the highest honors. This occurred at the time of the restoration, or about ten years after the death of Charles I. In 1813, i. e. one hundred and sixty-five years after that event, the body was accidentally discovered. To this fact, and to the examination by Sir Henry Halford, President of the Royal College of Physicians, I shall refer in my next.

No. XL

The passage, quoted in my last, from the Athenæ Oxonienses, shows plainly, that Charles I. was buried in 1648, in the same vault with the bodies of Henry VIII. and Jane Seymour; and this statement is perfectly sustained, by the remarkable discovery in 1813, which proves Lord Clarendon to have been mistaken in his account, Hist. Reb., Oxford ed., vol. vi. p. 243. The Duke of Richmond, the Marquis of Hertford, and the Earls of Southampton and Lindsey, who had been of the bed chamber, and had obtained leave, to perform the last duty to the decollated king, went into the church, at Windsor, to seek a place for the interment, and were greatly perplexed, by the mutilations and changes there—"At last," says Clarendon, "there was a fellow of the town, who undertook to tell them the place, where he said there was a vault, in which King Harry, the Eighth, and Queen Jane Seymour were interred. As near that place, as could conveniently be, they caused the grave to be made. There the king's body was laid, without any words, or other ceremonies, than the tears and sighs of the few beholders. Upon the coffin was a plate of silver fixed with these words only: 'King Charles, 1648.' When the coffin was put in, the black velvet pall, that had covered it, was thrown over it, and then the earth thrown in." *Such, clearly, could not have been the facts.*

Lord Clarendon then proceeds to speak of the impossibility of finding the body ten years after, when it was the wish of Charles II. to place it, with all honor, in the chapel of Henry VII., in Westminster Abbey. For this he accounts, by stating, that most of those present, at the *interment*, were dead or dispersed, at the restoration; and the memories of the remaining few had become so confused, that they could not designate the spot; and, after opening the ground, in several places, without success, they gave the matter up. Now there can be no doubt, that the body was placed in the vault, where it was found, in 1813, and that no *interment* took place, in the proper sense of that word. Had Richmond, Hertford, Southampton, or Lindsey been alive, or at hand, the *vault itself*, and not a spot *near the vault*, would, doubtless, have been indicated, as the resting place of King Charles. Wood, in the Athenæ Oxonienses, states, that the royal corpse was "well coffined, and all afterwards wrapped up in lead and covered with a new velvet pall." All this perfectly agrees with the account, given by Sir Henry Halford, and certified by the Prince Regent, in 1813.

Sir Henry Halford states, that George the Fourth had built a mausoleum, at Windsor; and, while constructing a passage, under the choir of St. George's Chapel, an opening was unintentionally made into the vault of Henry VIII., through which, the workmen saw, not only those two coffins, which were supposed to contain the bodies of Henry VIII. and Jane Seymour, but a third, covered with a black pall. Mr. Herbert's account, quoted in my last number, from the Athenæ, left little doubt, that this was the coffin of Charles I.; notwithstanding the statements of Lord Clarendon, that the body was interred *near* the vault. An examination was made, April 1, 1813, in the presence of George IV., then Prince Regent, the Duke of Cumberland, Count Munster, the Dean of Windsor, Benjamin Charles Stevenson, Esq., and Sir Henry Halford; of which the latter published an account. London, 1831. This account is exceedingly interesting. "On removing the pall, a plain leaden coffin, with no appearance of ever having been enclosed in wood, and bearing an inscription, King Charles, 1648, in large legible characters, on a scroll of lead encircling it, immediately presented itself to view.

"A square opening was then made, in the upper part of the lid, of such dimensions, as to admit a clear insight into its contents. These were an internal wooden coffin, very much decayed, and the body carefully wrapped up in cere-cloth, into the folds of which a quantity of unctuous or greasy matter, mixed with resin, as it seemed, had been melted, so as to exclude, as effectually as possible, the external air. The coffin was completely full; and from the tenacity of the cere-cloth, great difficulty was experienced, in detaching it successfully from the parts, which it enveloped. Wherever the unctuous matter had insinuated itself, the separation of the cere-cloth was easy; and when it came off, a correct impression of the features, to which it had been applied, was observed in the unctuous substance. At length the whole face was disengaged from its covering. The complexion of the skin of it was dark and discolored. The forehead and temples had lost little or nothing of their muscular substance; the cartilage of the nose was gone; but the left eye, in the first moment of exposure, was open and full, though it vanished, almost immediately; and the pointed beard, so characteristic of the period of the reign of King Charles, was perfect. The shape of the face was a long oval; many of the teeth remained; and the left ear, in consequence of the interposition of the unctuous matter, between it and the cere-cloth, was found entire.

"It was difficult, at this moment, to withhold a declaration, that, notwithstanding its disfigurement, the countenance did bear a strong resemblance to the coins, the busts, and especially to the pictures of King Charles I., by Vandyke, by which it had been made familiar to us. It is true, that the minds of the spectators of this interesting sight were well prepared to receive this impression; but it is also certain, that such a facility of belief had been occasioned, by the simplicity and truth of Mr. Herbert's narrative, every part of which had been confirmed by the investigation, so far as it had advanced; and it will not be denied, that the shape of the face, the forehead, an eye, and the beard, are the most important features, by which resemblance is determined.

"When the head had been entirely disengaged from the attachments, which confined it, it was found to be loose, and without any difficulty was taken up and held to view. It was quite wet, and gave a greenish and red tinge to paper and to linen, which touched it. The back part of the scalp was entirely perfect, and had a remarkably fresh appearance; the pores of the skin being more distinct, as they usually are, when soaked in moisture; and the tendons and ligaments of the neck were of considerable substance and firmness. The hair was thick, at the back part of the head, and in appearance, nearly black. A portion of it, which has since been cleansed and dried, is of a beautiful dark brown color. That of the beard was of a redder brown. On the back part of the head it was not more than an inch in length, and had probably been cut so short, for the convenience of the executioner, or perhaps, by the piety of friends, soon after death, in order to furnish memorials of the unhappy king."

"On holding up the head to examine the place of separation from the body, the muscles of the neck had evidently retracted themselves considerably; and the fourth cervical vertebra was found to be cut through its substance transversely, leaving the surfaces of the divided portions perfectly smooth and even, an appearance, which could have been produced only by a heavy blow, inflicted with a very sharp instrument, and which furnished the last proof wanting to identify King Charles, the First. After this examination of the head, which served every purpose in view, and without examining the body below the neck, it was immediately restored to its situation, the coffin was soldered up again, and the vault closed."

"Neither of the other coffins had any inscription upon them. The larger one, supposed, on good grounds, to contain the remains of Henry VIII., measured six feet ten inches in length, and had been enclosed in an elm one, of two inches in thickness; but this was decayed, and lay in small fragments. The leaden coffin appeared to have been beaten in by violence about the middle, and a considerable opening in that part of it, exposed a mere skeleton of the king. Some beard remained upon the chin, but there was nothing to discriminate the personage contained in it."

This is, certainly, a very interesting account. Some beard still remained upon the chin of Henry VIII., says Sir Henry Halford. Henry VIII. died Jan. 28, 1547. He had been dead, therefore, April 1, 1813, the day of the examination, two hundred and sixty-six years. The larger coffin measured six feet ten inches. Sir Henry means top measure. We always allow seven feet lid, or thereabouts, for a six feet corpse. Henry, in his History, vol. xi. p. 369, Lond. 1814, says that King Henry VIII. was tall. Strype, in Appendix A., vol. vi. p. 267, Ecc. Mem., London, 1816, devotes twenty-four octavo pages to an account of the funeral of Henry VIII., with all its singular details; and, at the last, he says—"Then was the vault uncovered, under the said corpse; and the corpse let down therein by the vice, with help of sixteen tal yeomen of the guard, appointed to the same." "Then, when the mold was brought in, at the word, pulverem pulveri et cinerem cineri, first the Lord Great Master, and after the Lord Chamberlain and al others in order, with heavy and dolorous lamentation brake their staves in shivers upon their heads and cast them after the corps into the pit. And then the gentlemen ushers, in like manner brake their rods, and threw them into the vault with exceeding sorrow and heaviness, not without grievous sighs and tears, not only of them, but of many others, as well of the meaner sort, as of the nobility, very piteous and sorrowful to behold."

No. XLI

My attention was arrested, a day or two since, by a memorial, referred to, in the Atlas, from the owner of the land, famous, in revolutionary history, as the birth-place of Liberty Tree; and, especially, by a suggestion, which quadrates entirely with my notions of the fitness of things. If I were a demi-millionaire, I should delight to raise a monument, upon that consecrated spot—it should be a simple colossal shaft, of Massachusetts granite, surmounted with the cap of liberty. I would not inscribe one syllable upon it—but, if any grey-headed *Boston boy*—born here, within the limits of the old peninsula—should be moved, by the spirit, to write below—

Hæc olim meminisse juvabit—

I should not deem that act any interference with my original purpose.

What days and nights those were! 1765! then, the man, who has now passed on to ninety-four, was the boy of ten! How perfectly the tablet of memory retains those impressions, made, by the pressure of great events, when the wax was soft and warm!

It is quite common, with the present generation, at least, to connect the origin of Liberty Tree with 1775-6. This is an error. It became celebrated, ten years earlier, during the disturbances in Boston, on account of the Stamp Act, which passed March 22, 1765, and was to be in force, on the first of November following. Intelligence arrived, that Andrew Oliver, Secretary of the Province, was to be distributor of stamps.

There was a cluster or grove of beautiful elms, in Hanover Square—such was the name, then given to the corner of Orange, now part of Washington Street, and Auchmuty's Lane, now Essex Street. Opposite the southwesterly corner of Frog Lane, now Boylston Street, where the market-house now stands, there was an old house, with manifold gables, and two massive chimneys, and, in the yard, in front of it, there stood a large, spreading elm. This was Liberty Tree. Its first designation was on this wise. During the night of August 13, 1765, some of the Sons of Liberty, as they styled themselves, assuming the appellation bestowed on them in the House of Commons, by Col. Barre, in a moment of splendid but unpremeditated eloquence, hung, upon that tree, an effigy of Mr. Oliver, and a boot, with a figure of the devil peeping out, and holding the stamp act in his hand; this boot was intended as a practical pun—wretched enough—upon the name of Lord Bute. In the morning of the 14th, a great crowd collected to the spot. Some of the neighbors attempted to take the effigy down. The *Sons of Liberty* gave them a forcible hint, and they desisted. The Lieutenant Governor, as Chief Justice, directed the sheriff to take it down: he reconnoitred the ground, and reported that it could not be done, without peril of life.

Business was suspended, about town. After dark, the effigy was borne, by the mob, to a building, which was supposed to have been erected, as a stamp-office. This they destroyed, and, bearing the fragments to Fort Hill, where Mr. Oliver lived, they made a bonfire, and burnt the effigy before his door. They next drove him and his family from his house, broke the windows and fences, and stoned the Lieutenant Governor and Sheriff, when they came to parley—all this, upon the night of August 14, 1765. On the 26th, they destroyed the house of Mr. Story, register-deputy of the Admiralty, and burnt the books and records of the court. They then served the house of Mr. Hollowell, Contractor of the Customs, in a similar manner, plundering and carrying away money and chattels. They next proceeded to the residence of the Lieutenant Governor, and destroyed every article not easily transported, doing irreparable mischief, by the destruction of many valuable manuscripts. The next day, a town meeting was held, and the citizens expressed their *detestation of the riots*—and, afterwards manifested their silent sympathy with the mob, by punishing nobody.

Nov. 1, 1765, the day, when the stamp act came into force, the bells were muffled and tolled; the shipping displayed their colors, at half mast; the stamp act was printed, with a death's head, in the place of the stamp, and cried about the streets, under the name of the Folly of England, and the Ruin of America. A new political journal appeared, having for its emblem, or political phylactery, a serpent, cut into pieces, each piece bearing the initials of a colony, with the ominous motto—join or die. More effigies were hung, upon "*the large old elm,*" as Gordon terms it—Liberty Tree. They were then cut down, and escorted over town. They were brought back, and hung up again; taken down again; escorted to the Neck, by an immense concourse; hanged upon the gallows tree; taken down once more; and torn into innumerable fragments. Three cheers were then given, and, upon a request to that effect, every man went quietly home; and a night of unusual stillness ensued.

Hearing that Mr. Oliver intended to resume his office, he was required, through the newspaper, by an anonymous writer, to acknowledge, or deny, the truth of that report. His answer proving unsatisfactory, he received a requisition, Nov. 16th, to appear "*tomorrow, under* Liberty Tree, *to make a public resignation."* Two thousand persons gathered then, beneath that Tree—not the rabble, but the selectmen, the merchants, and chief inhabitants. Mr. Oliver requested, that the meeting might be held, in the town house; but the sons of liberty seemed resolved, that he should be *treed*—no place, under the canopy of Heaven, would answer, but Liberty Tree. Mr. Oliver came; subscribed an ample declaration; and made oath to it, before Richard Dana, J. P. This exactitude and circumspection, on the part of the people, was not a work of supererogation: Andrew Oliver was a most amiable man, in private, but a most lubricious hypocrite, in public life; as appears by his famous letters, sent home by Dr. Franklin, in 1772. After his declaration under the tree, he made a short speech, expressive of his *"utter detestation of the stamp act."* What a spectacle was there and then! The best and the boldest were there. Samuel Adams and John—Jerry Gridley, Samuel Sewall, and John Hancock, *et id genus omne* were in Boston then, and the busiest men alive: their absence would have been marked—they must have been there. What an act of daring, thus to defy the monarch and his vicegerents! I paused, this very day, and gazed upon the spot, and put the steam upon my imagination, to conjure, into life and action, that little band of sterling patriots, gathered around; and that noble elm in their midst:—

> "In medio ramos annosaque brachia pandit
> Ulmus opaca, ingens."

Thenceforward, the Sons of Liberty seem to have taken the tree, under their special protection. On Valentine's day, 1776, they assembled, and passed a vote, that *it should be pruned after the best manner.* It is well, certainly, now and then, to lop off some rank, disorderly shoots of licentiousness, that will sometimes appear, upon Liberty Tree. It was pruned, accordingly, by a party of volunteer carpenters, under the direction of a gentleman of skill and judgment, in such matters.

News of the repeal of the stamp act arrived in Boston, May 16, 1766. The bells rang merrily—and the cannon were unlimbered, around Liberty Tree, and bellowed for joy. The tree, so skilfully pruned, in February, must have presented a beautiful appearance, bourgeoning forth, in the middle of May! The nineteenth of May was appointed, for a merrymaking. At one, in the morning, the bell of the Hollis Street Church, says a zealous writer of that day, *"began to ring"*—*sua sponte*, no doubt. The slumbers of the pastor, Dr. Byles, were disturbed, of course, for he was a tory, though a very pleasant tory, after all. Christ Church replied, with its royal peal, from the North, and *God save the king*, rang pleasantly again, in colonial ears. The universal joy was expressed, in all those unphilosophical ways, enumerated by Pope,

With gun, drum, trumpet, blunderbuss and thunder.

Liberty Tree was hung with various colors. Fireworks and illuminations succeeded. Gov. Hancock treated the people with "*a pipe of Madeira;*" and the Sons of Liberty raised a pyramid, upon the Common, with two hundred and eighty lamps. At twelve o'clock—midnight—a drum, upon the Common, beat the *tattoo*; and men, women, and children retired to their homes, in the most perfect order: verily, a soberness had come over the spirit of their dreams, and method into their madness. On the evening of the twentieth of May, it was resolved to have a festival of lanterns.

The inhabitants vied with each other; and, about dusk, they were seen streaming, from all quarters, to Hanover Square, every man and boy with his lamp or lantern. In a brief space, Liberty Tree was converted into a brilliant constellation. Like the sparkling waters, during the burning of Ucalegon's palace, described by Homer, the boughs, the branches, the veriest twigs of this popular idol

> — — — —"were bright,
> With splendors not their own, and shone with sparkling
> light."

It appears, by the journals of that day, from which most of these particulars are gathered, that our fathers—what inimitable, top-gallant fellows they were!—took a pleasant fancy into their heads, that these lamps would shed a brighter lustre, if the poor debtors, in jail, could join in the general joy, under Liberty Tree. Accordingly they made up a purse and paid the debts of them all! There was a general jail delivery of the poor debtors, for very joy. Well: a Boston boy, of the old school, was a noble animal—how easily held by the heart-strings!—with how much difficulty, by the head or the tail!

An antiquarian friend, to whom I am already under sundry obligations, has obligingly loaned me an interesting document, in connection with the subject of Liberty Tree; under whose shade I propose to linger a little longer.

No. XLII

March 22, 1765. George III. and his ministers took it into their heads to sow the wind; and, in an almost inconceivably short time, they reaped the whirlwind. They scattered dragons' teeth, and there came up armed men. They planted the stamp act, in the Colonial soil, and there sprang into life, mature and full of vigor, the Liberty Tree, like Minerva, fully developed, and in perfect armor, from the brain of Jupiter. Whoever would find a clear, succinct, and impartial account of the effect of the stamp act, upon the people of New England, may resort to Dodsley's Annual Register, page 49, of that memorable year. "The sun of liberty has set," wrote Franklin home, "but you must light up the candles of industry and economy."

The life of that act of oppression was short and stormy. March 18, 1766, its miserable requiem was sung in Parliament—"an event," says the Annual Register, of that year, page 46, "that caused more universal joy, throughout the British dominions, than, perhaps, any other, that can be remembered." How such a viper ever found its way into the cradle of liberty is quite a marvel—certain it is, the genius of freedom, with the power of Hercules, speedily strangled it there.

In America, and, especially, in Boston, the joy, as I have already stated, was very great; and some there were, beyond all doubt, who were delighted, to find an apology, for going back to monarchical usages. Even liberty may be, sometimes, irksome, at first, to him, who has long lived a slave; and it is no small grievance, I dare say, to such, to be deprived of the luxury of calling some one, Lord and Master, after the flesh. However monstrous, and even ridiculous, the idea of a king may seem to us, republicans, born in this wonderfully bracing atmosphere—there are some, who have a strong taste for *booing* and genuflection, and the doffing of beavers, and throwing up of "greasy caps," and rending their throats, for very ecstacy, when the royal coach is coming along, bearing the heir apparent, in diapers. This taste, I suppose, like that for olives, must be acquired; it cannot be natural.

May 19, and 20, 1766, the face of the town of Boston was dressed in smiles—a broad grin rather, from ear to ear, from Winnisimmet to Roxbury. Nothing was talked of but *"a grateful people,"* and *"the darling monarch"*— which amounts to this—the *"darling monarch"* had graciously desisted, from grinding their faces any longer, simply because he was convinced, that the *"grateful people"* would kick the grindstone over, and peradventure the grinder, should the *"darling"* attempt to give it another turn.

Under Liberty Tree, there was erected, during the rejoicings, an obelisk with four sides. An engraving of those four sides was made at the time, and is now, doubtless, very rare. A copy, loaned me by the friend, to whom I referred, in my last number, is lying before me. I present it, *verbatim, literatim, et punctuatim.*

It is thirteen and an half inches long, and nine and an half wide. On top are these words—"A view of the obelisk erected under liberty tree in Boston on the Rejoicings for the Repeal of the —— Stamp Act 1766." At the bottom—"To every Lover of Liberty this Plate is humbly dedicated by her true born Sons in Boston, New England." The plate presents, apparently, four obelisks, which are, in reality, the four sides of one. Every side, above the base, is divided horizontally, and nearly equally, into three parts. The superior division of each contains four heads, many of which may be readily recognized, and all of which have indicating letters. The middle division of each contains ten decasyllabic lines. The inferior division of each contains a sketch, of rude execution, and rather more patriotic, than tasteful, in the design. The principal portraits are of George III.; Queen Charlotte; Marquis of Rockingham; Duke of York; Gen. Conway; Lord Townshend; Colonel Barré; W. Pitt; Lord Dartmouth; Charles Townshend; Lord George Sackville; John Wilkes; Alderman Beckford; Lord Camden; &c. The first side is subscribed thus: *"America in distress, apprehending the total loss of* Liberty;" and is inscribed thus:

> Oh thou, whom next to Heaven we most revere
> Fair Liberty! thou lovely Goddess hear!
> Have we not woo'd thee, won thee, held thee long,
> Lain in thy Lap and melted on thy tongue.
> Thro' Deaths and Dangers rugged paths pursu'd
> And led thee smiling to this Solitude,
> Hid thee within our hearts' most golden cell
> And brav'd the Powers of Earth and Powers of Hell,
> Goddess! we cannot part, thou must not fly,
> Be Slaves! we dare to scorn it, dare to die.

Beneath is the sketch—America recumbent and dejected, in the form of an Indian chief, under a pine tree, the angel of Liberty hovering over; the Prime minister advancing with a chain, followed by one of the bishops, and others, Bute clearly designated by his Scotch plaid, and gaiters; over head, flying towards the Indian, with the stamp act in his right claw, is the Devil; of whom it is manifest our patriotic sires had a very clever conception.

The second side is subscribed thus: "*She implores the aid of her patrons;*" and is inscribed thus:

> While clanking chains and curses shall salute
> Thine Ears remorseless G——le, and thine O B——e,
> To you blest Patriots, we our cause submit,
> Illustrious Campden, Britain's Guardian, Pitt.
> Recede not, frown not, rather let us be
> Deprived of being than of Liberty,
> Let fraud or malice blacken all our crimes,
> No disaffection stains these peaceful climes.
> Oh save us, shield us from impending woes,
> The foes of Britain only are our foes.

Beneath is the sketch—America, on one knee, pointing over her shoulder towards a retreating group, composed, as the chain and the plaid inform us, of the Prime Minister Bute, and company, upon whose heads a thunder cloud is bursting. At the same time America—the Indian, as before—supplicates the aid of others, whose leader is being crowned, by Fame, with a laurel wreath. The enormous nose—a great help to identification—marks the Earl of Chatham; Camden may be known by his wig; and Barré by his military air.

The third side is subscribed thus: "*She endures the Conflict, for a short Season*" and is inscribed thus:

> Boast foul Oppression, boast thy transient Reign,
> While honest Freedom struggles with her Chain,
> But know the Sons of Virtue, hardy, brave,
> Disclaim to lose thro' mean Dispair to save;
> Arrowed in Thunder awfull they appear,
> With proud Deliverance stalking in their Rear,
> While Tyrant Foes their pallid Fears betray,
> Shrink from their Arms, and give their Vengeance way.
> See in the unequal War Oppressors fall,
> The hate, contempt, and endless Curse of all.

Beneath is the sketch—The Tree of Liberty, with an eagle feeding its young, in the topmost branches, and an angel advancing with an ægis.

The fourth side is subscribed thus: "*And has her* Liberty *restored by the Royal hand of* George *the Third;*" and is inscribed thus:

> Our Faith approv'd, our Liberty restor'd,
> Our Hearts bend grateful to our sov'reign Lord;
> Hail darling Monarch! by this act endear'd,

Our firm affections are thy best reward—
Sh'd Britain's self against herself divide,
And hostile Armies frown on either side;
Sh'd hosts rebellious shake our Brunswick's Throne,
And as they dar'd thy Parent dare the Son.
To this Asylum stretch thine happy Wing,
And we'll contend who best shall love our King.

Beneath is the sketch—George the Third, in armor, resembling a Dutch widow, in a long-short, introducing America to the goddess of liberty, who are, apparently, just commencing the Polka—at the bottom of the engraving are the words—*Paul Revere Sculp*. Our ancestors dealt rather in fact than fiction—they were no poets.

Gordon refers to liberty tree, i. 175.

The fame of liberty tree spread far beyond its branches. Not long before it was cut down, by the British soldiers, during the winter of 1775-6, an English gentleman, Philip Billes, residing at Backway, near Cambridge, England, died, seized of a considerable fortune, which he bequeathed to two gentlemen, not relatives, on condition, that they would faithfully execute a provision, set forth in his will, namely, that his body should be buried, under the shadow of liberty tree, in Boston, New England. This curious statement was published in England, June 3, 1774, and may be found in the Boston Evening Gazette, first page, Aug. 22, 1774, printed by Thomas & John Fleet, sign of the Heart and Crown, Cornhill.

No. XLIII

Josiah Carter died, at the close of December, 1774. Never was there a happier occasion, for citing the *Quis desiderio*, &c., and I would cite that fine ode, were it not worn threadbare, like an old coverlet, by having been, immemorially, thrown over all manner of corpses, from the cobbler's to the king's.

If good old Dr. Charles Chauncy were within hearing, I would, indeed, apply to him a portion of its noble passages:

> Multis ille bonis flebilis occidit,
> Nulli flebilior quam tibi — —.

> For good Josiah many wept, I fancy;
> But none more fluently than Dr. Chauncy.

Josiah Carter was sexton of the Old Brick. He died, in the prime of life— fifty only—a martyr to his profession—conscientious to a fault—standing all alone in the cold vault, after the last mourner had retired, and knocking gently upon the coffin lid, seeking for some little sign of animation, and begging the corpse, for Heaven's sake, if it were alive, to say so, in good English.

Carter was one of your real *integer vitæ* men. It is said of him, that he never actually lost his self-government, but once, in his life.

He was finishing a grave, in the Granary yard, and had come out of the pit, and was looking at his work, when a young, surgical sprig came up, and, with something of a mysterious air, shadowed forth a proposition, the substance of which was, that Carter should sell him the corpse—cover it lightly—and aid in removing it, by night. In an instant, Carter jerked the little chirurgeon into the grave—it was a deep one—and began to fill up, with all his might. The screams of the little fellow drew quite a number to the spot, and he was speedily rescued. When interrogated, years afterwards, as to his real intentions, at the time, Carter always became solemnized; and said he considered the preservation of that young doctor—a particular Providence.

Carter had a strong aversion to unburying—so have I—especially a hatchet. I have a rooted hatred of slavery; and I hope our friends, on the sunny side of Mason's and Dixon's line, will not censure me, for digging up the graves of the past, and exposing unsightly relics, while I solicit the world's attention to the following literary *bijoux*.

To be sold, a young negro fellow, fit for country or other business.—Will be sold to the highest bidder, a very good gold watch, a negro boy, &c.—Cheap, for cash, a negro man, and woman, and two children.—A very likely negro wench, about 16 years of age.—A likely negro woman, about 30, cheap for cash.—A likely negro boy, about 13.—Sold only for want of employ, a healthy, tractable negro girl, about 18 years of age.—To be sold, for want of employ, a strong, hearty negro fellow, about 25 years of age.—Ran away, a negro, named Dick, a well-looking, well-shaped fellow, right negro, little on the yellow, &c.—A likely negro woman, about 33 years old, remarkable for honesty and good temper.—Grant Webster has for sale new and second hand chaises, rum, wines, and male and female negroes.—At auction, a negro woman that is used to most sorts of house business.—A likely, healthy negro man, a good cook, and can drive a carriage.—Ran away, a negro man, named Prince, a tall, straight fellow; he is about 33 years old, talks pretty good English; his design was to get off in some vessel, so as to go to England, under the notion, if he could get there, he should be free, &c.—Ten dollars reward: ran away, negro Primus, five feet ten inches high, long limbs, very long finger nails, &c.—To be sold, for no fault, a negro man, of good temper.—A valuable negro man.—Ran away, my negro, Cromarte, commonly called Crum, &c., &c.; whoever will return said runaway to me, or secure him in some public jail, &c.—The cash will be given for a negro boy of good temper.—A fine negro male child, to be given away.—To be sold, a Spanish Indian woman, about 21 years old, also a negro child, about two years old. To be sold, a strong, hearty negro girl, and her son, about a week old.—Ran away, my negro man, Samson; when he speaks has a leering look under his eyes; whoever will return him, or secure him in any of the jails, shall receive ten dollars reward. For sale, a likely negro man; has had the smallpox.—A likely negro boy, large for his age, about 13.—To be sold, very reasonably, a likely negro woman, about 33 or '4 years of age.—To be sold or hired, for a number of years, a strong, healthy, honest, negro girl, about 16 years of age.

Ah, my dear, indignant reader, I marvel not, that you are grieved and shocked, that man should dare, directly under the eye of God, to offer his fellow for sale, as he would offer a side of mutton, or a slaughtered hog—that he should offer to sell him, from head to heel, liver and lights, and lungs, and heart, and bone, and muscle, and presume to convey over, to the buyer, the very will of the poor black man, for years, and for aye; so that the miserable creature should never draw in one single breath of freedom, but breathe the breath of a slave forever and ever. This is very damnable indeed—very. You read the advertisements, which I have paraded before you, with a sentiment of disgust towards the men of the South—*nimium ne crede colori*. These are northern negroes! these are northern advertisements!

> —— ——Mutato nomine, de te
> Fabula narratur—— ——.

Every one of these slaves was owned in Boston: every one of these advertisements was published in the Boston Gazette, and the two last on December 10, 1781. They are taken from one only of the public journals, and are a very Flemish sample of the whole cloth, which may be examined by him, who has leisure to turn over the several papers, then published here.

There is one, however, so awfully ridiculous, when we consider the profession of the deceased owner, and the place of sale, and which, in these connections, presents such an example of *sacra, commixta profanis*, that I must give the advertisement without defalcation. John Moorhead, the first minister of Bury, afterwards Berry Street Church, died Dec. 2, 1773. About a year after, his effects were sold, and the following advertisement appears, in the Boston Gazette, Jan. 2, 1775: "To be sold by Public Auction, on Thursday next, at ten o'clock in the Forenoon, all the Household Furniture, belonging to the Estate of the Rev. Mr. John Moorhead, deceased, consisting of Tables, Chairs, Looking Glasses, Feather Beds, Bedsteads and Bedding, Pewter, Brass, sundry Pieces of Plate, &c., &c. A valuable collection of Books—Also a likely Negro Lad—The sale to be at the House in Auchmuty's Lane, South End, not far from Liberty Tree."—Moses and the Prophets! *A human being to be sold as a* slave, *not far from* Liberty Tree, in 1775!

Let me be clearly comprehended. Two wrongs cannot, like two negatives, neutralize each other. It is true, there was slavery in Massachusetts, and probably more of it, than is supposed to have existed, by many of the present generation. Free negroes were not numerous, in Boston, in those years. In the Boston Gazette of Jan. 2, 1775, it is stated, that 547 whites and 52 blacks were buried in the town in 1774; and 533 whites and 62 blacks in 1773. Such was the proportion then.

The energy of our northern constitution has exorcised the evil spirit of slavery. Common sense and the grace of God put it into the minds and hearts of our fathers, when the accursed *Bohun Upas* was a sapling, to pull it up, by the roots. It follows not, therefore, that the people of the South are entitled to be treated by us, their brethren, like *outside barbarians*, because they do not cast it out from their midst, as promptly, and as easily, now that it has stricken down its roots into the bowels of the earth, and become a colossus, and overshadowed the land. Slavery, being the abomination that it is, in the abstract, and in the relative, we may well regret, that it ever defiled our peninsula; especially that a slave market, for the sale of one slave only, ever existed, *"not far from Liberty Tree."* In sober truth, we are not quite justified, for railing at the South, as we have done. The sins of our dear, old fathers are still so comparatively recent, in regard to slavery, that I am absolutely afraid to fire canister and grape, among the group of offenders, lest I should disturb the ashes of my ancestors. Neither may we forget, that we, of the North, consented, aided and abetted, constitutionally, in the confirmation of slavery. Some of the most furious of the abolitionists, in this fair city, are *descendants in the right line, from Boston slaveholders*—their fathers did not recognize the sinfulness of holding slaves!

The people of the South are entitled to civility, from the people of the North, because they are citizens of one common country; and, if there is one village, town, or city of these United States, that, more than any and all others, is under solemn obligations to cherish a sentiment of grateful and affectionate respect for the South, it is the city of Boston. I propose to refresh the reader's recollection, in my next.

No. XLIV

Delenda est Carthago—abolendum est servitium.—No doubt of it; slavery must be buried—decently, however. I cannot endure rudeness and violence, at a funeral. John Cades, in Charter Street, lost his place, in 1789, for letting old Goody Smith go by the run. The *naufragium* of Erasmus, was nothing at all, compared with that of the old lady's coffin. Our Southern confederates are entitled to *civility*, because they are men and brethren; and they are entitled to *kindness and courtesy from us, of Boston*, because we owe them a debt of gratitude, which it would be shameful to forget. Since we, of the North, have presumed to be *undertakers* upon this occasion, let us do the thing "*decenter et ornate.*" Besides, our friends of the South are notoriously testy and hot-headed: they are, geographically, children of the sun. John Smith's description of the Massachusetts Indians, in 1614, Richmond ed., ii. 194, is truly applicable to the Southern people, "*very kind, but, in their fury, no less valiant.*"

I am no more inclined to uphold the South, in the continued practice of a moral wrong, because they gave us bread when we were hungry, as they certainly did, than was Sir Matthew Hale, to decide favorably for the suitor, who sent him the fat buck. *Nullum simile quatuor pedibus currit*—the South, when they bestowed their kindness upon us, during the operation of the *Boston Port Bill*, had no possible favor to ask, in return.

This famous Port Bill, which operated like *guano* upon Liberty Tree, and caused it to send forth a multitude of new and vigorous shoots, was an act of revenge and coercion, passed March 31, 1774, by the British Parliament.

No government was ever so *penny wise* and *pound foolish*, as that of Great Britain, in 1773-'4. They actually sacrificed thirteen fine, flourishing colonies for *three pence*! In 1773 the East India Company, suffering from the bad effects of the smuggling trade, in the colonies, all taxation having been withdrawn, by Great Britain, excepting on tea, proposed, for the purpose of quieting the strife, to sell their tea, free of all duties, in the Colonies, and that sixpence a pound should be retained by the Government, on exportation. But the Government insisted upon *three pence* worth of dignity; in other words, for the honor of the Crown, they resolved, that the colonists *should pay three pence* a pound, import duty. This was a very poor bargain—a *crown* for *three pence!* Well; I have no room for detail—the tea came; some of it went back again; and the balance was tossed into the sea. It was not suffered to be landed, at Philadelphia and New York. Seventeen chests, brought to New York, on private account, says Gordon, vol. i. page 333, were thrown overboard, Nov. 18, 1773, and combustibles were prepared to burn the ships, if they came up from the Hook. Dec. 16, 1773, three hundred and twenty-four chests of tea were broken open, on board the ships, in Boston, and their contents thrown into the salt water, by a "number of persons," says Gordon, vol. i. page 341, "chiefly masters of vessels and shipbuilders from the north end of the town," dressed as Indians.

In consequence of this, the *Port Bill* was passed. The object of this bill was to beggar—commercially to neutralize or nullify—the town of Boston, by shutting the port, and cutting off all import and export, by sea, until full compensation should be made, for the tea destroyed, and to the officers of the revenue, and others, who had suffered, by the riots, in the years 1773 and 1774. Such was the *Port Bill*, whose destructive operation was directed, upon the port of Boston alone, under a fatal misunderstanding of the British government, in relation to the real unanimity of the American people.

It is no easy matter, to describe the effect of this act of folly and injustice. The whole country seemed to be affected, with a sort of political *neuralgia;* and the attack upon Boston, like a wound upon some principal nerve, convulsed the whole fabric. The colonies resembled a band of brothers— "born for affliction:" a blow was no sooner aimed at one, than the remaining twelve rushed to the rescue, each one interposing an ægis. In no part of the country, were there more dignified, or more touching, or more substantial testimonies of sympathy manifested, for the people of Boston, than in the Southern States; and especially in Virginia, Maryland, and both the Carolinas.

The *Port Bill* came into force, June 1, 1774. The Marylanders of Annapolis, on the 25th of May preceding, assembled, and resolved, that Boston was *"suffering in the common cause of America."* On the 30th, the magistrates, and other inhabitants of Queen Anne's County resolved, in full meeting, that they would *"make known, as speedily as possible, their sentiments to their distressed brethren of Boston, and that they looked upon the cause of Boston to be the common cause of America."* The House of Burgesses, in Virginia, appointed the day, when the Boston Port Bill came into operation, as a day of fasting and prayer, throughout the ancient dominion. A published letter, from Kent County, Maryland, dated June 7, 1774, says—"The people of Boston need not be afraid of being starved into compliance; if they will only give a short notice, they may make their town the granary of America."

June 24, 1774.—Twenty-four days after the Port Bill went into operation, a public meeting was held at Charleston, S. C. The moving spirits were the Trapiers and the Elliots, the Horries and the Clarksons, the Gadsdens and the Pinkneys of that day; and resolutions were passed, full of brotherly love and sympathy, for the inhabitants of Boston.

"Baltimore, July 16th, 1774.—A vessel hath sailed from the Eastern Shore of this Province, with a cargo of provisions as a free gift to our besieged brethren of Boston. The inhabitants of all the counties of Virginia and Maryland are subscribing, with great liberality, for the relief of the distressed towns of Boston and Charlestown. The inhabitants of Alexandria, we hear, in a few hours, subscribed £350, for that noble purpose. Subscriptions are opened in this town, for the support and animation of Boston, under their present great conflict, for the common freedom of us all. A vessel is now loading with provisions, as a testimony of the affection of this people towards their persecuted brethren."

"Salem, Aug. 23, 1774.—Yesterday arrived at Marblehead, Capt. Perkins, from Baltimore, with 3000 bushels of corn, 20 barrels of rye meal, and 21 barrels of bread, for the benefit of the poor of Boston, and with 1000 bushels of corn from Annapolis, for the same benevolent purpose."

"New York, Aug. 15, 1774.—Saturday last, Capt. Dickerson arrived here, and brought 376 barrels of rye from South Carolina, to be sold, and proceeds remitted to Boston, a present to the sufferers; a still larger cargo is to be shipped for the like benevolent purpose."

"Newport, R. I.—Capt. Bull, from Wilmington, North Carolina, arrived here last Tuesday, with a load of provisions for the poor of Boston; to sail again for Salem."

These testimonies of a kind and brotherly spirit, came from all quarters of the country. These illustrations might be multiplied to any extent. I pass by the manifestations of the most cordial sympathy from other colonies, and the contributions from the towns and villages around us—my business lies, at present with the South—and my object is to remind some of the more rampant and furious of my abolition friends, who are of yesterday, that the people of the South, however hasty they may be, living under the sun's fiercer rays, and however excited, when a Northern man, however respectable, comes to take up his quarters in their midst, and gather evidence against them, under their very noses—are not precisely *outside barbarians*.

Let the work of abolition go forward, in a dignified and decent spirit. Let us argue; and, so far as we rightfully may, let us legislate. Let us bring the whole world's sympathy up to the work of emancipation. But, let us not revile and vituperate those, who are, to all intents and purposes, our brethren, as certainly as if they lived just over the Roxbury line, instead of Mason's and Dixon's. Such harsh and unmitigated scoffing and abuse, as we too often witness, are equally ungracious, ungentlemanly, and ungrateful.

There is something strangely grotesque, to be sure, in the idea of calling a state, in which there are more slaves than freemen, the *land of liberty*. Our Massachusetts ancestors had a very good *theoretical* conception of its inconsistency and absurdity, as early as 1773; when the first glimmerings of independence began to come over the spirit of their dreams. In that year, the Massachusetts negroes caught the liberty fever, and presented a petition to have their fetters knocked off. May 17, 1773, the inhabitants of Pembroke addressed a respectfully suggestive letter to their representative in the General Court, John Turner; the last paragraph of which is well worthy of republication. The entire letter may be found in the Boston Gazette of June 14, 1773—"We think the negro petition reasonable—agreeable to natural justice and the precepts of the Gospel; and therefore advise that, in concurrence with the other worthy members of the assembly, you endeavor to find a way, in which they may be freed from slavery, without wrong to their present masters, or injury to themselves—and that a total abolition of slavery may in due time take place. Then we trust we may with humble confidence, look up to the Great Arbiter of Heaven and earth, expecting that he will in his own due time, look upon our affliction, and in the way of his Providence, deliver us from the insults, the grievances, and impositions we so justly complain of." This, as the reader will remember, had reference to slavery in Massachusetts.

No. XLV

In 1823, and in the month of May, something, in my line, caused me to visit the first ex-President Adams, at the old mansion in Quincy. By some persons, he was accounted a cold man; and his son, John Quincy, even a colder man: yet neither was cold, unless in the sense, in which Mount Hecla is cold—belted in everlasting ice, though liable, occasionally, to violent eruptions of a fiery character.

As I was taking my leave, being about to remove into a distant State, my daughter, between five and six years old, stepped timidly towards Mr. Adams, and placing her little hand upon his, and looking upon his venerable features, said to him—*"Sir, you are so old, and I am going away so far, that I do not think I shall ever see you again—will you let me kiss you before I go?"* His brow was suddenly overcast—the spirit became gently solemnized—*"Certainly, my child"* said he, *"if you desire to kiss a very old man, whom it is quite likely you will never see again."*—He bowed his aged form, and the child, rising on tiptoe, impressed a kiss upon his brow. I would give a great deal more than I can afford, for a fair sketch of that old man's face, as he resumed his position—I see it now, with the eye of a Swedenborgian. His features were slightly flushed, but not discomposed at all; tears filled his eyes; and, if one word must suffice to express all that I saw, that word is *benevolence*—that same benevolence, which taught him, on the day of his death, July 4, 1826, when asked if he knew what day it was, to exclaim—*"Yes, it is the glorious Fourth of July—God bless it—God bless you all."*

At the time of the little occurrence, which I have related, Mr. Adams was eighty-eight years old. I ventured to say, that I wished we could give him the years of Methuselah—to which he replied, with a faint smile,—*"My friend, you could not wish me a greater curse."*—As we wax older and grayer, this expression, which, in the common phrase, is *Greek* to the young and uninitiated, becomes sufficiently translated into every man's vernacular. Mr. Adams was born October 19, 1735, and had therefore attained his ninety-first year, when he died.

Nothing like the highest ancient standard of longevity is attained, in modern times. Nine hundred, sixty, and nine years, is certainly a long life-time. When baby Lamech was born, his father was a young fellow of one hundred and eighty-seven. Weary work it must have been, waiting so long, for one's inheritance!

The records of modern longevity will appear, nevertheless, somewhat surprising, to those, who have given but little attention to the subject. The celebrated Albert De Haller, and there can be no higher authority, enumerated eleven hundred and eleven cases of individuals, who had lived from 100 to 169. His classification is as follows:—

1000	from	100 to 110
60	"	110 to 120
29	"	120 to 130
15	"	130 to 140
6	"	140 to 150
1	of	169.

The oldest was Henry Jenkins, of Yorkshire, who died in 1670. Thomas Parr, of Wilmington, in Shropshire, died in 1635, aged 152. He was a poor yeoman, and married his first wife, when he was in his 88th year, or, as some say, his 80th, and had two children. He was brought to Court, by the Earl of Arundel, in the reign of Charles I., and died, as it was supposed, in consequence of change of diet. His body was examined by Dr. Harvey, who thought he might have lived much longer, had he adhered to his simple habits. Being rudely asked, before the King, what more he had done, in his long life, than other old men, he replied—"*At the age of 105, I did penance in Alderbury Church, for an illegitimate child.*" When he was 120, he married a second wife, by whom he had a child. Sharon Turner, in his Sacred History of the World, vol. iii. ch. 23, says, in a note, that Parr's son (by the second wife, the issue by the first died early) lived to the age of 113—his grandson to that of 109—his great-grandson to that of 124; and two other grandsons, who died in 1761 and 1763, to that of 127.

Parr's was a much longer life than Reuben's, Judah's, Issachar's, Abner's, Simeon's, Dan's, Zebulon's, Levi's, or Naphthali's. Dr. Harvey's account of the post mortem examination is extremely interesting. The quaint lines of Taylor, the water poet, as he was styled, I cannot omit:—

> "Good wholesome labor was his exercise,
> Down with the lamb, and with the lark would rise;
> In mire and toiling sweat he spent the day,
> And to his team he whistled time away:
> The cock his night-clock, and till day was done,

His watch and chief sundial was the sun.
He was of old Pythagoras' opinion,
That green cheese was most wholesome with an onion;
Coarse meslin bread, and for his daily swig,
Milk, buttermilk, and water, whey and whig.
Sometimes metheglin, and by fortune happy,
He sometimes sipp'd a cup of ale most nappy,
Cider or perry, when he did repair
T'a Whitsun ale, wake, wedding or a fair;
Or, when in Christmas time he was a guest
At his good landlord's house, among the rest.
Else he had very little time to waste,
Or at the alehouse huff-cap ale to taste.
His physic was good butter, which the soil
Of Salop yields, more sweet than candy oil.
And garlic he esteemed, above the rate
Of Venice treacle or best Mithridate.
He entertained no gout, no ache he felt,
The air was good and temperate, where he dwelt;
While mavises and sweet-tongued nightingales
Did sing him roundelays and madrigals.
Thus, living within bounds of nature's laws
Of his long, lasting life may be some cause.
From head to heel, his body had all over
A quickset, thickset, nat'ral, hairy cover."

Isaac lived to the age of 180, or five years longer than his father Abraham. I now propose to enter one or more well-known old stagers, of modern times, who will beat Isaac, by five lengths. Mr. Easton, of Salisbury, England, a respectable bookseller, and quoted, as good authority by Turner, prepared a more extensive list than Haller, of persons, who had died aged from 100 to 185. His work was entitled *Human Longevity*—1600 of his cases occurred, within the British Isles, and 1687 between the years 1706 and 1799. He sets down three between 170 and 185, giving their names and other particulars.

Mr. Whitehurst's tables contain several cases, not in Mr. Easton's work, from 134 years to 148. Some twenty other cases are stated, by Turner, from 130 to 150. I refer, historically, to the case of Jonathan Hartop, not because of the very great age he attained, but for other reasons of interest: "1791.— Died, Jonathan Hartop, aged one hundred and thirty-eight, of the village of Aldborough, Yorkshire. He could read to the last, without spectacles, and play at cribbage, with the most perfect recollection. He remembered

Charles II., and once travelled to London, with the facetious Killegrew. He ate but little; his only beverage was milk. He had been married five times. Mr. Hartop lent Milton fifty pounds, which the bard returned, with honor, though not without much difficulty. Mr. Hartop would have declined receiving it; but the pride of the poet was equal to his genius, and he sent the money with an angry letter, which was found, among the curious possessions of that venerable old man."

On the 4th of July, 1846, I visited Dr. Ezra Green, at his residence, in Dover, N. H. He showed me a couple of letters, which he had received, a short time before, from Daniel Webster and Thomas H. Benton, congratulating him, on having completed his one hundredth year, on the 17th of the preceding June, the anniversary of the battle of Bunker's Hill, and remarked, that those gentlemen had not regarded the difference, between the old style and the new. He told me, that in 1777, he had been a surgeon, in the Ranger, with John Paul Jones. Upon my taking out my glasses, to read a passage in a pamphlet, to which he called my attention, he told me he had never used spectacles, nor felt the need of any such assistance, in reading. Dr. Green died, in 1847.

He graduated, at Harvard, in 1765. At the time of his death, every other member of his own class, numbering fifty-four, was dead.

Previously to 1765, two thousand and seventy-five individuals are named, upon the catalogue. They were all dead at the time of his decease, though he died so recently, as 1847. Yet, from the year, when he graduated, to 1786, a period of twenty years, of seven hundred and seventy-three graduates, fifteen only appear, upon the catalogue of 1848, without the fatal star. One of the fifteen, Harrison Gray Otis, has recently died, leaving three survivors only, in his class of 1783, Asa Andrews, J. S. Boies, and Jonathan Ewins. Another of the fifteen has also recently died, being the oldest graduate, Judge Timothy Farrar, of the class of 1767. The oldest living graduate of Harvard is James Lovell, of the class of 1776.

I send my communication to the press, as speedily as possible, lest he also should be off, before I can publish.

No. XLVI

A few days ago, I saw, in the hands of the artist, Mr. Alvan Clarke, a sketch, nearly completed, from Stuart's painting of John Adams, in his very old age. This sketch is to be engraved, as an accompaniment of the works of Mr. Adams, about to be published, by Little & Brown. I scarcely know what to say of this sketch of Mr. Adams. His fine old face, such as it was in the flesh, and at the very last of his long and illustrious career, is fixed in my memory—rivetted there—as firmly as his name is bolted, upon the loftiest column of our national history. Never have I seen a more perfect fac simile of man, without the aid of relief—it is the resurrection and the life. If I am at a loss what to say of the sketch, I am still farther at fault, what to say of the artist. Like some of those heavenly bodies, whose contemplation occupies no little portion of his time, it is not always the easiest thing in the world, to know in what part of his orbit he may be found; if I desire to obtain a portrait, or a miniature, or a sketch, he can scarcely devote his time to it, he is so very busy, in contriving some new improvement, for his already celebrated rifle; or if it is a patent muzzled rifle that I want, he is quite likely to be occupied, in the manufacture of a telescope. Be all these matters as they may, I can vouch for it, after years of experience, Alvan Clarke is a very clever fellow, *Anglice et Americanice*; and this sketch of Mr. Adams does him honor, as an artist.

It was in the year 1822, I believe, that a young lady sent me her album, with a request, that I, of all people in the world, would occupy one of its pages. Well, I felt, that after all, it was quite in my line, for I had always looked upon a young lady's album, as a kind of cemetery, for the burial of anybody's bantlings, and I began to read the inscriptions, upon such as reposed in this place, appointed for the still-born. I was a little startled, I confess, at my first glance, upon the autograph of the late Bishop Griswold, appended to some very respectable verses. My attention was next drawn to some lines, over the name of Daniel Webster, *manu propria*. I forget them now, but I remember, that the American Eagle was invoked for the occasion, and flapped its wings, through one or more of the stanzas. Next came an article in strong, sensible prose, from John Adams, written by an amanuensis, but signed with his own hand. Such a hand—the "*manu deficiente*" of Tibullus. The letters, formed by the failing, trembling fingers, resembled the forked lightning. A solemnizing and impressive autograph it was: and, under the impulse of the moment, I had the audacity to spoil three pages of this consecrated album, by appending to this venerable name the following lines:—

High over Alps, in Dauphine,
There lies a lonely spot,
So wild, that ages rolled away,
And man had claimed it not:
For ages there, the tiger's yell
Bay'd the hoarse torrent as it fell.

Amid the dark, sequestered glade,
No more the brute shall roam;
For man, unsocial man, hath made
That wilderness his home:
And convent bell, with notes forlorn,
Is heard, at midnight, eve, and morn.

For now, amid the Grand Chartreuse,
Carthusian monks reside;
Whose lives are passed, from man recluse,
In scourging human pride;
In matins, vespers, aves, creeds,
With crosses, masses, prayers, and beads.

When hither men of curious mood,
Or pilgrims, bend their way,
To view this Alpine solitude,
Or, heav'nward bent, to pray,
Saint Bruno's monks their album bring,
Inscrib'd by poet, priest, and king.

Since pilgrim first, with holy tears,
Inscrib'd the tablet fair,
On time's dark flood, some thousand years,
Have pass'd like billows there.
What countless names its pages blot,
By country, kindred, long forgot!

Here chaste conceits and thoughts divine
Unclaim'd, and nameless, stand;
Which, like the Grecian's waving line,
Betray some master's hand.
And here Saint Bruno's monks display,
With pride, the classic lines of Gray.

While pilgrim ponders o'er the name,
He feels his bosom glow;
And counts it nothing less than fame,
To write his own below.
So, in this Album, fain would I,
Beneath a name, that cannot die.

Thrice happy book! no tablet bears
A nobler name than thine;
Still followed by a nation's pray'rs,
Through ling'ring life's decline.
The wav'ring stylus scarce obey'd
The hand, that once an empire sway'd!

Not thus, among the patriot band,
That name enroll'd we see—
No falt'ring tongue, no trembling hand
Proclaim'd an empire free!—
Lady, retrace those lines, and tell,
If, in thy heart, no sadness dwell?

And, in those fainting, struggling lines,
Oh, see'st thou naught sublime!
No tott'ring pile, that half inclines!
No mighty wreck of time!
Sighs not thy gentle heart to save
The sage, the patriot, from the grave!

If thus, oh then recall that sigh,
Unholy 'tis, and vain;
For saints and sages never die,
But sleep, to rise again.
Life is a lengthened day, at best,
And in the grave tir'd trav'llers rest;

Till, with his trump, to wake the dead,
Th' appointed angel flies;
Then Heav'n's bright album shall be spread,
And all who sleep, shall rise;
The blest to Zion's Hill repair,
And write their names immortal there.

I had as much pleasure, in composing these lines, as I ever had, in composing the limbs or the features of a corpse; and now that they are fairly laid out, the reader may bury them in oblivion, as soon as he pleases. The lines of Gray, referred to, in the sixth stanza, may be found in the collections of his works, and were written in the album of the Chartreuse, in 1741.

My recollections of John Adams, are very perfect, and preëminently pleasant. I knew nothing of him personally, of course, in the days of his power. I had nothing to ask at his hands, but the permission to sit and listen. How vast and how various his learning!—"Qui sermo! quæ præcepta! quanta notitia antiquitatis!... Omnia memoria tenebat, non domestica solum, sed etiam externa bella: cujus sermone ita tum cupide fruebar, quasi jam divinarem id, quod evenit, illo extincto, fore, unde discerem, neminem." Surpassingly delightful were the outpourings, till some thoughtless wight, by an ill-timed allusion, opened the fountain of bitter waters—then, history, literature, the arts, all were buried *in gurgito vasto*, giving place to Jefferson's injustice, the Mazzei letters, and Callender's prospect before us—*quantum mutatus ab illo!*

How forcibly the dead are quickened, upon the retina of memory, by the exhibition of some well known and personally associated article—the little hat of Napoleon—the mantle of Cæsar—*"you all do know this mantle!"* I have just now drawn, from my treasury, an autograph of John Adams, bearing date, Jan. 31, 1824, and a lock of strong hair, cut from his venerable brow, the day before. In October of that year, he was eighty-nine years of age; and that lock of hair is a dark iron gray. I have also taken from its casket a silver pen, and small portable inkstand attached, which also were his. The contemplation of these things—I came honestly by them—seems almost to raise that venerable form before me. I can almost hear him repeat those memorable words—"The Union is our Rock of Safety as well as our Pledge of Grandeur."

No. XLVII

I am rather surprised, to find how little is known, among the rising generation, about slavery, in the Old Bay State. One might delve for a twelve month, and not gather together the half of all, that is condensed, in Dr. Belknap's replies to Judge Tucker's inquiries, Mass. H. C., iv. 191.

I never was a sexton in the Berry Street Church, but I knew Dr. Jeremy Belknap well, in 1797, when he lived on the southeasterly side of Lincoln Street, near Essex. He died the following year. His garden was overrun with spiders. I had a great veneration for the doctor—he gave me a copy of his Foresters—and, to repay a small part of the debt, I was proceeding, one summer morning, with a strong arm, to demolish the spiders, when he pleasantly called to me to desist, saying, that he preferred them to the flies.

Slavery was here—negro slavery—at a very early day. Josselyn speaks of three slaves, in the family of Maverick, on Noddle's Island, Oct. 2, 1639, M. H. C., xxiii. 231. These were probably brought directly from Africa. In 1645, the General Court of Massachusetts ordered Mr. Williams, at Pascataqua, over which Massachusetts exercised jurisdiction, to send the negro he had of Captain Smith, to them, that he might be sent home; as Smith had confessed, that the negroes he brought were stolen from Guinea. Ibid. iv. 195. In the same year, a law was passed, against the traffic in slaves, those excepted, who were taken in war, or cast into servitude, for crime. Ibid.

The slave trade was carried on, in Massachusetts, to a very small extent. "In 1703," says Dr. Belknap, "a duty of £4 was laid on every negro imported." He adds—"By the inquiries which I have made of our oldest merchants, now living, I cannot find that more than three ships in a year, belonging to this port, were ever employed in the African trade. The rum distilled here, was the mainspring of this traffic. Very few whole cargoes ever came to this port. One gentleman says he remembers two or three. I remember one, between thirty and forty years ago, which consisted almost wholly of children. At Rhode Island the rum distillery and the African trade were prosecuted to a greater extent than in Boston; and I believe no other seaport, in Massachusetts, had any concern in the slave business." Ibid. 196. Dr. Belknap drew up his answers to Judge Tucker's inquiries, April 21, 1795: "*between thirty and forty years ago,*" therefore, was between 1755 and 1765.

Dr. Belknap remembered the arrival in Boston of a *"whole cargo"* of slaves, *"almost wholly children,"* between the years 1755 and 1765! If we have ever had an accurate and careful narrator of matters of fact, in New England, that man was Jeremy Belknap. The last of these years, 1765, was the memorable year of the Stamp Act, and Liberty Tree! Let us hope the arrival was nearer to 1755.

"About the time of the Stamp Act," says Dr. Belknap, "this trade began to decline, and, in 1788, it was prohibited by law. This could not have been done previous to the Revolution, as the governors sent hither from England, it is said, were instructed not to consent to any acts made for that purpose." Ibid. 197. In 1767, a bill was brought into the House of Representatives, "to prevent the unnatural and unwarrantable custom of enslaving mankind, and the importation of slaves into the Province:" but it came to nothing. "Had it passed both houses in any form whatever," says Dr. B., ibid. page 202, "Gov. Bernard would not have consented to it." One scarcely knows which most to admire, the fury against the South, of gentlemen, whose ancestors imported cargoes of slaves, or bought and sold them, at retail, or the righteous indignation of Great Britain, who instructed her colonial governors, to veto every attempt of the Massachusetts Legislature, to abolish the traffic in human flesh. A disposition existed, at an earlier period, to abolish the brutal traffic. In a letter to the Rev. Dr. Freeman from Timothy Pickering, which may found in M. H. C., xviii. 183, he refers to the following transcript, from the records of the Selectmen of Boston: "1701, May 26. The Representatives are desired to promote the encouraging the bringing of white servants, and to put a period to negroes being slaves."

"A few only of our merchants," says Dr. B., M. H. C., iv. 197, "were engaged in this traffic. It was never supported by popular opinion. A degree of infamy was attached to the characters of those, who were employed in it. Several of them, in their last hours, bitterly lamented their concern in it." Chief Justice Samuel Sewall wrote a pamphlet against it. Many, says Dr. B., who were wholly opposed to the traffic, would yet buy a slave, when brought here, on the ground that it was better for him to be brought up in a Christian land! For this, Abraham and the patriarchs were vouched in, of course, as supporters.

Our winters were unfavorable to unacclimated negroes; white laborers were therefore preferred to black. *"Negro children,"* says Dr. B., ibid. 200, *"were reckoned an incumbrance in a family; and, when weaned, were given away like puppies. They have been publicly advertised in the newspapers, to be given away."*

In answer to the question, how slavery had been abolished in Massachusetts? Dr. Belknap answered—"*by public opinion.*" He considers, that slavery came to an end, in our Commonwealth, in 1783. After 1781, there were, certainly, very few, who had the brass to offer negroes, for sale, openly, in the newspapers of Boston. Public opinion, as Dr. Belknap says, was accomplishing this work: and every calm, impartial person may opine for himself, how patiently we of the North should have endured, at that time, even a modicum of the galling abuse, of which such a *profluvium* is daily administered, to the people of the South. It seems to me, that such rough treatment would have been more likely to addle, than to hatch the ovum of public opinion in 1783.

Dr. Belknap's account, ibid. 203, is very clear. He says—"The present constitution of Massachusetts was established in 1780. The first article of the declaration of rights asserts that '*all men are born free and equal.*' This was inserted, not merely as a moral or political truth, but with a particular view to establish the liberation of the negroes, on a general principle; and so it was understood, by the people at large; but some doubted whether this were sufficient. Many of the blacks, taking advantage of the *public opinion*, and of this general assertion, in the bill of rights, asked their freedom and obtained it. Others took it without leave. Some of the aged and infirm thought it most prudent to continue in the families, where they had been well used, and experience has proved that they acted right. In 1781, at the court in Worcester County, an indictment was found against a white man for assaulting, beating, and imprisoning a black. He was tried at the Supreme Judicial Court, in 1783. His defence was that the black was his slave, and that the beating, &c., was the necessary restraint and correction of the master. This was answered by citing the aforesaid clause in the declaration of rights. The Judge and Jury were of opinion that he had no right to beat or imprison the negro. He was found guilty and fined forty shillings. This decision was a mortal wound to slavery in Massachusetts."

The reader will perceive, that a distinction was maintained, between the *slave trade*, eo nomine, and the *holding of slaves*, inseparably connected as it was, with the incidents of sale and transfer from man to man, in towns and villages. He, who was engaged in the *trade*, so called, was supposed *per se* or *per alium* to *steal* the slaves; but, contrary to the proverb, the *receiver* was, in this case, not accounted so bad as the *thief!* The prohibition of the *traffic*, in 1788, grew out of public indignation, produced by the act of one Avery, from Connecticut, who decoyed three black men on board his vessel, under pretence of employing them; and while they were at work below, proceeded to sea, having previously cleared for Martinico. The knowledge of this outrage produced a great sensation. Gov. Hancock, and

M. L'Etombe, the French Consul, wrote in favor of the kidnapped negroes, to all the West India Islands. A petition was presented to the Legislature, from the members of the association of the Boston Clergy; another from the blacks; and one, at that very time, from the Quakers, was lying on the table, for an act against equipping and insuring vessels, engaged in the traffic, and against kidnappers. Such an act was passed March 26, 1788.

The poor negroes, carried off by that arch villain, Avery, were offered for sale, in the island of St. Bartholomew. They told their story publicly—*magna est veritas*—the Governor heard and believed it—the sale was forbidden. An inhabitant of the island—a Mr. Atherton, of blessed memory—became their protector, and gave bonds for their good behavior, for six months. Letters, confirming their story, arrived. They were sent on their way home rejoicing, and arrived in Boston, on the following 29th day of July.

In 1763, according to Dr. Belknap, ibid. 198, there was 1 black to every 45 whites in Massachusetts; in 1776, 1 to every 65; in 1784, 1 to every 80. The whole number, in the latter year, 4377 blacks, 354,133 whites.

It appears, by a census, taken by order of Government, in the last month of 1754, and the first month of 1755, that there were then in the Province of Massachusetts Bay 2717 negro slaves of and over 16 years of age. Of these, 989 belonged to Boston. This table may be found in M. H. C., xiii. 95.

No. XLVIII

Of all sorts of affectation the affectation of happiness is the most universal. How many, whose domestic relations are full of trouble, are, abroad, apparently, the happiest of mortals. How many, after laying down the severest sumptuary laws, for their domestics, on the subject of *sugar* and *butter*, go forth, in all their personal finery, to inquire the prices of articles, which they have no means to purchase, and return, comforted by the assurance, that they have the reputation of fashion and wealth, with those, at least, who have, so deferentially, displayed their diamonds and pearls!

Who would not be thought wealthy, and wise, and witty, if he could!

Happiness is every man's *cynosure*, when he embarks upon the ocean of life. No man would willingly be thought so very unskilful, as that ill-starred Palinurus, who made the shores of Norway, on a voyage to the coast of Africa. Whether wealth, or fame, or fashion, or pleasure be the principal object of pursuit, no one is willing to be accounted a disappointed man, after the application of his best energies, for years. The man of wealth—the man of ambition, for example, are desirous of being accounted happy. It would certainly be exceedingly annoying to both, to be convinced, that they were believed, by mankind, to be otherwise. Their condition is rendered tolerable, only by the conviction, that thousands suppose them happy, and covet their condition accordingly. There is something particularly agreeable, in being envied, of course. Now, it is the common law of man's nature—a law, that executes itself—that *possession makes him poor* as Horace says, Sat. i. 1, 1.

> — — — —"Nemo, quam sibi sortem,
> Seu ratio dederit, seu fors objecerit illi,
> Contentus vivat." — — — —

All experience has demonstrated, that happiness is not to be bought, and that what there is of it, in this present life, is a home-made article, which every one produces for himself, in the workshop of his own bosom. It no more consists, in the accumulation of wealth, than in snuffing up the east wind. The poor believe the rich to be happy—they become rich, and find they were mistaken. But they keep the secret, and affect to be happy, nevertheless.

Seneca looked upon the devotion of time and talent to the acquirement of money, beyond the measure of a man's reasonable wants, with profound contempt. He called such, as gave themselves up to the unvarying pursuit of wealth, *short lived*; meaning that the hours and years, so employed, were carved out of the estate of a man's life, and utterly thrown away. There is a fine passage, in ch. 17, of Seneca's book, *De Brevitate Vitæ.*

"Misserrimam ergo necesse est, non tantum brevissimam, vitam eorum esse, qui magno parant labore, quod majore possideant: operose assequuntur quæ volunt, anxii tenent quæ assecuti sunt. Nulla interim nunquam amplius redituri temporis est ratio"—It is clear, therefore, that the life must be very miserable, and very brief, of those, who get their gains with great labor, and hold on to their gettings with greater—who obtain the object of their wishes, with much difficulty, and are everlastingly anxious for the safe keeping of their treasures. They seem to have no true estimate of those hours, thus wasted, which never can return.

In one of his admirable letters to Lucilius, the eightieth, on the subject of poverty, he says—"Si vis scire quam nihil in illa mali sit, compara inter se pauperum et divitum vultus. Sæpius pauper et fidelius ridet; nulla sollicitudo in alto est; etiamsi qua incidit cura, velut nubes levis transit Horum, qui felices vocantur, hilaritas ficta est, au gravis et suppurata tristitia; eo quidem gravior, quia interdum non licet palam esse miseros, sed inter ærumnas, cor ipsum exedentes, necesse est agere felicem"—If you wish to know, that there is no evil therein, compare the faces of the rich and the poor. The poor man laughs much oftener, and more heartily. There is no wearying solicitude pressing upon his inmost soul, and when care comes, it passes away, like a thin cloud. But the hilarity of these rich men, who are called happy, is affected, or a deep-seated and rankling anxiety, the more oppressive, because it never would answer for them to appear as miserable, as they are, being constrained to appear happy, in the midst of harassing cares, gnawing at their vitals.

If Seneca had been on 'Change, daily, during the last half year, and watched the countenances of our wealthy money-lenders, he could not have portrayed the picture with a more masterly pencil. The rate of usury has, of course, a relation to the hazard encountered, and that hazard is ever uppermost in the mind of the usurer: and it is extremely doubtful, if the hope, however sanguine, of realizing two per cent. a month, is always sufficient, to quiet those fears, which will occasionally arise, of losing the principal and interest together.

I never buried an old usurer, without a conviction, as I looked upon his hard, corrugated features, that, if he could carry nothing else with him, he certainly carried upon his checkered brow the very phylactery of his calling. We may talk about money, as an article of commerce, till we are tired—we may weary the legislature, by our importunity, into a repeal of the existing laws against usury—we may cudgel our brains, to stretch the mantle of the law over our operations, and make it appear *a regular business transaction*—it is a case, in which no refinement of the culinary art will ever be able to disguise, or neutralize, the odor of the opossum—there ever was—there is—there ever will be, I am afraid, a certain touch of moral *nastiness* about it, which no casuistical chemistry will ever be able entirely to remove.

Doubtless, there are men, who take something more, during a period of scarcity, than legal interest, and who are very worthy men withal. There are others, who are descendants, in the right line, from the horse-leech of biblical history—who take all they can get. Now, there is but one category: *they are all usurers*; and those, who are respectable, impart of their respectability to such, as have little or none; and give a confidence to those, who would be treated with contempt, for their merciless gripings, were they not banded together, with men of character, in the same occupation, as usurers. Those, who take seven or eight per cent. per annum, and those who take *one per cent. a day,* and such things have been, are not easily distinguished; but the question, who come within the category, as usurers, is a thing more readily comprehended. All are such, who exceed the law.

Usurer, originally, was not a term of reproach; for *interest* and *usury* meant one and the same thing. The earlier statutes against usury, in England, were directed chiefly against the Jews—whose lineal descendants are still in our midst. Usury was forbidden, by act of Parliament, in 1341. The rate then taken by the Jews, was enormous. In 1545, 37 Henry VIII., the rate established was ten per cent. This statute was confirmed by 13 Eliz. 1570. Reduced to eight per cent., 21 James I. 1623, when the word *interest* was first employed, instead of *usury.* Again reduced, by Cromwell, 1650, to six per cent. Confirmed by Charles II. 1660. Reduced to five per cent., 5 Anne, 1714.

There are not two words about it; extortion and usury harden the heart; soil the reputation; and diminish the quantum of happiness, by lowering the standard of self-respect. That unconscionable griper, whose god is Mammon, and who fattens upon misery, as surely as the vulture upon carrion, stalking up and down like a commercial buzzard, tearing away the substance of his miserable victim, by piecemeal—*two per cent. a month*—can he be happy! However much like a human being he may have looked, in his youth, the workings of his mercenary soul have told too truly upon his iron features, until that visage would form an appropriate figure-head for the portal of 'Change alley, or the Inquisition.

— — — —"Is your name Shylock?

Shylock is my name."

To how many, in this age of *anxious inquirers*, may we hold up this picture, and propound this interrogatory!

God is just, though Mahomet be not his prophet. Instead of exclaiming, that God's ways are past finding out, let us go doggedly to work, and study them a little. Some of them, I humbly confess, appear sufficiently intelligible, with common sense for an expositor. Does not the All-wise contriver say, in language not to be mistaken, to such as worship, at the shrines of avarice and sensuality—you have chosen idols, and your punishment shall consist, in part, in the ridicule and contempt, which the worship of these idols brings upon your old age. You—the victim of intemperance—shall continue, with your bloated lips, to worship—not a stone image—but a stone jug; and grasping your idol with your trembling fingers, literally stagger into the grave! And you, though last, not least, of all vermicular things, whose whole time and intellectual powers are devoted to no higher object than making money—shall still crawl along, heaping up treasure, day after day—day after day—to die at last, not knowing who shall come after you, a wise man or a fool!

> "Constant at Church and 'Change; his gains were sure,
> His givings rare, save farthings to the poor!
> The Dev'l was piq'd such saintship to behold,
> And long'd to tempt him, like good Job of old;
> But Satan now is wiser than of yore,
> And tempts, by making rich, not making poor."

No. XLIX

Self-conceit and vanity are very pardonable offences, till, stimulated by flattery, or aggravated by indulgence, they assume the offensive forms of arrogance and insolence. If we should drive, from the circle of our friends, all, who are occasionally guilty of such petty misdemeanors, we should restrict ourselves to the solitude of Selkirk. There are some worthy men, with whom this little infirmity is an intermittent, alternating, like fever and ague, between self-conceit and self-abasement. Like some estimable people, of both sexes, who, at one moment, proclaim themselves the chief of sinners, and the next, are in admirable working condition, as the spiritual guides and instructors of all mankind; these persons, under the influence of the wind, or the weather, or the world's smiles, or its frowns, or the state of their digestive organs, indicate, by their air and carriage, today, a feeling, far on the sunny side of self-complacency, and of deep humility, tomorrow.

William Boodle has been dead, some twenty years. He was my school-fellow. I would have undertaken anything, for Boodle, while living, but I could not undertake for him, when dead. The idea of burying Billy Boodle, my playmate from the cradle—we were put into breeches, the very same day—with whom I had passed, simultaneously, through all the epocha—rattles—drums—go-carts—kites—tops—bats—skates—the idea of shovelling the cold earth upon him, was too much. I would have buried the Governor and Council, with the greatest pleasure, but Billy Boodle—I couldn't. So I changed works, that day, with one of our craft, who comprehended my feelings perfectly.

I never shall forget my sensations, the first time he called me *Mr. Wycherly*. We had ever been on terms of the greatest intimacy, and had never known any other words of designation, than Abner and Bill. I was very much amazed; and he seemed a little confused, himself, when I laughed in his face, and asked him what the devil he meant by it. But he grew daily more formal in his manners, and more particular in his dress. His voice became changed—he began to use longer words—assumed an unusual wave of the hand, and a particular movement of the head, when speaking—and, while talking, on the most common-place topics, he had a way, quite new with him, of bringing down the fore-finger of his right hand, frequently and forcibly, upon the ball of the uplifted thumb of the left. He was a leather-breeches maker; and I caught him, upon two or three occasions, spouting in his shop, all by himself, before a small looking-glass. He once made a pair of buckskins, for old General Heath—they did not fit—the General returned them, and Boodle said he would have them *taken into a new draft*—I thought he was a little deranged: "taken where?" said the old General. Boodle colored, and corrected himself, saying he would have them *let out*. He had two turns of this strange behavior, in one year, during which, he was rather neglectful of his business, pompous in his family, and talked to his wife, who was a plain, notable woman, of nothing but first principles, and political economy. In the intervals between these attacks, he was perfectly himself again, and it was Abner and Bill, as in former days.

I have often smiled, at my own dullness, in not sooner apprehending the solution of this little enigma. Boodle was a member of the Legislature; and the fits were upon him, during the sessions. No man, probably, was ever more thoroughly confounded, than my old friend, when, it having been deemed expedient to compliment the leather-breeches interest, the committee requested him to permit his name to be put upon the list of candidates, as one of the representatives of the city of Boston, in the General Court. He could not think of it—the committee averred the utter impossibility of doing without him—he was ignorant of the duties—they could be learned in half a day—he was without education—the very thing, a self-taught man! He consented.

How much more easily we are persuaded to be great men, than to be Christians! There is but a step from conscious insignificancy to the loftiest pretension. Boodle was elected, and awoke the next morning, less surprised by the event, than at the extraordinary fact, that his talents had been overlooked, so long. He spoiled three good skins that day, from sheer absence of mind.

However disposed we may be to laugh at the airs of men, who so entirely misapprehend themselves and their constituents, our laughter should be tempered with charity. They are not honestly told, that they are wanted, only as makeweights—to keep in file—to follow, *en suite*—to register an edict: and their vanity is pardonable, in the ratio of that ignorance of themselves, which leads them to rely, so implicitly, upon the testimony of others.

Comparative mensuration is a very popular process, and a very comforting process, for all, who have made small progress in self-knowledge; and this category comprehends all, but a very small minority. There are a few, I doubt not, who think humbly of themselves; but there are very few, indeed, who cannot perceive, in themselves, or their possessions, some one or more points of imaginary superiority, over their fellows. This is an inexpensive mode of enjoying one's self, and I cannot see the wisdom, or the wit, of disturbing the self-complacency of any one, upon such an occasion, unless the delusion is of vital importance to somebody. What, if your neighbor prefers his Dutch domicil, with its overhanging gable, to your classic chateau—or sees more to admire, in his broad-faced squab of a wife, than in your faultless Helen—or vaunts the superiority of his short-legged cob, over your famous blood horse! Let him. Such things should be passed, with great forbearance, were it only for the innocent amusement they afford us. So far, however, is this from the ordinary mode of treating them, that I am compelled to believe vanity is often more apt, than criminality, to excite our irritable principle, and stimulate the spirit of resentment.

I have known some worthy men, generous and humane, whose very gait has rendered them exceedingly unpopular. I once heard a pious and reverend clergyman say, of one of his very best parishioners, but whose unfortunate air of hauteur was rather remarkable, that, with all his excellent qualities, "it would do the flesh good to give him a kick."

From a thousand illustrations, which are all around us, I will select one only. The anecdote, which I am about to relate, may be told without any apprehension of giving offence; as the parties have been dead, some thirty years. A worthy clergyman, residing in a neighboring state, grew old; and the parish, who entertained the most cordial respect and affection, for this venerable soldier of the cross, resolved to give him a colleague. After due inquiry, and a *quantum sufficit* of preaching on probation, they decided on giving a call to Parson Brocklebank. He was a little, red, round man, with a spherical head, a Brougham nose, and a gait, the like of which had never been seen, in that parish, before. It had not attracted particular notice, until after he was settled. To be sure, an aged single lady, of the parish, was heard to say, that she saw something of it, at the ordination, when Parson Brocklebank stepped forward, to receive the right hand of fellowship. Suffice it to say, for the reader's particular edification, that it was indescribable. It became the village talk, and is thought to have had an injurious influence, in retarding a revival, which seemed to be commencing, just before the period of the ordination. However lowly in spirit, the new minister may have been, all who ever beheld him move, were satisfied, at a glance, that he had a most exalted opinion of himself. And yet he was an excellent man.

This unfortunate trick of jerking out the hips, and those rotundities of flesh connected therewith, however it might have originated in "curs'd pride, that busy sin," had become, with Parson Brocklebank, an unchangeable habit. We often see it in a slight degree, but, as it existed in his particular case, it was a thing not known among men. I think I have seen it among women. Dr. Johnson would have called it a fundamental undulation, elaborated by the ostentatious workings of a pompous spirit. Whatever it was, it was fatal to the peace and prosperity of that parish. Every one talked of it. The young laughed at it; the old mourned over it; the middle aged were vexed by it; boys and girls were whipped, for imitating it; children were forbidden to look at it, for fear of their catching it; the very dogs were said to have barked at it.

The parish began to dissolve, *sine die*. The deacons waited upon their old clergyman, Father Paybody, and the following colloquy ensued:

"We're in a bad way, Father Paybody; and, if folks keep going off so, we don't see how we shall be able to pay the salaries.—Dismiss me: I am of little use now.—No, no, Father Paybody, while there's a potato in this parish, we'll share it together. We call'd for advice. Ever since Parson Brocklebank was settled, the parish has been going to pieces: what is the cause of it?—The shrewd old man shook his head, and smiled.—Parson Brocklebank is a good man, Father Paybody.—Excellent.—Sound doctrine.—Very.—Amazing ready at short notice.—Very.—Great at clearing a knotty passage.—Very.— We think him a very pious Christian.—Very.—In the parochial relation he is very acceptable.—Very.—I hear he has a winning way, and always has candy or gingerbread in his pockets, for the children, which helps the word greatly, with the little ones.—Well, nearly half our people are dissatisfied, and have left, or will leave soon. What is the cause of it, Father Paybody?—I will tell you: it's owing to no other cause under the sun, than that wriggle of Brother Brocklebank's behind."

No. L

I sincerely hope, that Daniel H. Pearson, now in prison, under suspicion of having murdered his wife and twin daughters, at Wilmington, in this Commonwealth, in the month of April last, may be proved to be an innocent man. For, should he be convicted, he will certainly be sentenced to be hung; and it is quite probable, that Governor Briggs, and his iron-hearted Council may do, as they recently did, in the case of poor Washington Goode, a most unfortunate man, who, unhappily, committed a most infernal murder, of which, after an impartial trial, he was duly convicted. Will it be believed, in this age of improved contrivances, moral and physical, that the Governor and Council of our Commonwealth have actually refused, to rush between the sentence and the execution, and save this egregious scoundrel from the gallows! They have solemnly decided, not to interfere with the operation of that ancient law of this Commonwealth, which decrees, that he, who kills his fellow man, with malice prepense, shall be hanged, by the neck, till he is dead!

It really seems to me, that the time has arrived when Massachusetts should be governed, by some compassionate person, who will prove himself, upon such unpleasant occasions, the murderer's friend. I am not unapprized of the fact, that there is a strong opposition to these opinions, among the wisest and best men in the community; and that, irrespectively of the operation of the *lex talionis* upon the murderer, his death is accounted necessary, *in terrorem*, for the rest of mankind; as Cicero has said—"*ut pœna ad paucos, metus ad omnes perveniat*"—that the punishment may reach the few, and fear the many. But Cicero was a heathen. There are also some individuals, having very little of that contempt for old wives' tales, which characterizes those profound thinkers, our interesting fellow-citizens of the Liberty Party, and who still venture, in these enlightened days, to cite the word of God—whoso sheddeth man's blood, by man shall his blood be shed. In the present condition of society, when there are so very few of us, who do not feel, that we are wise above what is written, this precept, delivered by God Almighty, to Noah, appears exceedingly preposterous, greatly resembling some of those *blue laws*, which were in operation, in the olden time, in a sister state. What was Noah to Jeremy Bentham! Although I am pained to confess the shortcomings of Jeremy; for, though he did much to meliorate the severity of the British penal code, he went not, by any means, to those happy lengths, which we approve, in shielding the unfortunate murderer from the halter.

There was a very amiable, old gentleman in England, who lived, through the times of Charles I., both Cromwells, and Charles II. He was reputed so wise, and learned, and just, and pious, that his judgment was highly prized, by all men. He was esteemed the greatest lawyer and the most upright, in all England; so much so, that, in 1671, he was created Lord Chief Justice of the realm. I desire to reason impartially, upon this subject, and therefore admit, that this great and good man, Sir Matthew Hale, believed death to be a very just punishment, for certain crimes, inferior to murder. Although Sir Matthew's crude notions are rapidly going out of fashion, it is but fair, to transcribe his words—"When offences grow enormous, frequent, and dangerous to a kingdom or state, destructive or highly pernicious to civil societies, and to the great insecurity and danger of the kingdom or its inhabitants, severe punishment and even death itself is necessary to be annexed to laws, in many cases, by the prudence of lawgivers." In all candor, we must admit, that Sir Matthew Hale was notoriously the very reverse of a sanguinary Judge. But Sir Matthew's days were the days of small things. We cannot sufficiently bless the Great Disposer of human affairs, for raising up the foolish, as He has done, in these latter days, and in such great numbers withal, to confound the wise. It is now no longer necessary, as of old, to pursue a particular course of study, to qualify mankind, for the work of legislation, or the practice of law, or physic, or the exposition of the more subtle points of religion, or ethics, or political economy.

This truly is an age of intuition. He, who learns, or half learns, one profession, is, instanter, competent to perform the duties of all. It is a heavenly stream of universal light and power, somewhat analogous to the miraculous gift of tongues. Nothing, in this connection, is more remarkable, than the rapid turgescence of every man's confidence, in his own abilities, upon the slightest encouragement, from his neighbor. There has been scarcely a blacksmith in New England, since the remarkable and merited success of Elihu Burritt, who, if you ask his opinion of the efficacy of pennyroyal for the stomach-ache, will not, with your permission, of course, prescribe for any acute or chronic complaint, with which you are afflicted. Tailors, in full measure, nine to a man, will readily solve you a point of theology, which would have been fearfully approached, by Tillotston or Horne. And, upon this solemn subject of capital punishment, there is scarcely a man-midwife in the land, who is not ready, with his instruments, to deliver the community of all their scruples at once.

This, certainly, is a blessed condition of things, for which we cannot be sufficiently thankful.

That we may do abundant justice to our opponents, I propose to offer, in this place, a quotation from the Edinburgh Review, vol. 86, p. 216. The article is entitled—*"What is to be done with our criminals?"* The passage runs thus—"Another circumstance, which renders legislation on this subject peculiarly difficult, is the lamentably perverted sentimentality, which is extensively diffusing itself among the people, and which may soon render it problematical, whether any penal code, really calculated to answer its objects, can be devised; a sentimentality, which weeps over the criminal, and has no tears to spare for the miseries he has caused—which transforms the felon into an object of interest and sympathy, and forgets the innocent sufferers from his cruelty or perfidy. So far as pity for the criminal is consistent with a more comprehensive compassion for those he has wronged, and is limited by the necessity of obtaining them redress and providing for the safety of society—so far as it prompts to a desire to see the statute-book cleared of every needless severity, and that no punishments shall be inflicted for punishment's sake it is laudable.

"But we must, with regret, profess our belief, that it has often far transcended these limits; and has exhibited itself in forms and modes, which, if permitted to dictate the tone of our criminal legislation, would tend to the rapid increase of crime. The people in question belong to a class, always numerous, who are led by the imagination, and not by their reason—by emotion rather than reflection. They see the felon in chains, and they are dissolved in commiseration; they do not stop to realize all the miseries, which have at last made *him* miserable—perhaps, in the present apathy of his conscience, much less miserable than many of those whom he has injured."

This is from an article, ably written, of some fifty-eight pages, published in 1847. I give it a place here, lest I should be suspected of suppressing all arguments, on the other side.

The idea of hanging a murderer, by form of law, instead of placing him for a few years, in some *anxious seat*, the treadmill or the state prison, where he might be converted perhaps—cutting him off, in the midst of his days, without time allowed for repentance, is a terrible thing. I am perfectly aware, that it will be replied—this is the very thing which he did for his wretched victim.

We are told, that the highest penalty known to the law is demanded. *All that a man hath will he give for his life*; and we are opposed, in our humane endeavors, by the scriptural edict referred to already. It is averred to be an all-important object in capital punishment, to operate upon the fears of others, *ut metus*, as we said before, *ad omnes perveniat*, which would be less likely to be the case, if the halter were abolished. It is true, that, while there is life, there is hope—hope of pardon; hope even of a natural and less horrible death; a fond, fearful hope of cutting the keeper's throat, and escaping from thraldom! How truly the poor murderer deserves our compassion!

What a revolting spectacle this hanging is! Here, however, I confess, the answer is complete—nobody, but the functionaries, is suffered to see it. It is much less of an entertainment, than it was, in the days of George Selwyn, who was in the habit of feeing the keeper of Newgate, for due notice of every execution, and a reservation of the best seat, nearest the gallows. It has been said, that hanging has become more unpopular, since it ceased to be a public amusement. It may be so—I rather doubt it.

In former times, there were very few inexpensive public amusements, in Boston, beside the Thursday lectures; and a hanging has always been highly attractive, in town and country. I well remember, not very many years ago, while riding into the city, in my chaise, having been compelled to halt, and remain at rest, for twenty minutes, in Washington, near Pleasant Street, while the immense mass of men, women and children rushed by, on their way to the execution of an Irishman, which took place at the gallows, near the grave-yard, on the Neck. The prisoner was in an open barouche, dressed in a blue coat and gilt buttons, white waistcoat, drab breeches, and white top boots, and his hair was powdered. He was accompanied by Mr. Larrassy, the Catholic priest, and the physician of the prison.

During the afternoon of July 30, 1794, on the morning of which day the great fire occurred in Boston, three pirates, brought home in irons, on board the brig Betsey, Captain Saunders, belonging to Daniel Sargent, were hung on the Common; and three governors, sitting in their chairs, would not have drawn half the concourse, then and there assembled.

No. LI

"Thy Clarence he is dead that stabb'd my Edward;
And the beholders of this tragic play
Untimely smothered in their dusky graves."

There were no humane and gentle spirits, in those days of old, to speak soft words of comfort in the ears of murderers and midnight assassins. Poor fellows! after they had let out the last drop of blood, in the hearts of their innocent victims, and reduced wives to widowhood, and children to orphanage—after the parricide had plunged the dagger in his father's heart—after the husband had murdered her, whom he had sworn, under the eye of God, to love and to cherish—after the wife, with the assistance of her paramour, had stealthily administered the poisonous draught to her confiding husband—they were respectively indicted—arraigned—publicly and deliberately tried—abundantly defended—and, when duly convicted at last, they were hanged, forsooth, by their necks, till they were dead!

Merciful God! where were the Marys and the Marthas! Was there no political lawyer, in those days, whom the desire of personal aggrandizement could induce to befriend the poor, afflicted cut-throat, by which parade of philanthropy he might ride into notice, as the patriot of the Anti-capital-punishment party! Was there no tender-hearted doctor, whose leisure hours, neither few nor far between, might have been devoted to the blessed work of relieving the murderer, from the gallows, and himself, from the excruciating misery of nothing to do!

Truly we live in a tragi-comical world. During the late trial of John Brown, the other day, for the murder of Miss Coventry, at Tolland, in regard to which the jury could not agree, a requisition arrived from the Governor of New York, for the prisoner, to answer, for the murder of Mrs. Hammond.—Dr. V. P. Coolidge, who murdered Matthews, at Waterville, committed suicide in prison, a few days since.—A precocious boy, eight years old, has, this month, chopped off the head of his sleeping father, with an axe, in the town of Lisle, N. Y.—Matthew Wood is to be hung in New York, June 22, for the murder of his wife.—Alexander Jones is to be hung, in the same State, on the same day, for arson.—Goode is to be hung here, in a few days.—On the 27th day of the last month, a man, named Newkirk, near Louisville,

Kentucky, shot and killed his mother, near one hundred years of age.—On the third day of the present month, Mr. Carroll, near Philadelphia, murdered his lady, by choking and pitching her down stairs.—J. M. Riley is to be hung, June 5, for the murder of W. Willis, in Independence, Tennessee.—Vintner is under sentence of death, for murdering Mrs. Cooper, in Baltimore.—Elder Enos G. Dudley is to be hung, in New Hampshire, May 23, for the murder of his wife.—The wife of John Freedly, of Philadelphia, is now in jail, for helping her husband, to murder his first wife.—Pearson is now in prison, under charge of murdering his wife and twin daughters, at Wilmington, in this Commonwealth, in April last.—Mrs. McAndrew has been convicted of murder, for killing her sister-in-law, in Madison, Mississippi.—Elisha N. Baldwin is to be hung, June 5, for the murder of his brother-in-law, Victor Matthews, at St. Louis.—The girl, Blaisdell, is to be hung, in New Hampshire, Aug. 30, for poisoning a little boy, two and a half years old. She was on trial for this act only. She had previously poisoned the child's grandmother, her friend and protectress, and subsequently attempted to poison both its parents. This *"misguided young lady"* was engaged to be married, and wanting cash, for an outfit, had forged the note of the child's father, for four hundred dollars.

Of Wood's case I know little more, than that he murdered his wife. Surely he is to be pitied, poor fellow. The case of Elder Enos is deeply interesting. This worthy Elder took his partner out, to give her a sleigh-ride, in life and health, and brought home her lifeless body. She had knocked her head against a tree—such, indeed, was the opinion, expressed by Elder Enos. He was also of opinion that it was not good for an Elder to be alone, for one minute; and he exhibited rather too much haste, perhaps, in taking to himself another partner. The jury were unanimously of opinion, that Elder Enos was mistaken, and that Mrs. Dudley came to her death, by the hands of Elder Enos himself. The Elder and the jury differed in opinion; and therefore, forsooth, Elder Enos must be hanged by the neck till he is dead! How much better to change this punishment, for perpetual imprisonment— and that, after a few years of good behavior, upon a petition, subscribed by hundreds, who care not the value of a sixpence, whether Elder Enos is in the State Prison, or out of it, for a pardon. Then the church will again be blessed with his services, as a ruling Elder; and the present Mrs. Dudley may herself be favored with a sleigh-ride, at some future day.

The case of the *"misguided"* Miss Blaisdell is truly affecting. It is quite inconceivable how the people of New Hampshire can have the heart to hang such an interesting creature by the neck, till she is dead. I am of opinion, that the remarks, with which Judge Eastman prefaced his sentence, must have hurt Miss Blaisdell's feelings. It seems that she only made use of the little innocent, as æronauts employ a pet balloon, to try the wind. She wished to ascertain, if her poison was first proof, before she tried it, upon the parents. Although it had worked to perfection, upon the old lady, Miss Blaisdell, who appears to have acted with consummate prudence, was not quite satisfied of its efficacy, upon more vigorous constitutions. It is quite surprising, that Judge Eastman should have talked so unkindly to Miss Blaisdell, in open court—"*An experiment is to be made; the efficiency of your poison is to be tried; and the helpless innocent boy is selected. He is left in your care, with all the confidence of a mother. He plays at your feet, he prattles at your side. You take him up, and give him the fatal morphia; and, when you see him sicken and dizzy, and stretching out his little arms to his mother, and trying to walk, your heart relents not. May God soften it.*" What sort of a Judge is this, to harrow up the delicate feelings of "*a misguided young lady*" after this fashion!

It has been proposed, by a medical gentleman, whose philanthropy has assumed the appearance of a violent eruption, breaking out in every direction, that, if this abominable punishment, this destruction of life, which God Almighty has prescribed, in the case of murder, must continue to be inflicted, the "*misguided young ladies*" and "*unfortunate men,*" who commit that crime, shall be executed under the influence of ether. This may be considered the happiest suggestion of the age. A tract may be expected from the pen of this gentleman, ere long, entitled "Crumbs of comfort for Cut-throats, or Hanging made easy." Jeremy Bentham gave his body to be dissected, for the good of mankind. Oh, that this worthy doctor, who has struck out this happy thought of hanging, under the influence of ether, would *verify the suggestion*!

There are some individuals, who had rather be hanged, than talked to, in such an unfeeling manner, as Judge Eastman talked to the unfortunate and misguided Miss Blaisdell: it has therefore been decided to improve, upon the suggestion of hanging murderers, under the influence of ether; and we propose to apply for an act, authorizing the sponge to be applied to the nostrils of the condemned, by the clerk *ex officio*, during the time, when the judge is pronouncing the sentence. The time of the murderer is short, and there are many little comforts, and even delicacies, which would greatly tend to soften the rigor of his imprisonment. We have it, upon the testimony of more than one experienced keeper of Newgate, that, with some few exceptions, the appetite of the misguided, who are about to be hanged, is remarkably good.

I fully comprehend the objections, which will be made to the use of ether, and granting such other little indulgences, to those, who are about to be sentenced, or are already condemned to be hanged. The Ciceronian argument,—*ut metus ad omnes perveniat*, will be neutralized. How many, it will be said, are now upon the earth, without God in this world, without the least particle of religious sensibility, disappointed men, desperate, degraded, men of utterly broken hopes, broken hearts, and broken fortunes, to whom nothing would be more acceptable, than an easy transition from this wide-awake world of pain and sadness to that region of negative happiness, which they anticipate, in their fancied state of endless oblivion beyond. They may be, nevertheless, disturbed, in some small degree, *in articulo*, by that indestructible doubt, which hangs over the mind, even the mind of the most sceptical, and deepens and darkens as death draws near, —suppose there should be a God! —what then! They are therefore unwilling to cut their own throats, however willing to cut the throats of other people. But, if the State will take the responsibility, and furnish the ether, there are not a few, who would very complacently embrace the opportunity.

That fear, which it is desirable to keep before the eyes of all men, say our opponents, is surely not the fear of the easiest of all imaginable deaths—the fear of meeting, not the King of terrors, but the very thing, which all men pray for, a placid exit from a world of care—a welcome spirit—an *etherial* deliverer. On the contrary, we wish, say they, to hold up to the world the fear of a terrible, as well as a shameful death: and we desire to give a certainty to this fear, which we cannot do, while the frequent exercise of the power of commutation and of pardon teaches that portion of our race, which is fatally bent upon mischief, that the gibbet is nothing but a bugbear; and that, let them commit as many murders, as they will, there is not one chance, in fifty, of their coming to the gallows, at last.

It is not easy to answer this argument, upon the spur of the moment; and it has been referred to a committee of our society, with instructions to prepare a reply, in season for the next execution.

We have the satisfaction of knowing, that no efforts have been spared by us, to save Washington Goode, one of the most interesting of murderers, from the gallows. We have endeavored to get up an excitement in the community, by posting placards, in numerous places—"a man to be hanged!" By this we intended to put an execution upon the footing of a puppet-show or play, and thereby to excite the public indignation. But, most unfortunately, there is too much common sense among the people of Boston, and too little enthusiasm altogether, for the successful advancement of our philanthropic views. However, importunity, if we faint not, will certainly prevail. The right of petition is ours. Let us follow, in the steps of Amy Darden and William Vans. The Legislature, at their last session, indefinitely postponed the consideration of the subject of the abolition of capital punishment. The Legislature is made of flesh and blood, and must finally give way, as a matter of course.

It cannot be denied, that gentlemen make use, occasionally, of strange arguments, while opposing our efforts, in favor of those *misguided* persons, who *unfortunately* commit rape, treason, arson, murder, &c. A few years since, when a bill was before our House of Representatives, for the abolition of capital punishment, in the case of rape, while it was proposed to retain it in the case of highway robbery—"Let us go home, Mr. Speaker," exclaimed an audacious orator, "and tell our wives and our daughters, that we set a higher value upon our purses, than upon the security of their persons, from brutal violation."

No. LII

To my anonymous correspondent who inquires, through the medium of the post-office, in what respect my "dealings with extortioners" can fairly be entitled *"dealings with the dead,"* I reply, because they are *alive* unto sin, and *dead* unto righteousness.

In Lord Bacon's Life of Henry VII., London edition of 1824, vol. v. 51, the Lord Chancellor Morton says to the Parliament—"His Grace prays you to take into consideration matters of trade, as also the manufactures of the kingdom, and to repress the bastard and barren employment of moneys to usury and unlawful exchanges, that they may be, as their natural use is, turned upon commerce, and lawful, and royal trading." Henry VIII. came to the throne, in 1509, and the rate of interest was fixed, in 1545, the 37th of that king's reign; and that rate was ten per cent. per annum. Before that time, no Christian was allowed to take interest for money; and the Jews had the matter of usury, all to themselves. It was shown, before Parliament, that, in 1260, two shillings was the rate, demanded and given, for the loan of twenty shillings for one week; and Stowe states, that the people were so highly excited against the Jews, on account of their extortion, as to massacre seven hundred of them, in London, in 1262. In 1274, a law was passed, compelling every Jew, lending money on interest, to wear a plate on his breast, signifying, that he was an usurer, or to quit the realm. What an exhibition we should have, in State Street, and the alleys, if this edict should be revived, against those, whose uncircumcision would avail them nothing, to disprove their Levitical propinquity.

In 1277, two hundred and sixty-seven Jews were hung, in London, for clipping the coin. Their usurious practices, at last, so highly exasperated the nation, that, according to Rapin, Lond., 1757, vol. iii. 246, 15,000 were banished the realm, in 1290. They had obtained great privileges from King Edward; but, says Rapin, "lost all these advantages, by not curbing their insatiable greediness of enriching themselves, by unlawful means, as usury, &c." I find Sir Edward Coke denies the fact of their banishment. His version is this: "They were not banished, but their usury was banished, by the statute, enacted in this parliament, and that was the cause they banished themselves into foreign countries, where they might live by their usury;

and because they were odious to the nation, that they might pass out of the realm in safety, they made a petition to the king, that a certain day might be prefixed for them to depart the realm, that they might have the king's writ to his sheriffs, for their safe conduct." 2d Institute, 507. Hume, nevertheless, Oxford ed., ii. 210, reaffirms the statement of Rapin.

Hume says, ibid., the practice of usury was afterwards carried on, "by the English themselves upon their fellow-citizens, or by the Lombards and other foreigners;" and he adds—"It is very much to be questioned, whether the dealings of these new usurers were equally open and unexceptionable with the old." Perhaps it may be questioned, whether the community would not fare better, at the present day, if some of the circumcised could be imported hither, from the Jews' Quarter, in Istampol. The following remark of Hume, on the same page, is of importance to the political economist:— "But as the canon law, seconded by the municipal, permitted no Christian to take interest, all transactions of this kind must, after the banishment of the Jews, have become more secret and clandestine, and the lender, of consequence, be paid both for the use of his money, *and for the infamy and danger, which he incurred by lending it.*" This is not from Aristotle, nor one of the school divines, but from David Hume, whose liberality is sufficiently notorious.

The English usurers, in those days, were more excusable, because they were not permitted to take *any interest whatever*, for the loan of money, while money lenders here have not the same excuse for being usurers, as they may lawfully take six per cent. per annum, or one per cent. above the legal rate of Great Britain, as established in 1714, the 13th of Queen Anne, and which has remained unaltered, to the present day.

I have heard of a fellow, who, upon being asked, after conviction of larceny, if he did not regret his conduct, replied, with an air of great sincerity, that he certainly did—for, instead of stealing a few pieces of gold, as he had done, he might easily have stolen enough, to bribe the court and jury. The Jews were wiser in their day and generation—they never suffered themselves to be placed in a predicament, which might cause them to suffer from any such regret. For many years, there subsisted a delightful understanding, between them and Edward I. Longshanks. Longshanks granted them many and various indulgencies; by his permission, they even had a synagogue in London. On their part, they were willing to relieve the necessities of Longshanks. In short, Longshanks was, vicariously, and upon the principle, that *qui facit per alium facit per se*, the very Apollyon of all usurers. He countenanced the extortion of the Jews, and shared the spoils. Sir Edward Coke, in his Second Institute, 506, states that, in seven years, covering portions of the reigns of Henry III. and Edward I., the Crown had four hundred and twenty thousand pounds, fifteen shillings, and four pence from the Jews.

After treating of the advantages and disadvantages of taking interest, on money loans, and arriving at the sensible conclusion, that it is impossible for society to get along without them, Lord Bacon remarks, ii. 354—"Let usury (the term for interest in those days) in general be reduced to five in the hundred, and let the rate be proclaimed to be free and current: and let the State shut itself out to take any penalty for the same. This will preserve borrowing from any stop or dryness. This will ease infinite borrowers in the country, &c." Lord Bacon was therefore in favor of an universal rate of interest, established by law. Of usury, in the opprobrious sense of the word, the taking of excessive and unlawful interest, this great man speaks in his tract on Riches, ii. 340, in no very complimentary terms—"Usury is the certainest means of gain, though one of the worst, as that whereby a man doth eat his bread, in *sudore vultus alieni*," by the sweat of another's brow.

I have heard it said of a rural governor of Massachusetts, now sleeping with his fathers, that, although addicted to the practice of virtual usury, he scrupulously abstained from lending money, at any rate, beyond six per cent. It became a by-word, in his district, however, when a farmer became straitened for a little money, and was inquiring among his neighbors—*that it was quite likely his excellency might have a yoke of cattle, that he did not care to winter over!* The cattle were sold at a high price to the needy man, who sold them forthwith, at auction, or otherwise, for a small one, giving the worthy governor his note in payment, and a mortgage on his farm, if required. The note was payable in six months, or a year, with "lawful interest."

This moral manœuvre appears to have been of ancient origin. There is the draught of a law for the punishment of it, in Lord Bacon's works, iv. 285. The preamble runs thus—"Whereas it is an usual practice, to the undoing and overthrowing of many young gentlemen and others, that where men are in necessity, and desire to borrow money, they are answered, that money cannot be had, but that they may have commodities sold unto them, upon credit, whereof they may make money, as they can: in which course it ever comes to pass, not only that such commodities are bought at extreme high rates, and sold again far under foot, at a double loss; but also that the party which is to borrow, is wrapt in bonds and counter bonds; so that upon a little money, which he receiveth, he is subject to penalties and suits of great value." Then follows the statute, taking away legal remedy, and punishing the broker or procurer with six months' imprisonment, and the pillory.

It has been commonly understood, that, before the act of 37th Henry VIII., though Christians were forbidden to take any interest for money, the Jews were not restrained; yet Lord Chief Baron Hale, Hard. 420, says that Jewish usury was forbidden, at common law, being forty per cent. and upwards, per annum, but no other. Lea, C. J., Palm. 292, says, that the usury, condemned at common law, was the *"biting usury"* of the Jews. To comprehend this expression, it must be understood, that, among the Jews, of old, there were two Hebrew words, signifying *usury, terebit,* which meant simply *increase,* and *Neshec,* which meant *devouring* or *biting usury.* Of this distinction, an account may be found in Calmet, vol. iii. Fragment 46.

When the statute of James I. was passed, in 1623, reducing the rate from ten to eight per cent., Orde says, in his Law of Usury, p. 5, that the Bishops "would not, at first, agree to it, for the sole reason, that there was no clause that disgraced usury, as in former statutes; and then the clause at the end of that statute was added, for their satisfaction." Usury was punished more severely in France, than in England. For the first offence, the usurer "was punished by a public and ignominious acknowledgment of his offence, and was banished. His second offence was capital, and he was hanged." Coke's 3d Institute, 152.

No. LIII

Our society, whose object is nothing less than the entire and unqualified abolition of capital punishment, have derived the greatest advantage, from an ample recognition of the rights of women—not only by a free participation of counsel with the softer sex, after the example of certain other societies, the value of whose services can never be understood, by the present generation; but by assigning equally to both sexes, all offices of honor and trust. We have adhered to this principle, with the most perfect impartiality, in the composition of our committees. Thus, our committee, for visiting the condemned, consists of the Rev. Mr. Puzzlepot, and the five Miss Frizzles—the committee on public excitement, prior to an execution, consists of Dr. Omnibus, Squire Farrago, Mrs. Pickett, and her daughters, the Misses Patience and Hopestill Pickett. In like proportion, all our committees are constructed.

We think proper, in this public manner, to express our warmest acknowledgments to Mrs. Negoose, Madam Moody, and Squire Bodkin, for their able report, on the iniquity of presumptive or circumstantial evidence. The notes, appended to this report, are invaluable—their authorship cannot be mistaken—every individual, acquainted with the peculiar style of the gifted author, will recognize the powerful hand of the justly celebrated Mrs. Folsom.

This committee are of opinion, that, under the show or pretence of punishing murder, our legal tribunals are constantly committing it. They *presume*, forsooth, that is, they guess, that the prisoner is guilty, and therefore take the awful responsibility of hanging him by the neck, till he is dead! This, says Mrs. Negoose, is *presumption* with a vengeance.

The committee refer to the statement of Sir Matthew Hale, as cited by Blackstone, iv. 358-9, that he had known two cases, in which, after the accused had been hung for murder, the individuals, supposed to have been murdered, had re-appeared, in full life. Upon this, the committee reason, with irresistible force and acumen. How many judges, say they, there have been, since the world began, we know not. *Two cases*, in which innocent persons were executed, on presumptive or circumstantial evidence, are proved to have occurred, within the knowledge of *one judge*. It is reasonable, say the committee, to conclude that, at a moderate calculation, *three cases* more, remaining undiscovered, occurred within the jurisdiction of that *one judge.* Now, we have nothing to do, but to ascertain the number of judges, who have ever existed, and then multiply that number by *five*; and thus, say the committee, "by the unerring force of figures, which cannot lie, we have the sanguinary result." "Talk not of ermine," exclaims Mrs. Negoose, the chairwoman of the committee, in a gush of scorching eloquence, "these blood-stained judges, gory with the blood of the innocents, let them be stripped of their ermine, and robed with the skins of wild cats and hyenas."

It has excited the highest indignation in the society, that Sir Matthew Hale, who has ever borne the name of a humane and upright judge, should have continued to decide questions, involving life, upon circumstantial evidence, after the cases, referred to above, had come to his knowledge, and in the very same manner, that he had been accustomed to decide them, in earlier times. Mrs. Moody openly expresses her opinion, that he was no better than he should be; and Squire Bodkin only wishes, that he could have had half an hour's conversation with Sir Matthew. The only effect, produced upon the mind of Sir Matthew Hale, by these painful discoveries, seems to have been to call forth an expression of opinion, that circumstantial evidence should be received with caution; and that, in trials for murder and manslaughter, no person should ever be convicted, till the body of the individual, alleged to have been killed, had been discovered.

An opinion, often repeated, as having been expressed by Chief Justice Dana, after the conviction of Fairbanks, for the murder of Miss Fales, at Dedham, in 1801, has frequently been a topic of conversation, among the members of our society, and Mrs. Negoose is satisfied, that if Chief Justice Dana expressed any such opinion, he must have been out of his head. Fairbanks was convicted and hung, on circumstantial evidence entirely. The concatenation, or linking together, of circumstances, in that remarkable case, was very extraordinary.

The sympathy for Fairbanks was very great, and began to exhibit itself, almost as soon, as the spirit had fled from the body of his victim. After his condemnation, his zealous admirers, for such they seemed to be, assisted him successfully, to break jail. He was retaken, on the borders of Lake Champlain; and, as the jail in Boston was of better proof, than the jail in Dedham, he was committed to the former. The genealogy of Fairbanks was shrouded in a sort of mystery. Ladies, of respectable standing, visited him, in his cell, and one, in particular, of some literary celebrity, in our days of small things, was supposed to have supplied him with a knife, of rather expensive workmanship, for the purpose of self-destruction. This knife was found upon his person, after her visits. There was no positive proof, to establish the guilt of Jason Fairbanks—not a tittle. Yet a merciless jury found him guilty, by a process, which our society considers mere *guess work*,—and after the execution, Judge Dana is reported to have said, that he believed Fairbanks murdered Miss Fales, more certainly, from the circumstantial evidence, produced at the trial, than if he had had the testimony of his own eyesight, at a short distance, in a dusky day. What sort of a Judge is this? cried Mrs. Negoose—sure enough, exclaimed Madam Moody.

I have no objection to give our opponents all the advantage, which they can possibly derive from a full and fair exposition of their arguments. When a witness, for example, swears, directly and unhesitatingly, that he saw the prisoner inflict a wound, with a deadly weapon, upon another person—that he saw that other person instantly fall, and die shortly after, this is *positive evidence of something*. Yet the act may be murder, or it may be manslaughter, or it may be justifiable homicide. Murder consists of three parts, the malice prepense, the blow inflicted or means employed, and the death ensuing, within a time prescribed by law. There can be no *murder*, if either of these parts be absent. Now, it is contended, by such as deem it lawful and right to hang the unfortunate, misguided, upon circumstantial evidence, that, however *positive* the evidence may be, upon the two latter points—the act done and the death ensuing—it is necessary, from the nature of things, in every case to depend on *circumstantial* evidence, to prove the malice prepense.

One or more of the senses enable the witness to swear positively to either of the two latter points. But the malice prepense must be *inferred*, from words, deeds, and *circumstances*. Upon this Dr. Omnibus sensibly observes, that this very fact proves the impropriety of hanging upon all occasions: and Mrs. Negoose remarks, that she is of the same opinion, on the authority of that ancient dictum, the authorship of which seems to be equally ascribed to Solomon and Sancho Panza—that *"circumstances* alter cases."

It is really surprising, that so grave and sensible a man, as Mr. Simon Greenleaf, should have made the remark, which appears vol. i., of his Treatise on Evidence,—*"In both cases* (civil and criminal) *a verdict may well be founded on circumstances alone; and these often lead to a conclusion far more satisfactory than direct evidence may produce."* Mr. Greenleaf refers, for illustration of this opinion, to the case of Bodine, N. Y. Legal Observer, vol. iv. p. 89, et seq. Lawyer Bodkin's work on evidence will, doubtless, correct this error.

Let us reason impartially. Compunction, in a dying hour, we cannot deny it, has established the fact, that innocent persons have been hung, now and then, upon *positive* evidence, the false witness confessing himself the murderer, *in articulo mortis*. Well, says Madam Moody, here is fresh proof of the great sinfulness of hanging.—To be sure.—But let our opponents have fair play. A. is found dead, evidently stabbed.—B. is seized upon suspicion.—C. heard B. declare he would have the heart's blood of A.—D. saw B. with a knife in his hand, ten minutes before the murder.—E. finds a knife bloody, near the place of the murder.—F. recognizes the knife as his own, and by him lent to B. just before the time of the murder.—G. says the size of the wound is precisely the size of the knife.—H. says, that, when he arrested B. his hand and shirt-sleeve were bloody.—I. says he heard B. say, just after the murder, "I've got my revenge." In the case supposed, C. D. E. F. G. H. and I. swear *positively*, each one to a particular fact. Here are seven witnesses. Here then is a chain of evidence, whereof each witness furnishes a single link. It is the opinion of Peake, Chitty, Starkie, Greenleaf, and all other writers, on the law of evidence, that this chain is often as strong or stronger, than it would be, were it fabricated by one man only. I will not deny, that Dr. Omnibus and Mrs. Negoose think differently.

An extraordinary example of circumstantial evidence, in a capital case, was related by Lord Eldon. A man was on trial for murder. The evidence against him, which was wholly circumstantial, was so very insufficient, that the prisoner, confident of acquittal, assumed an air of easy nonchalance. The officer, who had arrested the prisoner, and conducted the customary search, had exhibited, in court, the articles, found upon his person, at the time of his capture—a few articles of little value, and, among them, a fragment of a newspaper. The surgeon, who examined the body of the victim after death, produced the ball, which he had extracted from the wound, precisely as he found it. Enveloped in a wrapper of some sort, and with the blood dried upon it, it presented an almost unintelligible mass.

A basin of warm water was brought into court—the mass was softened— the wrapper carefully detached—it was the fragment of a newspaper, and fitted like the counterpart of an indenture to the fragment, taken by the officer from the prisoner's person. He was hung. Dear me! says Mrs. Negoose, what a pity!

I regret to learn from the late London papers, that Mr. Horace Twiss is recently dead. No one, I am confident, will fail to join in this feeling of regret, who has enjoyed, as I have done, the perusal of his truly delightful work, "The Public and Private Life of Lord Chancellor Eldon."

No. LIV

A pleasant anecdote is related by Nichols, of Dean Swift, who, when his servant apologized for not cleaning his boots, on a journey, because they would soon be dirty again, directed him to get the horses in readiness immediately: and, upon the fellow's remonstrance, that he had not eaten his breakfast, replied, that it was of little consequence, as he would soon be hungry again.

The American Irish are, undoubtedly, a very sweet people, when they are thoroughly washed; but they rarely think of washing themselves or their children—they are so soon dirty again. Hydrophobia is an Irish epidemic; and there are also some of the Native American Party, I fear, who have not been into water, since the Declaration of Independence.

When Peter Fagan applied to me, a few days since, to read for him a letter, from his cousin, Eyley Murphy, of Ballyconnel, in the county of Cavan, he was so insufferably filthy, that I gave him a quarter of a dollar, to be spent in sacrificing to the graces, that is, in taking a warm bath. While he was absent, I examined the letter; and found it to be a very interesting account of the execution of Fagan's fourth cousin, Rory Mullowny, for murder. As I thought its publication might be of importance here, at this time, I obtained Mr. Fagan's permission to place it before the community. I was, at first, disposed to correct the spelling, and give it rather more of an English complexion, but have, upon the whole, decided to publish it, as it is. Fagan tells me, that Eyley Murphy was the daughter of the hedge school-master, at Ballyconnel. The letter is written in a fair hand, and directed, "For Misther Pether Fagan, these—Boston, Capital of Amerriky."

Ballyconnel, Cavan, March 19, 1849.—Fagan dear, bad news and thrue for ye it is; Rory Mullowny, your own blood cousin o' the forth remove, by the mither's side, was pit up yestreen for the murther o' Tooley O'Shane, and there was niver a felly o' all that's been hung in Ballyconnel, with sich respictable attindance. The widdy Magee pit the divle into both the poor fellies, no more nor a waak arter the birril o' her forth husband, and so she kipt a flarting wid the one and the tither, till she flarted um out o' the warld this away.

Poor Rory—what a swaat boy he was—jist sax foot and fore inches in his brogans—och, my God! it's myself that wush'd I'd bin pit up along wid im. But he's claan gane now; whin we was childer togither how we used to gather the pirriwincles by the brook, and chase the fire-flaughts in the pasture o' a June evening—och my God—Pether—Pether—but there's no use waaping anyhow, so I'll be telling ye the shtory.

Poor Mullowny was found guilty o' what they call sircumstanshul ividunce. A spaach it was he made whin the cussid sherry was pittin im up, and he swore he died more innisent o' the crime nor the mither o' God, and he called God to witness what he sed. Himself it was that was rather hasty onyhow, in makin a confission to father Brian Bogle o' this very murther, and some other small mathers, a rape or too, may be, and sich like.

But the socyety that's agin pittin a body up—God bliss their sowls— they perswaded im to spaak at the gallows, and till the paaple how it was, and they rit im a spaach, in wich he toult 'em a body's last wull was the only wull that was gud in the law, and sure it was a poor body's last words and dyin spaach that was gud anunder the tree. And whin he had dun, the cursed divelsbird o' a sherry, wid a hart as coult as bog mud, swung im off in a minnit. It was himsilf was spaakin; and I jist pit my apurn to my face to wipe aff the saut wather, whin I heerd a shreek and a howl, louder and wilder nor ten thousand keenas at a birril, whin I lookd up and saw poor, daar Mullowny a swingin in the air. The like o' that yersilf niver saad, Pether Fagan, nor the mither that brot ye into this world o' care and confushon. The wimmin scraamed loud enuff to friten the little childer claan away in Ballymahon. The min swung their shillalies owr their heds. Father Brian Bogle was crossing himself, and a stone hurld by Jimmy Fitzgerald at the infarnal sherry, knocked father Bogle's taath down his throte. By the same token ye see, they was pit in for im the dee afore at considerable cost. Father Brian fell back, head foremost, ye see, on top o' Molly Mahoney's little bit table o' refrishments, and twas the wark o' a minnit.

Molly, who jist afore was wall to do in the warld, was a brukken marchant, immadiately, all claan gane; tumblers o' whiskey, cakes, custards, and cookies was all knocked in the shape o' bit o'chalk; and all the pennies she had took since bick o'dee—for more nor ten thousan was on the spot to see poor Rory pit up afore dee—was scattered and clutched up, by hunders o' little childher that was playing prop and chuck farding anunder the gallus. A jug o' buthermilk was capsized ower the widdy Magee's bran new dress, that was made for the hanging precesely, and ruinated it pretty considerably intirely. It was not myself that pittied the hussy—she to be there, as naar to the gallus as she could squaze hersel, and the very cause o' the dith o' poor Rory, and Tooley O'Shane into the bargin.

Och, Fagan, niver ye see was the likes o' it in Ballyconnel afore. Whin the sherry was for cuttin the alter and littin the corps o' poor, daar Mullowny down into the shell, that was all riddy below, the Mullownys swore they would have the body, for a riglar birrill, and a wake, and a keena, ye see—and the O'Shanes swore it should go to the risirictioners, to be made into a menotomy. Then for it, it was—such a cursin and swaring and howling—sich a swingin o' shillalies, sich a crackin o' pates, sich callin upon Jasus and the blissid mither, sich a scramin o' wimmin and childer, niver was herd afore in county Cavan. The sherry he gat on Molly Mahoney's little table to read the ryot act, and whin he opunt his mouth Phelim Macfarland flung a rottun egg atwaan his taath preceesly, and brot im to a spaady conclushon.

Poor Rory's vinrable oult mither was carried aff and murthered in the side o' the hid, wid a stone mint for the sherry, o' which she recovered diricly. They tried to kaap her quiet in her shanty, but she took on so gravous, that they let her attind the pittin up—poor ould sowl—she sed she had attinded the last moments o' her good man, and both her childer, Patrick and Pether, whin they wur pit up the same way, and it was not the like o' her to hart poor daar Rory's faalings onyhow.

Dolly Macabe was saved by a myrrikle, ye see. She took out wid her her siven childer, leading little Phelim by the hand, wid her babe at the brist, and hersilf in a familiar way into the bargin. She was knocked ower and trampled under the faat o' the fellies as was yellin and fitin, and stunted out o' her raason intirely. Only jist think o' it, Fagan daar, when she kim too, not one o' the childher was hart in the laast, nor Dolly naather; and the first thing she asked wos, whose was the two swaat babes, lyin together, and they toult her they war her own. Ye see, Patrick O'Shane and some more trod upon Dolly Macabe and hastened matters a leetle, and she was delivered o' twins, widout knowin anything about it. They gied her a glass o' whiskey, and O'Flaherty, the baker, pit the swaat babes in his brid cart, and Dolly, who priffird walking, wint home as well as could be expected. All the Macabes have ixcillint constitushons, and make no moor o' sich thrifles, than nothing at all.

But its for tellin the petiklars I'm writin. As I toult ye, twas about the widdy Magee. Rory toult more nor fifty, for a waak afore, that he'd have Tooley's hart's blood. When Tooley was found, it was ston ded he was, and his hed was bate all to paces, and Rory was o' tap o' im houltin im by the throte, wid a shillaly nigh by, covered wid blud, and the blood was rinnin out o' his eyes, and nose, and aars. Lawyer McGammon definded Rory, the poor unfortunit crathur, and he frankly admitted, that it was onlocky for him to be found jist that away, but he toult the jewry, that as he hoped for salvashun, Rory was an innysunt man, and he belaaved the foreman as guilty nor he. He brot half Ballyconnel to prove that Tooley was liable to blaad fraly at the nose, and was apt to have a rush o' blood to the hed, and he compared Rory to the good Summeritan, and sed he was there by the marest axidunt in the warld, and was tryin to stop the flow o' blud by houltin Tooley by the throte.

As to the bloody shillaly, McGammon brot more nor twenty witnesses, and ivery one a Mullowny, to sware it was more like Tooley's own shillaly nor two paas in a pud; and then he had three lunatic doctors, they call'd em, to prove that the O'Shane's were o' the silf-distructive persuashun. As to what Rory had sed about havin Tooley's hart's blud, lawyer McGammon provd that it was a common mode o' spakin in Ballyconnel and all owr the contree, among frinds and neybors, and thin he hinted, in a dillikit wey, that all the Mullownys wuld be after sayin that virry same thing o' the jewry, if thay brot Rory to the gallus by thair vardic, and that he was guilty o' nothin but circumstanshul ividunce. But the jewry brot in the poor felly guilty o' murther, and its all owr wid poor Rory.

It's no more I can rite—Your sister Betty Macnamarra has nine fine boys, at thraa births it is. From yours ever till the dee,

Eyley Murphy.

No impartial reader of Miss Eyley Murphy's letter will hesitate to pronounce Rory Mullowny an unfortunate man, and his case another example of the abominable practice of hanging innocent persons, upon circumstantial evidence.

No. LV

Poor Eli—as the old man was familiarly called by the Boston sextons of his time. He was a prime hand, at the shortest notice, in his better days. He has been long dead—died by inches—his memory first. For a year or more before his death, he was troubled with some strange hallucinations, of rather a professional character—among them, an impression, that he had committed a terrible sin, in putting so many respectable people under ground, who had never done him any harm. He said to me, more than once, while attempting to dissipate this film from his mental vision—"Abner, take my advice, and give up this wicked business, or you'll be served so yourself, one of these days." I was, upon one occasion, going over one of our farms, with the old man—the Granary burying-ground—and he flew into a terrible passion, because no grave had been dug for old Master Lovel!—the father. We tried to remind him, that Master Lovell, many years before, in 1776, had turned tory, and gone off with the British army; but poor old Eli was past conviction. He took his last favorite walk, among the graves on Copp's Hill, one morning in May—he there met a very worthy man, whom he was so fully persuaded he had buried, twenty years before, that he hobbled home, in the greatest trepidation, took to his bed, and never left it, but to verify his own suggestion, that we are all to be finally buried. During his last, brief illness, his mental wanderings were very manifest:—"Poor man—poor man"—he would mutter to himself—"I'm sure I buried him—deep grave, very—estate's been settled—his sons—very fast young men, took possession—gone long ago—poor weeping widow—married twice since—what a time there'll be—oh Lord forgive me, I'll never bury another." He was eighty-two then, and used to say he longed to die, and get among his old friends, for all, that he had known, were dead and gone.

A feeling, somewhat akin to this, is apt to gather about us, and grow stronger, as we march farther forward on our way, the numbers of our companions gradually lessening, as we go. Our ranks close up—those, with whom we stood, shoulder to shoulder, are cut down by the great leveller—and their places are filled by others. As we grow older, and the friends and companions of our earlier days are removed, we have a desire to do the next best thing—we cannot supply their places—but there are individuals—worthy people withal—whose faces have been familiar to our eyes, for fifty or sixty years—we have passed them, daily, or weekly—we chance to meet, no matter where—the ice is broken, by a mutual agreement, that it is very hot, or that it is very cold—very wet, or very dry—an allusion follows to the great number of years we have known each other, by name, and this results, frequently, in a relation, which, if it be not entitled to the sacred name of friendship, is not to be despised by those, who are deep in the valley:—out of such materials, an old craft, near the termination of its voyage, may rig up a respectable jury-mast, at least, and sail on comfortably, to the haven where it would be.

The old standard merchants, who transacted business, on the Long Wharf, Boston Pier, when I was a boy—are dead—*stelligeri*—almost every one of them; and, if all, that I have known and heard of them, were fairly told, it would make a very readable volume, highly honorable to many of their number, and calculated to operate, as a stimulus, upon the profession, in every age.

One little narrative spreads itself before my memory, at this moment, which I received from the only surviving son of the individual, to whom it especially refers. A merchant, very extensively engaged in commerce, and located.upon the Long Wharf, died February 18, 1806, at the age of 75, intestate. His eldest son administered upon the estate. This old gentleman used pleasantly to say, that, for many years, he had fed a very large number of the Catholics, on the shores of the Mediterranean, during Lent, referring to his very extensive connection with the fishing business. In his day, he was certainly well known; and, to the present time, is well remembered, by some of the "*old ones down along shore*," from the Gurnet's Nose to Race Point. Among his papers, a package, of very considerable size, was found, after his death, carefully tied up, and labelled as follows: "*Notes, due-bills, and accounts against sundry persons, down along shore. Some of these may be got by suit or severe dunning. But the people are poor: most of them have had fishermen's luck. My children will do as they think best. Perhaps they will think with me, that it is best to burn this package entire.*"

"About a month," said my informant, "after our father died, the sons met together, and, after some general remarks, our elder brother, the administrator, produced this package, of whose existence we were already apprized; read the superscription; and asked what course should be taken, in regard to it. Another brother, a few years younger than the eldest, a man of strong, impulsive temperament, unable, at the moment, to express his feeling, by words, while he brushed the tears from his eyes with one hand, by a spasmodic jerk of the other, towards the fireplace, indicated his wish to have the package put into the flames. It was suggested, by another of our number, that it might be well, first, to make a list of the debtors' names, and of the dates, and amounts, that we might be enabled, as the intended discharge was for all, to inform such as might offer payment, that their debts were forgiven. On the following day, we again assembled—the list had been prepared—and all the notes, due-bills, and accounts, whose amount, including interest, exceeded thirty-two thousand dollars, were committed to the flames."

"It was about four months after our father's death," continued my informant, "in the month of June, that, as I was sitting in my eldest brother's counting-room, waiting for an opportunity to speak with him, there came in a hard-favored, little, old man, who looked as if time and rough weather had been to windward of him, for seventy years. He asked if my brother was not the executor. He replied, that he was administrator, as our father died intestate. 'Well,' said the stranger, 'I've come up from the Cape, to pay a debt I owed the old gentleman.' My brother," continued my informant, "requested him to take a seat, being, at the moment, engaged with other persons, at the desk."

"The old man sat down, and, putting on his glasses, drew out a very ancient, leather pocket-book, and began to count over his money. When he had done—and there was quite a parcel of bank notes—as he sat, waiting his turn, slowly twisting his thumbs, with his old gray, meditative eyes upon the floor, he sighed; and I knew the money, as the phrase runs, *came hard*—and secretly wished the old man's name might be found, upon the forgiven list. My brother was soon at leisure, and asked him the common questions—his name, &c. The original debt was four hundred and forty dollars—it had stood a long time, and, with the interest, amounted to a sum, between seven and eight hundred. My brother went to his desk, and, after examining the forgiven list attentively, a sudden smile lighted up his countenance, and told me the truth, at a glance—the old man's name was there! My brother quietly took a chair, by his side, and a conversation ensued, between them, which I never shall forget.—'Your note is outlawed,' said my brother; 'it was dated twelve years ago, payable in two years; there is no witness, and no interest has ever been paid; you are not bound to pay this note, we cannot recover the amount.' 'Sir,' said the old man, 'I wish to pay it. It is the only heavy debt I have in the world. It may be outlawed here, but I have no child, and my old woman and I hope we have made our peace with God, and wish to do so with man. I should like to pay it'—and he laid his bank notes before my brother, requesting him to count them over. 'I cannot take this money,' said my brother. The old man became alarmed. 'I have cast simple interest, for twelve years and a little over,' said the old man. 'I will pay you compound interest, if you say so. The debt ought to have been paid, long ago, but your father, sir, was very indulgent—he knew I'd been unlucky, and told me not to worry about it.'

"My brother then set the whole matter plainly before him, and, taking the bank bills, returned them to the pocket book, telling him, that, although our father left no formal will, he had recommended to his children, to destroy certain notes, due-bills, and other evidences of debt, and release those, who might be legally bound to pay them. For a moment the worthy old man appeared to be stupefied. After he had collected himself, and wiped a few tears from his eyes, he stated, that, from the time he had heard of our father's death, he had raked, and scraped, and pinched and spared, to get the money together, for the payment of this debt.—'About ten days ago,' said he, 'I had made up the sum, within twenty dollars. My wife knew how much the payment of this debt lay upon my spirits, and advised me to sell a cow, and make up the difference, and get the heavy burden off my spirits. I did so—and now, what will my old woman say! I must get back to the Cape, and tell her this good news. She'll probably say over the very words she said, when she put her hand on my shoulder as we parted—*I have never yet seen the righteous man forsaken, nor his seed begging bread.*' After a hearty shake of the hand, and a blessing upon our old father's memory, he went upon his way rejoicing.

"After a short silence—taking his pencil and making a cast—'there,' said my brother, 'your part of the amount would be so much—contrive a plan to convey to me your share of the pleasure, derived from this operation, and the money is at your service.'"

Such is the simple tale, which I have told, as it was told to me.

No. LVI

*"Take heed that ye do not your alms before men, to be seen of them; otherwise ye
have no reward of your Father which is in Heaven. Therefore when thou doest thine
alms, do not sound a trumpet before thee, as the hypocrites do, in the synagogues,
and in the streets, that they may have glory of men. Verily I say unto you, they have
their reward. But when thou doest alms, let not thy left hand know what thy right
hand doeth. That thine alms may be in secret: and thy Father, which seeth in secret,
himself shall reward thee openly."*

This ancient word — *alms* — according to its derivative import,
comprehends not only those *oboli*, which are given to the wandering poor,
but all bestowments, great and small, in the blessed cause of charity.

In the present age, how limited the number, whose moral courage and
self-denial enable them to do their alms in secret, and without sounding
a trumpet, as the hypocrites do! How many, impatient of delay, prefer an
immediate reward — *to have glory of men* — rather than a long draft, upon far
futurity, though God himself be the paymaster!

The ability, to plan a magnificent, prospective charity, to provide the
means for its consummation, to preserve inviolate the secret of this high
and holy purpose, except from some confidential friend perhaps, until the
noble and pure-minded benefactor himself is beyond the reach of all human
praise — this is indeed a celestial and a rare accomplishment.

My thoughts have been drawn hitherward, by the public announcement
of certain testamentary donations of the late Theodore Lyman — ten
thousand dollars to the Horticultural Society — ten thousand dollars to
the Farm School — and fifty thousand dollars to the Reform School at
Westborough. The public have been long in doubt, who was the secret
patron of that excellent establishment, upon which he had previously
bestowed two and twenty thousand dollars. — While we readily admit, that,
in these unostentatious and posthumous benefactions, there is every claim
upon the grateful respect of the community — while we delight to cherish
a sentiment of reverence, for the memory of a good man, who would not
suffer the sound of his munificence to go forth, till he had descended to

that grave, where there is no device, nor work, and where his ears must be closed forever to the world's applause—still there are some, who, doubtless, will marvel at these magnificent, noiseless, and posthumous appropriations. With a very small portion of the amounts, bestowed upon these institutions, what glory might have been had of men, aye, and in his own life time! By distributing the aggregate into comparatively petty sums—by the exercise of rather more than ordinary vigilance and cunning, in the selection of fitting opportunities, what a reputation Mr. Lyman might have obtained! He would not only have been preceded, by the sound of a trumpet, but every penny paper would have readily converted itself into a penny trumpet, to spread the fame of his showy benefactions. His name would have been in every mouth—aye, and on every omnibus and engine. Add to all this a very small amount—a few hundred dollars, devoted to the procurement of plaster casts of himself, to be skilfully distributed, and verily he would have had his reward.

The Hon. Theodore Lyman is dead, and, today, my grateful and respectful dealings are with his memory. The practical benevolence of this gentleman has been well known to me, for years. There are quiet, unobtrusive charities, which are not likely to figure, in the daily journals, or to be known by any person, but the parties. For such as these I have occasionally solicited Mr. Lyman, and never in vain. On the other hand, there are individuals, whose names are forever before the public, in connection with some work, to be seen of men; but whose gold and silver, unless they are likely to glitter, *in transitu*, before the eye of the community, are parted with, reluctantly, if at all.

This great public benefactor, upon the present occasion, seems to have said, in the gentle, unobtrusive whisperings of his noble spirit—"A portion of that, which God has permitted me to gather, I believe it is my bounden duty to return, into the treasury of the Lord. This will I do. The secret shall remain, while I live, between God, who gives me this willing heart, and myself. And, when the world shall, at last, become unavoidably apprized of the fact, I shall have taken sanctuary in the grave, where the fulsome applause of the multitude can never reach me."

Between such apostolic charity as this, and certain flashy munificence, whose authors seem to be forever drawing drafts, at sight, and always *without grace*, upon the public, for fresh laudation—more votes of thanks— additional resolutions of all sorts of societies—and a more copious supply of vapid editorial adulation—between these, I say, there is all that real difference which exists, between the "gem of purest ray serene," and the wretched Bristol imitation—between the flower that blooms and sends abroad its perfume in secret, and that corruption whose veritable character can never be concealed; and I may be suffered to say, as truly as Jock Jabos of his professional relations, that one of my calling may be supposed to know something of corruption, by this time.

—— "My ear is pained,
My soul is sick with every day's report"

of *ad captandum* benefactions. Today, that generous benefactor, Mr. Pipkin, endows some village Lyceum, which is destined forever to glory in the euphonious name of Pipkin. Tomorrow our illustrious fellow-citizen, Mr. Snooks, presents a bell to some village church, and, the very next week, we are told, that the bell was cracked, while ringing peals in honor of the munificent Snooks. Even the Tonsons, whose ubiquity is a proverb, and whose inordinate relish for all sorts of notoriety surpasses their powers of munificence, are always in, for a pen'worth of this species of titillating snuff, at small cost.

The Hon. Theodore Lyman was born in Boston, in 1792. His father was Theodore Lyman, a shrewd, enterprising, and eminently successful merchant of this city. His mother's maiden name was Lydia Williams. She was a sister of Samuel Williams, the celebrated London Banker. The subject of this brief notice received his preparatory education, at Phillips Exeter Academy, under the charge of the venerable Dr. Abbott. He entered Harvard University in 1806, and took his degrees in the usual course.

In 1812, Mr. Lyman went to England, upon a visit to his maternal uncle, Mr. Williams, and, during his absence, travelled on the continent, with Mr. Edward Everett, visiting Greece, Palestine, &c., and remaining abroad, until 1816. He was in Paris, when the allied armies entered that city. Of this event he subsequently published an account, in a work, very pleasantly written, entitled *Three Weeks in Paris*.

In 1820, or very near that period, Mr. Lyman married Miss Mary Henderson of New York, a lady of rare personal beauty and accomplishments, who died in 1836. The issue of this marriage were three daughters and a son, Julia, Mary, Cora and Theodore. The two last survive. The elder children, Julia and Mary, in language of beautiful significancy, have "gone before."

Mr. Lyman published an octavo volume, on Italy, and compiled two useful volumes, on the Diplomacy of the United States with Foreign Nations. In 1834 and 1835, Mr. Lyman was Mayor of the City of Boston. He brought to that office the manners of a refined and polished gentleman; the independence of a man of spirit and of honor; a true regard for justice and the rights of all men; a lofty contempt for all time-serving policy; talents of a highly respectable order; a mind well stored and well balanced; and a cordial desire, exemplified in his own personal and domestic relations, and by his encouraging word and open hand, of promoting the best interests of the great temperance reform.

To the duties of this office, in which there is something less of glory than of toil, he devoted himself, during those two years, with great personal sacrifice and privation to those, whom he loved most. The period of his mayoralty was, by no means, a period of calm repose. Those years were scored, by the spirit of misrule, with deep, dark lines of infamy. Those years are memorable for the Vandal outrage upon the Ursuline Convent, and the Garrison riot; in which, a portion of the people of Boston demonstrated the terrible truth, that they were not to be outdone in fury, even by the most furious abolitionist, who ever converted his stylus into a harpoon, and his inkhorn into a vial of wrath.

Mr. Lyman, even in comparatively early life, filled the offices of a Brigadier and Major General of our Militia; and was in our Legislative Councils.

The temperament of Mr. Lyman was peculiar. Frigid, and even formal, before the world, he was one of the most warm-hearted men, among the noiseless paths of charity, and in the closer relations of life. I have sometimes marvelled, where he bestowed his keen sensibility, while going through the rough and wearying detail of official duty. In the spring of 1840 we met accidentally, at the South—in the city of Charleston. He was ill. His mind was ill at ease. He seemed to me, at that time, a practical illustration of the truth, that it is not good for man to be alone. Yet he had been long stricken then, in his domestic relation. His chief anxiety seemed to be about the health of his little boy. He told me, that he lingered there on his account. I never knew a more devoted father.

A gentleman, well-known to the community, by his untiring practical benevolence, to whom I applied for information, has sent me a reply, from which I must be permitted to extract one passage, for the benefit of the world—"I have known much of his benevolent acts, having been the frequent almoner of his bounty, with the injunction, '*Keep it to yourself.*' He often called, and spent one or two hours, to converse on temperance, and the poor, and would spend a long winter evening in my office, to learn of me what my situation enabled me to communicate, and always left a check for $50 or $100, to give to the Howard, or some other society. In the severe winter weather, I remarked that he would say, '*This weather makes one feel for the poor.*' He often sent his man with provisions to the houses of the destitute, and had a heart to feel for others' woe."

He has gone! But the memory of this good man shall never go! It shall be embalmed in the grateful tears of the reformed, from age to age. Thousands, now unborn, shall be snatched, like brands from the burning, through the agency of this heavenly charity; and, as they turn from the walls of this noble institution, in a moral sense, regenerate, they shall bless the name of their noble benefactor; and thus raise and perpetuate, to the memory of Theodore Lyman, the *monumentum ære perennius.*

No. LVII

It is scarcely credible, for what peccadilloes, life was forfeited, by the laws of England, within the memory of men, now living. One hundred and sixty offences, which may be committed by man, have been declared, by different acts of parliament, to be felony, without benefit of clergy; that is, punishable with death. It is truly wonderful, that, in the eighteenth century, it should have been a capital offence, in England, to break down the mound of a fish pond—to cut down a cherry tree in an orchard—or to be seen, for one month, in the company of those, who called themselves Egyptians.

We constantly refer to the laws of Draco, the Archon of Athens, as a code of unequalled cruelty; under whose operation, crimes of the highest order, and the most trifling offences, were punished, with equal severity. Draco punished murder with death, and he punished idleness with death. The laws of England punished murder with death, and they punished theft, over the value of twelve pence, with death. What is the necessity of going back to the time of Draco, 624 years before Christ, for examples of inhuman, and absurdly inconsistent legislation?

The Marquis of Beccaria, in his treatise, *De Delitti e Delle Pene*, seems to have awakened legislators from a trance, in 1764, by propounding the simple inquiry—*Ought not punishments to be proportioned to crimes, and how shall that proportion be established?* A matter, so apparently simple, seems not to have been thought of before.

Sir Samuel Romilly, Sir James Mackintosh, and Sir Robert Peel are entitled to great praise, for their efforts to soften and humanize the criminal code of Great Britain.

The distinction, between grand and petty larceny, was not abolished, until 1827, when, by the act 7th and 8th Geo. IV. chap. 29, theft was made punishable by transportation, or imprisonment and whipping. By this statute, robbery from the person, burglary, stealing in a dwelling-house to the value of £5, stealing cattle, and sheep-stealing are made punishable with death. So that the punishment was, even then, the same, for murdering a man, and stealing a sheep, or £5 from a dwelling-house. Death, by this statute, was also the punishment for arson, for setting fire to coal mines, and ships; and for riotously demolishing buildings or machinery.

In the following year, 1828, by the act 9th Geo. IV. ch. 31, death is made the punishment, for murder, maliciously shooting, cutting and maiming, administering poison, attempting to drown, suffocate, &c., and for rape and sodomy. By this act, more than fifty statutes, relative to offences against the person, are repealed.

The act 11th Geo. IV. and 1st Will. IV. ch. 66, passed in 1830, abolishes capital punishment, in all cases of forgery, excepting forgery of the royal seals, exchequer bills, bank notes, wills, bills of exchange, promissory notes, or money orders, transfers of stock, and powers of attorney. Death remained the penalty for all these forgeries, in 1830, and, for all other forgeries, transportation and imprisonment.

Two years after, in 1832, another step was taken. By 2d Will. IV. ch. 34, capital punishment was abolished, and transportation and imprisonment substituted, for all offences, relative to the coin. This was a prodigious stride.

This gave us a great hope, that misguided murderers might finally be suffered to live in security, at least, from the halter: for no object had been of greater moment with the British nation, than the coin of the realm, and the death penalty had often been exacted from those, who had dared to clip or counterfeit that sacred representative of majesty. The principle is well established, that men, who fly from one extreme, *in contraria currunt*. We trusted, therefore, that extremely lenient legislation would supervene, upon its very opposite.

We had great confidence in a system of "indefatigable teasing," as Butler calls it. In the same year, 1832, by 2d and 3d Will. IV. ch. 62, capital punishment was abolished, in cases of stealing from a dwelling-house to the value of £5, and sheep-stealing; and by the same act, ch. 123, capital punishment was abolished, in all cases of forgery, excepting in the cases of wills, and powers of attorney for stock.

In 1833, by 3d and 4th Will. IV. ch. 44, capital punishment was abolished in case of dwelling-house robbery; repealing so much of the larceny act of 1827.

Our good friends in England next thought it expedient to divest the process of hanging, of all its postmortuary terrors. I have heard of condemned persons, who expressed a greater horror, at the thought of being dissected, than of being hanged. It was deemed proper, therefore, to relieve the unfortunates, on this tender point. Accordingly, in 1834, by 4th Will. IV. ch. 26, dissecting murderers, and hanging them, in chains, were abolished.

It had been the law of England, that all persons returning, *sua sponte*, after transportation, should be hanged. But experience has shown how deep is the affection, which convicts bear to their former haunts, their native land. It is a perfect *nostalgia*. This law was therefore repealed, in 1834, by 4th and 5th Will. IV. ch. 67.

In 1835, by 5th and 6th Will. IV. ch. 33, sundry felonies, never before deemed bailable offences, were made so, notwithstanding the parties confessed themselves guilty.

Sacrilege and letter-stealing had long been capital offences in England. In the same year, they were no longer punished with death.

We had great hopes from Victoria. In 1837, 1 Vic. ch. 23, she began, by abolishing the pillory entirely;—and ch. 84, capital punishment is abolished, in all cases of forgery;—ch. 85, capital punishment is inflicted, for administering poison, or doing bodily injury with intent to mutilate; but other acts, with intent to murder, or maim, or disfigure, are punished with different degrees of transportation and imprisonment.—Ch. 86 takes away capital punishment, in burglary, unless accompanied with violence.—Ch. 87 takes away capital punishment, in case of robbery, unless attended with cutting or wounding. Ch. 88 leaves the punishment of death, transportation or imprisonment, to the discretion of the court, in case of piracy, where murder is attempted. Ch. 89 varies the laws of arson, making arson a capital offence, in regard to a dwelling-house, *any person being therein.*—Ch. 91 abolishes capital punishment in cases of riotous assemblies, seducing from allegiance, and certain offences against the revenue laws.

It is rather surprising, that there is such a general prejudice throughout the world, in favor of putting murderers to death. The Bible is an awful stumbling block, in this respect. We are also reminded that Solon, when he abolished the code of Draco, retained the punishment of death, in the case of murder. I have never thought much of Solon, since I became acquainted with this weak point in his character.

A writer in the Edinburgh Review, vol. 86, p. 217, speaking of death as the punishment for murder, observes—"The intense desire which now actuates a portion of the community, to get rid of capital punishment even for murder, may be taken as an indication of this excessive sensibility. The propriety of that punishment in the given case, would certainly appear to be distinctly sanctioned by that book, to which its opponents professedly appeal—by reason—and by the all but universal practice of nations. It is the only certain guarantee which society can have for the security of its members." Here we have it again—"that book"—the Bible. It cannot be denied that the Bible, or Solon, or Sir Matthew Hale, or somebody else, is everlastingly in the way of this and other modern, philanthropic movements.

What was Solon, in comparison with David Crockett—we are sure we are right, and why should we not go ahead?

For my own part, I have never been able to perceive the wisdom of attempting to conceal any of our prospective movements. Indeed, our future course must be sufficiently apparent, at a glance. When we have *agitated*, until capital punishment is abolished, and we have had a commemorative celebration, with emblematical banners, and an hundred guns on the Common, nothing will be further from our thoughts, than a dissolution, sine die. One of our chief arguments in favor of abolishing capital punishment, is the greater hardship of a life-long imprisonment. Availing of this argument, we shall be able to show, that we have placed these unfortunates, in a worse condition than before. A petition will be presented to the Governor and Council, from five thousand unhappy murderers, ravishers, house-burners, burglars and highway robbers—such we think will be the number, in a few years—representing their miserable condition, and respectfully requesting to be hanged, under the influence of ether or otherwise, as to the Governor and Council may seem fit. We shall then *agitate* anew, and endeavor, through public meetings and the press, to exhibit the barbarity of refusing their humble request.

This, we well enough know, will not be granted; and the only escape from the dilemma, will be to suffer them, to go at large, upon their parole of honor. It will not, of course, be expected, that this parole will be received from any, who cannot produce a certificate, under the hand of the warden, that they have committed no murder, rape, arson, burglary, or highway robbery, during the period of their confinement in the State Prison.

No. LVIII

The late Archbishop of Bordeaux, when Bishop of Boston, Dr. Cheverus, told me, that he had very little influence with his people, in regard to their extravagance at funerals. It is very hard to persuade them to abate the tithe of a hair, in the cost of a *birril*.

This post-mortuary profligacy, this pride of death, is confined to no age or nation of the world. It has prevailed, ever since chaos was licked into shape, and throughout all Heathendom and Christendom, begetting a childish and preposterous competition, who should bear off the corpses of their relations, most showily, and cause them to rot, most expensively.

This amazing folly has often required, and received, the sumptuary curb of legislation. I have briefly referred, in a former number, to the restraining edicts of the law-givers of Greece, and the laws of the Twelve Tables at Rome.

Even here, and among the earlier records of our own country, evidences are not wanting, that the attention of our worthy ancestors had been attracted to the subject of funereal extravagance. At a meeting, held in Faneuil Hall, October 28, 1767, at which the Hon. James Otis was the Moderator, the following resolution was passed: "*And we further agree strictly to adhere to the late regulations respecting funerals, and will not use any gloves but what are manufactured here, nor procure any new garments, upon such occasions, but what shall be absolutely necessary.*" This resolution was passed, *inter alia similia*, with reference to the Stamp Act of 1765, and as part of the system of non-importation.

There is probably no place like England—no city like London, for funereal parade and extravagance. The Church, to use the fox-hunting phrase, must be *in at the death*; and how truly would a simple funeral, without pageantry, in some sort—a cold, unceremonious burial, without mutes, and streamers, and feathers—without bell, book, or candle—flout and scandalize the gorgeous Church of England! The Church and the State are connected, so intimately and indissolubly connected, that he, who dies in the arms of Mother Church, must permit that particular old lady, in the matter of his funeral, to indulge her ruling passion, for costly forms and ceremonies.

It is more than forty years, since, with infinite delight, I first read that effusion—outpouring—splendid little eruption, if you like—of Walter Scott's, called Llewellyn. Apart from all context, a single stanza is to my present purpose; I give it from memory, where it has clung, for forty years:

> When a prince to the fate of a peasant has yielded,
> The tapestry waves dark, round the dim lighted pall,
> With scutcheons of silver the coffin is shielded,
> And pages stand mute in the canopied hall.
> Through the vault, at deep midnight, the torches are gleaming,
> In the proudly arched chapel the banners are beaming,
> Far adown the long aisle sacred music is streaming,
> Lamenting a chief of the people should fall.

In all this, the nobility ape royalty, the gentry the nobility, the commonalty the gentry: and there is no estate so low, as not, in this particular, to account the death of a near relative a perfect justification of extravagance.

There is scarcely one in a thousand, I believe, who has any just idea of the amount, annually lavished upon funerals, in Great Britain; or of the extraordinary fact, that joint stock burial companies exist there, and declare excellent dividends.

In 1843, at the request of her Majesty's principal Secretary of State, for the Home Department, Edwin Chadwick, Esquire, drew up "a report on the results of a special inquiry into the practice of interment, in towns."

Mr. Chadwick states, that, *upon a moderate calculation, the sum annually expended in funeral expenses, in England and Wales, is five millions of pounds sterling*, and that four of these millions may be justly set down as expended on the mere fopperies of death.

Evelyn says, that his mother requested his father, on her death bed, to bestow upon the poor, whatever he had designed, for the expenses of her funeral.

Speaking of this abominable misapplication of money, a writer, in the London Quarterly Review, vol. 73, p. 466, exclaims—"To what does it go? To silk scarfs and brass nails—feathers for the horses—kid gloves and gin for the mutes—white satin and black cloth for the worms. And whom does it benefit? Not those, whose unfeigned sorrow makes them callous, at the moment, to its show, and almost to its mockery—not the cold spectator, who sees its dull magnificence give the lie to the preacher's equality of death—but the lowest of all hypocrites, the hired mourner, &c." It is calculated by Mr. Chadwick, that £60 to £100 are necessary to bury an upper tradesman—£250 for a gentleman—£500 to £1500 for a nobleman.

High profits were obtained, by the joint stock burial companies in England, in 1843. The sale of graves in one cemetery was at the rate of £17,000 per acre, and a calculation, made for another, gave £45,375 per acre, not including fees for monuments, &c. One company, says Mr. Chadwick, has set forth an estimate, that seven acres, at the rate of ten coffins, in one grave, would accommodate 1,335,000—one million three hundred and thirty-five thousand—paupers. The following interrogatory was put, and repeated by members of the Parliamentary Committee, to the witnesses: "*Do you think there would be any objection to burying bodies with a certain quantity of quick lime, sufficient to destroy the coffin and the whole thing in a given time?*"

In 1843, Mr. J. C. Loudon published, in London, his work on the Managing of Cemeteries and the Improvement of Churchyards. The cool, philosophic style, in which Mr. Loudon handles this interesting subject, is rather remarkable. he expatiates, as follows: "*This temporary cemetery may be merely a field, rented on a twenty-one years' lease, of such an extent, as to be filled with graves in fourteen years. At the end of seven years more it may revert to the landlord, and be cultivated, planted, or laid down in grass, or in any manner that may be thought proper. Nor does there appear to us any objection to union workhouses having a portion of their garden ground used as a cemetery, to be restored to cultivation, after a sufficient time had elapsed.*"

This certainly is doing the utilitarian thing, with a vengeance. Quite a novel rotation of crops—cabbages following corpses. My long experience assures me, that the rapidity of decomposition depends, upon certain qualities in the subject and in the soil. Skeletons are sometimes found, in tolerably perfect condition, after an inhumation of two hundred years. Perhaps Mr. Loudon, in his eager festination for a crop, may have determined to bury in quicklime. Paupers and quicklime would make a capital compost, and scarcely require a top-dressing, of any kind, for years. What beets! what carrots, for the cockney market! Notwithstanding the quicklime, I should rather fear an occasional envelopment of some *unlucky* relic, in the guise of a *lucky* bone—a grinder, perhaps. And, when these vegetables shall again have been converted into animals, and these animals shall have served their day and generation, they shall again be converted into cabbages and carrots, as all their predecessors were. Well, this Mr. Loudon is a practical fellow; and his metastasis is admirable. Here are thousands of miserable wretches—*nullorum fiilii*, many of them—they have contributed scarcely anything to the common weal, while living; now let us put them in the way, with the assistance of a little quicklime, of doing something for their fellow-beings, after they are dead. The pauper squashes and cabbages must have been at a premium, in Leadenhall Market. Imagination is clearly worth something. After all my reason can accord, in the way of respect, for these utilitarian notions, I solemnly protest against marrowfats, cultivated in Mr. Loudon's pauper hotbeds. No doubt they would be larger, and the flavor richer and more peculiar—nevertheless, Mr. Loudon must excuse me—I say I protest. He gives an alternative permission, to lay down his mixture of dead bodies and quicklime to grass, or for the pasture of cows. Even then the milk would have a suspicious flavor, or *post-mortem* smell, I apprehend; it would be the same thing, by second intention, as the surgeons say.

The explanation of Mr. Loudon's monstrous proposition can be found nowhere, but in his concentrated interest in agriculture, to which he would have the living and the dead alike contribute. When contemplating the corpse of a portly pauper, he seems to think of nothing, but the readiest mode of converting it into cabbages.

I have heard of a cutaneous fellow, who had an irresistible fancy, for skinning animals—it had become a passion. Nothing came amiss to him. He sought with avidity, for every four-footed and creeping thing, that died within five miles of his dwelling, for the pleasure of skinning it. The insides of his apartments were covered with the expanded skins, not only of beasts and the lesser vermin, but of birds, serpents and fishes. His house was an exuvial museum. He had a little son, a mere child, who assisted his father, on these occasions, in a small way. He had the misfortune to lose his grandmother—a fine old lady—and the following brief colloquy occurred, between the father and the child, the day before she was buried: "I say, father." "What, Peter?" "When are you going to skin Granny?"

No. LIX

Last Sabbath morning, I read Cicero's *Dialogus de Amicitia*—simple Latinity, and very short—27 sections only. It seemed like enjoying the company of an old friend. It is now just forty-seven years, since I first read it, at Exeter. I marvel at Montaigne, for not thinking highly of it—but find some little motive, in the fact, that he had written a tract upon the subject, himself, which may be found, in his first volume, page 215, London, 1811, and which can no more be compared to the *Dialogus*, than—to use George Colman's expression—a mummy to Hyperion.

The Dialogus de Amicitia, of a Sabbath morning! Aye, my reverend, orthodox brother. Not having, in my system, one pulse of sympathy for disorganization, and liberty parties, I reverence the holy Sabbath, as much as you do yourself; and, to prevent the *Dialogus* from hurting me, I read one sermon before, and another immediately after—Jeremy Taylor's *Apples of Sodom*; and Fléchier's *Sur La Correction Fraternelle*—such sermons, as, in the concoction, would, perhaps, be very likely to burst your mental boiler, and which would not suit the appetites of many, modern congregations, who have ruined their powers of inwardly digesting such strong meat, by dieting upon theological *fricandises faites avec du sucre*.

And you was not at meeting then! Right again, my dear brother. I am deaf as a haddock; though Sir Thomas Browne has annihilated this favorite standard of comparison, by assuring us, that a haddock has as good ears, as any other fish in the sea. Mine, however, are quite unscriptural—ears not to hear. My ear is all in my eye.

Roscius boasted of his power to convey his meaning, by mute gesticulation. Our modern clergy have so little of this gift, that, with my impracticable ears, it is all dumb show for me. Now and then, when the wind is fair, I catch a word or two; and no cross-readings were ever more grotesque and comical, than my cross-hearings. I am convinced, that I do not always have the worst of it. When, in reply to an old lady, who once asked me how I liked the preacher, I told her I heard not a syllable—what a mercy! she exclaimed. But consider the example! True, there is something in that. Try the experiment—stop the *meatus auditorius* with beeswax, and try it, for half a dozen Sabbaths, even with the knowledge, that you can remove the impediment at will, which I cannot!

After I had finished the *Dialogus*, I found myself successfully engaged, in the process of mental exhumation:—up they came, one after another, the playmates of my childhood, with their tee-totums and merry-andrews— the companions of my boyhood, with their tops, kites, and marbles—the friends and associates of my youth, with their skates, bats, and fowling pieces. It is really quite pleasant to gather a party, upon such short notice, and with so little effort; and without the trouble of providing wine and sweetmeats. Upon the very threshold of manhood, how they scatter and disperse! There is a passage of the Dialogus—the tenth section—which is so true to life, at the present hour, that one can scarcely realize it was written, before the birth of Christ:—"Ille (Scipio) quidem nihil dificilius esse dicebat, quam amicitiam usque ad extremum vitæ permanere. Nam vel ut non idem expediret utrique, incidere sæpe; vel ut de republica non idem sentirent; mutari etiam mores hominum sæpe dicebat, alias adversis rebus, alias ætate ingravescente. Atque earum rerum exemplum ex similitudine capiebat incuentis ætatis, quod summi puerorum amores sæpe una cum prætexta ponerentur; sin autem ad adolescentiam perduxissent, dirimi tamen interdum contentione, vel uxoriæ conditionis, vel commodi allicujus, quod idem adipisci uterque non posset. Quod si qui longius in amicitia provecti essent, tamen sæpe labefactari, si in honoris contentionem incidissent: pestem esse nullam amicitiis, quam in plerisque pecuniæ cupiditatem, in optimis quibusque honoris certamen et gloriæ: ex quo inimicitias maximas sæpe inter amicissimos extitisse." Lord Rochester said, that nothing was ever benefited, by translation, but a bishop. This, nevertheless, I believe, is a fair translation of the passage—

He (Scipio) said, that nothing was more difficult, than for friendship to continue to the very end of life: either because its continuance was found to be inexpedient for one of the parties, or on account of political differences.

He remarked, that men's humors were apt to be affected, sometimes, by adverse fortune, and at others, by the heavy listlessness of age. He drew an example of these things, from a similar condition in youth—the most vehement attachments, among boys, were commonly laid aside with the prætexta, or at the age of maturity; or, if continued beyond that period, they were occasionally interrupted, by some contention about the state or condition of the wife, or the possessions or advantages of somebody, which the other party was unable to equal. Indeed, if some there were, whose friendship was drawn along to a later period, it was very apt to be weakened, if they became rivals, in the path of fame. The greatest bane of friendship, among the mass, was the love of money, and among some, of the better sort, the thirst for glory; by which the bitterest hatred had been generated, between those, who had been the greatest friends.

Unless it be orthodoxy, nothing has been so variously defined, as *friendship*. A man who stands by, and sees another murdered, in a duel, is his *friend*. Mutual endorsers are *friends*. Partisans are the *friends* of the candidate. Those gentlemen, who give their time and talents to eat and drink up some wealthy fool, who would pass for an Amphytrion, and laugh at the fellow's simplicity, behind his back, are his *friends*. The patrons of players and buffoons, signors and signorinas, are their *friends*. The venders of Havana cigars and Bologna sausages inform their *friends* and patrons, that they have recently received a fresh supply. Marat was the *friend* of the people. Eliphaz, Bildad, and Zophar were the *friends* of Job; and he told them rather uncivilly, I think, that they were miserable comforters. Matthew speaks of a *friend* of publicans and sinners.

Monsieur Megret, who, as Voltaire relates, the instant Charles XII. was killed, exclaimed—*Voila la piece finie, allons souper*—see, the play is over, let us go to supper, was the king's *friend*. William the First, like other kings, had many *friends*, who, the moment he died, ran away, and literally left the dead to bury the dead; of which a curious account may be found, in the Harleian Miscellany, vol. iii. page 160, London, 1809. Friendship flourishes, at Christmas and New Year, for every one, we are told, in the book of Proverbs, is a *friend* to him that giveth gifts. There seems to be no end to this enumeration of *friends*. The name is legion, to say nothing of the whole society of *Friends*. What then could Aristotle have meant, when he exclaimed, as Diogenes Laertius says he did, lib. v. sec. 21, *My friends, there is no such thing as a friend?* Menander is stated by Plutarch, in his tract, on Brotherly Love, cap. 3, to have proclaimed that man happy, who had found even *the shadow of a friend?*

It would be hard to describe the friend, whom Aristotle and Menander had in mind. Cicero has employed twenty-seven sections, and given us an imperfect definition after all. Such a friend comes not, within any one of the categories I have named.

Friends, in the common acceptation of that word, may be readily lost and won. The direction, ascribed to Rochefoucault, seems less revolting, when applied to such *friends* as these—*to treat all one's friends, as if, one day, they might be foes, and all one's foes, as if, one day, they might be friend*. This cold-blooded axiom is Rochefoucault's, only by adoption. Aristotle, in his Rhetoric, lib. ii. cap. 13, and Diogenes Laertius, in his life of Bias, lib. i. sec. 7, ascribe something like this saying to him. Cicero, in the sixteenth section of the *Dialogus de Amicitia*, after referring to the opinion—"*ita amare oportere, ut si aliquando esset ossurus*," and stating Scipio's abhorrence of the sentiment, expresses his belief, that it never proceeded from so good and wise a man, as Bias. Aulus Gellius, lib. i. cap. 3, imputes to Chilon, one of the seven wise men of Greece, substantially, the same sentiment—"*Love him, as if you were one day to hate him, and hate him, as if you were one day to love him.*" Poor Rochefoucault, who had sins enough to answer for, is as unjustly held to be author of this infernal sentiment, as was Dr. Guillotin of the instrument, that bears his ill-fated name.

Boccacio was in the right—*there is a skeleton in every house*. We have, all of us, our crosses to carry; and should strive to bear them as gracefully, as comports with the infirmity of human nature; and among the most severe is the loss of an old friend. Aristotle was mistaken—there is such a thing as a friend. Some fifty years ago, I began to have a friend—our professions and pursuits were similar. For some fifty years, we have cherished a feeling of mutual affection and respect; and, now that we have retired from the active exercise of our craft, we daily meet together, and, like a brace of veteran grasshoppers, chirp over days bygone. I believe I never asked of my friend an unreasonable or unseemly thing. God knows he never did of me. Thus we have obeyed Cicero's first law of friendship—*Hæc igitur prima lex in amicitia sanciatur, ut neque rogemus res turpes, nec faciamus, rogati.*

We are most happily adapted to each other. I have always taken pleasure in regurgitating, from the fourth stomach of the mind, some tale or anecdote, and chewing over the cud of pleasant fancy. No man ever had a friend with a more willing ear, or a shorter memory. But for this, which I have always accounted a Providence, my stock would have been exhausted, long ago. After lying fallow, for two or three months, every tale is as good as new.

God bless my friend, and compensate the shortness of his memory, by giving him length of days, and every good thing, in this and a better world.

No. LX

Much has been said and written, of late, here and elsewhere, on the subject of *intra mural* interment—burial within the *walls* or *confines* of cities. This term, though commonly employed by British writers, is wholly inapplicable, in all those rural cities, which have recently sprung up among us, and in which there are still many broad acres of meadow and pasture, plough-land and forest. In these almost nominal cities, the question must be, in relation to the propriety of burying the dead, not within the confines, but in the more densely peopled portions—in the very midst of the living.

I have an opinion, firmly fixed, and long cherished, upon this important subject; and, considering myself, professionally, an expert, in these matters, I shall devote the present article to their consideration.

There is no doubt, that a cemetery, from its improper location, or the mass of putrefying material, which the madness, or folly, or avarice of its proprietors has accumulated there, or from the indecent and almost superficial deposition of half-buried corpses, may become, like the burden of our sins—*intolerable*. It is not less certain, that it may become a *public nuisance*—not merely in the *popular* sense—but *legally*, and, as such, indictable at common law. Neither can there be any doubt, that the city authorities, without a resort to the process of indictment, and as conservators of the public health, have full power, to prevent all future interments in that cemetery. This is true of a cemetery in the suburbs—*a fortiori*, of a cemetery in the city.

At the present day, it may seem astonishing to many, that any doubt ever prevailed, in the minds of respectable members of the medical faculty, as to the unhealthy influences of the effluvia, arising from *animal* corruption. Orfila, Parant Duchâtelet, and other Frenchmen, of high professional reputation, have maintained, that such effluvia are perfectly innocuous. It seems to be almost universally agreed, at the present day, to reject such extraordinary doctrines entirely; although it is admitted, by the highest authorities, that the exhalations from *vegetable* corruption are the more pernicious of the two.

So far as the decision of this question concerns the remedy, by legal process, it is of no absolute importance. The popular impression, that exhalations, of any kind, cannot constitute a *public nuisance*, in the technical import of those words, unless those exhalations are injurious to health, is erroneous. Lord Mansfield held this not to be necessary; and that it was enough, if the air were so affected, as to be breathed by the public, with less comfort and pleasure, than before.

Interment, beyond the confines of the city, was enjoined, some eighteen hundred years ago. It was decreed in Rome, by the twelve tables—*hominem mortuum in urbe ne sepelito*.

A writer, in the London Quarterly Review, vol 73, p 446, has written, very ably, on this interesting topic. He supplies some facts of importance, connected with the history of interment. A. D. 381.—The Theodosian code forbade all interment within the walls of the city, and even ordered, that all the bodies and monuments, already placed there, should be carried out.

A. D. 529.—The first clause was confirmed by Justinian. A. D. 563.—The Council of Brague decreed, that no dead body should be buried, within the circle of the city walls.

A. D. 586.—The Council of Auxerre decreed, that no one should be buried in their temples. A. D. 827.—Charlemagne decreed, that no person should be buried in a church. A. D. 1076.—The Council of Winchester decreed, that no person should be buried in the churches. A. D. 1552.—Latimer, on Saint Luke vii. ii., says, "the citizens of Nain had their burying places without the city; and I do marvel, that London, being so great a city, hath not a burial place without," &c. A. D. 1565.—Charles Borromeo, the good bishop of Milan, ordered the return to the ancient custom of suburban cemeteries.

Sir Matthew Hale used to say, "churches were made for the living, not for the dead." The learned Anthony Rivet observed—"I wish this custom, which covetousness and superstition first brought in, were abolished; and that the ancient custom were revived to have burying places, in the free and open fields, without the gates of cities." In 1832, fifteen Archbishops, Bishops, and others, ecclesiastical commissioners, in London, recommended the abolition of all burials in churches.

At great expense, the City Government of Roxbury have judiciously selected a spot, eminently beautiful, and remote from the peopled portion of the city, for the burial of the dead. The great argument—the manifest motive—was *a just regard for the health of their constituents*. If the present nuisance should continue much longer, and grow much greater, may not the question be respectfully asked, with some little pertinency, *what has become of that just regard?*

Surely there is no lack of power. In 1832, the government of Boston said to the town of Roxbury, not in the language of David to Moab—thou shalt be *"my wash pot"* —but thou shalt be the receptacle of our offal—of all, that is filthy, and corruptible, within our borders. The City Government of Boston went extensively then into the carrion and garbage business, and furnished the provant for a legion of hogs, the property of an influential citizen of Roxbury. This awful hoggery was located on the road, now called East Street. The carrion carts of the metropolis of New England, *eundo, redeundo, et manendo,* dropping filth and fatness, as they went, became an abominable nuisance; and, as Commodore Trunnion beat up to church, on his wedding day, so every citizen, as soon as he discovered one of these aromatic vehicles, drawn by six or eight horses, tossing up their heads, and snorting sympathetically, was obliged to close-haul his nose, and struggle for the weather gage.

Then again, the proprietor of this colossal hog-sty, with his burnery of bones, and other fragrant contrivances, created a stench, unknown among men, since the bituminous conflagration of the cities of the plain—Sodom and Gomorrah; and which terrible stench, in the language of Sternhold & Hopkins, *"came flying all abroad."* In the keeping of the varying wind, this *"arria cattiva,"* like that from a graveyard, surcharged with half-buried corpses, visited, from day to day, every dwelling, and nauseated every man, woman, and child in the village. Four town meetings were held, upon this subject. Roxbury calmly remonstrated,—Boston doggedly persisted; and, at last, patience having had its perfect work, the carrion carts, while attempting to enter Roxbury, were met, by the yeomanry, on the line, and driven back to Boston. Chief Justice Shaw having refused an application for an *injunction*, the complaint was brought before the grand jury of Norfolk. Bills were found, against the owner of the hogs, and the city of Boston. My learned and amiable friend, the late John Pickering, then the City Solicitor, defended them both, with great ability; and the present Judge Merrick, then County Attorney, opposed the whole swinish concern, with the spirit of an Israelite, and the power of a Rabbi. The owner of the hogs and the city of Boston were both duly convicted, and, entering into a written obligation to sin no more, in this wise, the indictment was held over them, for a reasonable period, until they had given satisfactory evidence of their sincerity.

In the testimony of Dr. George Cheyne Shattuck, which was published, at the time, after sustaining the prosecutors amply, in their allegation, in respect to the deleterious effect of the nuisance, he remarks—"*The Creator has established, in the sense of smelling, a sentinel, to descry distant danger of life. The alarm, sounded through this organ, seldom passes unheeded, with impunity.*"

Dr. John C. Warren and sixteen other respectable physicians concurred in this opinion.

No. LXI

How long—oh Lord—how long will thy peculiar people disregard the simple, unmistakable teachings of common sense, and the admonitions of their own, proper noses, and bury the dead, in the very midst of the living!—Above all, how long will they continue to perpetrate that hideous folly of burying the dead, in tombs! What a childish effort, to keep the worm at bay—to stave off corruption, yet a little while—to procrastinate the payment of nature's debt, at maturity—dust thou art and unto dust thou shalt return!—For what? That the poor, senseless tabernacle may have a few more months or years, to rot in—that friends and relatives may, from time to time, be enabled, upon every re-opening of the tomb, to gratify their morbid curiosity, and see how the worms are getting on—that, whenever the tomb is unbarred, for another and another tenant, as it may often happen, at the time, when corruption is doing its utmost—its rankest work—the foul quintessence—the reeking, deleterious gases may rush back upon the living world; and, blending with ten thousand kindred stenches, in a densely peopled city, promote the mighty work of pestilence and death.

Who does not sympathize with Cowper!

Oh for a lodge, in some vast wilderness,
Some boundless contiguity of shade,
Where the atrocious smells of docks, and sewers,
Eruptive gas, and rank distillery
May never reach me more. My lungs are pain'd,
My nose is sick, with this eternal stench
Of corpse and carrion, with which earth is fill'd.

I am not unmindful, that, in a former number of these Dealings with the Dead, I have passed over these burial-grounds, and partially exhibited the interior of these tombs already. But there really seems to be a great awakening, upon this subject, at the present moment, at home and abroad; and I rejoice, that it is so.

I am aware, that, within the bounds of old, peninsular Boston, no inhumations—burials in graves—are permitted. This is well.—Burials in tombs are still allowed.—Why? This mode of burial is much more offensive. In grave burial, the gases percolate gradually; and a considerable portion may be reasonably supposed to be neutralized, *in transitu*. This is unquestionably the case, unless the grave is kept open, or opened, six times, or more, on the speculation principle, for the reception of new customers. In *tomb burial*, it is otherwise. The tomb is opened for new comers, and sometimes, most inopportunely, and the horrible smell fills the atmosphere, and compels the neighboring inhabitants, to close their windows and doors.

As, with some persons, this may seem to require authentication, without leading the reader to every offensive graveyard in this city, I will take a single, and a sufficient example—I will take the oldest graveyard in the Commonwealth, and the most central, in the city of Boston. I refer to Isaac Johnson's lot, where, in 1630, his bones were laid—the Chapel burying-ground. The Savings Bank building bounds upon that cemetery. The rooms of the Massachusetts Historical Society are over the Bank.

The stench, produced, by burials in the tombs, in that yard, during the summer of 1849, has compelled the Librarian to close his windows. *Tomb burial*, in this yard, has not been limited to deceased proprietors, and their relatives; it has, in some instances, been a matter of traffic. I have been struck with the present arrangement of the gravestones, in this yard. Some ingenious person has removed them all, from their original positions, and actually planted them, *"all of a row,"* like the four and twenty fiddlers—or rather, in four straight rows, near the four sides of the graveyard. This is a queerer metamorphosis, than any I ever read of. Ovid has nothing to compare with it. There they are, every one, with its *"Here lies,"* &c., compelled to stand forever, a monument of falsehood.

Of all the pranks, ever perpetrated in a graveyard, this, surely, is the most amusing. In defiance of the *lex loci*, which rightfully enjoins solemnity of demeanor, in such a place—and of all my reverence for Isaac Johnson, and those illustrious men, who slumber there, I was actually seized with a fit of uncontrollable laughter; and came to the conclusion, that this sacrilegious transposition must have been the work of Punch, or Puck, or some Lord of misrule. As I proceeded to read the inscriptions, my merriment increased, for the gravestones seemed to be conferring together, upon the subject of these extraordinary changes, which had befallen them; and repeating over to one another—*"As you are now, so once was I."* As it happened, in the case of Major Pitcairn, should any person desire to remove the ashes of his ancestor, these misplaced gravestones would surely lead to the awakening of the wrong passenger; and some venerable old lady, who died in her bed, may be transported to England, and buried under arms, for a major of infantry, who died in battle.

Why continue to bury in tombs? *Surely the sufferance on the part of the City Government, does not arise, from a respect for vested rights!!!* If the City Government has power to close the offensive cellars in Broad Street, and elsewhere, being private property, because they are accounted injurious to public health, why may they not close the tombs, being private property, for the very same reason? Considerations of public health are paramount. When, upon an application from a number of the liquor-sellers, wholesale and retail, in this city, Chancellor Kent gave his opinion, adverse to their hearts' desire, that the license laws were *constitutional*, he alluded, analogically, to the power of the Commonwealth, to pass sanatory laws. If the municipal power were deemed inadequate, legislation would give all the power required. For it would, indeed, be monstrous, having settled the fact, that the public health suffered, from burial in tombs, to suppose it a remediless evil.

The slaughter-houses and tanneries, which once existed, in Kilby Street and Dock Square, would not be tolerated now. Originally, they were not nuisances. Population gathered around them—their precedency availed them nothing—they became nuisances, by the force of circumstances. The tombs, in the churchyard, were not nuisances, when population was sparse—though they are so now. But the fact I have stated will increase the evil, from day to day: there can be no more burials, in graves, within the city proper—people will die—and, as we have not the taste nor courage to burn—they must be buried—where? In the tombs—which, as I have stated, is the most offensive and mischievous mode of burial. I have already alluded to some instances of traffic, connected with certain tombs, in the Chapel yard. If some plan be not adopted, a new line of business will spring up, in which the members of my profession will figure, to some extent: many of the present owners of tombs will sell out, and move their dead to Mount Auburn, or Forest Hills; and the city tombs will be crammed with as many corpses, as they can hold, by their speculating proprietors. Rather than this, it would have been better to continue the old mode of earth burial. The remedy is plain—the fields are before you—*carry out* "your dead!"

A famous preacher of eternal torment, and who always, in addition to the sulphurous complexion of his discourses throughout, devoted three or four pages, at the close, exclusively to brimstone and fire; is said, upon a special occasion, to have produced a prodigious effect, upon the more devoted of his intensely agitated flock, by causing the sexton, when he heard the preacher scream brimstone, at the top of his lungs, to throw two or three rolls, into the furnace below, whose fumes speedily ascended into the church.

This anecdote came instantly to my recollection, some twenty years ago, one Sabbath morning, while attending the services in St. Paul's church, in this city. The rector was absent, and a very worthy clergyman supplied his place. In the course of his sermon, he repeated, in a very solemn tone, pointing downward with his finger, in the direction of the tombs below, those memorable words of Job—*If I wait, the grave is mine house: I have made my bed in darkness. I have said to corruption, Thou art my father: to the worm, Thou art my mother and my sister.* Almost immediately—the coincidence was wonderful—I was oppressed by a most offensive stench, which certainly seemed to be *germain* to the subject. It became more and more powerful. It seemed to me, and I call myself a pretty good judge, to be posthumous, decidedly. I certainly believed it proceeded from the charnel house below. My eyes turned right and left, to see how my neighbors were impressed. The females bowed their heads, and used their handkerchiefs—the males were evidently aware of it; but, with a slight compression of their noses, kept their eyes fixed upon the preacher. Two medical gentlemen, then present, and yet living, pronounced it to be *the worm and corruption*, and connected it with the burial of a particular individual, not long before.

The case was carefully investigated, by the wardens and others; who were perfectly satisfied, that this horrible effluvium was, very probably, produced, by the burning of a heretic, in the form of a church mouse, that had taken up his quarters, in the pipe or flue, and was thus converted into an unsavory *pastille.*

No. LXII

Draco, I think, would have been perfectly satisfied with some portions of the primitive, colonial and town legislation of Massachusetts. Hutchinson, i. 436, quotes the following decree—"Captain Stone, for abusing Mr. Ludlow, and calling him *Justass*, is fined an hundred pounds, and prohibited coming within the patent, without the Governor's leave, upon pain of death."

Hazard, Hist. Coll. i. 630, has preserved a law against the Quakers, published in Boston, by beat of drum. It bears date Oct. 14th, 1656. The preamble is couched, in rather strong language—"Whereas there is a cursed sect of heretics lately risen up in the world, which are commonly called Quakers, who take upon them to be immediately sent of God," &c. The statute inflicts a fine of £100 upon any person, who brings one of them into any harbor, creek, or cove, compels him to carry such Quaker away—the Quaker to be put in the house of correction, and severely whipped; no person to speak to him. £5 penalty, for importing, dispersing, or concealing any book, containing their "devilish opinions;" 40 shillings for maintaining such opinions. £4 for persisting. House of correction and banishment, for still persisting.

The poor Quakers gave our intolerant ancestors complete vexation. Hazard, ii. 589, gives an extract from a law, for the special punishment of two of these unhappy people, Peter Pierson and Judah Brown—"That they shall, by the constable of Boston, be forthwith taken out of the prison, and stripped from the girdle upwards, by the executioner, tied to the cart's tail, and whipped through the town, with twenty stripes; and then carried to Roxbury, and delivered to the constable there, who is also to tie them, or cause them to be tied, in like manner, to the cart's tail, and again whip them through the town with ten stripes; and then carried to Dedham, and delivered to the constable there, who is again, in like manner, to cause them to be tied to the cart's tail, and whipped, with ten stripes, through the town, and thence they are immediately to depart the jurisdiction, at their peril."

The legislative designation of the Quakers was *Quaker rogues, heretics, accursed rantors, and vagabonds.*

In 1657, according to Hutchinson, i. 197, "an additional law was made, by which all persons were subjected to the penalty of 40 shillings, for every hour's entertainment, given to a known Quaker, and every Quaker, after the first conviction, if a man, was to lose an ear, and a second time the other; a woman, each time, to be severely whipped; and the third time, man or woman, to have their tongues bored through, with a red-hot iron." In 1658, 10 shillings fine were levied, on every person, present at a Quaker meeting, and £5 for speaking at such meeting. In October of that year, the punishment of death was decreed against all Quakers, returning into the Colony, after banishment. Bishop, in his "New England Judged," says, that the ears of Holden, Copeland, and Rous, three Quakers, were cut off in prison. June 1, 1660, Mary Dyer was hanged for returning, after banishment. Seven persons were fined, some of them £10 apiece, for harboring, and Edward Wharton whipped, twenty stripes, for piloting the Quakers. Several persons were brought to trial—"for adhering to the cursed sect of Quakers, not disowning themselves to be such, refusing to give civil respect, leaving their families and relations, and running from place to place, vagabond-like." Daniel Gold and Robert Harper were sentenced to be whipped, and, with Alice Courland, Mary Scott, and Hope Clifford, banished, under pain of death. William Kingsmill, Margaret Smith, Mary Trask, and Provided Southwick were sentenced to be whipped, and Hannah Phelps admonished.

Sundry others were whipped and banished, that year. John Chamberlain came to trial, with his hat on, and refused to answer. The verdict of the jury, as recorded, was—"*much inclining to the cursed opinions of the Quakers.*" Wendlock Christopherson was sentenced to death, but suffered to fly the jurisdiction. March 14, 1660.—William Ledea, "*a cursed Quaker,*" was hanged. Some of these Quakers, I apprehend, were determined to exhibit the naked truth to our Puritan fathers. "Deborah Wilson," says Hutchinson, i. 204, "went through the streets of Salem, naked as she came into the world, for which she was well whipped." At length, Sept. 9, 1661, an order came from the King, prohibiting the capital, and even corporal, punishment of the Quakers.

Oct. 13, 1657.—Benedict Arnold, William Baulston, Randall Howldon, Arthur Fenner, and William Feild, the Government of Rhode Island, addressed a letter, on the subject of this persecution, to the General Court of Massachusetts, in reply to one, received from them. This letter is highly creditable to the good sense and discretion of the writers—"And as concerning these Quakers, (so called)" say they, "which are now among us, we have no law, whereby to punish any, for only declaring by words, &c., their mindes and understandings concerning the things and ways of God, as to salvation and an eternal condition. And we moreover finde that in those places, where these people aforesaid, in this Coloney, are most of all suffered to declare themselves freely, and are only opposed by arguments in discourse, there they least of all desire to come; and we are informed they begin to loath this place, for that they are not opposed by the civil authority, but with all patience and meekness are suffered to say over their pretended revelations and admonitions, nor are they like or able to gain many here to their way; and surely we find that they delight to be persecuted by the civil powers, and when they are soe, they are like to gaine more adherents by the conseyte of their patient sufferings than by consent to their pernicious sayings."

One is taken rather by surprise, upon meeting with such a sample of admirable common sense, in an adjoining Colony, and on such a subject, at that early day—so opposite withal to those principles of action, which prevailed in Massachusetts.

The laws of the Colony, enacted from year to year, were first collected together, and ratified by the General Court, in 1648. Hutchinson, i. 437, says, "Mr. Bellingham of the magistrates, and Mr. Cotton of the clergy, had the greatest share in this work."

This code was framed, by Bellingham and Cotton, with a particular regard to Moses and the tables, and a singular piece of mosaic it was. "Murder, sodomy, witchcraft, arson, and *rape of a child*, under ten years of age," says Hutchinson, i. 440, "were the only crimes made capital in the Colony, which were capital in England." Rape, in the general sense, not being a capital offence, by the Jewish law, was not made a capital offence, in the Colony, for many years. High treason is not even named. The worship of false gods was punished with death, with an exception, in favor of the Indians, who were fined £5 a piece, for powowing.

Blasphemy and reproaching religion were capital offences. Adultery with a married woman, whether the man were married or single, was punished with the death of both parties; but, if the woman were single, whether the man were married or single, it was not a capital offence, in either. Man-stealing was a capital offence. So was wilful perjury, with intent to take away another's life. Cursing or smiting a parent, by a child over sixteen years of age, unless in self-defence, or provoked by cruelty, or having been "unchristianly neglected in its education," was a capital offence. A stubborn, rebellious son was punished with death. There was a conviction under this law; "but the offender," says Hutchinson, ibid. 442, "was rescued from the gallows, by the King's commissioners, in 1665." The return of a "cursed Quaker," or a Romish priest, after banishment, and the denial of either of the books, of the Old or New Testament, were punished with banishment or death, at the discretion of the court. The jurisdiction of the Colony was extended, by the code of Parson Cotton and Mr. Bellingham, over the ocean; for they decreed the same punishment, for the last-named offence, when committed upon the high seas, and the General Court ratified this law. Burglary, and theft, in a house, or in the fields, on the Lord's day, were, upon a third conviction, made capital crimes. The distinction, between grand and petty larceny, which was recognized in England, till 1827, 7th and 8th Geo. IV., ch. 29, was abolished, by the code of Cotton and Bellingham, in 1648; and theft, without limitation of value, was made punishable, by fine or whipping, and restitution of treble value. In some cases, only double. Thus, ibid. 436, we have the following entry—"Josias Plaistowe, for stealing four baskets of corn from the Indians, is ordered to return them eight baskets, to be fined five pounds, and hereafter to be called by the name of Josias, and not Mr., as formerly he used to be."

Thus lenity, in regard to larceny, Mr. Cotton seems to have been willing to counterbalance, by a terrible severity, on some other occasions.

Mr. Hutchinson, ibid. 442, states, that he has seen the first draught of this code, in the hand-writing of Mr. Cotton, in which there are named six offences, made punishable with death, all which are altered, in the hand of Gov. Winthrop, and the death penalty stricken out. The six offences were—"Prophaning the Lord's day, in a careless or scornful neglect or contempt thereof—Reviling the magistrates in the highest rank, viz., the Governor and Council—Defiling a woman espoused—Incest within the Levitical degrees—The pollution, mentioned in Leviticus xx. 13 to 16—Lying with a maid in her father's house, and keeping secret, till she is married to another." Mr. Cotton would have punished all these offences with death.

On the subject of divorce, the code of 1648 differed from that of the present day, *with us*, essentially. Adultery in the wife was held to be sufficient cause, for divorce *a vinculo*: "but male adultery," says Hutchinson, i. 445, "after some debate and consultation with the elders, was judged not sufficient." The principle, which directed their decision, was, doubtless, the same, referred to and recognized, by Lord Chancellor Eldon, in the House of Lords, in 1801, as reported by Mr. Twiss, in his Memoirs, vol. i. p. 383.

No. LXIII

If the materials, of which history and biography are made—the sources of information—were accessible to every reader, and the patience and ability were his, to examine for himself, there is, probably, no historian nor biographer, in whose accuracy and impartiality, his confidence would not be occasionally weakened. The statement or assertion, the authority for which lies scattered, among the pages of fifty different writers, perhaps, and which the historian has compressed within ten short lines, would, now and then, be found tinctured, and its true complexion materially altered, by the religious or political coloring of the writer's mind.

The entire history of one or more ages has been written, to support a particular code of religious or political tenets. The prejudices of an annalist have, occasionally, from long indulgence, become so habitual, that his offences, in this wise, become almost involuntary.

It is very probable, that the devoted followers—the wholesale admirers—of William Penn, who have presented their conceptions of his character, and their constructions of his conduct, to the world, from time to time, have been led into some little excesses, by the force of habitual idolatry. On the other hand, few readers, I believe, have failed to be surprised, by some of the statements and opinions, in regard to Penn, which are presented, on the pages of Mr. Macaulay's History of England.

In my last number, I alluded to the persecution of the Quakers in Massachusetts. It is my purpose, to say something more of these "*cursed*" Quakers, and, particularly, of William Penn. My remarks may extend over several consecutive numbers of these Dealings with the Dead; and, I flatter myself, that, from the nature of the subject, they will not be wholly uninteresting to the reader.

I have always cherished a feeling of regard and respect, for these "cursed" Quakers, originating in early impressions, and increased, by some personal intercourse, with certain members of the Society of Friends.

It appears, by the Salem Records, that John Kitchen was fined thirty pence, for "unworthy and malignant carriages and speeches, in open court, Sept. 25, 1662." I was very much chagrined, when I first glanced at this record; for he was my great, great, great-grandfather, by the mother's side; and grandfather of the Hon. Col. John Turner, of Salem, who commanded, at the battle of Haverhill. Great was my satisfaction, when I discovered, that John Kitchen's offence was neither more nor less, than an absolute refusal to take off his hat, in presence of the magistrate. For the luxury of keeping it on, and absenting themselves from the ordinances, he appears to have paid £40 stirling, in fines, for himself and Elizabeth, his wife. The "*cursed*" Quakers appear to have had a hard time of it, about the middle of the seventeenth century. Felt tells us, in his Annals, p. 204, that Robinson and Stevenson were hung in 1659, for returning from banishment; and, on p. 206, that Mary Dyer, of the Friends, was hung, June 1, 1660.

The deposition of John Ward and Thomas Mekens, is still of record, taken in that very month and year, showing that they saw Mrs. Kitchen pulled off her horse, and heard one Batter tell her, she was "*a base, quaking slut,*" and had been "*a powowing.*"

Now, John Kitchen was a good Quaker, doubtless, so far as regarded the essential qualification of obstinately wearing his hat, and refusing to take an oath. But he was made of flesh and blood, like all other Quakers; and this outrage, in pulling my gr. gr. gr. grandmother down from her horse, was more than flesh and blood could bear. A copy of the deposition of Giles Corey is now before me, showing, that John, upon other occasions, was not so pacific, as he might have been—and that, upon one occasion, "*he struck up Mr. Edward Norris his heels*"—and, upon another, he beat Giles Corey himself, "*till he was all blody.*" He seems to have been moved, by the spirit, to thrash them both. I take this Giles Corey to be the man, or the father of the man, who, as Felt says, was pressed to death, in Salem, for standing mute, during the witch mania, September 19, 1692.

William Penn was, for many years, engaged in controversy, chiefly in defence of the peculiar, religious opinions of the Quakers. Wood, in his Athenæ Oxonienses, iv. p. 647, Lond. 1820, gives the titles of fifty-two tracts and pamphlets, published by Penn, between 1668 and 1690. In the heat of controversy, his character was rudely assailed, and his conduct grossly misrepresented. The familiar relation, subsisting between him and James II., gave color, with some persons, to the report, that Penn, at heart, was a Papist and a Jesuit. These groundless imputations have, long ago, been swallowed up, in their own absurdity. So strong, however, was the hold, which these ridiculous fancies had taken of the public mind, that, after the revolution of 1688, he was examined before the Council, and obliged to give bond, for his appearance, from time to time; till, at last, he obtained a hearing before King William, and effectually established his innocence.

Among the few men, of elevated standing, who gave, or pretended to give credit to the rumor, that Penn was a Papist, Burnet appears in the foremost rank. He, who could speak of Prior, as *"one Prior,"* might be expected to speak of William Penn, as *"Penn the Quaker."* The appearance of Penn, at the Court of the Prince of Orange, could, on no account, have been agreeable to a Bishop, and, least of all Bishops, to Burnet; who saw, in the new comer, the confidential agent of his bitterest enemy, King James the Second; and who might, on other scores, have been jealous of the influence, even of *"Penn the Quaker."* Burnet's words are these, vol. ii. p. 318, Lond., 1818—"Many suspected that he was a concealed Papist; it is certain he was much with father Peter, and was particularly trusted by the Earl of Sunderland." On the preceding page Burnet thus describes the Quaker—"He was a talking vain man, who had been long in the King's favor, he being the Vice Admiral's son. He had such an opinion of his own faculty of persuading, that he thought none could stand before it; though he was singular in that opinion; for he had a tedious, luscious way, that was not apt to overcome a man's reason, though it might tire his patience." It is impossible not to perceive, in this description, some touches, which, historians have told us, were singularly applicable to Burnet himself.

William, who perfectly comprehended the character of Halifax and Burnet, perceived the propriety of keeping them apart, when the former came to Hungerford, as a commissioner from the King, Dec. 8, 1688. How far I judge rightly, in applying a part of Burnet's description of Penn, to Burnet himself, may appear, in the following passage from Macaulay, vol. ii. p. 538: "Almost all those, who were admitted to his (William's) confidence, were men, taciturn and impenetrable as himself. Burnet was the only exception. He was notoriously garrulous and indiscreet. Yet circumstances had made it necessary to trust him; and he would, doubtless, under the dexterous management of Halifax, have poured put secrets, as fast as words. William knew this well; and, when he was informed, that Halifax was asking for the Doctor, could not refrain from exclaiming, *'If they get together, there will be fine tattling.'"*

Mr. Macaulay remarks, that—*"To speak the whole truth, concerning Penn, is a task, which requires some courage."* He then, vol. i. page 505, delivers himself as follows—"The integrity of Penn had stood firm against obloquy and persecution. But now, attacked by royal wiles, by female blandishments, by the insinuating eloquence and delicate flattery of veteran diplomatists and courtiers, his resolution began to give way. Titles and phrases, against which he had often borne his testimony, dropped occasionally from his lips and his pen. It would be well, if he had been guilty of nothing worse than such compliances with the fashions of the world. Unhappily it cannot be concealed, that he bore a chief part in some transactions, condemned, not merely by the rigid code of the society, to which he belonged, but by the general sense of all honest men. He afterwards solemnly protested that his hands were pure from illicit gain, and that he had never received any gratuity from those, whom he had obliged, though he might easily, while his interest at court lasted, have made a hundred and twenty thousand pounds. To this assertion full credit is due. But bribes may be offered to vanity, as well as to cupidity; and it is impossible to deny that Penn was cajoled into bearing a part, in some unjustifiable transactions of which others enjoyed the profits."

This passage will tend, in the ratio of Mr. Macaulay's influence, to disturb the popular opinion of William Penn. It is very carefully written, and will not always be so carefully read. It is, perhaps, unfortunate for Penn, that Mr. Macaulay felt obliged, in pursuing the course of his history, to postpone the presentation of the facts, upon which his opinions rest, until they arise, in their chronological order. Thus the impression, instead of being removed, qualified, or confirmed, by instant examination, is suffered to become imbedded in the mind. Having carefully collated this passage, with every other passage, relative to Penn, in Mr. Macaulay's work, I must confess, that the exceedingly painful impression, produced by the paragraph, presented above, has been materially relieved, by a careful consideration of all the evidence, subsequently offered, by Mr. Macaulay himself, and by the testimony of other writers. Perhaps the reader will consent to go along with me, in the examination of this question.

No. LXIV

Mr. Macaulay's second mention of William Penn may be found, vol. i. page 650. A number of young girls, acting under the direction of their school-mistress, had walked in procession, and presented a standard to Monmouth, at Taunton, in 1635. Some of them had expiated their offence already. That hell-hound of a judge, Jeffreys, had literally frightened one of them to death. It was determined, under menace of the gibbet, to extort a ransom from the parents of *all* these innocent girls. Who does not apply those lines of Shakspeare to this infernal judge!

> "Did you say all? What, all? Oh, hell-kite, all?
> What, all my pretty chickens and their dam,
> At one fell swoop?"

"The Queen's maids of honor," says Mr. Macaulay, "asked the royal permission, to wring money out of the parents of the poor children; and the permission was granted." They demanded £7000, and applied to Sir Francis Warre, to exact the ransom. "He was charged to declare, in strong language, that the maids of honor would not endure delay," &c.

Warre excused himself. Mr. Macaulay proceeds as follows: "The maids of honor then requested William Penn to act for them, and Penn accepted the commission. Yet it should seem that a little of the pertinacious scrupulosity, which he had often shown, about taking off his hat, would not have been altogether out of place on this occasion. He probably silenced the remonstrances of his conscience, by repeating to himself, that none of the money, which he extorted, would go into his own pocket; that, if he refused to be the agent of the ladies, they would find agents less humane; that by complying he should increase his influence at the court; and that his influence at the court had already enabled him, and might still enable him to render greater services to his oppressed brethren. The maids of honor were at last forced to content themselves with less than a third part of what they had demanded."

Now it seems to me, that no clear-headed, whole-hearted, *impartial* reader will draw the inference, from this passage, which Mr. Macaulay would manifestly have him draw. Penn well understood the resolute brutality of Jeffreys, the never-dying obstinacy and vindictive malevolence of James, and the heartless greediness of these maids of honor. He knew, as Mr. Macaulay says, that "*if he refused to be the agent of the ladies they would find agents less humane.*" There was no secrecy here—this thing was not done in a corner. Mr. Macaulay says, "they *charged* Sir Francis Warre," &c.: and after he refused, they "*requested* William Penn," &c. Penn acted as a peacemaker. He stood between these she wolves—these shameless maids of honor—and the Taunton lambs; and, instead of £7000, he persuaded those vampyres, who, under the royal grant, had full power in their hands to do their wicked will—to receive less than £2300. Mr. Macaulay admits, that Penn received not a farthing; and, that, had he refused, matters might have been worse for the oppressed.

The known character of Penn demands of us the presumption, in his favor, that he entered upon this business conscientiously, and not as an *extortioner*—and that he made, as the result leads us to believe he did, the very best terms for the parents. Wherein was ever the sin or the shame of negotiating, between the buccaneers of the Tortugas, and the parents of captive children, for their ransom? Does not Mr. Macaulay present the reign of James II. before us, as blotted all over, with official piracy and judicial murder? If the adjustment of this odious business increased the influence of Penn, at court, and thereby enabled him to "*render great services to his oppressed brethren*"—these were the natural consequences of the act; without them, there was enough of just and honorable motive, for a mediator, to step between the oppressor and the oppressed, and lessen, as much as possible, the weight of the oppression.

If the conduct of William Penn, upon this occasion, was the humane and Christian thing, which it certainly appears to have been, "*the pertinacious scrupulosity, which he had often shown, about taking off his hat*" would have been wholly out of place. And if so, what justification can be found for Mr. Macaulay's expressions—"*the remonstrances of his conscience,*" and "*the money, which he extorted.*"

It is proverbially hard, for an old dog to learn new tricks. He, to whose hand the hatchet is familiar, when he substitutes the rapier, will still hack and hew with it, as though it were a hatchet. It may well be doubted, if an impartial history, especially those parts of it, wherein the writer deals with character and motive, can ever be trustworthily and impartially written, by a veteran, professional reviewer, of the tomahawk school, however splendid his talents may be.

Upon this occasion, Penn, doubtless, persuaded the maids of honor to moderate their demands; at the same time, representing to the parents the uncompromising character of those, with whom they had to deal, and the unavoidable necessity of making terms. It is impossible to judge of the transaction aright, without taking into view the character of those dark days of tyranny and misrule, and the little security, then enjoyed by the subject.

Mr. Macaulay, once more, introduces Penn to his readers—"William Penn, for whom exhibitions, which humane men generally avoid, seem to have had a strong attraction, hastened from Cheapside, where he had seen Cornish hanged, to Tyburn, in order to see Elizabeth Gaunt burned. He afterwards related that, when she calmly disposed the straw about her, in such a manner, as to shorten her sufferings, all the bystanders burst into tears." Here is another attempt to lower the Quaker, in public estimation.

That Penn ever, from the cradle to the grave, gazed, unsympathizingly, upon human suffering, nobody, but a madman, will credit, for a moment. Nor would Mr. Macaulay, notwithstanding the rather peculiar construction of the paragraph, venture *directly* so to represent him. It has been my fortune to know several men, of kind and warm affections, who have confessed, without reserve, a strong desire to witness the execution of criminals. Cornish and Gaunt were executed on the same day, and their fate excited universal attention. Penn's account of the last moments of both was very minute; and shows him to have been a deeply interested observer. I am not aware, that he ever attended any other execution. And if he did not, the remark of Mr. Macaulay, which is *general*, can never be justified, in relation to Penn; though it would fairly apply to the celebrated George Selwyn, who, though remarkable for the keenness of his sensibility, and the kindness of his heart, was in the habit of attending every execution in London; and who, upon one remarkable occasion of this kind, actually embarked for the Continent.

Why could not Mr. Macaulay, who often refers to Clarkson, have adopted some of his charitable and gentlemanly constructions of Penn's conduct, upon this occasion? Clarkson says—"Men of the most noted benevolence have felt and indulged a curiosity of this sort. They have been worked upon, by different motives; some, perhaps, by a desire of seeing what human nature would be, at such an awful crisis; what would be its struggles; what would be the effects of innocence or guilt; what would be the power of religion on the mind." * * * * "I should say that he consented to witness the scenes in question, with a view to do good; with a view of being able to make an impression on the King's mind, by his own relation," &c.

In vol. ii. page 222, 1687, Mr. Macaulay says—"Penn had never been a strong-headed man: the life which he had been leading, during two years, had not a little impaired his moral sensibility; and, if his conscience ever reproached him, he comforted himself by repeating, that he had a good and noble end in view, and that he was not paid for his services in money."

Again, ibid., referring to the effort of the King, to propitiate William Kiffen, a great man, among the Baptists, no phraseology would suit Mr. Macaulay, but this—*"Penn was employed in the work of seduction."* What *seduction?* Indeed, whenever a good chance presents itself to reach the Quaker, anywhere and anyhow, through the joints of the harness, the phylactery of Mr. Macaulay seems to have been—*semper paratus.*

It was enough, that Penn was, in some sense, the confidant, and, occasionally, the *unconstrained and perfectly conscientious* agent of this most miserable King.

That posterity will sanction these politico-historical flings, at the character of William Penn, I cannot believe.

Tillotson knew him well. He had once expressed a suspicion that Penn was a Papist. A correspondence ensued. "In conclusion," says Chalmers, "Tillotson declared himself fully satisfied, and, as in that case he had promised, he heartily begs pardon of Penn."

Chalmers himself, who had no sympathy with the *"cursed Quakers,"* closes his account of Penn, as follows—*"It must be evident from his works, that he was a man of abilities; and from his conduct through life, that he was a man of the purest conscience. This, without acceding to his opinions in religion, we are perfectly willing to allow and to declare."*

No. LXV

There was a couple of unamiable, maiden ladies, who had cherished, for a long time, an unkindly feeling to the son of their married sister; and, whenever her temporary absence afforded a fitting opportunity, one of them would inquire of the other, if it was not *a good time to lick Billy*. Mr. Macaulay suffers no convenient occasion to pass, without exhibiting a practical illustration of this opinion, that it is *a good time to lick Billy*.

In vol. ii. page 292, Mr. Macaulay says—"Penn was at Chester (in 1687,) on a pastoral tour. His popularity and authority among his brethren had greatly declined since he had become a tool of the King and the Jesuits." In proof of this assertion Mr. Macaulay refers to a letter, from Bonrepaux to Seignelay, and to Gerard Croese's Quaker History. Let us see, for ourselves, what Bonrepaux says—"Penn, chef des Quakers, qu'on sait être dans les intérêts du Roi d'Angleterre, est si fort décrié parmi ceux de son parti qu'ils n'ont plus aucune confiance en lui."

Now I ask, in the name of historical truth, if Mr. Macaulay is sustained in his assertion, by Bonrepaux? Is there a jot or tittle of evidence, in this reference, that Penn *"had become a tool of the King and of the Jesuits;"* or that Bonrepaux was himself of any such opinion?

Let us next present the passage from Croese—"Etiam Quakeri Pennum non amplius, ut ante, ita amabant ac magnifaciebant, quidam aversabantur ac fugiebant."

I ask, in reference to this quotation from Croese, the same question? No possible version of these passages into English will go farther, than to show, that the Quakers were dissatisfied with Penn, about that time: in neither is there the slightest reference to Penn, as *"a tool of the King and of the Jesuits."* Mr. Macaulay's passage is so constructed, that his citation of authorities goes, not only to the fact of Penn's unpopularity, for a time, but to the cause of it, as assigned by Mr. Macaulay himself, namely, that Penn *"had become a tool of the King and of the Jesuits."*

Now it is well known, that Penn, in 1687, was in bad odor with some of the Quakers. He was *suspected*, by some persons, of being a Jesuit—George Keith, the Quaker renegade, called him a deist—he was said by others to be a Papist. Even Tillotson had given countenance to this foolish story, which Penn's intimacy with King James tended to corroborate. How far Tillotston believed Penn to be a *Papist*, or a *tool* of the King, or of the *Jesuits*, will appear, upon the perusal of a few lines from Tillotson to Penn, written in 1686, the year before that, of which Mr. Macaulay is writing—"I am very sorry that the suspicion I had entertained concerning you, of which I gave you the true account in my former letter, hath occasioned so much trouble and inconvenience to you: and I do now declare with great joy, that I am fully satisfied, that there was no just ground for that suspicion, and therefore do heartily beg your pardon for it." Clarkson's Memoirs, vol. i. chap. 22.

If the authorities, cited, sustained the statement of Mr. Macaulay, their credibility would still form a serious question. In vol. ii. pages 305-7-8, Mr. Macaulay refers to Bonrepaux's "complicity with the Jesuits." It would have been quite agreeable to that crafty emissary of Lewis, to have had it believed, that Penn was of their fraternity. As for Gerard Croese, Chalmers speaks of him and his history, with very little respect; and states, that it dissatisfied the Quakers. However this may have been, there is not a syllable in Gerard Croese's Historia Quakeriana, giving color to Mr. Macaulay's assertion, that Penn *"had become a tool of the King and of the Jesuits."* On the contrary, Croese, as I shall show hereafter, speaks of Penn, with great respect, on several occasions.

In the same paragraph, of which a part is quoted, at the commencement of this article, Mr. Macaulay, after stating, that, when the King and Penn met at Chester, in 1687, Penn preached, or, to use Mr. Macaulay's word, *harangued*, in the tennis court, he says—"*It is said indeed, that his Majesty deigned to look into the tennis court, and to listen, with decency, to his friend's melodious eloquence.*" What does Mr. Macaulay mean?—that the King did not laugh outright?—that he made some little exertion, to suppress a disposition to make a mock of Penn and his preaching? No intelligent reader, though he may not catch the invidious spirit of this remark, can fail to perceive the writer's design, to speak disparagingly of Penn.

Well: what is Mr. Macaulay's authority for this? He quotes "Cartwright's Diary, Aug. 30, 1687, and Clarkson's Life of William Penn"—but without any indication of volume, chapter, or page. This loose and unsatisfactory kind of reference is quite common with Mr. Macaulay; and one might almost as well indicate the route to the pyramids, by setting up a finger post in Edinburgh, pointing in the direction of Cairo. No eminent historian, English or Scotch, has ever been thus regardless of his reader's comfort; neither Rapin nor Tindal, Smollett nor Hume, nor Henry, nor Robertson, nor Guthrie, nor any other. Of this the reader may well complain. This may all be well enough, in a historical romance—but in a matter, pretending to be true and impartial history, no good reader will walk by faith, altogether, and upon the staff of a single narrator; and he will too often find, that the spirit of the context, in the authority, is very different, from that of the citation.

He, who imparts to any historical fact the coloring of his own prejudice, and *dresses up* a statement, after his own fancy, has no right to vouch in, as his authority, for the *whole thing,* however grotesque he may have made it—the writer, who has stated the *naked fact.* If Clarkson said simply, that the King had listened to Penn's preaching, Mr. Macaulay has no right to quote Clarkson, as having said so, in a manner to lower Penn, the tithe of a hair, in the estimation of the world. *A fortiori,* if Clarkson has said, that the King listened to Penn's preaching, *on several occasion, with respect,* Mr. Macaulay had no right to quote Clarkson, as his authority, for the sneering and ill-natured statement, to which I have referred. This is not history, it is gross misrepresentation; and, the more forcibly and ingeniously it is fabricated, the more unjust and the more ungenerous the libel, upon the dead.

The reader, if he will, may judge of Mr. Macaulay's impartiality, by comparing his words with the *only words* uttered by Clarkson, on this point. They may be found, vol. i. chap. 23—"Among the places he (Penn) visited, in Cheshire, was Chester itself. The King, who was then travelling, arriving there at the same time, went to the meeting-house of the Quakers, to hear him preach. This mark of respect the King showed him also, at two or three other places where they fell in with each other, in the course of their respective tours."

This is the only passage, which can be referred to, in Clarkson, by Mr. Macaulay, to sustain his ill-natured remark, whose evil spirit is entirely neutralized, by the very authority he cites. But there will be many, who will rather give Mr. Macaulay credit, for stating the point impartially; and few, I apprehend, who will take the trouble to look, through two octavo volumes, for a passage, thus vaguely referred to, without any indication of the volume, chapter, or page.

This rude assault, upon the character and motives of William Penn, Mr. Macaulay commences, by saying—"*To speak the whole truths concerning Penn, is a task, which requires some courage.*" It is becoming, in every historian, to speak the truth, the whole truth, and *nothing but the truth.* It certainly requires some courage—audacity, perhaps, is the better word—to present citations, in French and Latin, to sustain an assertion, which those citations do not sustain; and to refer to a highly respectable author, as having stated that, which he has nowhere stated.

It may not be amiss, to present my views of Mr. Macaulay's injustice, more plainly than I have done. It is obvious to all, that a fact—the same fact—may, by the very manner of stating it, raise or lower the character of him, in regard to whom it is related. The *manner* of representing it may become *material*, or, substantially, part and parcel of the fact, as completely, as the coloring is part and parcel of a picture. No man has a right to take the sketch or outline of an angel, and, having given it the sable complexion of a devil, ascribe the entire thing, such as he has made it, to the author of the original sketch. No man, surely, has a right to seize a wreath, respectfully designed for the brows of his neighbor; distort it into the shape of a fool's cap; clap it upon that neighbor's head; and then charge the responsibility upon him, who prepared the original chaplet, as a token of respect.

Mr. Macaulay represents King James, as listening to the preaching of Penn, with concealed contempt—such are the force and meaning of his words; and he quotes Clarkson, as authority for this, who says precisely the contrary.

Every reader, who is uninstructed in the French and Latin languages, will view the quotations from Bonrepaux and Croese, as authorities for Mr. Macaulay's assertion, that Penn had *"become the tool of the King and the Jesuits"* —for, whether carelessly, or cunningly, contrived, the sentence will certainly be understood to mean precisely this. A large number, even of those, who understand the languages, will take these quotations, as evidence, upon Mr. Macaulay's word, without examination. Now, as I have stated, there is not the slightest authority, in these passages, for Mr. Macaulay's assertion.

No. LXVI

Mr. Macaulay's last attack upon William Penn will be found, in vol. ii., pages 295-6-7. The Fellows of Magdalen College had been most abominably treated, by James II., in 1687. The detail is too long for my limits, and is, withal, unnecessary here, since there is neither doubt nor denial of the fact. The mediatorial agency of Penn was employed. The King was enraged, and resolved to have his way. His obstinacy was a proverb. There were three courses for Penn—right, left, and medial—to side with the King—to side with the Fellows—or to act as a mediator. Mr. Macaulay is pleased, in his Index, to speak of the transaction, as "*Penn's mediation.*"

Had he sided with the Fellows entirely, he would have lost his influence utterly, to serve them, with the King. Had he sided with the King entirely, he would have lost all confidence with the Fellows. Mr. Macaulay, here, as elsewhere, is evidently bent upon showing up Penn, as the "*tool of the King:*" and, if there is anything more unjust, upon historical record, I know not where to look for it.

[1] With manifest effort, and in stinted measure, Mr. Macaulay lets down a few drops of the milk of human kindness, in the outset, and says of Penn— "*He had too much good feeling to approve of the violent and unjust proceedings of the government, and even ventured to express part of what he thought.*" Here, that which proceeded from *fixed and lofty principle*, is ascribed to a less honorable motive—"*good feeling,*" or *bonhommie*; and the "*part of what he thought,*" was neither more nor less, than a bold and frank remonstrance, committed to writing, and sent to the King, by Penn.

When they met at Oxford, says Clarkson, vol. i. chap. 23, "William Penn had an opportunity of showing not only his courage, but his consistency in those principles of religious liberty, which he had defended, during his whole life." After giving an account of the Prince's injustice, Clarkson says— "Next morning William Penn was on horseback, ready to leave Oxford, but knowing what had taken place, he rode up to Magdalen College, and conversed with the Fellows, on the subject. After this conversation, he wrote a letter, and desired them to present it to the King." * * * * "Dr. Sykes, in relating this anecdote of William Penn, by letter to Dr. Chazlett, who was then absent, mentions that Penn, after some discourse with the Fellows of Magdalen College, wrote a short letter, directed to the King. He wrote to this purpose—that their case was hard, and that, in their circumstances, they could not yield obedience."

This was confirmed by Mr. Creech, as Clarkson states, and by Sewell, who states, in his History of the Rise and Progress of the Quakers, that Penn told the King the act *"could not in justice be defended, since the general liberty of conscience did not allow of depriving any of their property, who did what they ought to do, as the Fellows of the said College appeared to have done."* This is the *"part of what he thought,"* referred to by Mr. Macaulay, who has not found it convenient, upon this occasion, to quote a syllable from Clarkson, nor from Sewell, of whose work Chalmers and others have spoken with respect.

I know of no better mode of presenting this matter fairly, than by laying before the reader contrasted passages, from Mr. Macaulay, and from Clarkson, relating to the conduct of Penn, upon this occasion. Mr. Macaulay shall lead off—"James, was as usual, obstinate in the wrong. The courtly Quaker, therefore, did his best to seduce the college from the path of right."—Therefore!—Wherefore? Penn did his best to *seduce* the college from the path of right, *because* James was, as usual, obstinate in the wrong! This is based, of course, upon Mr. Macaulay's favorite hypothesis, that Penn was *"the tool of the King and the Jesuits."* —"He tried first intimidation. Ruin, he said, impended over the society. The King was highly incensed. The case might be a hard one. Most people thought it so. But every child knew that his Majesty loved to have his own way, and could not bear to be thwarted. Penn, therefore, exhorted the Fellows not to rely on the goodness of their cause, but to submit, or at least to temporize. Such counsel came strangely from one, who had been expelled from the University for raising a riot about the surplice, who had run the risk of being disinherited, rather than take off his hat to the princes of the blood, and who had been more than once sent to prison, for haranguing in conventicles. He did not succeed in frightening the Magdalen men."

It may be thought scarcely worth while, to charge a Quaker, at the age of *forty-three*, with inconsistency, because his views had somewhat altered, since he was a wild young man, at *twenty-one*.

It is also clear, that Penn viewed the Magdalen question, as one quite as much of *property* as of *conscience*; and that he could see no good reason, with his eyes of toleration wide open, why all the great educational institutions should be forever, in the hands of one denomination.

Mr. Macaulay again—"Then Penn tried a gentler tone. He had an interview with Hough and some of the Fellows, and after many professions of sympathy and friendship, began to hint at a compromise. The King could not bear to be crossed. The college must give way. Parker must be admitted. But he was in very bad health. All his preferments would soon be vacant. 'Dr. Hough,' said Penn, 'may then be Bishop of Oxford. How should you like that, gentlemen?' Penn had passed his life in declaiming against a hireling ministry. He held, that he was bound to refuse the payment of tithes, and this even when he had bought lands, chargeable with tithes, and had been allowed the value of the tithes in the purchase money. According to his own principles, he would have committed a great sin, if he had interfered, for the purpose of obtaining a benefice, on the most honorable terms, for the most pious divine. Yet to such a degree had his manners been corrupted by evil communications, and his understanding obscured by inordinate zeal for a single object, that he did not scruple to become a broker in simony of a peculiarly discreditable kind, and to use a bishopric as a bait to tempt a divine to perjury."

Are these the words of truth and soberness? I rather think they are not. In the sacred name of common sense—did Penn become a *broker in simony of a peculiarly discreditable kind, and use a bishopric, as a bait to tempt a divine to perjury,* by stating, that Parker was very infirm, and, that, should he die, Hough might be his successor! If this is history, give us fiction, for Heaven's sake, which is said to be less marvellous than fact. There is not the least pretence, that he offered, or was authorized to offer, any such "*bait*." He spoke of a mere contingency; and did the best he could to mediate, between the King and the Fellows, both of whom were highly incensed.

As to the matter of tithes, Penn was mediating, between men, *who had no scruples about tithes.* He recognized, *pro hac vice,* the usages of the parties; and a Christian judge may, as shrewdly, be charged with infidelity, for conforming to the established law of evidence, and permitting a disciple of Mahomet to be sworn, upon the Koran.

When Hough replied, that the Papists had robbed them of University College, and Christ Church, and were now after Magdalen, and would have all the rest, "Penn," says Mr. Macaulay, "was foolish enough to answer, that he believed the Papists would now be content. 'University,' he said, 'is a pleasant college. Christ Church is a noble place. Magdalen is a fine building. The situation is convenient. The walks by the river are delightful. If the Roman Catholics are reasonable, they will be satisfied with these.'"

And now I will present Clarkson's just and sensible view of this transaction. Mr. Macaulay has said, vol. ii. page 295, that "*the agency of Penn was employed,*" meaning, as the context shows, employed *by the King.* Clarkson, vol. i. chap. 23, says expressly, that, Oct. 3, 1687, Dr. Bailey wrote to Penn, "stated the merits of the case, and solicited his mediation." Penn told the Fellows, as appears from *Dr. Hough's own letter, written the evening after their last interview,* that he "feared they had come too late. He would use, however, his endeavors; and, if they were unsuccessful, they must attribute it to want of power in him, and not of good will to serve them." The mediation came to nothing. The Fellows grew dissatisfied with Penn;

falling, doubtless, into the very common error of parties, highly excited, and differing so widely, that all, who are not *for them; in toto, are against them.* They seem to have been specially offended, by the following liberal remark of Penn's—"For my part, I have always declared my opinion, that the preferments of the Church should not be put into any other hands but such as they at present are in; but I hope you would not have the two Universities such invincible bulwarks of the Church of England, that none but they must be capable of giving their children a learned education."

In the same volume and chapter, Clarkson remarks—"They (the delegates from Magdalen) thought, strange to relate, that Penn had been rambling; and because he spoke doubtfully, about the success of his intended efforts, and of the superior capacity of the established clergy, that they alone should monopolize education, that his language was not to be depended upon as sincere. How this could have come into their heads, except from the terror, into which the situation of the College had thrown them, it is not easy to conceive; for certainly William Penn was as explicit, as any man could have been, under similar circumstances. He informed them, that, after repeated efforts with the King, he feared they had come too late. This was plain language. He informed them again, that he would make another trial with the King; that he would read their papers to him, unless peremptorily commanded to forbear; but that, if he failed, they must attribute his want of success not to his want of will, but want of power."

"This, though expressive of his doubts and fears, was but a necessary caution, when his exertions had already failed; and it was still more necessary, when there was reason to suppose, that, though the King had a regard for him, and was glad to employ him, as an instrument, in forwarding his public views, yet that he would not gratify him, where his solicitations directly opposed them. That William Penn did afterwards make a trial with the King, to serve the College, there can be no doubt, because no instance can be produced, wherein he ever forfeited his word or broke his promise. But all trials with this view must of necessity have been ineffectual. The King and his ministers had already determined the point in question."

Such were the sentiments of Clarkson.

No. LXVII

Charles I. was King, when William Penn was born; and, when he died, George I. was on the throne. Penn therefore lived in the reins of nine rulers of the realm—Charles I.—the Cromwells, Oliver and Richard—Charles II.—James II.—William and Mary as joint sovereigns—William alone—Anne—and George I.

He was the son of Admiral, Sir William Penn, and was born on Tower Hill, London, Oct. 4, 1644. The spirit and the flesh strove hard for the mastery, before young William came forth a Quaker, fully developed. He was remarkable at Oxford, for his fine scholarship, and athletic performances.

Penn believed, that the Lord appeared to him, when he was very young. The devil seems to have made him a short visit afterwards, if we may rely upon the testimony of Penn's biographers. Wood, in his Athenæ, iv. 645, gives this brief account of the Lord's visit—Penn was "educated in puerile learning, at Chigwell in Essex, where, at eleven years of age, being retired in a chamber alone, he was so suddenly surprised with an inward comfort, and, as he thought, an external glory in the room, that he has, many times, said that, from that time, he had the seal of divinity and immortality, that there was also a God, and that the soul of man was capable of enjoying his divine communications."

His biographer, Clarkson, says, that Penn, at the age of sixteen, was led to a sense of the corruptions of the established faith, by the preaching of Thomas Loe, a Quaker; and broke off at the chapel, and began to hold prayer meetings. For this he was fined and admonished. It is remarkable, that Wood, though he states, that Penn, after he became a Quaker, in good earnest, was imprisoned, once in Ireland, once in the Tower, and three times in Newgate, does not even allude, in his Athenæ, to the expulsion from Oxford, which is related, by Chalmers, Clarkson, and others.

It seems, that, after he had become impressed, by Loe's preaching, an order came down from court, that the students should wear surplices. This so irritated Penn, that, instead of letting his yea be yea, and his nay nay—in company with others, says Clarkson, "he fell upon those students, who appeared in surplices, and tore them everywhere over their heads." On the subject of his conversion, Wood says—"If you'll believe a satirical pamphlet—'*The history of Will Penn's conversion from a gentleman to a Quaker,*' printed at London, in 1682—you'll find, that the reason of his turning Quaker was the loss of his mistress, a delicate young lady, that then lived in Dublin; or, as others say, because he refused to fight a duel."

For two, good and sufficient reasons, this statement, contained in the "*satirical pamphlet,*" and referred to by Wood, is unworthy of the slightest credit. In the first place, though Penn met Loe, in Dublin, after the expulsion from Oxford, and became more fully impressed, yet his first meeting with Loe was at Oxford, before the expulsion, and the serious impression, produced by his preaching, led, albeit rather oddly, to the affair of the surplices.

In the second place, the notion, that Penn would put on Quakerism, to avoid a duel, is still more incredible. Nothing could be more unfortunate, than any imputation upon Penn's courage, moral or physical. We have seen, that he was famous for his athletic exercises. Strange, though it may seem, to such as have contemplated Penn, as the quiet non-combatant, he was an accomplished swordsman, and, upon one occasion, was actually engaged in an affair, which had all the aspect, and all the peril, of the *duellium*, however it may have lacked the preliminary forms and ceremonies. "During his residence in Paris," says Chalmers, "he was assaulted in the street, one evening, by a person with a drawn sword, on account of a supposed affront; but among other accomplishments of a gay man, he had become so good a swordsman, as to disarm his antagonist."

After his expulsion from Oxford, in 1662, he returned home. His father, the Admiral, was greatly provoked, to see his son resorting to the company of religious people, who were, of all, the least likely, in the licentious reign of Charles II., to advance his worldly interest. The old gentleman tried severity, and finally, as Penn himself relates, gave the Quaker neophyte a thrashing, and turned him out of doors.

Ere long, the father got the better of the admiral. He relented: and, probably, supposing there was as little vitality in Paris, for a Quaker, as some of the old philosophers fancied there might be, in a vacuum, for an angel, he sent young William thither, as one of a fashionable travelling party.

After his return, he was admitted of Lincoln's Inn, and continued there, till the year of the plague, 1665. The following year, his father sent him to Ireland, to take charge of an estate. At Cork, he met Loe once more—attended his meetings, became an unalterable Quaker, preached in conventicles— was committed to prison—released upon application to the Earl of Orrery— and summoned home, by his indignant father. The old Admiral loved his accomplished son, then twenty-three years old—but abhorred his Quakerish airs and manners. In all points, save one—the point of conscience—William was unexceptionably dutiful. At length, the Admiral agreed to compound, on conditions, which seem not to have been very oppressive: in short, he consented to waive all objections, and let William do as he pleased, in regard to his religion, provided he would yield, in one particular—doff his broad brim—take off his hat—in presence of the King, the Duke of York, and his own father, the Admiral. Young William demanded time for consideration. It was granted; and he earnestly sought the Lord, on an empty stomach, as he says himself, with prayer. He finally informed his father, that he *could not do it*; and, once again, the Admiral, in a paroxysm of wrath, turned the rebellious young Quaker out of doors, broad brim and all.

William Penn now began to figure, as a preacher, at the Quaker meetings. The *friends*, and the fond mother, ever on hand, in such emergencies, supplied his temporal necessities. Even the old Admiral, becoming satisfied of William's perfect sincerity, although too proud to tack about, hoisted private signals, for his release, when imprisoned, for attending Quaker meetings; and evidently lay by, ready to bear down, in the event of serious difficulty.

In 1668, Penn's brim grew broader and broader, and his coat became buttonless behind. He was a writer and a preacher, and a powerful defender of the *"cursed and depised"* Quakers. The titles of his various works may be found in Clarkson, and in Wood's Athenæ. They conformed to the fashion of the age, and were, necessarily, quaint and extended. I have room for one only, as a specimen,—the title of his first tract—*"Truth exalted, in a short but sure testimony, against all those religious faiths and worships, that have been formed and followed in the darkness of apostacy; and for that glorious light, which is now risen, and shines forth in the life and doctrine of the despised Quakers, as the alone good old way of life and salvation; presented to princes, priests, and people, that they may repent, believe, and obey. By William Penn; whom Divine love constrains, in an holy contempt, to trample on Egypt's glory, not fearing the King's wrath, having beheld the majesty of Him, who is invisible."* In this same year 1668, he was imprisoned in the Tower, for publishing his Sandy Foundation Shaken. There he was confined seven months, doing infinitely more mischief, for the cause of lawn sleeves and white frocks, forms, ceremonies, and hat-worship, as he calls it, than if he had been loose. For, then and there, he wrote his most able pamphlets, especially, No Cross no Crown, which gained him great praise, far beyond the pale of Quakerdom. His treatise has been often reprinted, and translated into foreign tongues.

In 1670, his influence was so great, that he obtained an order in Council, for the release of the Quakers then in prison. At a later day, he again assumed the office of St. Peter's angel, and set three thousand captives free. In 1685, says Mr. Macaulay, "he strongly represented the sufferings of the Quakers to the new King," &c. "In this way, about fifteen hundred Quakers, and a still greater number of Roman Catholics regained their liberty." No wonder he was mistaken for a Papist, by those, who adopt that bastard principle, that charity begins at home, and ends there; whose religious circle forms the exclusive line of demarcation, for the exercise of that celestial principle; and who look, with the eye of a Chinaman, upon all beyond the holy sectarian wall, as outside barbarians. I was delighted and rather surprised, that Mr. Macaulay suffered the statement of this fact to pass, without some ill-natured expression, in regard to Penn—who, I say it reverentially, was less the tool of the King, than of Jesus Christ.

No. LXVIII

In 1670, William Penn was, for the third time, committed to Newgate, for preaching. His fines were paid by his father, who died this year, entirely reconciled to his son; and, upon his bed of death, pronounced these comforting words—*"Son William, let nothing in this world tempt you to wrong your conscience: I charge you, do nothing against your conscience. So will you keep peace at home, which will be a feast to you in a day of trouble."*

Penn inherited from his father an estate, yielding about £1500 per annum. About this time he wrote his *"Seasonable caveat against Popery;"* though he knew it was the faith of the Queen and his good friend, the Duke of York. Shortly after, he travelled in Holland and Germany. In 1672, he married Gulielma Maria Springett. In 1675, he held his famous dispute with Richard Baxter; and, in 1677, he again visited the continent, in company with George Cox and Robert Barclay, constantly preaching, and writing, and importuning, in behalf of his despised and oppressed brethren. About this period, and soon after his return to England, we find him petitioning Parliament, in their behalf. Twice, he was permitted to address the committee of the House of Commons, upon this subject.

Whoever coveted the honor of being the creditor of royalty found a willing customer, in Charles the Second. In 1681, that monarch, in consideration of £16,000 due from him to the estate of Admiral Penn, conveyed to William the district, now called Pennsylvania. He himself would have given it the name of Sylvania, but the King insisted, on prefixing the name of the grantee. Full powers of legislation and government were bestowed upon the proprietor. The only limitation was a power, reserved to the Privy Council, to rescind his laws, within six months, after they were laid before that body. The charter bears date March 4, 1681. He first designed to call his domain "New Wales," and nothing saved the Philadelphians from being Welchmen, but an objection, from the under-secretary of state, who was himself a Welchman, and was offended at the Quaker's presumption.

He encouraged emigrants, judiciously selected, to embark for his Province; and followed, himself, with about a hundred Quakers, in September, 1682. His arrival in the Delaware, his beneficent administration, and the whole story of his negotiation, with the Indians, are full of interest, and overflowing. It is a long story withal, too long, altogether, for our narrow boundaries. I have indicated the sources of information, and this is all my limits will allow.

After two years, he returned to England, and became a greater favorite than ever, with James II.—was calumniated, of course—pursued by the unholy alliance of churchmen, and sectaries, and apostate Quakers— grossly insulted—"chastened but not killed"—and finally deprived of his government. Justice, at length, prevailed. Penn's rights were restored, by William III. Having lost his wife and son, he went again, upon his travels, and again married. In 1699, he returned to Pennsylvania, and remained there, for the term of two years. He then went home to England; and, after continuing to employ his tongue and his pen, as freely as ever, for several years, he died, July 30, 1718, at the age of seventy-two years, at Jordan, near Beaconsfield, in Buckinghamshire.

Such is the mere *skeleton* of this good man's life; and it is my purpose to *flesh it up*, with some few of those highly interesting, and well authenticated, incidents, which may be found, on the pages of trust worthy writers.

I do not believe, that the pen of any past, present, or future historian, or biographer, however masterly the hand that holds it—however bitter and pungent the gall of bigotry or political venom, in which it may dipped—will ever be able, very grievously, or lastingly, to soil the character of William Penn. The world's opinion has settled down, upon firm convictions. If new facts can be produced, then, indeed, a writer may justly move, for a reconsideration of the public sentiment—but Mr. Macaulay does not present *a single fact*, in relation to William Penn, not known before—he gives a *construction* of his own, so manifestly tinctured with ill nature, as, at once, to excite the suspicion of his reader.

I wear a narrow brim, and have buttons behind—I am no Quaker—and, indeed, have a quarrel with them all—chiefly grammatical—though I esteem and respect the principles of that moral and religious people—but I simply describe the impulse of my own heart, when I say, that Mr. Macaulay's ill natured treatment of William Penn painfully disturbed my confidence, in his impartiality; and constrained me to "read, mark, learn and inwardly digest," the highly seasoned *provant*, which he has furnished—*cum grano salis*; and with great care, not to swallow the *flummery*. Scotchmen have not always written thus of William Penn; and the sentiments of mankind, now and hereafter, if I do not strangely err, will be found, embodied in the concluding passage of an article in the Edinburgh Review, vol. xxi. page 462.

"We shall not stop to examine what dregs of ambition, or what hankerings after worldly prosperity may have mixed themselves with the pious and philanthropic principles, that were undoubtedly his chief guides in forming, that great settlement, which still bears his name, and profits by his example. Human virtue does not challenge nor admit of such a scrutiny: and it should be sufficient for the glory of William Penn, that he stands upon record, as the most humane, the most moderate, and most pacific of all governors." All this may be enough for his *glory*. But there are some simple, touching truths, to be told of William Penn, and some highly interesting personal details; which, though they may have little about them, in accordance with the ordinary estimate of *glory*, will long continue to envelop the memory of this extraordinary man, with a purer and a milder light.

I know no better mode of concluding the present article, than by presenting a few extracts, from the valedictory letter of William Penn to his wife and children, written on the eve of his first visit to Pennsylvania, September, 1682. If the *saints* write such admirable love letters, it would greatly benefit the *sinners*—the men of this world—to follow the example, and surpass it, if they can.

"My dear wife and children. My love, which neither sea, nor land, nor death itself can extinguish nor lessen towards you, most endearingly visits you, with eternal embraces, and will abide with you forever. My dear wife! remember thou wast the love of my youth, and much the joy of my life; the most beloved, as well as most worthy of all my earthly comforts; and the reason of that love was more thy inward than thy outward excellencies, which yet were many. God knows, and thou knowest it, I can say it was a match of Providence's making; and God's image in us both was the first thing, and the most amiable and engaging ornament in our eyes. Now I am to leave thee, and that, without knowing whether I shall ever see thee more in this world. Take my counsel into thy bosom, and let it dwell with thee, in my stead, while thou livest."

Here follows some domestic advice. Penn then proceeds—"And now, my dearest, let me recommend to thy care, my dear children, abundantly beloved of me, as the Lord's blessings, and the sweet pledges of our mutual and endeared affection. Above all things, endeavor to breed them up, in the knowledge and love of virtue, and that holy plain way of it, which we have lived in, that the world, in no part of it, get into my family. * * *

"For their learning, be liberal. Spare no cost. For by such parsimony all is lost, that is saved: but let it be useful knowledge, such as is consistent with truth and godliness, not cherishing a vain conversation, or idle mind.

* * * I recommend the useful parts of mathematics, &c., but agriculture is especially in my eye: let my children be husbandmen and housewives: it is industrious, healthy, honest and of good example. * * * Be sure to observe their genius, and do not cross it as to learning. * * * I choose not they should be married to earthly, covetous kindred; and of cities and towns of concourse, beware. The world is apt to stick close to those, who have lived and got wealth there. A country life and estate, I like best for my children. I prefer a decent mansion, of an hundred pounds per annum, before ten thousand pounds, in London, or such like place, in a way of trade."

He then addresses his children, and finally his elder boys, in the following admirable strain, honorable alike to his understanding and his heart.

"And, as for you, who are likely to be concerned, in the government of Pennsylvania, I do charge you, before the Lord God and his holy angels, that you be lowly, diligent and tender, fearing God, loving the people, and hating covetousness. Let justice have its impartial course, and the law free passage. Though to your loss, protect no man against it—for you are not above the law, but the law above you. Live therefore the lives, yourselves, you would have the people live; and then you have right and boldness to punish the transgressor. Keep upon the square, for God sees you: therefore do your duty, and be sure you see with your own eyes, and hear with your own ears. Entertain no lurchers; cherish no informers for gain or revenge; use no tricks; fly to no devices, to support or cover injustice but let your heart be upright before the Lord, trusting in him, above the contrivances of men, and none shall be able to hurt or supplant."

The letter, from which I have made these few extracts, concludes—"So farewell to my thrice dearly beloved wife and children! Yours as God pleaseth, in that, which no waters can quench, no time forget, nor distance wear away."

It is truly pleasant to get behind the curtain of form and ceremony, and look at these eminent men, in their night-gowns and slippers, and listen to them thus, while talking to their wives and their children.

No. LXIX

It is remarkable, that such a genuine Quaker, as William Penn, should have sprung from such a belligerent stock. His father, as I have stated, was a British admiral; and his grandfather, Giles, was a captain in the navy. William Penn may, nevertheless, have derived, from this origin, and from his Dutch mother, Margaret Jasper, of Rotterdam—a certain quality, eminently characteristic of the Quaker—that resolute determination, which the coarser man of the world calls *pluck*, and the Quaker, *constancy*.

This constancy of purpose, in William Penn, seems never to have been shaken. It appeared, in his refusal to doff his brim, before his father, the Duke of York, and the King. It was manifested, when, being imprisoned in the Tower, for printing his *Sandy Foundation Shaken*, and hearing, that the Bishop of London had declared the offender should publicly recant, or remain there, for life; he replied, "*he would weary out the malice of his enemies by his patience, and that his prison should be his grave, before he would renounce his just opinions, for he owed his conscience to no man.*"

This same constancy was signally exhibited, during the disputation, between himself and George Whitehead, for the Quakers, and Thomas Vincent and others, for the Presbyterians. Vincent had a parish, in Spitalfields. Two of his parishioners went to listen, perhaps to laugh, at the Quakers. Like Goldsmith's scoffers, who came to laugh, and remained to pray—they went in, Presbyterians, and came out, Quakers. They were converted. At this, Vincent lost his patience; and seems to have become a persecutor of the *cursed Quakers*; and, as Clarkson states, said all manner of "*unhandsome*" things of them, and their *damnable* doctrines. Penn and Whitehead invited Vincent to a public discussion. After much delay and evasion, Vincent consented. As every fowl is bravest on his own *stercorium*, Vincent selected his own Presbyterian meeting-house, as the place for the discussion; and, before the appointed hour, filled it with his own people, so completely, that the disputants themselves, Penn and Whitehead, could scarcely gain admittance. They were instantly insulted, by a charge, suddenly made, that the Quakers held "*damnable doctrines.*" Whitehead began a reply; Vincent interrupted him, and proposed, as the proper course, that he should put questions to the Quakers. He put the motion, and, as almost all present were of his party, it was agreed to, of course. He then put a question concerning the Godhead, which he knew the Quakers would answer in the negative. Whitehead and Penn attempted to explain. Several rose on the other side. Whitehead desired to put a question to Vincent. This the Presbyterians refused. They proceeded to laugh, hiss and stigmatize. Penn they called a Jesuit. Upon an answer from Whitehead, to a question from Vincent, uproar ensued, and Vincent "went instantly to prayer," that the Lord would *come short* with heretics and blasphemers.

When he had, by this manœuvre, discharged his battery upon the Quakers, effectually securing himself from interruption—for no one would presume to interrupt a minister at prayer—he cut off all power of reply, by telling the people to go home immediately, at the same moment setting them the example.

The closing part, which especially exhibits that constancy, for which the Quakers have ever been remarkable, cannot be more happily related, than in the language of Mr. Clarkson himself.

"The congregation was leaving the meeting-house, and they had not yet been heard. Finding they would soon be left to themselves, some of them, at length, ventured to speak; but they were pulled down, and the candles, for the controversy had lasted till midnight, were put out. They were not, however, prevented by this usage, from going on: for, rising up, they continued their defence in the dark; and what was extraordinary, many staid to hear it. This brought Vincent among them with a candle. Addressing himself to the Quakers, he desired them to disperse. To this, at length, they consented, but only, on the promise, that another meeting should be granted them, for the same purpose, in the same place."

Vincent did not keep his promise. He was, doubtless, fearful that more of his parishioners would be converted. Penn and Whitehead, at last, went to Vincent's meeting-house, on a lecture day; and, when the lecture was finished, rose and begged an audience: but Vincent went off, as fast as possible; and the congregation, as speedily, followed. Finding no other mode before him, Penn wrote and published his celebrated *Sandy Foundation Shaken*, which caused his imprisonment in the Tower, as already related.

Another remarkable example of the constancy of Penn is recorded, in the history of his trial, before the Lord Mayor, for a breach of the conventicle act, in 1670. Mr. Macaulay is pleased to say, Penn had never been "*a strong-headed man*." This is one of those sliding phrases, that may mean anything, or nothing. It may mean, that not being a *strong-headed man*, he necessarily belonged to the other category, and was a *weak-headed man*. Or, it may mean, that he was not as strong-headed as Lord Verulam, or Mr. Macaulay. I wish the reader would decide this question for himself; and, for that end, read the history of this interesting trial, as given by Clarkson, in the first volume, and sixth chapter of his Memoirs of Penn. If the evidences of a strong head and a strong heart were not abundantly exhibited, by the accused, upon that occasion, I know not where to look for them.

The jury returned a verdict of *guilty of speaking in Grace Street Church.* Sir Samuel Starling, the Mayor, and the whole court abused the jurors, after the example of Jeffreys, and sent them back to their room. After half an hour, they returned the same verdict, in writing, signed with their names. The court were more enraged than before; and, Mr. Clarkson says, the Recorder addressed them thus—"You shall not be dismissed, till we have a verdict, such as the court will accept; and you shall be locked up without meat, drink, fire, and tobacco; you shall not think thus to abuse the court; we will have a verdict, by the help of God, or you shall starve for it." After being out all night, the jury returned the same verdict, for the third time. They were severely abused by the court, after the fashion of that day, and sent to their room, once more. A fourth time, they returned the same verdict. Penn addressed the jury, and the court ordered the jailor to stop his mouth, and bring fetters, and stake him to the ground. Friend William, for an instant, merged the Quaker in the Englishman, and exclaimed—"Do your pleasure, I matter not your fetters."

On the fifth of September, the jury, who had received no refreshment, for two days and two nights, returned a verdict of *not guilty.* Such was the condition of things, at that day, that, for the rendition of that verdict, the jury were fined forty marks apiece, and imprisoned in Newgate. Penn was, at this time, five-and-twenty years of age.

The peculiar position of William Penn, at the court of Charles and James the Second, may be explained, without laying, at his door, the imputation of being a time-server, and a man of the world. Between the latter monarch and the Quaker, there existed a relation, akin to friendship. Penn, in keeping with his Quaker principles, was forgetful of injuries, and mindful of benefits. It is impossible to say, how long he would have remained in the tower, when imprisoned there, through the agency of the Bishop of London, had he not been released, upon the unsolicited importunity of James II., when Duke of York. When the Admiral, his father, was near his end, "he sent one of his friends," says Mr. Clarkson, "to the Duke of York, to desire of him, as a death-bed request, that he would endeavor to protect his son, as far as he consistently could, and to ask the King to do the same, in case of future persecution. The answer was gratifying, both of them promising their services, upon a fit occasion."

Perhaps it would not be going too far—with Mr. Macaulay's permission, of course—to ascribe that personal consideration, which Penn exhibited, for Charles and James—a part of it, at least—to a grateful recollection of their favors, to his father and himself.

"Titles and phrases," says Mr. Macaulay, *"against which he had often borne his testimony, dropped occasionally from his lips and his pen."* I rather doubt, if the recording angel, who will never *"set down aught in malice,"* has noted the unquakerish sins of William Penn, in doing grammatical justice to personal pronouns. This, truly, is a mighty small matter. If Penn was not so particular, in these little things, as some others of his brotherhood, his birth and education may be well considered. He was not a Quaker born. His residence in France may also be taken into the account. "He had contracted," says Clarkson, "a sort of polished or courtly demeanor, which he had insensibly taken from the customs of the people, among whom he had lately lived."

In the matter of the hat, even Mr. Macaulay will never charge William Penn with inconsistency. In Granger's Biographical History of England, iv. 16, I find the following anecdote—"We are credibly informed, that he sat with his hat on before Charles II., and that the King, as a gentle rebuke for his ill manners, put off his own: upon which Penn said to him—'Friend Charles, why dost thou not put on thy hat?' The King answered, ''Tis the custom of this place, that never above one person should be covered at a time.'" This tale is told also, in a note to Grey's Hudibras, on canto ii. v. 225, and elsewhere.

No. LXX

The pride of life—that omnipresent frailty—that universal mark of man's congenital naughtiness—in William Penn, seemed scarcely an earthly leaven, springing, as it did, from a comforting consciousness of the purity of his own. *The pride of life*, with him, was essentially *humility*; for, when compelled to rest his defence, in any degree, upon his individual character, he vaunted not himself, but gave all the glory to the Giver.

No man, however, more keenly felt the assaults, which were made upon his character, by the tongue and the pen of envy and hatred, ignorance and bigotry, because he knew, that the shaft, though aimed, ostensibly, at him, was frequently designed, for that body, whose prominent leader he was.

In the very year of his father's death, and shortly after that event, he was seized, by a file of soldiers, sent purposely, for his apprehension, while preaching, in a Quaker meeting-house, and carried before Sir John Robinson, who treated him roughly, and sent him, for six months, to Newgate. In the course of the trial, Robinson said to Penn—"*You have been as bad as other folks*"—to which Penn replied—"*When and where? I charge thee to tell the company to my face.*" Robinson rejoined—"Abroad, and at home too." This was so notoriously false and absurd, that an ingenuous member of the court, Sir John Shelden, exclaimed—"*No, no, Sir John, that's too much.*" Penn, turning to the assembly, and with all the chastened indignation of an insulted Christian—Quaker as he was—delivered himself, with a strength and simplicity, which would have done honor to Paul, in the presence of Agrippa; and which must forever, so long as the precious record shall remain, touch a responsive chord—even in the bosoms of those, whose practice it is, upon ordinary occasions, to let their yea be yea, and their nay—nay.

I am sure it would have cheered the old Admiral's heart, and elevated his respect for the broad brim, to have heard the manly language of his Quaker son, that day.

"I make this bold challenge to all men, women, and children upon earth, justly to accuse me, with having seen me drunk, heard me swear, utter a curse, or speak one obscene word, much less that I ever made it my practice. I speak this to God's glory, who has ever preserved me from the power of these pollutions, and who, from a child, begot an hatred in me, towards them."

"But there is nothing more common, than, when men are of a more severe life than ordinary, for loose persons to comfort themselves with the conceit, that these were once as they themselves are; as if there were no collateral or oblique line of the compass or globe, by which men might be said to come to the Arctic pole, but directly and immediately from the Antarctic. Thy words shall be thy burden, and I trample thy slanders, as dirt, under my feet."

Mr. Clarkson is quoted, as good authority, by Mr. Macaulay. Such he has ever been esteemed. A brief quotation may not be amiss, in regard to Penn's relation to James II. Having referred to the Admiral's dying request to Charles and James, to have a regard for his Quaker son, Clarkson says— "From this period a more regular acquaintance grew up between them (William Penn and James II.) and intimacy followed. During this intimacy, however William Penn might have disapproved, as he did, of the King's religious opinions, he was attached to him, from a belief, that he was a friend to liberty of conscience. Entertaining this opinion concerning him, he conceived it to be his duty, now that he had become King, to renew this intimacy with him, and that, in a stronger manner than ever, that he might forward the great object, for which he had crossed the Atlantic, namely, the relief of those unhappy persons, who were then suffering, on account of their religion. * * * * He used his influence with the King solely in doing good."

The relation, between William Penn and the Papist King, was indeed remarkable. Gerard Croese published his Historia Quakeriana, at Amsterdam, in 1695, which was translated into English, in the following year. It was greatly disliked, by the Quakers; and, in 1696, drew forth an answer from one of the society. The testimony of Croese, in relation to Penn, may therefore be deemed impartial. He says— "The king loved him, as a singular and entire friend, and imparted to him many of his secrets and counsels. He often honored him with his company in private, discoursing with him of various affairs, and that not for one but many hours together."

When a peer, who had been long kept waiting for Penn to come forth, ventured to complain, the King simply said— "*Penn always talked ingeniously and he heard him willingly.*" Croese says, that Penn was unwearied, as the suitor on behalf of his oppressed people, making constant efforts for their liberation, and paying their legal expenses, from his private purse. The King's remark certainly does not quadrate with Burnet's statement, that Penn *"had a tedious luscious way of talking."* With Queen Anne he was a great favorite; and Clarkson says, vol. ii. chap. 15, "she received him always in a friendly manner, and was pleased with his conversation." So was Tillotson. So was a better judge than Queen Anne, Tillotson, or Burnet. In Noble's continuation of Granger, Swift is stated to have said—*"Penn talked very agreeably and with much spirit."*

Somewhat of Penn's relation to King James may be gathered, from Penn's answer, when examined, in 1690, before King William, in regard to an intercepted letter from King James to Penn. In that letter, James desired Penn to *"come to his assistance and express to him the resentments of his favor and benevolence."* When asked what *resentments* were intended, he replied that "he did not know, but he supposed the King meant he should compass his restoration. Though, however he could not avoid the suspicion of such an attempt, he could avoid the guilt of it. He confessed he had loved King James; and, as he had loved him, in his prosperity, he could not hate him, in his adversity—yes, he loved him yet, for the many favors he had conferred on him, though he could not join with him, in what concerned the state or kingdom." This answer, says Pickart, *"was noble, generous, and wise."*

One of the most able and eloquent compositions of William Penn is his justly celebrated letter of October 24, 1688, to William Popple. Mr. Popple was secretary to the Lords Commissioners, for the affairs of trade and plantations, and a particular friend of Penn and of his schoolfellow, John Locke. Had Mr. Macaulay flourished then, he would have had readier listeners to these cavils, than he has at present. Penn, in 1688, was excessively unpopular. He was not only *the tool of the King and the Jesuits,* but a rank *Papist* and *Jesuit* himself—the *friend of arbitrary power,*—bred at *St. Omers in the Jesuits College*—he had *taken orders at Rome*—*married under a dispensation*—*officiated as a priest at Whitehall*—no charge against William Penn was too absurd, to gain credit with the people, at the period of the Revolution.

Upon this occasion, Mr. Popple addressed to Penn a letter, eminently beautiful, in point of style, and containing a most forcible appeal to Penn's sense of duty to himself, to the society of Friends, to his children, and the world, to put down these atrocious calumnies, by some public written declaration. His letter will be found, in Clarkson's Memoirs, vol. ii. chap. i.

I truly regret, that I have space only, for some brief disconnected extracts, from William Penn's reply.

"Worthy Friend; it is now above twenty years, I thank God, that I have not been very solicitous what the world thought of me, &c. The business, chiefly insisted on, is my Popery and endeavors to promote it. I do say then, and that, with all simplicity, that I am not only no Jesuit, but no Papist; and which is more, I never had any temptation upon me to be so, either from doubts in my own mind, about the way I profess, or from the discourses or writings of any of that religion. And in the presence of Almighty God I do declare, that the King did never once directly or indirectly, attack me or tempt me upon that subject." * * * * "I say then solemnly, that so far from having been bred at St. Omers, and having received orders at Rome, I never was at either place; nor do I know anybody there, nor had I ever a correspondence with anybody in those places." After alluding to the absurdity of charging him with having officiated as a Catholic Priest, he adverts to his opinion of the views of King James, on the subject of toleration—"And in his honor, as well as in my own defence, I am obliged in conscience to say, that he has ever declared to me it was his opinion; and on all occasions, when Duke, he never refused me the repeated proof of it, as often as I had any poor sufferers for conscience' sake to solicit his help for." * * * * "To this let me add the relation my father had to this King's service; his particular favor in getting me released out of the Tower of London in 1669, my father's humble request to him, upon his death-bed, to protect me from the inconveniences and troubles my persuasion might expose me to, and his friendly promise to do it, and exact performance of it, from the moment I addressed myself to him. I say, when all this is considered, anybody, that has the least pretence to good nature, gratitude, or generosity, must needs know how to interpret my access to the King."

This letter contains sentiments, on the subject of religious toleration, which would be highly ornamental, if placed in golden characters, upon the walls of all our churches—"Our fault is, we are apt to be mighty hot upon speculative errors, and break all bounds in our resentments; but we let practical ones pass without remark, if not without repentance! as if a mistake about an obscure proposition of faith were a greater evil, than the breach of an undoubted precept. Such a religion the devils themselves are not without, for they have both faith and knowledge; but their faith doth not work by love, nor their knowledge by obedience." * * * "Let us not think religion a litigious thing; nor that Christ came only to make us disputants." * * * * "It is charity that deservedly excels in the Christian religion." * * * * * "He that suffers his difference with his neighbor, about the other world, to carry him beyond the line of moderation in this, is the worse for his opinion, even if it be true. It is too little considered by Christians, that men may hold the truth in unrighteousness; that they may be orthodox, and not know what spirit they are of."

Verily, this *"courtly Quaker"* — this *"tool of the King and the Jesuits,"* who was *"never a strong-headed man"* — was quite a Christian gentleman after all.

No. LXXI

In the latter days of William Penn, *the sun and the light were darkened—the clouds returned after the rain—the grasshopper became a burden—*and the years had drawn nigh, when he could truly say he had *no pleasure in them.* No mortal, probably, ever enjoyed a more continual feast from the consciousness of a life, devoted to the glory of God, and the welfare of man; but many of his temporal reliances had crumbled under him; and trouble had gathered about his path, and about his bed.

He had not much more comfort in his government, I fear, than Sancho Panza enjoyed, in that of Barataria. Its commencement was marked, by a vexatious dispute with Lord Baltimore; and the Governor's absence was ever the signal for altercation, between different cliques and parties, and vexatious neglect, on the part of his tenants and agents. In his letters to Thomas Lloyd, the President of his Council, he complains of some in the government, for drinking, carousing, and official extortion.

In his letters to Lloyd and Harrison in 1686, he complains of the Council, for neglecting and slighting his letters; that he cannot get *"a penny"* of his quit-rents; and adds—"God is my witness, I lie not. I am now above six thousand pounds out of pocket, more than ever I saw by the province; and you may throw in my pains, cares, and hazard of life, and leaving of my family and friends to serve them."

It is even stated by Clarkson, vol. i. ch. 22, that want of funds from the Province prevented his returning to America, in 1686. In the following year, he renews these complaints.

In 1688, and after the revolution, he was examined, before the Lords of Council, on the charge of being a Papist and a Jesuit; gave bonds for his attendance, on the first day of the next term; and, no witness then appearing against him, he was discharged.

In 1690, he was again arrested, and bound over as before, and, no witness appearing, was again discharged. In the same year, he was once more arrested, and committed to prison. On the day of trial, no witness appeared, and he was again discharged. He resolved to fly from such continual persecution, to America, and, while making his preparation, he was again arrested, upon the information of one Fuller, who was afterward set in the pillory, for his crime.

Penn sought safety, in privacy and retirement from the world. In 1691, a new proclamation was issued for his arrest; and his American affairs wore a gloomy aspect. In 1693, he was deprived of his government, by King William; and pursued with unrelenting rage, by his enemies. In the words of Clarkson, he was *"a poor, persecuted exile."*

"Canonized to-day and cursed to-morrow" —such seems to have been the fortune of William Penn. His only prudent course seemed to be to bow down, before the wrath of that popular hurricane, which swept furiously over him, and went upon its way. This good and great man was not wholly forgotten. He had never forfeited the affectionate respect of some persons, who have left bright names, for the admiration of future ages. Such were Locke and Tillotson. They marked their time, and moved in behalf of the oppressed. Lords Ranelagh, Rochester, and Sidney went to King William— they *"considered it a dishonor to the Government, that a man, who had lived such an exemplary life, and who had been so distinguished for his talents, disinterestedness, generosity, and public spirit, should be buried in an ignoble obscurity, and prevented from rising to future eminence and usefulness, in consequence of the charge of an unprincipled wretch, whom Parliament had publicly stigmatized, as a cheat and an impostor."*

King William replied to these truly noble lords, "that William Penn was *an old friend of his, as well as theirs,* and that he might follow his business, as freely as ever, for he had nothing to say against him." The principal Secretary of State, Sir John Trenchard, and the Marquis of Winchester bore these joyful tidings to William Penn. And how did he receive them? He went instantly, of course, to tender the homage of his humble acknowledgments to King William—not so. He was then greatly embarrassed in his pecuniary affairs. Foes were on every side. The wife whom, in his parting letter, he bade remember, that she was *the love of his youth and the joy of his life,* was on her death-bed, prostrated there, according to Clarkson, in no small degree, by her too keen sympathy for her long suffering husband. His *heart* was broken—his *spirit* was not. He preferred rights before favors, and desired permission publicly to defend himself, before the King in council. This was granted, and he was abundantly acquitted, after a deliberate hearing.

The last hours of his wife, Gulielma Maria, were cheered by this intelligence. In about a month after this event, she died. "She was an excelling person," said he, "as wife, child, mother, mistress, friend, and neighbor."

In 1694, a complete reconciliation took place between Penn and the society of Friends; and, in the same year, he was restored to the Government of Pennsylvania. In 1696, he married Hannah Callowhill, of Bristol. These gleams of returning happiness were soon obscured. A few weeks after this marriage, he lost his eldest son. This young man was upon the eve of twenty-one. His father's simple narrative of the dying hour is truly affecting. "His time drawing on apace, he said to me—'My dear father, kiss me. Thou art a dear father. How can I make thee amends?' He also called his sister, and said to her, 'poor child, come and kiss me,' between whom seemed a tender and long parting. I sent for his brother, that he might kiss him too, which he did. All were in tears about him. Turning his head to me, he said softly, 'Dear father, hast thou no hope for me?' I answered, 'My dear child, I am afraid to hope, and I dare not despair, but am and have been resigned, though one of the hardest lessons I ever learned.'" When the doctor came, he was very weak, and the narrative continues thus. "He said—'Let my father speak to the doctor, and I'll go to sleep,' which he did and waked no more; breathing his last upon my breast, the tenth day of the second month, between nine and ten in the morning, 1696. So ended the life of my dear child and eldest son, much of my comfort and hope, and one of the most tender and dutiful, as well as ingenuous and virtuous youths I knew, if I may say so of my own dear son, in whom I lost all that any father can lose in a child; since he was capable of anything, that became a sober young man, my friend and companion, as well as most affectionate and dutiful child."

About this time Penn was sorely grieved, by the conduct of George Keith, the apostate Quaker, who had been excommunicated, and now spent his time, in abusing the society.

Penn had become well convinced of many solemn truths, presented in the last chapter of Ecclesiastes, and of none more fully, than that there is no end of making books. He continued to pour forth pamphlets, on various subjects. In this year, 1696, he became acquainted, and had several interviews, with Peter the Great, who was then working, as a common shipwright, in the dock yards at Deptford. In 1699 he once more visited Pennsylvania. In 1701 he returned to England. In 1702 and 1703 he continued to preach and publish, as vigorously as ever.

In 1707 he became involved in a lawsuit, with the executors of one Ford, his former steward, or agent. Ford was undoubtedly a knave. Penn suffered severely from this cause. The decision was against him; and, though Chancery could not relieve, many thought him greatly wronged. He was compelled, in 1708, to live within the rules of the Fleet. This, doubtless, was the occasion of Mr. Burke's erroneous statement, many years after, that Penn died in the Fleet Prison. An amusing anecdote may be referred to this period, which, though not mentioned by Clarkson, nor in the life by Chalmers, may be found in the Encyclopædia Britannica, of 1798, and is repeated, in Napier's edition of 1842. Penn is said to have had a peep-hole, through which, unseen, he could see every visitor. A creditor, having often knocked, and becoming impatient, knocked more violently; "will not your master see me?" said he, when the door was opened—"He hath *seen* thee, friend," the servant replied, "but he doth not like thee."

In 1709, his necessities were such, that he mortgaged his whole Province of Pennsylvania, for £6600. This necessity, as Oldmixon says, in his "Account of the British Empire in America," arose from "his bounty to the Indians, his generosity in minding the public affairs of the Colony more than his own private ones, his humanity to those, who have not made suitable returns, his confidence in those, who have betrayed him."

In 1712, he had three apoplectic fits, followed by those painful effects, which are usual in such cases. His friend, Thomas Story, the first recorder of Philadelphia, made him yearly visits, after this period, till his death, which took place July 30, 1718. It is impossible to read the account of these visits, as given by Thomas Story himself, and presented by Clarkson, vol. ii. chap. 18, without emotion.

It has too often befallen those, whose lives have been devoted to the benefit of mankind, to be outraged, after they were dead and buried. Malice delights to meddle with their ashes. Political prejudice and priestly bigotry seek, in graves, undisturbed by ages, for something to gratify their unnatural appetites, and satisfy the gnawings of a mean, vindictive spirit.

Penn had not long been committed to the tomb, when a wretch, Henry Pickworth, an excommunicated renegade, spread abroad, with all the industry and energy of a malicious spirit, the report that Penn had died a raving maniac, at Bath. This rumor became so general, that it was thought necessary to destroy it, by the publication of certificates from those, who had ministered about his dying bed.

For one hundred and thirty years, William Penn has slumbered in the grave. That *hutesium et clamor*, that spirit of persecution, by which this excellent man was pursued, vilified, impoverished, and exiled, has long been hushed. The high churchman, the bigot, the Quaker renegade, the false accuser, have worn out their viperous teeth upon the file. All, that bore the primeval impress of human weakness, in William Penn, had well nigh perished, and departed from the minds of men. All, that was excellent, and lovely, and of good report, had become case hardened, as it were, into a sort of precious immortality. That his spirit had found a celestial niche, among the just made perfect, was the firm faith of all, who believe, that their Father in Heaven is a God of toleration and of mercy. I have paid my imperfect tribute of affectionate respect to the memory of William Penn.

Notwithstanding Mr. Macaulay's efforts to disturb the popular opinion, in regard to William Penn, his History of England is one of the most amusing books, in the English language. Relationship is worth something, even in a library; I have placed the two volumes, already published, between the works of Sir Walter Scott, and a highly prized edition of the Arabian Nights.

No. LXXII

Death has taken away, within a brief space, several of our estimable citizens—Mr. Joseph Balch, an excellent and amiable man, who filled an official station, honorably for himself, and profitably for others—Mr. Samuel C. Gray, a gentleman of taste and refinement, who graduated at Harvard College, in 1811, and, at the time of his death, was President of the Atlas Bank—Mr. John Bromfield, a man of a sound head, and a kind heart. Having bestowed five and twenty thousand dollars, in his life-time, upon the Boston Athenæum, he modestly left the more extended purposes of his benevolent heart, to be proclaimed, after his decease; and, by his will, distributed, among eight charitable institutions, and his native town, the sum of one hundred and ten thousand dollars.

The features of these good men are still upon the retina of our memories; the tones of their voices yet ring in our ears; we almost expect their wonted salutation, upon the public walk. But there is no mockery here—they are gone—the places, that knew them, shall know them no more!

Death has laid his icy hand upon these men, as he has ever laid the same cold palm upon their fathers, since time began. Such exits are common. Disease triumphed over the flesh, and they ceased to be.

But Death has done his dismal work, of late, in our very midst, by the hand of cruel violence—not sitting like the King of Terrors, in quiet dignity, upon his throne, and casting his unerring shafts abroad; but darting down upon his unsuspecting victim, and, with a murderous grasp, crushing him at once. I allude, as every reader well knows, to the fate of the late Dr. George Parkman.

As the Coroner's Inquest, after long and laborious investigation, has declared, that he was "*killed*," we must assume it to be so. I have known this gentleman, for more than forty years; and have had occasion to observe some of the peculiarities of his character, in the relations of business, as well as in those of ordinary intercourse—I say the *peculiarities* of his character, for he certainly must be classed in the category of *eccentric* men. Having heard much of this ill-fated gentleman, for many years, before the late awful occurrence, and still more since the event—for he was extensively known, and all, who knew him, have something to relate—I am satisfied, that those very traits of eccentricity, to which I refer, have led the larger part of mankind, to form erroneous impressions of his character.

Dr. George Parkman was the son of Samuel Parkman, an enterprising, and successful merchant, of Boston, who was a descendant of Ebenezer Parkman, who graduated at Harvard College, in 1721, and was ordained Oct. 28, 1724, the first minister of Westborough; and who, after a ministry of sixty years, died, Dec. 9, 1782, at the age of 79, and whose wife was the daughter of Robert Breck, minister of Marlborough, who was the grandson of Edward Breck, one of the early settlers of Dorchester, in 1636.

Dr. George Parkman graduated, at Harvard College, in 1809. When he commenced his junior year, John White Webster, now Erving Professor of Chemistry and Mineralogy, entered the University, as freshman. Dr. Webster, who is now in prison, charged with the *"killing"* of Dr. Parkman, will, in due time, be tried, by a jury of his countrymen. Will it not be decorous, and humane, and in accordance with the golden rule, for the men, women, and children of Massachusetts, to permit the accused to have an impartial trial? Can this be possible, if, upon the *on dits* of the day, of whose value every man of any experience can judge, this individual, whose past career seems not to have been particularly bloodthirsty, is to be morally condemned, without a hearing?

Hundreds, whose elastic intellects have been accustomed to jump in judgment, are already assured, that we believe Dr. Webster innocent. Now we *believe* no such thing—nor do we *believe* he is guilty. His reputation and his life are of some little importance to himself, and to his family; and we should be heartily ashamed, to carry a head upon our shoulders, which would not enable us to suspend our judgment, until all the *true facts* are in, and all the *false facts* are out.

How much beautiful reasoning has been utterly and gratuitously wasted, upon premises, which have turned out to be not a whit better, than stubble and rottenness! The very readiness, with which everybody believes all manner of evil, of everybody, furnishes evidence enough, that the devil is in everybody; and goes not a little way, in support of the doctrine of original sin.

Let us, by all means, and especially, by an avoidance of the topic, give assurance to the accused of a fair and impartial trial. If he shall be proved to be innocent, who will not blush, that has contributed to fill the atmosphere, with a presentiment of this poor man's guilt? If, on the other hand, he shall be proved to be guilty of an incomparably foul and fiendish murder—let him be hanged by the neck till he is dead, for God's sake—aye, for God's sake—for God hath said—whoso sheddeth man's blood, by man shall his blood be shed.

The personal appearance of Dr. Parkman was remarkable—so much so, that his identity could not well be mistaken, by any one, who had carefully observed his person. His body was unusually attenuated, and I have often, while looking at his profile, perceived a resemblance to Hogarth's sketch of his friend Fielding, taken from memory, after death.

The talents of Dr. George Parkman were highly respectable. His mind was of that order, which took little rest—its movements, like those of his body, were always quick; more so, perhaps, upon some occasions, than comported with the formation of just and permanent judgment. He was a respectably well read man, not only in his own profession, but he possessed a very creditable store of general information, and was an entertaining and instructive companion. In various ways, he promoted the best interests of medical science; and nothing, probably, prevented him from attaining very considerable eminence, in his calling, but the accession of hereditary wealth; whose management occupied, for many years, a large portion of his time and thoughts.

By some persons, he has been accounted over sharp and hard, in his pecuniary dealings—mean and even miserly. No opinion can be more untrue. Dr. Parkman's eccentricity was nowhere so manifest, as in his money relations. The line was singularly well defined, in his mind, between charity, or liberality, and traffic. He adhered to the time-honored maxim, that *there is no love in trade*. There are persons, who, in their dealings, give up fractions, and suffer petty encroachments, for the sake of popularity; and who make, not only their own side of a bargain, but, in a very amiable, patronizing way, a portion of the other. Dr. Parkman did none of these things. He gave men credit, for a full share of selfishness and cunning—made his contracts carefully—performed them strictly—and expected an exact fulfilment, from the other party.

It is perfectly natural, that the promptness and the pertinacity of Dr. Parkman, in exacting the punctual payment of money, and the strict performance of contracts, should be equally surprising and annoying to those, whose previous dealings had been with men, of less method and vigilance. But no man, however irritated by the daily repetition of the dun, has ever charged, upon Dr. Parkman, the slightest departure from the line of strict integrity. He was a man of honor, in the true acceptation of that word. His domestic arrangements were of the most liberal kind—his manners were courteous—and he possessed the high spirit of a gentleman—and, with all the occasional evidences, which his conduct *openly* supplied, of his particular care, in the gathering of units; he could be *secretly* liberal, with hundreds.

It may well be doubted, if any individual has ever lived, for sixty years, in this city, whose real character has been so little understood, by the community at large. The reason is at hand—he exposed that regard for pittances, which most men conceal—and he concealed many acts of charity, which most men expose. He had many tenants of the lower order—he was frequently his own collector, and brought upon himself many murmurs and complaints, which are commonly the agent's portion.

The charities of Dr. Parkman wore an aspect, now and then, of whimsicality, and were strangely contrasted with *apparent* meanness. Thus, upon one occasion, he is said to have insisted upon being paid a paltry balance of rent, some twenty-five cents, by a poor woman, who assured him it was all she had to buy her dinner. *"Now we have settled the rent,"* said he, and immediately gave her a couple of dollars.

A gentleman, an old college acquaintance of Dr. Parkman's, told me, a day or two since, that the Dr. came to him, after this gentleman's failure, some years ago, and said to him, with great kindness and delicacy—"You want a house—there is mine in — — street, empty and repaired—take it—you shall pay no rent for a year, and as much longer, as may suit your convenience."

In 1832, this city was visited by the cholera. Mr. Charles Wells was Mayor, and a very good Mayor was he. Had his benevolence induced him to labor, for the more extensive diffusion of the blessing of alcohol, among the poor, the liquor trade would certainly have voted him a punch-bowl, for his vigorous opposition to the cholera. Upon the occasion, to which I refer, Dr. Parkman said to the city authorities—"You are seeking for a cholera hospital—take any of my houses, that may suit you, rent free, in welcome. If you prefer that, which I occupy, I will move out, with pleasure."

When Dorcas died, the good people of Joppa began to display her handiwork. I am surprised, though much of it was known to me before, at the amount of evidence, which is now produced, from various quarters, to prove, that this unfortunate gentleman was a man of the most kind affections, and of extensive, practical benevolence.

Let me close these remarks, with one brief anecdote; which, though once already related of Dr. Parkman, by the editor of the Transcript, is worthy of many republications, and is not at all like news, on the stock exchange, good only while it is new.

"A politician stopped the Doctor in the street and asked him to subscribe for the expense of a salute, in honor of some political victory. The Doctor put his arm in his, and invited him to take a little walk. He led him round the corner into a dismal alley, and then up three flights of rickety stairs into a room where a poor woman was sitting, propped by pillows, feebly attempting to sew. Some pale, hungry-looking children were near. The Doctor took six dollars out of his pocket-book, and handed it to the politician, and, simply remarking, "do with it as you please," he darted out of the room in his usually impulsive way."

I must close this feeble tribute of respect to the memory of one, who truly deserved a milder fate and an abler pen. Had we the power of recall— how well and wisely might we pay his ransom, with scores of men, quite as *eccentric* in their way, but whose *eccentricity* has very rarely assumed the charitable type!

No. LXXIII

When I was a very young man, I had the honor of a slight acquaintance with a most worthy gentleman, my senior by many years, who represented the town of Hull, in the Legislature of our Commonwealth. As I marked the solemn step, with which he moved along the public way, towards the House of Representatives, and the weight of responsibility, which hung upon his anxious brow—if such, thought I, is the effect, produced upon the representative of Hull—what an awful thing it must be, to represent the whole United States of North America, at the court of the greatest nation in the world!

In harmony with this opinion, every nation of the earth has selected, from the *élite* of the whole country, for the high and responsible employment of standing before the world, as the legitimate representative of itself, a man of affairs—I do not mean the affairs of trade, and discounts, and invoices, and profits—I use the word, in its most ample diplomatic sense—a man of great wisdom, and knowledge, and experience—a man familiar with the laws of nations—a man of dignity—not that arrogated dignity, which looks supremely wise, while it feels supremely foolish—but that conscious dignity, which is innate, and sits upon the wearer, like an easy garment—a man of liberal education, and great familiarity, not with the whole circle of sciences, but with the whole circle of historical and correlative knowledge—a man of classical erudition, and a scholar, competent to bear a becoming part, in that elevated intercourse of mind, which forms the dignified and delightful recreation of the diplomatist, in the first society of Europe.

Men, who have been bred up, amid the pursuits of trade, have been, with great propriety, selected, to fill the offices of *consuls*, in foreign lands; agreeably to the long established distinction, that *consuls* represent the *commercial affairs*—*ambassadors* the *state and dignity* of the country, from whence they come.

Oh! for the wand of that enchantress, the glorious witch of Endor! to turn up the sod of memory, and conjure, from their honorable graves, the train of illustrious, and highly gifted men, who, from time to time, have been sent forth, to represent this great Republic, before the throne of England!

First, on that scroll of honor, is a name, which shall prove coeval with the first days, and with the last, of this Republic. It shall never perish, till the whole earth itself shall be rolled up, like a scroll. On the second day of June, 1785, John Adams was presented to King George, the third. The very man, whom that obstinate, old monarch had never contemplated, in his royal visions, but as a rebel, suing for pardon, with a rope about his neck, then stood before him, calm and erect—the equal of that king, in all things, that became a man, and his mighty superior in many—the representative of a nation, which his consummate wisdom, and invincible, moral courage had contributed, so materially, to render free and independent.

What a tribute was conveyed, in the words of Jefferson, his political rival—"*The great pillar and support to the declaration of independence, and its ablest advocate and champion on the floor of the house was* John Adams. *He was the Colossus of that Congress: not graceful, not eloquent, not always fluent, in his public addresses, he yet came out with a power both of thought and expression, which moved the hearers from their seats.*"

In those thoughtful days, secretaries of legation were carefully selected, and with some reference, of course, to their contingent responsibilities, in the event of the absence, or illness, of their principals. When, in 1779, Mr. Adams went, on his mission to France, a gentleman of high qualifications, Mr. Francis Dana, gave up his seat, *as a member of Congress,* to follow that great man, *as secretary of legation.* Mr. Dana subsequently figured, ably and gracefully, in the highest stations. In 1780, he was minister to Russia. In 1784, he was a delegate to Congress. In 1797, he declined the office of envoy extraordinary to France. From 1792 to 1806, he was the able, impartial, and eminently dignified Chief Justice of the Supreme Judicial Court of Massachusetts.

In 1794, it was thought, by the appointing power, that John Jay might be trusted to represent our Republic, at the British Court. With what a reputation, for wisdom, and talents, and learning, that great man crossed the sea! Mr. Jay, an eminent lawyer, uniting the wisdom and dignity of years, with the vigor and zeal of early manhood, was a member of the first American Congress, at the age of twenty-nine. Chairman of the Committee, of which Lee and Livingston were members, he was the author of the eloquent "*Address to the People of Great Britain.*" He was Chief Justice of the State of New York, from 1777 to 1779, and relinquished that elevated station, as incompatible with the due performance of his duties, as President of Congress. From his skilful hand came the stirring address of that assembly, to its constituents, of Sept. 8, 1779. He was appointed minister plenipotentiary to Spain, at the close of that year—a commissioner, to negotiate peace with Great Britain, in 1782—Chief Justice of the Supreme Judicial Court of the United States, in 1789—Governor of New York, in 1795, being then abroad, as minister plenipotentiary of the United States, to Great Britain, to which office he was appointed in 1794—and again Governor of New York, in 1798.

Rufus King graduated at Harvard College, in 1777, with a high reputation, as a classical scholar and an orator; and studied his profession, with the late Chief Justice Parsons. In 1784, he was a delegate to Congress. He was a member of the Convention of 1787, to form the Constitution of the United States. In 1789, he was a member of the United States Senate. Of the celebrated Camillus papers, commonly ascribed to Hamilton, all, excepting the ten first, were from the pen of Rufus King. In 1796, he was nominated, by Washington, minister plenipotentiary to the Court of Great Britain. He filled that high station, till the close of the second year of the Jefferson administration. After a long retirement, he was again in the Senate of the United States, in 1813. After quitting the Senate, in 1825, he was once more appointed minister to Great Britain; but, after remaining abroad, about a year, in ill health, he returned, and died at Jamaica, Long Island, April 29, 1827.

"And what shall I more say? For the time would fail me, to tell of" Pinckney, and Gore, and the younger Adams, that incarnation of wisdom and learning, and Gallatin, and Maclean, and Everett, and Bancroft, every one of whom has been preceded, by the well-earned reputation of high, intellectual powers and attainments, whatever may have been the difference of their political opinions.

Knowledge is power; talent is power; and fine literary tastes and acquirements are, preëminently, power; and, in no spot, upon the surface of the earth, are they more truly so, than in the great British metropolis. The wand of a man of letters can there do more, than can be achieved, by the power of Midas, or the wonder-working lamp of Aladdin.

Our fathers, therefore, preferred, that the nation should be represented, in its simplicity and strength, by men of long heads, strong hearts, and short purses. They considered a regular, thorough, and polished education, literary attainments of a very high order, a clear and comprehensive knowledge of the law of nations, and an extensive store of general information, absolutely essential, in a minister plenipotentiary, from this Republic, to the Court of Great Britain; for our *state and dignity* were to be represented there, not less than our *commercial relations.*

They well knew, that our representative should be qualified to represent the refined and educated portions of our community, in the presence of those elevated classes, among whom he must frequently appear; and "*whose talk*," to use the expression of Dr. Johnson, was not likely to be "*of bullocks*." They therefore invariably selected, for this exalted station, one, who would be abundantly able to represent the nation, with gravity, and dignity, and wisdom, and knowledge, and power; and who would never be reduced, whatever the subject might be, to believe his safety was in sitting still, or of suffering the secret of his impotency to escape, by opening his mouth.

If I have passed too rapidly for the reader's willingness to linger, over the names of some highly distinguished men, who have so ably represented our country, at the British Court, and who still *survive*—it is because *my dealings are with the dead.*

No. LXXIV

"An immense quantity of fuel was always of necessity used, when dead bodies were burned, instead of buried; and a friend, learned in such lore, as well as in much that is far more valuable, informs us that the burning of a *martyr* was always an expensive process."

This passage was transferred, from the New York Courier and Enquirer, to the Boston Atlas, December 29, 1849, and is part of an article having reference to the partial cremation of Dr. Parkman's remains.

I must presume, as a sexton of the old school, to doubt the accuracy of this statement, in the very face of the averment, that the editor's authority is *"a friend, learned in such lore."*

To enable my readers to judge of the comparative expense of burial, in the ordinary mode, by interment or entombment, and by cremation, I refer, in the first place, to Mr. Chadwick's Report, made by request of Her Majesty's Principal Secretary of State, for the Home Department, Lond. 1843, in which it is stated, that a Master in Chancery, when dealing with insolvent estates, will pass, *"as a matter of course,"* such claims as these—from £60 to £100 for burying an upper tradesman—£250 for burying a gentleman—£500 to £1500 for burying a nobleman.

But let us confine our remarks to the particular allegation. The *"friend, learned in such lore,"* has greatly diminished the labor of refutation, by confining his statement to the burning of *martyrs*—*"the burning of a martyr was always an expensive process,"* requiring, says the Courier and Enquirer, *"an immense quantity of fuel."*

I well remember to have read, though I cannot recall the authority, that aromatic woods and spices were occasionally used in the East, during the *suttees*, to correct the offensive odor. In addition to the reason, assigned by Cicero, De Legibus, ii. 23, for the law against intramural burning, that conflagration might be avoided—Servius, in a note, on the Æneis, vi. 150, states another, that the air might not be infected with the stench. To prevent this, we know that costly perfumes were cast upon the pile; and the respect and affection for the defunct came to be measured, at last, by this species of extravagance; just as the funereal sorrow of the Irish is supposed to be graduated, by the number of coaches, and the quantity of whiskey.

But our business is with the *martyrs*. What was the cost of burning John Rogers I really do not know. I doubt if the process was very expensive; for good old John Strype has told us, almost to a fagot, how much fuel it took, to burn Cranmer, Latimer, and Ridley. The fuel, employed to burn Latimer and Ridley, cost fifteen shillings and four pence sterling for both; and the fuel for burning Cranmer, nine shillings and four pence only. Then there were chains, stakes, laborers, and cartage; and the whole cost for burning all three, was *one pound, sixteen shillings, and six pence!* Not a very expensive process truly. The authority is not at every one's command: I therefore give it entire, from Strype's Memorials of Cranmer, Oxford ed., 1840, vol. i. p. 563:—

	s.	d.
"For three loads of wood fagots to burn Ridley and Latimer,	12	0
Item, one load of furs fagots,	3	4
For the carriage of these four loads,	2	0
Item, a post,	1	4
Item, two chains,	3	4
Item, two staples,	0	6
Item, four laborers,	2	8
"For Burning Cranmer.		
For an 100 of wood fagots,	6	0
For an 100 and half of furs fagots,	3	4
For the carriage of them,	0	8
To two laborers,	1	4."

£1500 to *bury* a nobleman, and £1 16 6, to *burn* three martyrs! Leaving the Courier and Enquirer, and the *"friend, learned in such lore,"* to *bury* or to *burn* this record, as they please, I turn to another subject, referred to, on the very same page of Strype's Memorials, and which is not without some little interest, at the present moment.

A prisoner, charged with any terrible offence, innocent or guilty, lies under the *surveillance* of all eyes and ears. The slightest act, the shortest word, the very breath of his nostrils are carefully reported. The public resolves itself into a committee of anxious inquirers, to ascertain precisely how he eats, and drinks, and sleeps. There are persons of lively fancies, whose imaginations fire up, at the mere sight of his prison walls, and start off, under high pressure, filling the air with rumors, too horribly delightful, to be doubted for an instant.

If the topic were not the terrible thing that it is, it would be difficult to preserve one's gravity, while listening to some portion of the testimony, upon which, it may be our fortune, one of these days, to be convicted of murder, by the charitable public.

Of the guilt or innocence of John White Webster I *know* nothing, and I *believe* nothing. But it has been currently reported, that, since his confinement, he has been detected, in the crime of eating oysters. I doubt, if this ordeal would have been considered entirely satisfactory, even by Dr. Mather, in 1692. Man is a marvellous monster, when sitting, self-placed, in judgment, on his fellow! The very thing, which is a sin, in the commission or observance, is no less a sin, in the omission and the breach—for who will doubt the blood-guiltiness of a man, that, while confined, on a charge of murder, can partake of an oyster pie! And if he cannot do this, who will doubt, that a consciousness of guilt has deprived him of his appetite!

I have heard of a drunken husband, who, while staggering home, after midnight, communed with himself, as follows—*"If my wife has gone to bed, before I get home to supper, I'll beat her,—and if she is sitting up, so late as this, burning my wood and candles, I'll beat her."*

Good John Strype, ibid. 562, says of Cranmer, Latimer and Ridley, while in the prison of Bocardo—"They ate constantly suppers as well as dinners. Their meals amounted to about three or four shillings; seldom exceeding four. Their bread and ale commonly came to two pence or three pence; they had constantly cheese and pears for their last dish, both at dinner and supper; and always wine." It is not uninteresting to note the prices, paid for certain articles of their diet, in those days, 1555. While describing the *provant* of these martyrs, Strype annexes the prices, *"it being an extraordinary dear time.—*A goose, 14d. A pig, 12 oz. 13d. A cony, 6d. A woodcock, 3d. and sometimes 5d. A couple of chickens, 6d. Three plovers, 10d. Half a dozen larks, 3d. A dozen of larks and 2 plovers, 10d. A breast of veal, 11d. A shoulder of mutton, 10d. Roast beef, 12d." He presents one of Cranmer's bills of fare:—

"Bread and ale,	2.d.
Item oisters,	1.d.
Item butter,	2.d.
Item eggs,	2.d.
Item lyng,	8.d.

Item a piece of fresh salmon,	10.d.
Wine,	3.d.
Cheese and pears,	2.d."

Two bailiffs, Wells and Winkle, upon their own responsibility, furnished the table of these martyrs, and appear never to have been reimbursed. Strype says, ibid. 563, that they expended £63 10s. 2d., and never received but £20, which they obtained from Sir William Petre, Secretary of State. Ten years after, a petition was presented to the successor of Cranmer, that these poor bailiffs might receive some recompense.

After the pile had burnt down, in the case of Cranmer, upon raking among the embers, his heart was found entire. Upon this incident, Strype exclaims—"Methinks it is a pity, that his heart, that remained sound in the fire, and was found unconsumed in his ashes, was not preserved in some urn; which, when the better times of Queen Elizabeth came, might, in memory of this truly good and great Thomas of Canterbury, have been placed among his predecessors, in his church there, as one of the truest glories of that See."

In 1821, Mr. William Ward, of Serampore, published, in London, his "Farewell Letters." Mr. Ward was a Baptist missionary; and, at the time of the publication, was preparing to return to Bengal. This work was very favorably reviewed in the Christian Observer, vol. xxi. p. 504. I have never met with a description, so exceedingly minute, of the *suttee*, the process of burning widows. He thus describes the funeral pile—"The funeral pile consists of a quantity of fagots, laid on the earth, rising, in height, about three feet from the ground, about four feet wide, and six feet in length." Admitting these fagots to be closely packed, the pile contains seventy-two cubic feet of wood, or fifty-six less than a cord. "*A large quantity of fagots are then laid upon the bodies,*" says Mr. Ward. As the widow often leaps from the pile, and is chased back again, into the flames, by the benevolent Bramins, the fagots, which are not heaped *around* the pile, but "*laid on the bodies,*" cannot be a very oppressive load; and the quantity, thus employed in the *suttee*, is for the cremation of two bodies, at least, the dead husband, and the living widow.

There can be no doubt of the superior economy of cremation, over earth-burial. The notions of an "*expensive process,*" and the "*immense quantities of fuel,*" have no foundation in practice. If the ashes, as has been sometimes the case, were given to the winds, or cast upon the waters, the expense of cremation would be exceedingly small. But cremation, however inexpensive, in itself, has led to unmeasured extravagance, in the matter of urns of the most costly materials, and workmanship, of which an ample account may be found, in the *Hydriotaphia* of Sir Thomas Browne, London, 1835, vol. iii. p. 449.

More remarkable changes have occurred, in modern times, than a revival of the practice of cremation. It is an error, however, to suppose this practice to have been the original mode of dealing with the dead. It was very general about the year 1225, B. C., but the usage, at the present day, was, doubtless, the primitive practice of mankind. So thought Cicero, De Legibus ii. 22. "Ac mihi quidem antiquissimum sepulturæ genus id fuisse videtur, quo apud Xenophontem Cyrus utitur. Redditur enim terræ corpus, et ita locatum ac situm, quasi operimento matris obducitur."

Nevertheless, there is a strong cremation party among us. Who would not save sixpence, if he could, even in a winding-sheet! Should the wood and lumber interest be fairly represented, in our city councils, it would not be surprising, if there should be a majority, in favor of taking the remains of our citizens to Nova Scotia, to be burnt, rather than to Malden, to be buried. My friends, Birch, Touchwood, and Deal, are of this opinion; and would be happy to receive the citizens on board their regular coasters, for this purpose, at a reasonable price, per hundred, or by the single citizen—packed in ice.

An experienced person will be always on hand, to receive the corpses. Religious services will be duly performed, during the burning, without extra charge; and, should the project find favor with the public, a regular line of funeral coasters, with appropriate emblems, and figure-heads, will, in due time, be established. Those, who prefer the more economical mode of water-burial, for their departed relatives, thereby saving the expense of fuel altogether, will be accommodated, if they will leave orders in writing, with the masters on board, who will personally superintend the dropping of the bodies, off soundings.

No. LXXV

While attempting to rectify the supposed mistakes of other men, we sometimes commit egregious blunders ourselves. In turning over an old copy of John Josselyn's Voyages to New England, in 1638 and 1663, my attention was attracted, by a particular passage, and a marginal manuscript note, intended to correct what the annotator supposed, and what some readers might suppose, to be a blunder of the printer, or the author. The passage runs thus—"In 1602, these North parts were further discovered by Capt. *Bartholomew Gosnold*. The first *English* that planted there, set down not far from the *Narragansetts Bay*, and called their Colony *Plimouth*, since old *Plimouth, An. Dom., 1602.*" The annotator had written, on the margin, "*gross blunder*," and, in both instances, run his indignant pen through 1602, and substituted 1620. There are others, doubtless, who would have done the same thing. The first aspect of the thing is certainly very tempting. The text, nevertheless, is undoubtedly correct. It is altogether likely, that the matter, stated by Josselyn, can be found, so stated by no other writer. In 1602, Gosnold discovered the Elizabeth Islands, and built a house, and erected palisades, on the "Island Elizabeth," the westernmost of the group, whose Indian name was Cuttyhunk. In 1797, Dr. Jeremy Belknap visited this interesting spot. "*We had the supreme satisfaction,*" says he, Am. Biog. ii. 115, "*to find the cellar of Gosnold's store-house!*"

Hutchinson, i. 1, refers expressly to the passage, in Josselyn; and after stating that Gosnold discovered the Elizabeth Islands, in 1602, and built a fort there, and intended a settlement, but could not persuade his people to remain, he adds, in a note—"*This, I suppose, is what Josselyn, and no other author, calls the first colony of New Plimouth, for he says it was begun in 1602, and near Narragansett Bay.*"

The writer of a "Topographical Description of New Bedford," M. H. C., iv. 234, states, that the island, on which Gosnold built his fort and store-house, was *Nashaun*, and refers to Dr. Belknap's Biography. The New Bedford writer is wrong, in point of fact, and right, in point of reference. Dr. Belknap published the first volume of his Biography, in 1794, containing a short notice of Gosnold, in which, p. 236, he says—"The island, on which

Gosnold and his companions took up their abode, is now called by its Indian name, *Nashaun*, and is the property of the Hon. James Bowdoin, of Boston, to whom I am indebted for these remarks on Gosnold's journal." The writer of the description of New Bedford published his account, the following year, and relied on Dr. Belknap, who unfortunately relied on his informant, who, it seems, was entirely mistaken.

Dr. Belknap published his second volume, in 1798, with a new and more extended memoir of Gosnold, in which, p. 100, he remarks—"The account of Gosnold's voyage and discovery, in the first volume of this work, is so erroneous, from the misinformation, which I had received, that I thought it best to write the whole of it anew. The former mistakes are here corrected, partly from the best information which I could obtain, after the most assiduous inquiry; but principally from *my own observations*, on the spot; compared with the journal of the voyage, more critically examined than before."

Here is abundant evidence of that scrupulous regard for historical truth, for which that upright and excellent man was ever remarkable. With most writers, the pride of authorship would have revolted. The very thought of these *vestigia retrorsum*, would not have found toleration, for a moment. Some less offensive mode might have been adopted, by the employment of *errata*, or *appendices*, or *addenda*. Not so: this conscientious man, however innocently, had misled the public, upon a few historical points, and nothing would give him satisfaction, but a public recantation. His right hand had not been the agent, like Cranmer's, of voluntary falsehood, but of unintentional mistake, like Scævola's; and nothing would suffice, in his opinion, but the actual cautery.

In this second life of Gosnold, p. 114, after describing "the island Elizabeth," or Cuttyhunk, Dr. Belknap says—"To this spot I went, on the 20th day of June, 1797, in company with several gentlemen, whose curiosity and obliging kindness induced them to accompany me. The protecting hand of nature had reserved this favorite spot to herself. Its fertility and its productions are exactly the same, as in Gosnold's time, excepting the wood, of which there is none. Every species of what he calls 'rubbish,' with strawberries, pears, tansy, and other fruits, and herbs, appear in rich abundance, unmolested by any animal but aquatic birds. We had the supreme satisfaction to find the cellar of Gosnold's store-house."

"*We had the supreme satisfaction to find the cellar of Gosnold's store-house!*"—A whole-souled ejaculation this! I reverence the memory of the man who made it. It is not every other man we meet on 'Change, who can estimate a sentiment like this. My little Jew friend, in Griper's Alley, entirely mistakes the case. Never having heard of Bart Gosnold before, he takes him, for the like of Kidd; and the venerable Dr. Jeremy Belknap, for a gold-finder. What *supreme satisfaction* could there be, in discovering the cellar of a store-house, nearly two hundred years old, unless hidden treasures were there concealed! How, in the name of two per cent. a month, and all the other gods we worship, could a visit down to Cuttyhunk ever *pay*, only to stare at the stones of an ancient cellar!

Dr. Belknap's ejaculation reminds one of divers interesting matters—of Archimedes, when he leaped from his bath, and ran about naked, for joy, with *eureka* on his lips, having excogitated the plan, for detecting the fraud, practised upon Hiero.—It also recalls—*parvis componere magna*—Johnson's memorable exclamation, upon walking over the graves, at Icolmkill—"To abstract the mind from all local emotion would be impossible, if it were endeavored, and would be foolish, if it were possible. Whatever withdraws us from the power of our senses; whatever makes the past, the distant or the future predominate over the present, advances us in the dignity of thinking beings. Far from me and from my friends be such frigid philosophy, as may conduct as indifferent and unmoved over any ground, which has been dignified by wisdom, bravery or virtue. That man is little to be envied, whose patriotism would not gain force upon the plains of Marathon, or whose piety would not grow warmer among the ruins of Iona."

Dr. Jeremy Belknap was a Boston boy, born June 4, 1744. He learned his rudiments, under the effective birch of Master Lovell; graduated A. M. at Harvard, 1762, S. T. D. 1792. He was ordained pastor of the church in Dover, N. H. 1767; and in 1787, he became pastor of the church in Berry Street, formerly known as Johnny Moorehead's, who was settled there in 1730, and succeeded, by David Annan, in 1783, and which is now Dr. Gannett's.

Dr. Belknap was the founder of the Massachusetts Historical Society, and one of the most earnest promoters of the welfare of Harvard College.

Dr. Belknap published sermons, on various occasions; a volume of dissertations, on the character and resurrection of Christ; his history of New Hampshire in three volumes; his American Biography, in two volumes; and the Foresters, an American Tale, well worthy of republication, at the present day. He wrote extensively, in the newspapers, and published several essays, on the slave trade, and upon the early settlement of the country.

I have the most perfect recollection of this excellent man; for I saw him often, when I was very young; and I used to wonder, how a man, with so rough a voice, could bestow such a benign and captivating smile, upon little boys.

The churchman prays to be delivered from *sudden* death. Dr. Belknap prayed for *sudden* death—that he might be translated *"in a moment"*—such were his words. Yet here is no discrepancy. No man, prepared to die, will pray for a lingering death—and to him, who is not prepared, no death, however prolonged, can be other than *sudden* and premature. On the ninth of February, 1791, Dr. Belknap was called to mourn the loss of a friend, whose death was immediate. Among the Dr.'s papers, after his decease, the following lines were found, bearing the date of that friend's demise, and exhibiting, with considerable felicity of language, his own views and aspirations:—

"When faith and patience, hope and love
Have made us meet for Heav'n above;
How blest the privilege to rise,
Snatch'd, in a moment, to the skies!
Unconscious, to resign our breath,
Nor taste the bitterness of death!
Such be my lot, Lord, if thou please
To die in silence, and at ease;
When thou dost know, that I'm prepared,
Oh seize me quick to my reward.
But, if thy wisdom sees it best,
To turn thine ear from this request;
If sickness be th' appointed way,
To waste this frame of human clay;
If, worn with grief, and rack'd with pain,
This earth must turn to earth again;
Then let thine angels round me stand;
Support me, by thy powerful hand;
Let not my faith or patience move,
Nor aught abate my hope or love;
But brighter may my graces shine,
Till they're absorbed in light divine."

The will of the Lord coincided with the wish of this eminent disciple; and his was the sudden death, that he had asked of God. At 4 o'clock in the morning of June 20, 1798, paralysis seized upon his frame, and, before noon, he was no more.

Personal considerations of the flesh cannot be supposed, alone, to have moved the heart of this benevolent man. Who would not wish to avoid that pain, which is reflected, for days, and weeks, and months, and years, from the faces of those we love, who watch, and weep, about the bed of disease and death! Who can imagine this veteran soldier of the cross, with his armor of righteousness, upon the right hand and upon the left, awaiting the welcome signal to depart—without adopting, in the spiritual, and in the physical, sense, the language of the prophet—"*Let me die the death of the righteous, and let my last end be like his.*"

No. LXXVI

I never dream, if I can possibly avoid it—when the thing is absolutely forced upon me, why that is another affair. On the evening of the second day of January, 1850, from some inexplicable cause, I lost all appetite for my pillow. I had, till past eleven, been engaged, in the perusal of Goethe's Confessions of a Fair Saint. After a vain trial of the commonplace expedients, such as counting leaping sheep, up to a thousand and one; humming Old Hundred; and fixing my thoughts upon the heads of good parson Cleverly's last Sabbath sermon, on perseverance; I, fortunately, thought of Joel Barlow's Columbiad, and, after two or three pages, went, thankfully, to bed. I threw myself upon my right side, as I always do; for, being deaf—very—in the sinister ear, I thus exclude the nocturnal cries of fire, oysters, and murder.

I think I must have been asleep, full half an hour, by a capital Shrewsbury clock, that I keep in my chamber. It was, of course, on the dawning side of twelve—the very time, when dreams are true, or poets lie, which latter alternative is impossible. I was aroused, by the stroke of a deep-toned bell; and, in an instant, sat bolt upright, listening to the sound. I should have known it, among a thousand—it was the old passing bell of King's Chapel. I am confident, as to the bell—it had the full, jarring sound, occasioned by the blockhead of a sexton, who cracked it, in 1814. I counted the strokes—one—two—three—an adult male, of course—and then the age—seventy-four was the number of the strokes of that good old bell, corresponding with the years of his pilgrimage—and then a pause—I almost expected another—so, doubtless, did he, poor man—but it came not!—Some old stager, thought I, has put up, for the long night; and the power of slumber was upon me, in a moment.

I slept—but it was a fitful sleep—and I dreamt such a dream, as none but a sexton of the old school can ever dream—

> — — — "velut ægri somnia, vanæ
> Fingentur species, ut nec pes, nec caput uni
> Reddatur formæ."

"Funeral baked meats," and bride's cake, and weepers, and wedding rings seemed oddly consorted together. At one moment, two very light and airy skeletons seemed to be engaged, in dancing the polka; and, getting angry, flung their skulls furiously at each other. I then fancied, that I saw old Grossman, driving his hearse at a full run, with the corpse of an intemperate old lady, not to the graveyard, but, by mistake, to the very shop, where she bought her Jamaica. I dare not relate the half of my dream, lest I should excite some doubt of my veracity. For aught I know, I might have dreamt on till midsummer, had not a hand been laid on my shoulder, and a change come over the spirit of my dream, in a marvellous manner—for I actually dreamt I was wider awake, than I often am, when Sirius rages, of a summer afternoon, and I am taking my comfort, in my postprandial chair.

Starting suddenly, I beheld the well known features of an old acquaintance and fellow-spadesman—"Don't you know me?" "Yes," said I—"no, I can't say I do"—for I was confoundedly frightened—"Not know me! Haven't we lifted, head and foot, together, for six and thirty years?" "Well, I suppose we have; but you are so deadly pale; and, will you be so kind as to take your hand from my shoulder; for it's rather airy, at this season, you know, and your palm is like the hand of death." "And such it is," said he—"did you not hear my bell?" "*Your* bell?" I inquired, gazing more intently, at the little, white-haired, old man, that stood before me. "Even so, Abner," he replied; "your old friend, and fellow-laborer, Martin Smith, is dead. I always had a solemn affection, for the passing bell. It sounded not so pleasantly, to be sure, in the neighborhood of theatres and gay hotels; and its good, old, solemnizing tones are no longer permitted to be heard. I longed to hear it, once more; and, after they had laid me out, and left me alone, I clapped on my great coat, over my shroud, as you see, and ran up to the church, and tolled my own death peal. When, more than one hundred years ago, in 1747, Dr. Caner took possession, in the old way, by entering, and closing the doors, and tolling the bell, as the Rev. Roger Price had done before, in 1729, he did not feel, that the church belonged to him, half so truly as I have felt, for many years, whenever I got a fair grip of that ancient bell-rope."

"Martin," said I, "this is rather a long speech, for a ghost; and must be wearying to the spirit; suppose you sit down." This I said, because I really supposed the good, little, old man, contrary to all his known habits, was practising upon my credulity—perhaps upon my fears; and was playing a new year's prank, in his old age: and I resolved, by the smallest touch of sarcasm in the world, to show him, that I was not so easily deceived. He made no reply; but, drawing my hand between his great coat and shroud, placed it over the region of his heart—"Good God! you are really dead then, Martin!" said I, for all was cold and still there. "I am," he replied. "I have lived long—did you count the strokes of my bell?"—I nodded assent, for I could not speak.—"Four years beyond the scriptural measure of man's pilgrimage. You are not so old as I am" — "No," I replied. — "No, not quite," said he. — "No, no, Martin," said I, adjusting my night cap, "not by several years." — "Well," said the old man, with a sigh, "a few years make very little difference, when one has so many to answer for; those odd years are like a few odd shillings, in a very long account. I have come to ask you to go with me." — A cold sweat broke through my skin, as quickly, as if it had been mere tissue paper; and my mind instantly sprang to the work of finding devices, for putting the old man off. "Surely," said he, observing my reluctance, "you would not deny the request of a dying man." "Perhaps not," I replied, "but now that you are dead, dear Martin, for Heaven's sake, what's the use of it?"

The old man seemed to be pained, by my hesitation — "Abner," said he, after a short pause, "you and I have had a goodly number of strange passages, at odd hours, down in that vault — are ye afeard, Abner — eh!" — "Why, as to that, Martin," said I, "if you were a real, live sexton, I'd go with pleasure; but our relations are somewhat changed, you will admit. Besides, as I told you before, I cannot see the use of it." I felt rather vexed, to be suspected of fear.

"You have the advantage of me, Abner Wycherly," said Martin Smith, "being alive; and I have come to ask you to do a favor, for me, which I cannot do, for myself." — "What is it?" said I, rather impatiently, perhaps. — "I want you to embalm my" — "Martin," said I, interrupting him — "I can't — I never embalmed in my life." "You misunderstand me" — the old man replied — "I want you to embalm my memory; and preserve it, from the too common lot of our profession, who are remembered, often, as resurrectionists, and men of intemperate lives, and mysterious conversations. I want you to allow me a little *niche*, among your *Dealings with the Dead*. I shall take but little room, you see for yourself" — and then, in an under-tone, he said something about thinking more of the honor, than he should of a place in Westminster Abbey; which was very agreeable, to be sure, notwithstanding the sepulchral tone, in which it was uttered. Indeed I was surprised to find how very refreshing, to the spirits of an author, this species of extreme unction might be, administered even by a ghost.

"Martin," said I, "I have always thought highly of your good opinion; but what can I say — how can I serve you?" "I am desirous," said he, "of transmitting to my children a good name, which is better than riches." — "Well, my worthy, old fellow-laborer," I replied, "if that is all you want, the work is done to your hand, already. You will not suspect me of flattering you to your face, now that you are dead, Martin; and I can truly say, that I have heard thousands speak of you, with great kindness and respect, and never a lisp against you. All this I am ready to vouch for—but, for what purpose, do you ask me to go with you?"

"I wish you to go with me, and examine for yourself," said the old man; "and then you can speak, of your own knowledge. Don't refuse me—let us have one more of those cozy walks, Abner, under the old Chapel, and over that yard. I desire to talk over some things with you there, which can be better understood, upon the spot—and I want to explain one or two matters, so that you may be able to defend my reputation, should any censure be cast upon it, after I am gone."—"I cannot go with you tonight, Martin," said I; "I see a gleam in the East, already."—"True," said he, "I may be missed."— For not more than the half of one second, I closed my eyes—and, in that twinkling of an eye, he was gone—but I heard him whisper, distinctly, as he went—"*tomorrow night!*"

No. LXXVII

I verily believe, that ghosts are the most punctual people in the world, especially if they were ever sextons, after the flesh. The last stroke of twelve had not ceased ringing in my ears, when that icy palm was again laid upon my shoulder; and Martin Smith stood by the side of my bed.

"Well, Martin," said I, "since you have taken the trouble to come out again, and upon such a stormy night withal, I cannot refuse your request." — It seemed to me, that I rose to put on my garments, and found them already on; and had scarcely prepared to go, with my old friend, to the Chapel, before we were in the middle of the broad aisle. Dreams are marvellous things, certainly — all this was a dream, I suppose — for, if it was not — what was it?

There seemed to be an oppressive weight, upon the mind of my old friend, connected, doubtless, with those explanations, which he had proposed to make, upon the spot. We sat down, near Governor Shirley's monument. "Abner," said he, "I wish, before I am buried, to make a clean breast, and to confess my misdeeds." — "I cannot believe, Martin," I replied, "that there is a very heavy, professional load upon your conscience. If there is, I know not what will become of the rest of us. But I will hearken to all you may choose to reveal." — "Well," resumed the old man, with a sigh, "I have tried to be conscientious, but we are all liable to error — we are are all fallible creatures, especially sextons. I have been sexton here, for six and thirty years; and I am often painfully reminded, that, in the year 1815, I was rather remiss, in dusting the pews." — "Have you any other burden upon your conscience?" — "I have," he replied; and, rising, requested me to follow him.

He went out into the yard, and walked near the northerly corner, where Dr. Caner's house formerly stood, which was afterwards occupied, as the Boston Athenæum, and, more recently, gave place to the present Savings Bank. "Here," said he, "thirty years ago, Dinah Furbush, a worthy, negro woman, was buried. The careless carpenter made her coffin one foot too short; and, to conceal his blunder, chopped off Dinah's head, and, clapping it between her feet, nailed down the lid. This scandalous transaction came to my knowledge, and I grieve to say, that I never communicated it to the wardens."—"Well, Martin," said I, "what more?"—"Nothing, thank Heaven!" he replied. Giving way to an irresistible impulse, I broke forth into a roar of laughter, so long and loud, that three watchmen gathered to the wall, and seeing Martin Smith, whom they well knew, with the bottom of his shroud, exhibited below his great coat, they dropped their hooks and rattles, and ran for their lives. Martin walked slowly back to the church, and I followed.

He walked in, among the tombs—thousands of spirits seemed to welcome his advent—but, as I crossed the threshold, at the tramp of a living foot, they vanished, in a moment.

"How many corpses have you lifted, my old friend, in your six and thirty years of office?" "About five thousand," he replied, "exclusive of babies. It is a very grateful employment, when one becomes used to it."

"I have heard," continued Martin, "that the office of executioner, in Paris, is highly respectable, and has been hereditary, for many years, in the family of the Sansons. I have done all in my power, to elevate our profession; and it is my highest ambition, that the office should continue in my family; and that my descendants may be sextons, till the graves shall give up their dead, and death itself be swallowed up in victory." I was sensibly touched, by the enthusiasm of this good old official; for I honor the man, who honors his calling. I could not refrain from saying a few kind and respectful words, of the old man's son and successor. He was moved—"The eyes of ghosts," said he, "are tearless, or I should weep. You have heard," continued the old man, in a low, tremulous voice, "that, when the mother of Washington was complimented, by some distinguished men, upon the achievements of her son, she went on with her knitting, saying, 'Well, George always was a good boy'—now, I need say no more of Frank; and, in truth, I can say no less. I knew he would be a sexton. He has forgotten it, I dare say; but he was not satisfied with the first go-cart he ever had, till he had fashioned it, like a hearse. He took hold right, from the beginning. When I resigned, and gave him the keys, and felt, that I should no more walk up and down the broad aisle, as I had done, for so many years, I wept like a child."

"Yours has been a hale old age. You have always been *temperate*, I believe," said I.—"No," the old man replied, "I have always been *abstinent*. Like yourself, I use no intoxicating drink, upon any occasion, nor tobacco, in any of its forms, and we have come, as you say, to a hale old age. I have seen drunken sextons squirt tobacco juice over the coffin and pall; and let the corpse go by the run; and I know more than one successor of St. Peter, in this city, who smoke and chew, from morning to night; and give the sextons great trouble, in cleaning up after them."

We had advanced midway, among the tombs.—"It is awfully cold and dark here, Martin," said I, "and I hear something, like a mysterious breathing in the air; and, now and then, it seems as if a feather brushed my cheek."—"Is it unpleasant?" said the old man.—"Not particularly agreeable," I replied.—"The spirits are aware, that another is added to their number," said he, "and even the presence of one, in the flesh, will scarcely restrain them from coming forth. I will send them back to their dormitories." He lighted a spirit lamp, not in the vulgar sense of that word, but a lamp, before whose rays no spirit, however determined, could stand, for an instant.

There is comfort, even in a farthing rush light—I felt warmer. "What a subterraneous life you must have had of it," said I, "and how many tears and sighs you must have witnessed!" "Why yes," he replied, with a shake of the head, and a sigh, "the duties of my office have given to my features an expression of universal compassion—a sort of omnibus look, which has caused many a mourner to say—'Ah, Mr. Smith, I see how much you feel for me.' And I'm sure I did; not perhaps quite so keenly as I might, if I had been less frequently encored in the performance of my melancholy part. Yes," continued the old man—"I have witnessed tears and sighs, and deep grief, and shallow, and raving—for a month, and life-long; very proper tears, gushing from the eyes of widows, already wooed and won; and from the eyes of widowers, who, in a right melancholy way, had predetermined the mothers, for their orphan children. But passages have occurred, now and then, all in my sad vocation, pure and holy, and soul-stirring enough, to give pulse to a heart of stone."

The old man took from his pocket a master key, and beckoned me to follow. He opened an ancient tomb. The mouldy shells were piled one upon another, and a few rusty fragments of that flimsy garniture, which was in vogue of old, had fallen on the bricks below.

"*Sacred to the memory!*" said the old man, with a sad, significant smile, upon his intelligent features, as he removed the coffin of a child. I looked into the little receptacle, as he raised the lamp. "This," said he, "was the most beautiful boy I ever buried." "This?" said I, for the little narrow house contained nothing but a small handful of grayish dust. "Aye," he replied, "I see; it is all gone now—it is twelve years since I looked at it last—there were some remnants of bones then, and a lock or two of golden hair. This small deposit was one of the first that I made, in this melancholy savings bank. Six-and-thirty years! So tender and so frail a thing may well be turned to dust.

"Time is an alchymist, Abner, as you and I well know. If tears could have embalmed, it would not have been thus. I have never witnessed such agony. The poor, young mother lies there. She was not seventeen, when she died. In a luckless hour, she married a very gentlemanly sot, and left her native home, for a land of strangers. Hers was the common fate of such unequal bargains. He wasted her little property, died of intemperance, and left her nothing, but this orphan boy. And all the love of her warm, young heart was turned upon this child. It had, to be sure, the sweetest, catching smile, that I ever beheld.

"Their heart strings seemed twisted together—the child pined; and the mother grew pale and wan. They waned together. The child died first. The poor, lone, young mother seemed frantic; and refused to part with her idol. After the little thing was made ready for the tomb, she would not suffer it to be removed. It was laid upon the bed, beside her. On the following day, I carried the coffin to the house; and, leaving it below, went up, with a kind neighbor, to the chamber, hoping to prevail upon the poor thing, to permit us to remove the body of the child. She was holding her little boy, clasped in her arms—their lips were joined together—'It is a pity to awaken her,' said the neighbor, who attended me—I put my hand upon her forehead—'Nothing but the last trump will awaken her,' said I—'she is dead.'"

"Well, Martin," said I, "pray let us talk of something else—where is old Isaac Johnson, the founder of the city, who was buried, in this lot, in 1630?"—"Ah"—the old man replied—"the prophets, where are *they*! I believe you may as well look among the embers, after a conflagration, for the original spark."

"You must know many curious things, Martin," said I, "concerning this ancient temple."—"I do," said he, "of my own knowledge, and still more, by tradition; and some things, that neither the wardens nor vestry wot of. If I thought I might trust you, Abner, in a matter of such moment, but"—"Did I ever deceive you, Martin," said I, "while living; and do you think I would take advantage of your confidence, now you are a ghost?"—"Pardon me, Abner," he replied, for he saw, that he had wounded my feelings, "but the matter, to which I allude, were it made public, would produce terrible confusion—but I will trust you—meet me here, at ten minutes before twelve, on Sabbath night—three low knocks upon the outer door—at present I can reveal no more."—"No postponement, on account of the weather?" I inquired.—"None," the old man replied, and locked up the tomb.

"Did you ever see Dr. Caner," I inquired, as we ascended into the body of the church.—"That," replied Martin Smith, "is rather a delicate question. In the very year, in which I was born, 1776, the Rev. Doctor Henry Caner, then an old man, carried off the church plate, 2800 ounces of silver, the gift of three kings; of which not a particle has ever been recovered: and, in lieu thereof, he left behind his fervent prayers, that God would "*change the hearts of the rebels.*" This the Almighty has never seen fit to do—so that the society have not only lost the silver, but the benefit of Dr. Caner's prayers. No, Abner, I have never seen Dr. Caner, according to the flesh, but—ask me nothing further, on this highly exciting subject, till we meet again."

I awoke, sorely disturbed—Martin had vanished.

No. LXXVIII

I know not why, but the idea of another meeting with Martin Smith, notwithstanding my affectionate respect, for that good old man, disturbed me so much, that I resolved, to be out of his way, by keeping awake. But, in defiance of my very best efforts, strengthened by a bowl of unsugared hyson, at half past eleven, if I err not, I fell into a profound slumber; and, at the very appointed moment, found myself, at the Chapel door. At the third knock, it opened, with an almost alarming suddenness—I quietly entered—and the old man closed it softly, after me.

"In ten minutes," said he, "the congregation will assemble."—"What," I inquired, "at this time of night?"—"Be silent," said he, rather angrily, as I thought; and, drawing me, by the arm, to the north side of the door, he shoved me against the Vassal monument, with a force, that I would not have believed it possible, for any modern ghost to exert. "Be still and listen," said he. "In 1782, my dear, old pastor, Dr. Freeman, came here, as Reader; and became Rector, in 1787. Dr. Caner was inducted, in 1747, and continued Rector, twenty-nine years; for, as I told you, he went off with the plate, in 1776. There were no Rectors, between those two. Brockwell and Troutbeck were Caner's assistants only: the first died in 1755, and the last left, the year before Dr. Caner."

"Well," continued the old man, "never reveal what I am about to tell you, Abner Wycherly—the Trinitarians have never surrendered their claims, upon this Church; and, precisely at midnight, upon every Sabbath, since 1776, Dr. Caner and the congregation have gathered here; and the Church service has been performed, just as it used to be, before the revolution. They make short work of it, rarely exceeding fifteen minutes—hush, for your life—they are coming!"

A glare of unearthly light, invisible through the windows, as Martin assured me, to all without, filled the tabernacle, in an instant—exceedingly like gas light; and, at the same instant, I heard a rattling, resembling the down-sitting, after prayers, in a village meeting-house, where the seats are clappers, and go on hinges. Observing, that my jaws chattered, Martin pressed my hand in his icy fingers, and whispered, that it was nothing but

Dr. Caner's congregation, coming up, rather less silently, of course, than when they were in the flesh.

Being the first Sunday in the month, all the communion plate, that Caner carried off, was paraded, on the altar. I wish the twelve apostles could have seen it. It glittered, like Jones, Ball & Poor's bow-window, viewed from the old, Donnison corner. The whole interior of the Chapel was marvellously changed. I was much struck, by a showy, gilt crown, over the organ, supported by a couple of gilt mitres. This was the famous organ, said to have been selected by Handel, and which came over in 1756.

At this moment, a brief and sudden darkness hid everything from view; succeeded, instantly, by a brighter light than before; and all was changed. The organ had vanished; the monuments of Shirley and Apthorp, and the tablet of Price, over the vestry door, were gone; I looked behind me, for the Vassal monument, against which I had been leaning; it was no longer there. Martin Smith perceived my astonishment, and whispered, that Dr. Caner was never so partial to the Stone Chapel, which was opened in 1754, as he was to the ancient King's Chapel, in which he had been inducted in 1747, and in which we then were.

The pews were larger than any Hingham boxes I ever saw; but very small. The pulpit was on the north side. In front of it was the governor's pew, highly ornamented, lined with China silk; the cushions and chairs therein were covered with crimson damask, and the window curtain was of the same material. Near to this, I saw an elevated pew, in which were half a dozen fine looking skeletons, with their heads up and their arms akimbo. This pew, Martin informed me, was reserved, for the officers of the army and navy. A small organ was in the western gallery, said to be the first, ever heard in our country. From the walls and pillars, hung several escutcheons and armorial bearings. I distinguished those of the royal family, and of Andros, Nicholson, Hamilton, Dudley, Shute, Belcher, and Shirley.

I had always associated the *hour-glass* with my ideas of a Presbyterian pulpit, in the olden time, when the very length of the discourse gave the hearer some little foretaste of eternity. I was rather surprised to see an hour-glass, of large proportions, perched upon the pulpit, in its highly ornamented stand of brass. The altar-piece was at the easterly end of the Church, with the Glory, the Ten Commandments, the Lord's Prayer, the Creed, and some texts of Scripture.

The congregation had taken their seats; and a slender, sickly looking skeleton glided into the reading desk. "Dr. Caner?" said I. "Brockwell, the assistant," replied Martin, in a whisper, "the very first wardens, of 1686, are in the pew, tonight, Bullivant and Banks. They all serve in rotation. Next Sabbath, we shall have Foxcroft and Ravenscroft. Clerke Hill, and Rutley are sextons, tonight."

The services were very well conducted; and, taking all things into consideration, I was surprised, that I comprehended so well, as I did. The prayer, for the royal family, was very impressively delivered. The assistant made use, I observed, of the Athanasian creed, and every one seemed to understand it, at which I was greatly surprised. Dr. Caner seemed very feeble, and preached a very short discourse upon the loss of Esau's birthright, making a pointed application, to the conversion of King's Chapel, by the Unitarians. He made rather a poor case of it, I thought. Martin was so much offended, that he said, though being a ghost, he was obliged to be quiet, he wished I would call the watch, and break up the meeting. I told him, that I did not believe Dr. Caner's arguments would have any very mischievous effect; and it seemed not more than fair, that these ancient worshippers should have the use of the church, at midnight, so long as they conducted themselves orderly—consumed no fuel—and furnished their own light.

One of the sextons, passing near me, accidentally dropped a small parcel. I was seized with a vehement desire of possessing it; and, watching my opportunity, conveyed it to my pocket. When Dr. Caner pronounced his final amen, light was instantly turned into darkness—a slight noise ensued—"*the service is over!*" said Martin, and all was still. I begged Martin to light his lamp; and, by its light, I examined the parcel the sexton had dropped. It was a small roll, containing some extracts from the records. They were not without interest. "Sept. 21, 1691.—It must not be forgot that Sir Robert Robertson gave a new silk damask cushion and cloth pulpit-cover." "1697.—Whit Sunday. Paid Mr. Coneyball, for buying and carting Poses and hanging the Doares 8s." "Dec. 20.—Paid for a stone Gug Clark Hill broak." "March 29, 1698.—Paid Mr. Shelson for Loucking after the Boyes £1." "1701, Aug. 4.—Paid for scouring the brass frame for the hour-glass 10s." "1733, Oct. 11.—Voted that the Brass Stand for the hour-glass be lent to the church of Scituate, as also three Diaper napkins, provided Mr. Addington Davenport, their minister, gives his note to return the same to the Church wardens of the Church, &c." "April 3, 1740.—Rec'd of Mr. Sylvester Gardner Sixteen Pounds Two Shills, in full for wine for the Chapple for the year past. John Hancock."

I was about to put this fragment of the record into my pocket—"If," said Martin, "you do not particularly covet a visit from Clark Hill, or whichever of the old sextons it was, that dropped that paper, leave it, as you found it." I did so, most joyfully.

"If you have any questions to ask of me," said the old man, "ask them now, and briefly, for we are about to part—to meet no more, until we meet, as I trust we shall, in a better world." "As a mere matter of curiosity," said I, "I should like to know, if you consider your venerable pastor, now dead and gone, Dr. Freeman, as the successor of Saint Peter?" "No more," said Martin Smith, with an expression almost too comical for a ghost, "than I consider you and myself successors of the sexton, who, under the directions of Abraham, buried Sarah, in the cave of the field of Machpelah, before Mamre." "Do you consider the Apostolical succession broken off, at the time of Dr. Freeman's ordination?" "Short off, like a pipe stem," he replied. "And so you do not consider the laying on of a Bishop's hand necessary, to empower a man to preach the Gospel?" "No more," said he, "than I consider the laying on of spades, necessary to empower a man, to dig a grave. We were a peculiar people, but quite as zealous for good works, as any of our neighbors. The Bishop of New York declined to ordain our pastor, because we were Unitarians; and we could not expect this service from our neighbors, had it been otherwise, on account of our adherence to the Liturgy, though modified, and to certain Episcopal forms—so we ordained him ourselves. The senior warden laid his hands upon the good man and true—said nothing of the thirty-nine articles—but gave him a Bible, as the sole compass for his voyage, in full confidence, that, while he steered thereby, we should be upon our course, to the haven, where we would be. We have never felt the want of the succession, for a moment, and, ever since, we have been a most happy and u— —."

Just then a distant steam whistle struck upon the ear, which Martin, undoubtedly, mistook, for cock-crowing—for his lamp was extinguished, in an instant, and he vanished.

If my confidence in dreams needed any confirmation, nothing more could be required, than a careful comparison of many of these incidents, with the statements, in the history of King's Chapel, published by the late, amiable Rector, seventeen years ago. A copy is, at this moment, beneath my eye; and, upon the fly leaf, in the author's own hand writing, under date Jan. 1, 1843, I read—"*Presented to Martin Smith, for many years, a sexton of this church, from his friend F. W. P. Greenwood.*" Aye; every one was the *friend* of good old Martin Smith. Here, deposited among the leaves of this book, is an order, from that excellent man, my honored friend, Colonel Joseph May, then junior warden. It bears date "Saturday, 18 June, 1814." It is laconic, and to the point. "*Toll slow!*" This also is subscribed "*Your friend.*"

Yes, every one was the friend of Martin Smith. He was a spruce, little, old man—especially at Christmas.

No. LXXIX

Nothing can be more entirely unfounded, than the popular notion, that circumstantial evidence is an inferior quality of proof. The most able writers, on the law of evidence, have always maintained the contrary.

Sir William Blackstone and Sir Matthew Hale, it is true, have expressed the very just and humane opinion, that circumstantial evidence should be weighed with extreme caution; and the latter has expressly said, that, in trials, for murder and manslaughter, no conviction ought ever to be had, until the fact is clearly proven, or the body of the person, alleged to have been killed, has been discovered; for he stated, that two instances had occurred, within his own knowledge, in which, after the execution of the accused, the persons, supposed to have been murdered, had reäppeared alive.

Probably, one of the most extraordinary cases of fatal confidence in circumstantial evidence, recorded, in the history of British, criminal jurisprudence, is that, commonly referred to, as the case of "*Hayes and Bradford.*" In that case, a murder was certainly committed; the body of the murdered man was readily found; the murderer escaped; and, after many years, confessed the crime, in a dying hour; and another person, who had designed to commit the murder, but found his intended victim, already slain, was arrested, as the murderer; and, after an elaborate trial, suffered for the crime, upon the gallows.

There is a case in the criminal jurisprudence of our own country, in all its strange particulars, far surpassing the British example, to which I have referred; and attended by circumstances, almost incredible, were the evidence and vouchers less respectable, than they are. I refer to the case of Stephen and Jesse Boorn, who were tried, for the murder of Russell Colvin, and convicted, before the Supreme Judicial Court of the State of Vermont, in October, 1819. In this remarkable case, it must be observed, that the Judges appeared to have acted, in utter disregard of that merciful caution of Sir Matthew Hale, to which I have alluded; and that these miserable men were rescued, from their impending fate, in a most remarkable manner.

It is my purpose to present a clear and faithful account of this occurrence; and, to enable the reader to go along with me, step by step, with perfect confidence, in a matter, in which, from the marvellous character of the circumstances, to doubt would be extremely natural, I will first exhibit the sources, from which the elements of this narrative are drawn. I. The public journals of the day, published in Vermont. II. "Mystery developed, &c., by the Rev. Lemuel Haynes, Hartford, 1820." III. A sermon, on the occasion, by the same. IV. "A brief sketch of the Indictment, Trial, and Conviction of Stephen and Jesse Boorn, for the murder of Russell Colvin, by S. Putnam Waldo, Hartford." V. "A Collection of remarkable events, by Leonard Deming. Middlebury, 1825." VI. "Journals of the General Assembly of the State of Vermont, for 1819, October session," in which, page 185, may be found the minutes of the testimony, taken on the trial, and certified up, by Judge Chace, to the Legislature, by request, on petition, for a commutation of punishment. VII. Law Reporter, published in Boston, vol. v. page 193. VIII. Trial of Stephen and Jesse Boorn, Rutland, 1820. IX. Remarks thereon, N. A. Review, vol. x. page 418. X. Greenleaf's Treatise on Evidence, vol. 1. page 320, note 2. XI. Cooley's Memoir of Rev. Lemuel Haynes, N. Y., 1839.

In the village of Manchester, Bennington County, and State of Vermont, there resided in 1812, an old man, whose name was Barney Boorn, who had two sons, Stephen and Jesse, and a daughter Sarah, who had married Russell Colvin. Like the conies of the Bible, these people were *a feeble folk*—their mental powers were slender—they grew up in ignorance—their lot was poverty. Colvin, in particular, was, notoriously, an *imbecile*. He had been, for a long period, partially deranged. He was incompetent to manage the concerns of his family. He moved about in an idle, wandering way, and was perfectly inoffensive; and the wilful destruction of such a man would have been the murder of an *innocent.*

In May, 1812, Russell Colvin was missing from home. This, in consideration of his uncertain habits, occasioned, at first, but little surprise. But his continued absence, for days, and weeks, and months, produced very considerable excitement, in the village of Manchester. This excitement naturally increased, with the term of his absence; and the contagion began, ere long, to catch upon the neighboring towns; until the most exciting topic of the day, throughout that portion of the Hampshire Grants, in the absence of mad dogs and revivals, was the mysterious disappearance of Russell Colvin.

Rumors began to spread, from lip to lip. Suspicion, like a hungry leech—"a German one"—fastened upon the Boorns. Nor was this suspicion groundless. Thomas Johnson, a neighbor of all the parties, a credible witness, who swore to the facts, seven years after, on the trial, reported, that the last time he saw Russell Colvin was immediately before his remarkable disappearance, and that he and the Boorns were then quarrelling, while engaged in picking up stones.

Lewis Colvin, the son of Russell, with manifest reluctance, stated, that, just before his father's disappearance, a quarrel took place, between his father and Stephen—that his father struck Stephen first—that Stephen then knocked his father down twice with a club—that he, the boy, was frightened and ran away—that Stephen told him never to mention what had happened—and that he had never seen his father since.

Here, doubtless, was legitimate ground, for suspicion, and the village of Manchester, on the Battenkill, was in a state of universal fermentation— the very atmosphere seemed redolent of murder. It is marvellous, in what manner the Boorns escaped from being lynched, without trial; and, more especially, how Stephen was preserved, from the fate of his namesake, the martyr. A shortlived calm followed this tempest of popular feeling—parties were formed—some were sure the Boorns were the murderers of Colvin— some were inclined to believe they were not. The Boorns continued to dwell in the village, *without any effort to escape*; and the evidence against them was not deemed legally sufficient then, even to authorize their arrest.

It appeared, upon the statement of Mrs. Colvin, that Stephen and Jesse, her brothers, had told her, upon a certain occasion, that she might be satisfied her husband was dead, and that *they knew it*. This additional fact gave fresh impulse to the popular excitement.

In such miserable society, as may be supposed to have remained to these suspected men, it is not wonderful, that they should often have encountered the most unsparing allusions, and vulgar interrogatories—nor that they should have met this species of persecution, with equally vulgar and unflinching replies. It became well established, ere long, upon the declarations of a Mr. Baldwin and his wife, that, when asked where Colvin had gone, one of the Boorns replied, that he had *"gone to hell"* —and the other that he had *"gone where potatoes would not freeze."*

It is not wonderful, that, upon such evidence, the daughters of Manchester should begin to prophecy, and the young men to see visions, and the old men to dream dreams. In the language of one, who has briefly described the condition of that village, during this period of intense excitement—*"Every house was haunted with the ghost of Colvin."*

At length, a respectable man, a paternal uncle of the Boorns, began to dream, in good earnest. The ghost of Colvin appeared to him, and told him, upon his honor, that he had been murdered; and indicated the place, with unmistakable precision, where his body lay concealed. Like a bill, which cannot pass to enactment, until after a third reading, the declarations of a ghost are not entitled to the slightest regard, until after a third repetition. Every sensible ghost knows this, of course. The ghost of Colvin seems to have understood his business perfectly; and he manifested a very commendable delicacy, in selecting one of the family, for his confidant. Three times, in perfect conformity with acknowledged precedent, the ghost of Colvin announced the fact of his murder, and indicated the place, where his body was concealed.

To put a slight upon a respectable ghost, in perfectly good standing, who had taken all this trouble, was entirely out of the question. Accordingly, the uncle of the Boorns summoned his neighbors—announced these revelations—gathered a posse—proceeded to dig in the hole, so particularly indicated by the ghost—and, after digging to a great depth, succeeded completely, in discovering nothing of any human remains. Indeed he was as unsuccessful, as our worthy friend, the Warden of the Prison, in his recent search for hidden treasure—excepting, that it does not appear, that the ghost made the slightest effort to bury him alive.

This movement was productive, nevertheless, of additional testimony, against the Boorns. In the hole, were found a jack-knife and a button, both which Mrs. Colvin solemnly declared to have belonged to her husband.

In regard to the location of the body, the ghost was certainly mistaken; perhaps Mr. Boorn, the uncle, being dull of hearing, might have misunderstood the revelation; and perhaps the memory of the ghost was treacherous. Evidence, gathered up by piecemeal, was, nevertheless, gradually enveloping the fate of these miserable men—evidence of a much more substantial material, than dreams are made of.

Thomas Johnson, the witness, above referred to, having purchased the field, where the quarrel took place, between Colvin and the Boorns, the children of Johnson found, while playing there, an old mouldy hat; which Johnson asserted, at the time, and afterwards, at the trial, swore, positively, had belonged to Colvin.

Nearly seven years had passed, since the disappearance of Russell Colvin. Stephen Boorn had removed from Manchester, about five years after the supposed murder; and resided in Denmark, Lewis County, New York; at the distance of some two hundred miles. Jesse still continued in Manchester; and *neither of these wretched men, upon any occasion, appears to have attempted flight, or concealment.*

Stephen Boorn, who, as the sequel will abundantly show, seems not to have been entirely deficient, in natural affection, had discovered, after a bitter experience of five long years, that the burden of his sins was not more intolerable, than the oppressive consciousness of the tenure, by which he lived, and moved, and had his being; which tenure was no other, than that, by which Cain walked upon the earth, after the murder of Abel. Stephen

Boorn gathered up the little, that he had, and went into a far country—not hastily, nor by night—but openly, and in the light of day.

Jesse, who was, evidently, the weaker brother—the poorer spirit—remained behind; deeming it easier, doubtless, to endure the continued suspicion and contempt of mankind, than to muster enough of energy, to rise and walk.

Well nigh seven years, as I have stated, had passed, since the disappearance of Colvin. A discovery was made, at this period, which left very little doubt, upon the minds of the good people of Manchester, that the Boorns were guilty of the murder of this unhappy man, and of attempting to conceal his remains, by cremation.

No. LXXX

At this period, about seven years after the disappearance of Russell Colvin, a lad, walking near the house of Barney Boorn, was attracted, by the movements of a dog, that seemed to have discovered some object of interest, near the stump of an ancient tree, upon the banks of the Battenkill river. This stump was about sixty rods from the hole, in which, upon the suggestion of the ghost, the uncle of the Boorns, and his curious neighbors had sought for the body of Colvin. The lad examined the stump, and discovered the cavity to be filled with bones!

Had the magnetic been then in operation, the tidings could not have been telegraphed more speedily. The affair was definitively settled—the bones of Colvin were discovered; and the ghost appeared to have been only sixty rods out of the way, after all. Murder will find a tongue. Manchester found thousands. The village was on fire. Young men and maidens, old men and children came forth, to gaze upon the bones of the murdered Colvin; and to praise the Lord, for this providential discovery! Whatever the value of it might be—the merit seemed clearly to belong, in equal moieties, to the dog and the ghost.

How prone we are—the children of this generation—to reason upon the philosophy, before we weigh the fish! This was a case, if there ever was a case, for the recognition of the principle, *cuique in sua arte credendum est*. Accordingly the medical magi of Manchester and of its highly excited neighborhood were summoned, to sit in judgment, upon these bones. The question was not—*"can these dry bones live?"*—but are they the bones of the murdered Colvin? One, thoughtful practitioner believed there was a previous question, entitled to some little consideration—are these bones the bones of a man, or of a beast? Never were scruples more entirely out of place. Imagine the indignation of the good people of Manchester, at the bare suggestion, that they had wasted so much excellent sympathy, upon the bones, peradventure, of a horse or a heifer!

The doubter, as might have been expected, stood alone: but he sturdily persisted. The regular faculty, with the eyes of their well-persuaded patients riveted, encouragingly, upon theirs, expressed their clear conviction, that the bones were human bones, and, if human bones, whose—aye whose—but the murdered Colvin's! This gave universal satisfaction, of course.

It was evident, that some of these bones had been broken and pounded—the quantity was small, for an entire skeleton—some few bones had been found, beneath a barn, belonging to the father of the Boorns, which had been, previously, consumed by fire—and some persons may have supposed, that the murderers, having deposited the dead body there, had destroyed the barn, to conceal their crime—and, finding a part of the body unconsumed, after the conflagration, had deposited that part, in the hollow stump, to be disposed of, at some future moment of convenience.

A very plausible theory, beyond all doubt. But the doubting doctor continued to turn over these bones, with an air of provoking unbelief; now and then, perhaps, holding aloft, in significant silence, the fragment of a cranium, of remarkably sheepish proportions.

This was not to be endured. Anatomical knowledge appears not to have made uncommon strides, in that region, in 1819; for, when it was finally decided to compare these bones with those of the human body, there actually seems to have been nothing in that region, which would serve the purpose of the faculty, but the leg of a citizen, long before amputated, and committed to the earth. I will here adopt the words of the Rev. Mr. Haynes—"A Mr. Salisbury, about four years ago, had his leg amputated, which was buried, at the distance of four or five miles. The limb was dug up, and, by comparing, it was universally determined that the bones were not human." This was a severe disappointment, undoubtedly; but not absolutely total: for two nails, or something, in the image thereof, were found, amid the mass, which nails, says Mr. Haynes, "were human, and so appeared to all beholders."

Let us now turn to the murderers, or rather to Jesse, for Stephen was two hundred miles away, entirely unsuspicious of the gathering cloud, which was destined, ere long, to burst upon his devoted head.

When the discovery of these bones had excited the feelings and suspicions of the people, to the utmost, it was deemed proper to take Jesse into custody. An examination took place, on Tuesday, May 27, 1819, and continued, till the following Saturday. This examination was conducted, in the meeting-house, as it appears, from the testimony of Truman Hill, upon the subsequent trial; who says of Jesse, that—"when the knife was presented to him, in the meeting-house, and also when the hat was presented to him, his feelings were such, as to oblige him to take hold of the pew, to steady himself—he appeared to be much agitated—I asked him what was the matter—he answered there was matter enough—I asked him to state—he said he feared, that Stephen had killed Colvin—that he never believed so, till the spring or winter, when he went into William Boorn's shop, where were William and Stephen Boorn—at which time he gained a knowledge of the manner of Colvin's death; and that he thought he knew, within a few rods, where Colvin was buried."

Such was the evidence of Truman Hill, upon the trial; and he related the facts, very naturally, at the time, to his neighbors. The statement was considered, by the community, as tantamount to a confession. At this time, the examination of Jesse Boorn had nearly closed—no ground for detention appeared against him—the bones, discovered in the stump, were acknowledged to have belonged to some brute animal—it was the general opinion, that Jesse should be released; when this declaration of his to Truman Hill, turned the tide of popular sentiment entirely; and Jesse Boorn was remanded to prison.

Truman Hill was the jailer; or, in his own conservative phraseology, he *"kept the keys of the prison."* Jailers are rather apt to look upon their prisoners, as great curiosities, in proportion to the crimes, with which they are charged, and themselves as showmen. Most men are sufficiently willing to be distinguished, for something or other:—to see Jesse Boorn—to catechise the wretched man—to set before him the fear of death, and the hope of pardon—to beg him to confess—nothing but the truth, of course—these were privileges—favors—and Truman Hill had the power of granting them. Thus he says—he *"let in"* Mr. Johnson; and, when Mr. Johnson came out, he went in himself, and found Jesse "in great agitation"—and then he, himself, urged Jesse to confess—the truth of course—if he said anything—assuring him, that every falsehood he told, would sink him deeper in trouble. It must have been evident to the mind of Jesse, that a confession of the murder would be particularly agreeable to the public, and that a continued protestation of his innocence would disappoint the reasonable expectations of his fellow-citizens.

Jesse confessed to Judge Skinner, that Stephen had, probably, buried Colvin's body in the mountain; and that the knife, found with the button, in the hole, indicated to his uncle by the ghost, was, doubtless, Colvin's; for he had often seen Colvin's mother use it, to cut her tobacco. Judge Skinner and Jesse took an edifying walk up the mountain, in search of the body—they did not find it, which is very surprising.

About the middle of the month of May, 1819, Mr. Orange Clark, a neighbor of Stephen Boorn, in the town of Denmark, some two hundred miles from Manchester, entered his dwelling, in the evening. He took a chair, and commenced a friendly conversation with Stephen and his wife—for Stephen had married a wife—the sharer of all his sorrows—his joys, probably, were few, and far between, and not worth the partition. Shortly after, a Mr. Hooper, another neighbor, dropped in. He had scarcely taken his seat, before another entered the apartment, Mr. Sylvester, the innkeeper, who, upon some grave testimony, then recently imported into Denmark, had arrived at the solemn conclusion, that there was something rotten there.

Stephen and his helpmate were, doubtless, somewhat surprised, at this unusual gathering, in their humble dwelling. Their surprise was greatly increased, of course, by the appearance, almost immediately after, of Messieurs Anderson and Raymond, worthy men of Manchester. If the ghost of Russell Colvin had stalked in, after them, Stephen Boorn could not have been more astonished, than he was, when he beheld, closing up the rear of all this goodly company—no less a personage, than Captain Truman Hill, the jailer of Manchester—the gentleman, I mean, who *"kept the keys of the prison."*

To Stephen there must have been something not wholly incomprehensible in this. His ill-starred partner was not long left in doubt. The very glances of the party were of evil omen. Their business was soon declared. The gentleman, that *kept the keys,* kept also the *handcuffs*. They were speedily produced. Stephen Boorn must go back to the place, from whence he came—and from thence—so opined the men, women and children of Manchester—to the place of execution. But, when the process commenced, of putting the irons upon that wretched man—the poor woman—the wife of his bosom—for he had a bosom, and a human heart therein, full of tenderness, as the sequel will demonstrate, for her; however inconceivable to the gentleman, that *"kept the keys"* —and to those learned judges, who, in the very teeth, and in utter contempt, of the law, so clearly laid down by Sir Matthew Hale, of glorious memory, would have hanged this miserable man, but for the signal Providence of Almighty God—this poor woman was completely overwhelmed with agony.

The estimate of many things, in this nether world, is a vastly relative affair. That, which would be in excellent taste, among a people, without refinement, however moral, will frequently appear to the enlightened portion of mankind, as absolutely barbarous.

The idea of allaying the anguish of a wife, produced by the forcible removal of her husband, in chains, on a charge of murder, by *making her presents*, hurries one's imagination to the land of the Hottentots, or of the Caffres; where the loss of a child is sometimes forgotten, in the contemplation of a few glass beads—and no consolation proves so effectual for the loss of wife, as a nail or a hatchet.

And yet it is impossible—and it ought to be—to read the short and simple statement of that good man, the Rev. Mr. Haynes, without emotion—

"The surprise and distress of Mrs. Boorn, on this occasion, are not easily described: they excited the compassion of those, who came to take away her husband; and they made her some presents."

"The prisoner," continues Mr. Haynes, "was put in irons, and brought to Manchester, on the 15th of May. He peremptorily asserted his innocence, and declared he knew nothing about the murder of his brother-in-law. The prisoners were kept apart, for a time. They were afterwards confined in one room. Stephen denied the evidence, brought against him by Jesse, and treated him with severity."

These men, imprisoned in May, 1819, were not tried, until October of that year. The *evidence*, upon which they were convicted of murder, in the first degree, lies now before me, certified up to the General Assembly of the State of Vermont, upon their request, by Judge Dudley Chace, Nov. 11, 1819. Let us now turn from *on dits*, and dreams, and ghosts, and doubtful relics, to the *duly certified testimony, upon which these men were sentenced to be hung.*

No. LXXXI

The grand jurors of Bennington County found a bill of indictment, against Stephen and Jesse Boorn, September 3, 1819, for the murder of Russell Colvin, May 10, 1812, charging Stephen, as principal, in the first count, and Jesse, in the second.

The facts, proved, upon the trial, by witnesses, whose testimony was unimpeached, and which facts appear, in the minutes of evidence, certified by Judge Dudley Chace to the General Assembly, November 11, 1819, were, substantially, these. Before the time of the alleged murder, Stephen had complained that his brother-in-law, Colvin, was a burden to the family; and Stephen had said, if there was no other way of preventing him from multiplying children, for his father-in-law, Barney Boorn, to support, he would prevent him himself.

At the time of the alleged murder, Stephen and Jesse Boorn had a quarrel with Colvin. The affair, in part, was seen and heard, by a neighbor, from a distance. Lewis Colvin, then ten years old, the son of Russell, was present; and, when seventeen, testified at the trial, that the last time he saw his father was, when the quarrel took place, which arose, at the time they were all engaged, in picking up stones—that Colvin struck Stephen first, with a small stick—that Stephen then struck Colvin, on his neck, with a club, and he fell—that Colvin rose and struck Stephen again—that Stephen again struck Colvin with the club, and knocked him down—whereupon the witness, being frightened, ran away; and was afterwards told, by Stephen, that he would kill him, if he ever told of what had happened. The witness further stated, that he ran, and told his grandmother.

Stephen appears to have been gifted with a lively fancy. It was testified, that, before this occurrence, speaking of his sister and her husband, he had said he wished Russell and Sal were both dead; and that he would *kick them into hell if he burnt his legs off*. This piece of evidence, after having produced the usual effect upon the jury, was rejected.

Upon another occasion, four years after the alleged murder, Stephen stated to Daniel D. Baldwin, and Eunice, his wife, that Colvin went off very strangely; that the last he saw of him was when he, Stephen, and Jesse were together, and Colvin went off to the woods; that Lewis, the son of Colvin, upon returning with some drink, for which he had been sent, asked where his father was, and that he, Stephen, replied, that Colvin had gone to hell; and Jesse, that they had put him where potatoes would not freeze; and Stephen added, while making this statement to the Baldwins, that it was not likely he or Jesse would have said this to the boy, if they had killed his father.

When the body was sought for, before the bones were discovered, which were mistaken for human remains, a girl said to Stephen, "they are going to dig up Colvin for you; aren't they?" He became angry, and said, that Colvin often went off and returned—and that, when he went off, the last time, he was crazy; and went off without his hat.

About four years after his disappearance, an old mouldy hat was discovered, in the field, where the quarrel took place; and was identified, positively, as the hat of Colvin, by the witness who had seen the quarrel, from a distance, as I have stated.

Stephen denied, to Benjamin Deming, that he, Stephen, was present, when Colvin went off, and stated, that he was then, at a distance.

To Joseph Lincoln he said, that he never killed Colvin—that he, and Colvin, and Jesse were picking up stones, and that Colvin was crazy, and went off into the woods, and that they had not seen nor heard from him since.

To William Wyman, Stephen reäffirmed his statement, made to Benjamin Deming—called on Wyman to clear up his statement, that he, Stephen, had killed Colvin—asserted, that he knew nothing of what had become of Colvin; and that he had never worked with him an hour.

The minutes of the Judge furnish other examples of similar contradiction and inconsistency, on the part of Stephen Boorn.

But the reader will bear constantly in mind, that, through a period of seven years, during which the suspicion of the vicinage hung over them, like an angry cloud, sending forth occasional mutterings of judgment to come, and threatening to burst upon their heads, at any moment; *neither of these miserable men attempted flight or concealment.* Two years before his arrest, Stephen removed from Manchester, as I have related; but, in an open manner. There was not the slightest disguise, in regard to his abode; and there, when it was thought proper to arrest him, he was readily found, in the bosom of his family.

In 1813, Jesse Boorn was asked, by Daniel Jacobs, where Russell Colvin was; and replied, that he had enlisted, as a soldier in the army.

Thus far, the evidence, certified by Judge Chace, appears to have proceeded from perfectly credible witnesses. Silas Merrill, *in jail, on a charge of perjury*, testified to the following confession—that, when Jesse returned to prison, after his examination, he told Merrill, that *"they"* had encouraged him to confess, *with promise of pardon*, and that he, Merrill, had told him, that, perhaps, he had better confess the whole truth, and *obtain some favor*. In June, 1819, Jesse's father visited him in jail—after he went away, Jesse seemed much afflicted. After falling asleep, Jesse awoke, and shook the witness, Merrill—told him that he, Jesse, was frightened—had seen a vision—and wished the witness to get up, for he had something to tell him. They both arose; and Jesse made the following disclosure. He said it was true, that he, and Stephen, and Colvin, and Lewis were in the lot, picking stones—that Stephen struck Colvin with a club—that the boy, Lewis, ran— that Colvin got up—that Stephen struck him again, above the ear, and broke his skull—that his, Stephen's father came up, and asked if Colvin was dead; and that he repeated this question three times—that all three of them carried Colvin, not then dead, to an old cellar, where the father cut Colvin's throat, with a small penknife of Stephen's—that they buried him, in the cellar— that Stephen wore Colvin's shoes, till he, Jesse, told him it would lead to a discovery.

Jesse, as the witness stated, informed him, that he had told his brother Stephen, that he had confessed. When Stephen came into the room, witness asked him, if he did not take the life of Colvin; to which he replied, that *"he did not take the main life of Colvin."* Stephen, as the witness stated, said, that Jesse's confession was true; and that he, Stephen, had made a confession, which would only make manslaughter of it. The witness, Merrill, then proceeded to say, that Jesse further confessed, that, eighteen months after they had buried the body, they took it up, and placed it under the floor of a barn, that was afterwards burnt—that they then pounded the bones, and put them in the river; excepting a few, which their father gathered up, and hid in a hollow stump.

At this stage of the trial, the prosecuting officer offered the written confession of Stephen Boorn, dated Aug. 27, 1819. The document was authenticated. An attempt was made by the prisoners' counsel, to show, that this confession was made, under the fear of death and hope and prospect of pardon. Samuel C. Raymond testified, that he had often told the prisoner to confess, *if guilty*, but not otherwise. Stephen said he was *not guilty*. The witness then told him *not to confess*. The witness said he had heard Mr. Pratt, and Mr. Sheldon, the prosecuting officer, tell Jesse, that, if he would confess, *in case he was guilty*, they would petition the legislature in his favor. The witness had made the same proposition to Stephen himself, and *always told him he had no doubt of his guilt; and that the public mind was against him.*

The court, of course, rejected the *written confession* of Stephen, made, obviously, under the fear of death, and the hope and prospect of pardon. William Farnsworth was then produced, to prove the *oral confession* of Stephen, much to the same effect. To this the prisoners' counsel objected, very properly, as it occurred after the very statement and proposal, made to the prisoner, by Mr. Raymond. *The court, nevertheless, permitted the witness to proceed.* Mr. Farnsworth then testified, that, about two weeks *after* the date of the written confession, Stephen confessed, that he killed Russell Colvin—that Russell struck at him; and that he struck Russell and killed him—hid him in the bushes—buried him—dug him up—buried him again, under a barn, that was burnt—threw the unburnt bones into the river—scraped up some few remains, and hid them in a stump—and that the nails found he knew were Russell Colvin's. The witness told him his case looked badly; and, probably, gave him no encouragement. Stephen then said they should have done well enough, had it not been for Jesse, and wished he *"had back that paper,"* meaning the written confession.

After Mr. Farnsworth had been, thus absurdly, permitted to testify, there was no cause for withholding the written confession; and the prisoners' counsel called for its production. This confession embodies little more, with the exception of some particulars, as to the manner of burying the body; but is entirely inconsistent with the confession of Jesse. It is a full confession, that he killed Russell Colvin, and buried his remains. But, unlike the confession of Jesse, there is not the slightest implication of their father.

The evidence, in behalf of the prisoners, was of very little importance, excepting in relation to the fact, that *they were persuaded, by divers individuals, that the only chance of escaping the halter was, by an ample confession of the murder.* They were told to confess *nothing but the truth*—but this was accompanied, by ominous intimations, that their case *"looked dark"*—that they were *"gone geese"*—or, by the considerate language of *Squire Raymond*—as he is styled in the minutes—that he *"had no doubt of their guilt;"* and if they would confess *the truth*—that is, *what the Squire had no doubt of*—he would petition the legislature in their favor! What atrocious language to a prisoner, under a charge of murder!

It would be quite interesting to read the instructions of Judge Dudley Chace, while submitting the case of Stephen and Jesse Boorn to the jury; that we might be able to comprehend the measure of his respect, for the law, touching the inadmissibility of such extra judicial confessions, and for the solemn, judicial declaration of Sir Matthew Hale, that *no conviction ought ever to take place in trials, for murder or manslaughter, until the fact was clearly proven, or the dead body of the person, alleged to have been killed, was discovered.*

In *"about an hour,"* the jury returned a verdict of guilty, against Stephen and Jesse Boorn. And, in *"about an hour"* after, the prisoners were brought into court again, and sentenced to be hung, on the twenty-eighth day of January, 1820. Judge Chace is said to have been *"quite moved,"* while passing sentence on Stephen and Jesse Boorn. It would have been well, for the cause of humanity, and not amiss, for the honor of his judicial station, if he had shed tears of blood, as the reader of the sequel will readily admit.

No. LXXXII

Sentenced, on the last day of October, 1819, to be hung, on the 28th of January following, the Boorns were remanded to their prison, and put in irons.

From this period, their most authentic and interesting prison history is obtained, from the written statement of the clergyman, who appears to have performed his sacred functions, in regard to these men, with singular fidelity and propriety. This clergyman, the Rev. Lemuel Haynes, belonged to that class of human beings, commonly denominated *colored people*—a term, to which I have always sturdily objected, because drunkards, who are often a highly-colored people, may thus be confounded with temperate and respectable men of African descent.

[2] Mr. Haynes was, in part, of African parentage; and the author of the narrative, and occasional sermon, to which I have referred, at the commencement of these articles. There flourished, in this city, some five and thirty years ago, a number of very respectable, negro musicians, associated, as a band; and Major Russell, the editor of the Centinel, was in the habit of distinguishing the music, by the color of the performers. He frequently remarked, in his journal, that the *"black music"* was excellent. If this phraseology be allowable, I cannot deny, that the black, or colored, narrative of Mr. Haynes is very interesting; and that I have seldom read a black or colored discourse, with more satisfaction; and that I have read many a white one, with infinitely less.

Previously to their trial, and after the arrest of Stephen, the Rev. Mr. Haynes expressly states, that Jesse, having had an interview with Stephen, positively denied his own former statement, that Stephen had admitted he killed Colvin. These are the words of Mr. Haynes—"During the interval, the writer frequently visited them, in his official capacity; and did not discover any symptoms of compunction; but they persisted, in declaring their innocence, with appeals to Heaven. Stephen, at times, appeared absorbed in passion and impatience. One day, I introduced the example of Christ, under sufferings, as a pattern, worthy of imitation: he exclaimed—'I am as innocent, as Jesus Christ!' for which extravagant expression I reproved him: he replied—'I don't mean I am guiltless, as he was, I know I am a great sinner; but I am as innocent of killing Colvin, as he was.'"

The condition of the Boorns, immediately after sentence, cannot be more forcibly exhibited, than in the language of this worthy clergyman— "None can express the confusion and anguish, into which the prisoners were cast, on hearing their doom. They requested, by their counsel, liberty to speak, which was granted. In sighs and broken accents, they asserted their innocence. The convulsion of nature, attending Stephen, at last, was so great, as to render him unable to walk, and he was supported to the prison."

Compassion was excited, in the hearts of some—doubts, peradventure, in the minds of others. A petition was presented to the General Assembly; and the punishment of Jesse was changed to imprisonment, for life. Ninety-seven deadly noes, against forty-two merciful ayes, decided the fate of Stephen.

On the 29th of October, 1819, Jesse bade Stephen a last farewell; and was transferred to the State prison, at Windsor.

"I visited him—Stephen"—says Mr. Haynes, "frequently, with sympathy and grief; and endeavored to turn his mind upon the things of another world; telling him, that, as all human means had failed, he must look to God, as the only way of deliverance. I advised him to read the Holy Scriptures; to which he consented, if he could be allowed a candle, as his cell was dark. This request was granted; and I often found him reading. He was at times calm, and again impatient."

Upon another occasion, still nearer the day of the prisoner's doom— "the last of earth"—Mr. Haynes remarks, that Stephen addressed him thus—"'Mr. Haynes, I see no way but I must die: everything works against me; but I am an innocent man: this you will know, after I am dead.' He burst into a flood of tears, and said—'What will become of my poor wife and children; they are in needy circumstances; and I love them better than life itself.'—I told him, God would take care of them. He replied—'I don't want to die. I wish they would let me live, even in this situation, somewhat longer: perhaps something will take place, that will convince people I am innocent.' I was about to leave the prison, when he said—'will you pray with me?'—He arose with his heavy chains on his hands and legs, being also chained down to the floor, and stood on his feet, with deep and bitter sighings."

On the 26th day of November, 1819—two brief months before the time, appointed, for the execution of Stephen Boorn, the following notice appeared in the Rutland Herald—"Murder.—*Printers of Newspapers, throughout the United States, are desired to publish, that Stephen Boorn of Manchester, in Vermont, is sentenced to be executed for the murder of Russell Colvin, who has been absent about seven years. Any person, who can give information of said Colvin, may save the life of the innocent, by making immediate communication. Colvin is about five feet five inches high, light complexion, light hair, blue eyes, about forty years of age. Manchester, Vt., Nov. 26, 1819."*

This notice, published by request of the prisoner, was, doubtless, prepared, by one of his counsel:—by whomsoever prepared, it bears, in its very structure, unmistakable evidence of the writer's entire confidence, in the innocency, of Stephen Boorn, of the *murder* of Russell Colvin. No man, who had a doubt upon his mind, could have put these words together, in the very places, where they stand. Had it been otherwise, some little hesitancy of expression—some conservative syllable—one little if, *ex abundanti cautela*, to shelter the writer from the charge of a most miserably weak and merciful credulity, would have characterized this last appeal—this short, shrill cry for mercy—as the work of a doubter, and a hireling.

There may have been a few, whose strong confidence, in the bloodguiltiness of Stephen Boorn, had become slightly paralyzed, by his entire and absolute retractation of all his confessions, made before trial. There may have been a few, who believe, that they, themselves, might have confessed, though innocent, in the same predicament—assured by the *squires*, the *magnates* of the village, whom they supposed powerful to save, that *no doubt existed of their guilt*—that they were *gone geese*—and who proffered an effort in their favor—to save them from the gallows—if they would confess *the truth*, which *truth* could, of course, be nothing, but their *guilt*. If they would confess a crime, though innocent, they might still live! If not, they must be deemed liars, and murderers, and die the death!

The prisoner, Stephen Boorn, even supposing him to be innocent, but of humble station in society, and of ordinary mental powers—oppressed by the chains he wore, and, more heavily, by the dread of death—clinging to life—not only because it is written, by the finger of God, in the members of man, that all a man hath will be given for his life—but because, as the statement of Mr. Haynes convincingly shows, poor degraded outcast as Stephen was, he was deeply and tenderly attached to his wife and children—might well fall under the temptation, so censurably spread before him.

There may have been a few, who were compelled to doubt, if Stephen were a murderer, upon hearing the simple narrative, spread through the village, by the worthy clergyman, of the fervent and awful declaration of Stephen Boorn, in a moment of deep and energetic misery—"I am as innocent of the murder of Russell Colvin, as Jesus Christ."

But the strong current of popular indignation ran, overwhelmingly, against him. By a large number, the brief notice, published in the Rutland Herald, was, undoubtedly, accounted a mere personal, or professional attempt, to produce an impression of the murderer's innocence, in the hope of commutation, or of pardon—and, with many, it certainly tended to confirm the prejudice against him. Days of unutterable anguish were succeeded, by nights of frightful slumber. The cell was feebly lighted, by the taper allowed him—with unpractised fingers, the prisoner turned over the pages of God's holy word—but a kind, faithful guide was at his elbow—the voice of fervent prayer, amid the occasional clanking of the prisoner's fetters, went up to that infallible ear, that is ever ready to hear.—The Judicial power had consigned this victim to the gallows—the general sense had decided, that Stephen Boorn ought not to live—to prepare him to die was the only remaining office, for the man of God.

No. LXXXIII

In April, 1813, about a year after poor Colvin was murdered, by the Boorns, according to the indictment—there came to the house of a Mr. Polhamus, in Dover, Monmouth County, New Jersey, a wandering man—he was a stranger, and Mr. Polhamus was a good man, and took him in—he was hungry, and he fed him—he was ragged, if not absolutely naked, and he clothed him. He was a man of mean appearance, rapid utterance, and disordered understanding. He was harmless withal, perfectly tractable, capable of light service, and grateful for kindness. In the family of Mr. Polhamus, this poor vagrant had continued, to the very time, when the Boorns were convicted of the murder of Russell Colvin.

Not far from Dover, lies the town of Shrewsbury, near Long Branch, the Baiæ of the Philadelphians. There dwelt in Shrewsbury, in the year 1819, Mr. Taber Chadwick, the brother-in-law of Mr. Polhamus, and familiarly acquainted with the domestic affairs of his relative. He also was a man of kind and generous feelings. He had accidentally read in the New York Evening Post, a paper which he rarely met with, the account of the conviction of the Boorns, for the murder of Colvin. The notice in the Rutland Herald, he had never seen. He was firmly persuaded, that the stranger, who arrived at the house of his brother-in-law, some six years before, was Russell Colvin. What reasons he had, for this conviction, the reader will gather from a perusal of the following letter, which appeared in the Evening Post:—

"Shrewsbury, Monmouth, N. J., Dec. 6, 1819. To the Editor of the New York Evening Post: Sir. Having read in your paper of Nov. 26th last, of the conviction and sentence of Stephen and Jesse Boorn, of Manchester, Vermont, charged with the murder of Russell Colvin, and from facts, which have fallen within my own knowledge, and not knowing what facts may have been disclosed on their trial, and wishing to serve the cause of humanity, I would state as follows, which may be relied on. Some years past, (I think between five and ten), a stranger made his appearance in this county: and, upon being inquired of, said his name was Russell Colvin, (which name he answers to at this time)—that he came from Manchester, Vermont—he appeared to be in a state of mental derangement; but, at times, gave considerable account of himself—his connections, acquaintances,

&c.—He mentions the names of Clarissa, Rufus, &c.—Among his relations he has mentioned the Boorns above—Jesse as Judge (I think,) &c., &c. He is a man rather small in stature—round favored—speaks very fast, and has two scars on his head, and appears to be between thirty and forty years of age. There is no doubt but that he came from Vermont, from the mention that he has made of a number of places and persons there, and probably is the person supposed to have been murdered. He is now living here, but so completely insane, as not to be able to give a satisfactory account of himself, but the connections of Russell Colvin might know, by seeing him. If you think proper to give this a place in your columns, it may possibly lead to a discovery, that may save the lives of innocent men—if so, you will have the pleasure, as well as myself, of having served the cause of humanity. If you give this an insertion in your paper, pray be so good as to request the different editors of newspapers, in New York, and Vermont, to give it a place in theirs. I am, sir, with sentiments of regard, yours, &c.,

Taber Chadwick."

To render a certain part of this letter intelligible to the reader, it is proper to state, that Clarissa and Rufus, as it appeared from the evidence, were the names of Colvin's children; and that "*the judge*" was a title, or sobriquet, frequently bestowed upon Jesse, by Stephen.

Upon the arrival of a printed copy of Mr. Chadwick's letter, in Manchester, it produced little or no effect. Very few of the inhabitants gave any credit to the story; and it might have been very reasonably supposed, that St. Thomas had begotten a large majority of the population. Squire Raymond was certain of Stephen's guilt; and to differ from Squire Raymond, was probably accounted, by the villagers, as one of the presumptuous sins. Besides, if a doubt of their guilt had existed, would not those most learned judges have given the prisoners the full advantage of that doubt! How little the good people of Manchester imagined, that, upon the trial of the Boorns, the well established rules of evidence had been outrageously violated, and a great fundamental principle of criminal jurisprudence shamefully disregarded, by the court! Such, however painful and disgraceful the admission, was manifestly the fact. Judges, who sit thus, in judgment, upon the lives of men, would do well to doff their ermine, and assume the robe, commended by Faulconbridge to Austria. To the enforcement of this simple truth I shall turn hereafter.

Let us now go to the dungeon, taking with us, of course, the newspaper, containing these living lines—these tidings of exceeding great joy. But the details of all that occurred within the prison, are related with great simplicity and power, by the good clergyman, who stood by Stephen Boorn, in his deepest need. Let Mr. Haynes, himself, describe in a few words, the effect of this communication, upon the prisoner—"Mr. Chadwick's letter was carried to the prison, and read to Stephen. The news was so overwhelming, that, to use his own language, nature could scarcely sustain the shock; but, as there was some doubt as to the truth of the report, it tended to prevent an immediate dissolution. He observed to me, that, if Colvin had then made his appearance before him, he believed it would have caused immediate death. Even now a faintness was created, that was painful to endure."

Not a few very charitable people, who shrink, instinctively, from the very thought of giving pain, marvelled at the cruelty of those, who presumed to raise the poor prisoner's hopes, upon such frail and improbable grounds.

Soon, intelligence arrived in Manchester, that a Mr. Whelpley, of New York, formerly of Manchester, who knew Colvin well, having seen Mr. Chadwick's letter, had gone to New Jersey, to settle the question of identity. This, according to Mr. Deming's account, was done, at the instance of the city authorities of New York.

Doubt fell, fifty per cent., in the market of Manchester, when a brief letter, in the well known handwriting of Mr. Whelpley, was received, in that village, immediately upon his return to New York, containing these vital words—"I have Colvin with me!" This letter was immediately followed by another from a Mr. Rempton, who knew him well, in which he says—"*while writing, Russell Colvin is before me!*" The New York journals now published the notice, that *Colvin had arrived, and would soon proceed to Vermont.* Doubt dies hard, in the bosoms of those, whose pride of opinion forbids them to recant. Squire Raymond, and his tail, as the Scotch call a great man's followers, could not believe the story. Their honors, who sentenced the Boorns to death, in one hour, after the verdict had been delivered—were very naturally inclined to take a longer time, for consideration, before they sentenced themselves to merited reproach, for their rash and unjustifiable conduct. Bets were made, says Mr. Haynes, that the man, on his way to Vermont, notwithstanding the positive averments of Whelpley and Rempton, was not the true Colvin, but an impostor.

Whoever he was, he was soon upon his way. He passed through Albany. The streets, says Mr. Deming, were literally crowded to get a glimpse of the man, who was dead and alive again. He passed through Troy. The Trojan horse could not have produced a greater measure of amazement, in the days of Priam. Dec. 22, he arrived with Mr. Whelpley, at Bennington. The court then in session, suspended business, to look upon him, for several hours.

Towards evening, upon that memorable day, Dec. 22, 1819, the stage was seen, driving into Manchester, and the driving was like the driving of

Jehu, for it drove furiously. When the dust cleared away, sufficiently, to enable the excited population to obtain a clearer view, an unusual signal was observed floating above the advancing vehicle. A shout broke forth from the crowd—Colvin has come! Hundreds ran to their houses to communicate the tidings—*Colvin has come!* The stage drove up to the tavern door; and a little man, of mean appearance, and wild, disordered look, came forth into the middle of the eager multitude. His bewildered eyes turned, rapidly and feverishly, in all directions, encountering eyes innumerable, that seemed to drink him in, with the strong relish of wonder and delight. Hundreds upon hundreds pressed forward, to grasp this poor, little, demented creature, by the hand; and enough of sense and memory remained, to enable him, feebly, to return the smiles of his former neighbors, and to call them, by their names. All was uproar and frantic joy. The people of Manchester believed it to be their bounden duty to go partially mad; and they did their duty to perfection. Guns were fired, amid wild demonstrations of excitement; and Colvin was tumultuously borne to the cell of the condemned. The meeting shall be described by Mr. Haynes—*"The prison door was unbolted—the news proclaimed to Stephen, that Colvin had come! The welcome reception, given it by the joyful prisoner, need not be mentioned. The chains, on his arms, were taken off, while those on his legs remained. Being impatient of an interview with him, who had come to bring salvation, they met. Colvin gazed upon the chains, and asked—'What is that for?'—Stephen answered—'Because, they say, I murdered you'—'You never hurt me'—replied Colvin."*

Colvin recognized his children; but marvelled how they came in Manchester, asserting, that he left them, at the house of his kind benefactor, Mr. Polhamus, in New Jersey. Of his wife, who came to see him, he took little notice, asserting, that she did not belong to him. There may have been enough of method, in his madness, to enable him to appreciate, correctly, the value of his marital relation. The breath of Manchester may have blown the truth into his ear. An ingenious person may find some little resemblance between the wanderings of Ulysses and those of Colvin the *Oudeis* of Manchester—but the testimony, upon the trial, peremptorily forbids the slightest comparison, between Penelope and Mrs. Colvin, who appears not to have embarrassed her suitors, with the preliminary ordeal of the bow.

There is an admirable painting, in the Boston Athenæum, by Neagle, of Patrick Lyon, the blacksmith, who was long imprisoned, in Philadelphia, for the robbery of a bank, of which crime he was perfectly innocent, as it finally appeared, to the entire satisfaction of the government, by whom he was, consequently, discharged. Lyon is represented, at his forge; and he desired the artist to introduce the Walnut Street prison in the rear, where he had suffered, so unjustly, and so long.

The graphic hand of a master might do something here. I would pay more than I can well afford, for a couple of illustrative paintings—I. The Judges, with tears in their eyes, sentencing Stephen and Jesse to be hanged, for the murder of Colvin—the best books on evidence, before them, and open at the pages where it is expressly stated that extra-judicial confession, under fear of death, and hope of pardon, shall never be received—and the leaf turned down, at the authority of Sir Matthew Hale, that no conviction ought ever to take place, upon trials for murder and manslaughter, till the fact be clearly proven, or the *dead body* be discovered.

II. The dungeon, Dec. 22, 1819, just thirty-six days, before the time, appointed for the execution of Stephen—the murderer and the murdered man, standing face to face, in full life—Squire Raymond still avowing his conviction of Stephen's guilt, and holding aloft his written confession—Judge Chace seen in the distance, burying the *"certified minutes of evidence"* in the very hole, pointed out, to Nathaniel Boorn, by Colvin's ghost—and Judge Doolittle evidently regretting, that he had not done less, in this unhappy transaction, which came so near the consummation of judicial murder.

In the succeeding number, I shall endeavor to present a simple version of the motives and conduct of the parties—and some brief remarks, upon this extraordinary trial.

No. LXXXIV

After a little reflection, the true explanation of this apparent mystery appears to be exceedingly simple. Colvin had become an object of contempt and hatred to the Boorns; and especially to Stephen. His mental feebleness had produced their contempt—the burdensomeness of himself and his family had begotten their hatred. The poor, semi-demented creature happened, in a luckless hour, to boast, most absurdly, no doubt, of his great importance and usefulness, as a member of this interesting family. This gave a doubly keen edge to the animosity of Stephen; and he berated his brother-in-law, in terms, almost as vulgar and abusive, as those we daily meet with, in so many of our leading political journals, of all denominations.

Forgetful of his inferiority, this miserable worm exemplified the proverb, and turned upon his oppressor, in a feeble way. He struck Stephen with *"a small riding stick."* This was accounted sufficient provocation by Stephen; and, in the language of the witness, *"Stephen then struck Russell on his neck with a club, and knocked him down."* He rose, and made a slight effort to renew the battle, and then Stephen again knocked him down. Upon this, Colvin rambled off, towards the mountain, and was seen in that region, no more, till he was brought back, after the expiration of seven years, in December, 1819.

He went off without his hat and shoes; whether, in his effort to shake off the dust of that city, he unconsciously shook off his shoes, is unknown. The discovery of the hat, some years after, formed a part of that wretched *rope of sand*, for it is not worthy of being called a *chain of evidence*, upon which Stephen and Jesse were sentenced to death. Colvin had, doubtless, long been aware, that he was an object of hatred to the Boorns. The blows, inflicted upon this occasion, undoubtedly, aggravated his insanity; yet enough remained of the instinctive love of life, to teach him, that his safety was in flight. How he found his way to that part of New Jersey, which lies near the Atlantic Ocean, is of little importance. He was, notoriously, a wanderer. It was the spring of the year. He moved onward, without plan, camping out, among the bushes, or sleeping in barns; the world before him, and Providence his guide. He, probably, rambled from Manchester, which is in the southwest corner of Vermont, into the State of New York, which lies very near; and, wandering, in a southerly direction, along the westerly boundary lines of Massachusetts and Connecticut, he would, before many days, have entered the northerly part of New Jersey.

Accustomed to his occasional absences, the Boorns, undoubtedly, expected his return, for weeks and months, even though the summer had past, and the harvest had ended. But, after the snows of winter had come, and covered the mountains; and the spring had returned, and melted them away; and Colvin came not; then Stephen Boorn, doubtless, began to fear, that he had, unintentionally, killed him—that he had wandered away, and died of the effects of the blows he had received—and that his bones were bleaching, in some unknown part of the mountain, whither he had wandered, immediately after the occurrence.

Upon this hypothesis, alone, can we explain one remarkable word, in the answer of Stephen to Merrill's question, in the jail, as certified, by Judge Chace, in his minutes—"*I asked him, if he did take the life of Colvin.—He said he did not take the* main *life of Colvin. He said no more at that time.*"

Does any reflecting man inquire—what could have induced these men to confess the crime, with such a particular detail of minute, and extraordinary, circumstances? The answer has already been given, in part.—Stephen, doubtless, believed it to be quite probable, that he had been the means of Colvin's death. To explain the motive for confession, more fully, it is only necessary to stand, for one moment, in the prisoner's shoes. He was assured, by "Squire Raymond," and others, in whom he confided, that no doubt was entertained of his guilt—that his case was dark—and that his only hope lay in confession.

His mind was brought to the full and settled belief, that he should be hung, before many days, *unless he confessed*. If he had confessed the simple truth—the quarrel—the blows—the departure of Colvin—all this would have availed him nothing. It was not this, of which "Squire Raymond," and others, had *no doubt he was guilty*. They had no doubt he was guilty of the *murder* of Colvin. No confession of anything, short of *the murder of Colvin*, would satisfy "Squire Raymond," and induce him to "petition the legislature in favor" of the prisoner! Stephen well knew, that, if he confessed the murder of Colvin, it would be immediately asked—where he had buried the body—a puzzling question, it must be confessed, for one, who had committed no murder. But it was a delicate moment, for Stephen. It was necessary for him to stand, not only *rectus in curia*—but *rectus* with "Squire Raymond," and all his other attentive patrons. He therefore, to save his life, and secure the patronage of the "Squire," strung together a terrible tissue of lies, too manifestly preposterous and improbable, even for the credulous brain of Cotton Mather, in 1692. He relieved himself of all embarrassment, in regard to the dead body of the *living* Colvin, by *confessing*, that he first buried it, in the earth—then took it up and reburied it, under a barn—and, after the barn had been burnt, took up the bones again, and cast them into the Battenkill river.

The confession of Jesse was made, when he was aroused from sleep, at midnight, under the impression, as he stated, at the time, that *"something had come in at the window, and was on the bed beside him"* —somewhat extra-judicial, this confession, to be sure. This Jesse appears to have been a most unfilial scoundrel; for, instead of *confessing*, as Stephen had *confessed*, that Stephen himself killed Colvin, single-handed and alone; Jesse catered, more abundantly, to the popular appetite for horrors, by *confessing* that his old father, Barney Boorn, *"damned"* his son-in-law, Colvin, very frequently, and *"cut his throat with a small penknife."* All this clotted mass of inconsistent absurdity, extorted by hope and fear, his honor, Judge Chace, received, as legal evidence, and gravely certified up to the General Assembly of Vermont.

It is true, Judge Chace, as we have stated, rejected the written confession of Stephen, because Raymond swore, as follows—*"I have heard Mr. Pratt and Mr. Sheldon tell Jesse Boorn, that if he would confess, in case he was guilty, they would petition the legislature for him—I have made the same proposition to Stephen myself, and always told him I had no doubt of his guilt, and that the public mind was against him."* It is needless to expatiate on the gross impropriety of addressing such language to a prisoner, under such circumstances.

But the witness, Farnsworth, was then produced to prove Stephen's oral confession, that he killed Colvin. It appears, by the minutes, certified by Judge Chace, that he put the preliminary questions, and that the witness swore, "that neither he nor anybody else, *to his knowledge*, had done anything, directly or indirectly, to influence the said Stephen to the *talk* he was about to communicate." In vain, the prisoners' counsel protested, that the evidence was inadmissible, because the "*talk*" between Stephen and Farnsworth was subsequent to the proposition made to Stephen by Raymond. In vain they pressed the consideration, that if, on this ground, the written confession had been rejected, the oral confession should also be rejected. In vain they offered to prove other proposals and promises, made to the prisoners, at other times, *before* the conversation, now offered to be proved. Nothing, however, would stay their honors, from gibbetting their judicial reputation, in chains, which no time will ever knock off. They suffered Farnsworth to testify; and he swore, that Stephen told him, "about two weeks *after* the written confession, that he killed Colvin," &c. This must have been about September 10, 1819, and, of course, before the trial, when he was still relying on the promises of Squire Raymond, and others.

The prisoners' counsel very judiciously moved, for the reception of the written confession, and it was read accordingly. Unable to restrain the judicial antics of the Court, it appeared to be the only course, for the prisoners' counsel, to throw the whole crude and incongruous mass before the jury, and leave its credibility, or rather, its palpable incredibility, to their decision. It would be desirable, as a judicial curiosity, to possess a copy of Judge Chace's charge. Of his instructions to the jury he says nothing, in his certified statement to the General Assembly.

Now, apart from the confessions of these men, extorted, so clearly, by the fear of death, and the hope of pardon, there was evidence enough to excite *suspicion*, and there was no more: but, the law of our country convicts no man of murder, or manslaughter, upon *suspicion*. I shall conclude my remarks, upon this interesting case, in the following number.

No. LXXXV

The chains of Stephen Boorn were stricken off, and Jesse was liberated from prison. They were men of note. If there were not *giants*, there were *lions*, in those days. Colvin soon became weary of standing upon that dizzy eminence, where circumstances had placed him. He had a painful recollection, no doubt, more or less distinct, of the past: and, after he had served the high purpose, for which he had been brought from New Jersey, he expressed an earnest wish to return to the home of his adoption; where he had found, in the good Mr. Polhamus, a friend, who had considered the necessities and distresses of his body and mind; and, who had been willing, in return for his feeble services, to give him shelter and protection.

The Boorns had, undoubtedly, a fortunate, and, almost a miraculous, escape. So had their honors, the Judges, Chace and Doolittle. Their first meeting, after the *denouement*, must have been perfectly tragi-comical.

Their escape from an awful precipice may admonish all, who sit, in judgment, upon the lives of their fellow-men, to administer the law, with extreme caution, and with a high and holy regard, for those well-established principles, and rules, which can never be disregarded, with impunity. God forbid, that any humble phraseology of mine should, for an instant, be perverted, to mislead the meanest understanding — to foster those principles, which, for the purpose of extending mercy, undeserved, to the murderer, would heap gross injustice and cruelty, upon the whole community — to break down the positive law of God, which Jesus Christ declared, that he came to confirm; and, in its place and stead, to erect the sickly decrees of a society of philandering puppets, whose wires are notoriously pulled, by certain professional and political managers.

In the commencement of my remarks, upon this romance of real life, I endeavored to forefend, against the suspicion of undervaluing that species of evidence, which is called presumptive, or circumstantial. It is accounted, by the most able writers, on this branch of jurisprudence, of the highest quality. Thus, in his admirable work, on Evidence, vol. i. sec. 13, Professor Greenleaf remarks, that, in both civil and criminal cases, "*a verdict may well be founded on circumstances alone; and these often lead to a conclusion, far more satisfactory than direct evidence can produce.*"

The errors, committed by the Judges, upon the trial of the Boorns—and those errors were egregious—were twofold—the admission of extra-judicial confessions, manifestly extorted by hope and fear—and suffering a conviction to take place, before the dead body of the person, alleged to have been murdered, had been discovered.

The rule, on the subject of confessions, is sufficiently plain. *"Deliberate confessions of guilt,"* says Mr. Greenleaf, ibid. sec. 215, "are among the most effectual proofs in the law." But they should be received and weighed with caution; for, as he remarks, sec. 214—"it should be recollected, that the mind of the prisoner himself, is oppressed by the calamity of his situation, and that he is often influenced by motives of hope or fear, to make an untrue confession." Mr. Greenleaf then proceeds to say, in a note on this passage—"of this character was the remarkable case of the two Boorns," &c., and proceeds to give a summary of the case.

"In the United States," says Mr. Greenleaf, ibid. sec. 217, "the prisoner's confession, when the *corpus delicti* is not otherwise proved, has been held insufficient, for his conviction; and this opinion, certainly, best accords with the humanity of the criminal code, and with the great degree of caution, applied in receiving and weighing the evidence of confessions, in other cases; and it seems countenanced by approved writers, on this branch of the law."

Again, ibid. sec. 219, he remarks—"Before any confession can be received, in evidence, in a criminal case, it must be shown, that it was *voluntary.* * * * * 'A free and voluntary confession,' said Eyre, C. B., 'is deserving of the highest credit, because it is presumed to flow from the strongest sense of guilt, and therefore it is admitted as proof of the crime, to which it refers; but a confession forced from the mind, by the flattery of hope, or by the torture of fear, comes in so questionable a shape, when it is to be considered as the evidence of guilt, that no credit ought to be given to it; and therefore it is rejected.'" Unfortunately, Judges Chace and Doolittle thought otherwise; and brought themselves and the condemned, upon the very threshold of a terrible catastrophe.

Mr. Greenleaf, in the note, above referred to, alludes to an article, in the North American Review, vol. 10, p. 418, in which this case of the Boorns is examined. It was from the pen of a gentleman, whose high professional prospects were blasted, by an early death. This writer had seen nothing, however, but *"a very imperfect report of the trial."* His article was published, in April, 1820, about four months after the discovery of Colvin. The conclusions, at which he arrives, that the confessions ought not to have been admitted, would have gained additional strength, had he inspected the *certified minutes*, taken on the trial, by the Chief Justice.

Had he seen those certified minutes of the evidence, he would scarcely have described the utter inconsistency of the two confessions, by the inadequate phrase—"*there are differences between them*:" for Stephen's claims the whole act of killing to himself—while Jesse's charges the father, who was notoriously not present, with cutting Colvin's throat, while he was yet living, and after Stephen had given him a blow.

This writer relies strongly, upon the humane caution of Sir Matthew Hale, to which I have alluded, that no conviction in case of murder or manslaughter should ever take place, till the fact were proved—or the dead body had been discovered.

A perfect horror of induction seems to have settled down, like a dense cloud, upon the southwestern corner of Vermont. Judges and jurymen appear to have been stupefied, by its power. The important *consequence*, vital to the whole, they assumed to be true, without trial or experiment. I have looked, attentively, into every document, that I could lay my hands upon, connected with this subject; and I cannot discover, that any effort whatever was made, by any one, *till after the trial*, to discover the *living* body of Colvin. The interesting ramble of Jesse and Judge Skinner, upon the mountain, was in search of Colvin's *dead* body! But, upon the publication of the notice, in the Rutland Herald, Nov. 26, 1819, stating the facts, and calling for information, in regard to Colvin, and a similar notice, of the same date, in the New York Evening Post—in ten days, that is, Dec. 6, the most ample and satisfactory information was published, by Mr. Taber Chadwick, in regard to the *living* body of Russell Colvin!

The great caution of Sir Matthew Hale was meant, not less for the prisoner, than for the whole community; no one of whom can be sure, through a long life, of escaping from the oppressive influence of circumstances, accidentally, or purposely, combined against him. His *discreet* humanity spread no mantle of imitation charity or morbid philanthropy over the guilty. He was a bold practitioner—too bold, by far, occasionally, as in the case of Cullender and Duny. But this great, good man, well knew, that prisoners, charged with murder, were entitled to all the benefit of *reasonable* doubt. He well knew, that no judicial caution could go farther, to save, than the fierce suspicion of an excited community would go, to destroy. He well knew, that, with not a small number, the very enormity of the crime seems to supply the want of legal evidence; and, that, in many cases, to be suspected is to be condemned. We have all heard of the jury, who, having convicted a prisoner of murder, in direct opposition to the Judge's instructions, and being questioned and reproved—replied, that an enormous crime had been committed, and ought to be atoned for; and they saw no good reason, why the prisoner, the only person *suspected*, should not be selected, as the victim!

Sir Matthew Hale's forbearance extended to cases of reprieve, after conviction, before another judge. Thus in H. P. C., vol. ii. ch. lvi., he says—"I have generally observed this rule, that I would never give judgment, or award execution, upon a person, reprieved by any other judge but myself, because I could not know, upon what ground or reason he reprieved him."

Upon this, there is the following pertinent note—"The usefulness of this caution may be seen, from what is observed, by Sir John Hawles, in his remarks on Cornish's trial, where he relates the case of some persons, who had been convicted of the murder of a person absent, barely by inferences from foolish words and actions; but the judge, before whom it was tried, was so unsatisfied in the matter, because the body of the person, supposed to be murdered, was not to be found, that he reprieved the persons condemned; yet, in a circuit afterwards, a certain unwary judge, without inquiring into the reasons of the reprieve, ordered execution, and the persons to be hanged in chains, which was done accordingly; and afterwards, to his reproach, the person, supposed to be murdered, appeared alive."

The death of the person, alleged to have been murdered, is, manifestly, not less a constituent part of the crime, than the malice prepense, or the employment of the means. These three things are necessary to constitute murder, in the eye of the law. Thus, an acquittal has taken place, where the *murder* was alleged to have been committed, *on the high seas*; and the *malice* and the *blow* only were proved to have occurred *on the high seas*—and the *death*, in the harbor of Cape François. Such was the case of the U. S. against McGill, reported in Dallas. This extreme particularity appears, to some persons, exceedingly ridiculous; but not quite as much so, as certain commentaries, upon legal proceedings which we sometimes meet with, in the ordinary journals of the day.

Aaron Burr, whom I desire not to quote, too frequently, once shrewdly remarked—"*he, who despises forms, knows not what he despises.*" To infer the death, from the malice, and the employment of the means, in all cases, would be absurd. If one man maliciously knocks another into the sea, here is, certainly, a violent assault and battery—perhaps an assault with intent to kill. But, before we join, in the popular *hutesium et clamor*, we have two important points to settle, beyond all *reasonable* doubt—first, if the person, knocked overboard, be dead, for he may have swum to land, or have been picked up, at sea, alive, in which case, unless he die of the blow, within the time prescribed, there can be neither murder nor manslaughter. And, secondly, if he be proved to have died of the injury within that time, we must duly weigh the previous circumstances and the provocation, to ascertain, if the act done be manslaughter or murder.

Those, who vociferate, most loudly, against the law, for its hesitancy, and demand the immediate descent of the executioner's axe, upon the neck of the victim, will be the very first fervently to supplicate, for the law's most merciful carefulness of life, should a father, a brother, or a son be charged with crime, and involved in the complicated meshes of presumptive evidence.

No. LXXXVI

The transition state, when the confidence of youth begins to give place to that wholesome distrust, which is the usual—by no means, the invariable—accompaniment of riper years, is often a state of disquietude and pain. It is no light matter to look upon the visions of our own superiority, and imaginary importance, as they break, like bubbles, one after another, and leave us abundantly convinced, that we are of yesterday, and know nothing.

The confidence of ignorance, however venial in youth, is not altogether so excusable, in full grown men. Its exhibitions, however ridiculous and absurd, are daily manifested, by mankind, in relation to those arts and sciences, which have little or nothing in common with their own respective vocations. The physician, the lawyer, the clergyman, the deeper they descend into their respective, professional wells, where truth is proverbially said to abide, proceed with increasing caution. Yet it is quite amazing, to witness the boldness, with which they dive into the very depths, that lie entirely beyond their professional precincts. The physician, who proceeds, in the cure of bodies, with the extremest caution, seems to be quite at home, in the cure of souls; and has very little doubt or difficulty, upon points, which have perplexed the brains of Hale and Mansfield. The lawyer, who, in his own department, moves warily; weighs evidence with infinite care; and consults authorities, with great deliberation—looks upon physic and theology, as rather speculative matters, and of easy acquirement. The clergyman frequently practises physic gratuitously; and holding the doctrine in perfect contempt, that the *viginti studia annorum* are necessary to make a tolerable lawyer, he rather opines, that, as *majus implicat minus*, so his knowledge of the Divine law necessarily comprehends a perfect knowledge of mere human jurisprudence.

This confidence of ignorance is nowhere more perfectly, or more briefly, expressed, than in four oft-repeated lines, in Pope's Essay on Criticism:

> "A *little* learning is a dangerous thing;
> Drink deep, or taste not the Pierian spring:

These shallow draughts intoxicate the brain,
And drinking largely sobers us again."

The editors of public journals are, in many instances, men of education and highly respectable abilities—men of taste and learning—men of integrity, and refinement, cherishing a just regard for the rights of individuals, and of the community. There is a very different class of men, who, however incompetent to improve the minds or the manners of the public, have a small smattering of knowledge; hold a reckless, rapid pen; and, by the aid of the scavengers, whom they employ, to rake the gutters for slander and obscenity, cater, daily, to the foulest appetites of mankind. There are some, who descend not thus, to the very nadir of all filth and corruption, but whose columns, nevertheless, are ever open, like the mouths of so many *cloacæ*, for the filthy contributions of every dirty depositor; and who are ever on hand, like the Scotch cloak-man, in *Auld Reekie*, to serve the occasions of a customer.

The very phraseology of the craft has a tendency to the amplification of an editor; and to give confirmation to the confidence of ignorance. The broken merchant, the ambitious weaver, the briefless lawyer, the literary tailor are speedily sunk, in "*we*," and "*our sheet*," and "*our columns*," and "*our-self.*"

This confidence of ignorance has rarely been manifested, more extensively, upon any occasion, than in connection with the indictment, trial, and condemnation of Dr. Webster, for the murder of Dr. George Parkman.

The indictment was no sooner published, than three *religious* journals began to criticise this *legal* instrument, which had been carefully, and, as the decision of the learned Chief Justice and of the Court has decided, sufficiently, prepared, by the Attorney General of the Commonwealth. This indictment contained several counts, a thing by no means unusual, the object of which is well understood, by professional men. "If the crime was committed with a knife, or with the fists, how could it be committed with a hammer?" It would not be an easy task to convince these worthy ministers of the Gospel, how exceedingly ridiculous such commentaries appear, to men of any legal knowledge.

Judge, Jurymen, and Counsellors are severely censured, for the parts they have borne, in the trial and condemnation of Dr. Webster. By whom? By the editors of certain far-away journals, upon the evidence, *as it has reached them*. The evidence has been very variously reported. A portion of the evidence, however deeply graven upon the hearts, and minds, and memories of the highly respectable jury, and of the court, and of the multitude, present at the trial, is, from its peculiar nature, not transferable. I refer to the appearance, the air, the manner, the voice of the prisoner, especially, when, in opposition to the advice of his counsel, he fatally opened his mouth, and said precisely nothing, that betokened innocence.

I do not believe there was ever, in the United States, a more impartial trial, more quietly conducted, than this trial of Dr. Webster. Party feeling has had no lot, nor share, in this matter. The whole dealing has been calmly and confidingly surrendered to the laws of the land. With scarcely an exception, from the moment of arrest to the hour of trial, the public journals, in this vicinity, have borne themselves, with great forbearance to the prisoner. The family connexions of Dr. Parkman have held themselves scrupulously aloof, unless summoned to bear witness to facts, within their knowledge.

It has been asserted, in one or more journals, that even the body of Dr. Parkman has not been discovered. The reply is short, and germain—the coroner's jury, twenty-four grand jurors, and twelve jurors in the Supreme Judicial Court have decided, that the mutilated remains were those of the late George Parkman; and that John White Webster was his murderer; and the Court has gravely pronounced the opinion, that the verdict is a righteous verdict, and in accordance with the law and the evidence. This opinion appears to meet with a very general, affirmative response, in this quarter. The jury—and the members of that panel, one and all, after twelve days' concentration of thought, upon this solemn question of life and death, appear to have been conscientious men—the jury have not recommended the prisoner, as a person entitled to mercy.

In view of all this, the editor of a distant, public journal may be supposed to entertain a pretty good opinion of his qualifications, who ventures to pronounce his ex-cathedral decree, either that Dr. Webster is innocent, or, if guilty, that, on technical grounds, he has been illegally convicted. There is something absolutely melancholy in the contemplation of such presumption as this. But, under all the circumstances of this heart-sickening occurrence, it is impossible to behold, without a smile, the extraordinary efforts of some exceedingly benevolent people, in the city of New York, who are circulating a petition to the Governor of Massachusetts, not merely for a commutation of punishment, but for a pardon. This, to speak of it forbearingly, may be safely catalogued among the works of supererogation.

If the Governor of Massachusetts needs any guidance from man, upon the present occasion, his Council is at hand. The highest judicial tribunal of the Commonwealth, entirely approving the verdict of an impartial and intelligent jury, has sentenced Dr. Webster to be hung, for a murder, as foul and atrocious, as was ever perpetrated, within the borders of New England. Talents, education, rank aggravate the criminality of the guilty party. "To kill a man, upon sudden and violent resentment, is less penal than upon cool deliberate malice."

If there be any substantial reasons, for pardon or commutation of punishment—any new matter, which has not been exhibited, before the court and jury—those reasons will be duly weighed—that matter will be gravely considered, by the Governor and Council. But, if the objections to the execution of the sentence, upon the present occasion, rest upon any imaginary misdirection, on the part of the Court, or any misunderstanding, on the part of the jury, those objections must be unavailing. After a careful comparison of the evidence, in the case of Dr. Webster, with the evidence, in the case of Jason Fairbanks, who was executed, for the murder of Betsy Fales, the *concatena*—the chain of circumstances—seems even less perfect in the latter case. Yet, after sentence, in that memorable trial, Chief Justice Dana, who sat in judgment, upon that occasion, was reported to have said, that he believed Fairbanks to be the murderer, more firmly, upon the evidence before the court, than he should have believed the very same thing, upon the evidence of his own eyesight, in a cloudy day—the first could not have deceived him—the latter might.

If an application, for pardon or commutation, be grounded, on the objection to all capital punishment, that objection has been too recently disposed of, in the case of Washington Goode. The majesty of the law, the peace of society, the decree of Almighty God call for impartial justice—whoso sheddeth man's blood by man shall his blood be shed!

With the eye of mercy turned upon all—aye upon all—who have any relation to the murderer, the better course is Christian submission to the decrees of God and man. What may be the value of a few more years of misery and contempt! God's high decree, that the murderer shall die, is merciful and just. His judgment upon Cain was far more severe—not that he should die—but *that he should live!*—that he should walk the earth, and wear the brand of terrible distinction forever—"*And now thou art cursed from the earth, which hath opened her mouth to receive thy brother's blood from thy hand. When thou tillest the ground, it shall not henceforth yield unto thee her strength; a fugitive and a vagabond shalt thou be upon the earth. And Cain said unto the Lord, my punishment is greater than I can bear. Behold thou hast driven me out, this day, from the face of the earth; and from thy face shall I be hid; and I shall be a fugitive and a vagabond in the earth; and it shall come to pass, that every one that findeth me shall slay me. And the Lord said unto him, therefore whosoever slayeth Cain, vengeance shall be taken on him seven fold. And the Lord set a mark upon Cain, lest any one finding him should slay him."*

No. LXXXVII

It may be said of a proud, poor man—especially, if he be a fearless, godless man, as Dirk Hatteraick said of himself, to Glossin—that he is *"dangerous."* It is quite probable, there are men, even in our own limited community, of an hundred and thirty thousand souls, who would rather die an easy death, than signify abroad their inability to maintain, any longer, their expensive relations to the fashionable world.

What will not such a man occasionally do, rather than submit gracefully, under such a trial, to the will of God? He will beg, and he will borrow—he will lie, and he will steal. Is there a crime, in the decalogue, or out of it, which he will not, occasionally, perpetrate, if its consummation be likely to save him from a confession of his poverty, and from ceasing to fill his accustomed niche, in the *beau monde*? Not one—*no, not one!*

Well may we, who profess to be Republicans, adopt the wisdom and the words of Montesquieu—*"The less luxury there is in a Republic, the more it is perfect. * * * * Republics end with luxury."*

A significant illustration of these remarks will readily occur, to every reader of American History, in the conduct and character of Benedict Arnold. Among the dead, who, with their own hands, have prepared themselves graves of infamy, there are men of elevated rank, who have made shipwreck of the fairest hopes, in a similar manner. But, far in advance of them all, Arnold is entitled to a terrible preëminence.

The last turn of the screw crushes the victim—it is the last feather, say the Bedouins, that breaks the camel's back—and the train, which has been in gradual preparation for many years, may be exploded, in an instant, by a very little spark, at last.

There are periods, in the lives of certain individuals, when, upon the approach of minor troubles—baleful stars, doubtless, but of the third or fourth magnitude—it may be said, as Rochefoucault said of the calamities of our friends, that there is something in them, not particularly disagreeable to us. A man, whose afflictions, especially when self-induced, are chafing, at every turn, against his already lacerated pride, and who is seeking some apology, for deeds of desperation, often discovers, with a morbid satisfaction, in some petty offence, or imaginary wrong, ample excuse, for deeds, absolutely damnable.

Such were the influences, at work, in the case of Benedict Arnold. In 1780, in obedience to the sentence of a court martial, he was reprimanded by the Commander-in-Chief; but in terms so highly complimentary, that it is impossible to read them, without a doubt, whether this official reprimand were a crown of thorns, or a crown of glory. At that very time, Arnold's pecuniary embarrassments were overwhelming. Without the rightful means of supporting a one-horse chaise, he rattled up and down, in the city of Philadelphia, in a chariot and four. The splendid mansion, which he occupied, had, in former times, been the residence of the Penns. Here he gave a sumptuous repast to the French ambassador, and entertained the minister and his suite, for several days.

Hunger, it is said, will break through stone walls; even this is a feeble illustration of that force and energy, which characterized Arnold's *passion* for parade. To support his career of unparalleled extravagance and folly, he resorted to stratagems, which would have been contemptible, in a broker of the lowest grade—petty traffic and huckstering speculation—the sale of permits, to do certain things, absolutely forbidden—such were among the last, miserable shifts of this "brave, wicked" man, when his conscience came between the antagonist muscles of poverty and pride. For some of these very offences, he had been condemned, by the court martial. Even then, he had secretly become, at heart, a scoundrel and a renegade; and, covertly, under a feigned name, had already tendered his services to the enemy.

The sentence of the court, sheer justice, but so graciously mingled with mercy, as scarcely to wear the aspect of punishment, supplied him with the very thing he coveted—a pretence, for complaining of injustice and oppression. He sought the French ambassador; and, after a plain allusion to his own needy condition, shadowed forth, in language, not to be mistaken, his willingness to become the secret servant of France. The prompt reply of the French minister is of record, most honorable for himself, and sufficiently humiliating to the spirit of the applicant.

The result is before the world—Arnold became a traitor, detested by those, whose cause he had forsaken, and utterly despised by those, whose cause he affected to espouse—trusted by them, only, because they well knew he might safely be employed against an enemy, who would deal with him, if captured, not as a prisoner of war, but as a traitor. I have, thus briefly, alluded to the career of Arnold, only for the purpose of illustration.

No truth is more simple—none more firmly established by experience—none more universally disregarded—than, that the growth of luxury must work the overthrow of a republic. As the largest masses are made up of the smallest particles, so the characteristic luxury of a whole people consists of individual extravagance and folly. The ambition to be foremost becomes, ere long, the ruling, and almost universal, passion—in still stronger language, *"it is all the rage."* In a certain condition of society, talent takes precedence of virtue, and men would rather be called knaves than fools: and, where luxury abounds, as the poorer and the middling classes will imitate the wealthier, there must be a large amount of indebtedness, and many men and women of desperate fortunes. We cannot strut about, in unpaid-for garments, nor ride about, in unpaid-for chariots, nor gather the world together, to admire unpaid-for furniture, without an inward sense of personal degradation.

It would be a poor compliment to our race, to deny the truth of this assertion. True or false, the argument goes steadily forward—for, if not true, then that callous, case-hardened condition of the heart exists, which takes off all care for the common weal, and turns it entirely upon one's self, and one's own aggrandizement. Nothing can be more destructive of that feeling of independence, which ever lies, at the bottom of republican virtue.

This condition of things is the very hot-bed of hypocrisy,—and it makes the heart a forcing-house, for all the evil and bitter passions, envy, hatred, malice, and all uncharitableness. Pastors, of all denominations, may well unite, in the chorus of the churchman's prayer, and cry aloud—*Good Lord deliver us!*

A very fallacious and mischievous estimate of personal array, equipage, and furniture has always given wonderful preëminence to this species of emulation. It is perfectly natural withal. Distinction, of some sort, is uppermost, in most men's minds. It is comforting to many to know there is a *tapis*—*"the field of the cloth of gold"*—on which the wealthy fool is more than a match, for the poor, wise man; and, as this world contains such an overwhelming majority of the former class, the ayes have it, and luxury holds on, *vires acquirens eundo.*

None but an idiot will cavil, because a rich man adorns his mansion, with elegance and taste, and receives his friends in a style of liberal hospitality. Even if he go beyond the bounds of republican simplicity, and waste his substance, it matters not, beyond the circle of his creditors and heirs; if the example be not followed by thousands, who are unable, or unwilling, to be edified, by Æsop's pleasant fable of the ox and the frog.

But it never can be thus. The machinery is exceedingly simple, in these manufactories, from which men of broken fortunes are annually turned out upon the world.

When once involved in the whirl of fashion, extrication is difficult and painful—the descent is wonderfully easy—*sed revocare gradum*! The maniac hugs not his fetters, more forcibly, than the devotee of fashion clings, with the assistance, occasionally, of his better half, to his *position in society.*

These remarks are, by no means, exclusively applicable to those, who move in the higher circles. This is a world of gradation, and there are few so humble, as to be entirely without their imitators.

What shall we do to be saved? This anxious inquiry is not always offered, I apprehend, in relation to the concerns of a better world. How often, and how oppressively, the spirit of this interrogatory has agitated the bosom of the impoverished man of fashion! What shall I do to be saved, from the terrible disgrace of being exposed, in the court of fashion, as being guilty of the awful crime of *poverty*, and disfranchised, as one of the *beau monde*? And what will he not do, to work out this species of salvation, with fear and trembling? We have seen how readily, under the influence of pride and poverty, treason may be committed by men of lofty standing. It would be superfluous, therefore, to inquire, if there be any crime, which men, heavily oppressed by their embarrassments, and restrained thereby, from drinking more deeply of that luxury, with which they are already drunk, will hesitate to commit.

No. LXXXVIII

There is a popular notion, that sumptuary laws are applicable to monarchies—not to republics. The very reverse is the truth. Montesquieu says, Spirit of Laws, book vii. ch. 4, that *"luxury is extremely proper for monarchies, and that, under this government, there should be no sumptuary laws."*

Sumptuary laws are looked upon, at present, as the relics of an age gone by. These laws, in a strict sense, are designed to restrain pecuniary extravagance. It has often been attempted to stigmatize the wholesome, prohibitory laws of the several States, in regard to the sale of intoxicating liquor, by calling them *sumptuary laws*. The distinction is clear—sumptuary laws strike at the root of extravagance—the prohibitory, license laws, as they are called, strike, not only at the root of extravagance, but at the root of every crime, in the decalogue.

The *leges sumptuariæ* of Rome were numerous. The Locrian law limited the number of guests, and the Fannian law the expense, at festivals. The Didian law extended the operation of all these laws over Italy.

The laws of the Edwards III., and IV., and of Henry VIII., against shoes with long points, short doublets, and long coats, were not repealed, till the first year of James I. Camden says, that, "in the time of Henry IV., it was proclaimed, that no man should wear shoes, above six inches broad, at the toes." He also states, "that their other garments were so short, that it was enacted, 25 Edward IV., that no person, under the condition of a lord, should wear any mantle or gown, unless of such length, that, standing upright, it might cover his buttocks."

Diodorus Siculus, lib. xii. cap. 20, gives an amusing account of the sumptuary laws of Zeleucus, king of the Locrians. His design appears to have been to accomplish his object, by casting ridicule upon those practices, against which his laws were intended to operate. He decreed, that no free woman should have more than one maid to follow her, unless she was drunk; nor should she stir out of the city by night, nor wear jewels of gold, or an embroidered gown, unless she was a professed strumpet. No men, but ruffians, were allowed to wear gold rings, nor to be seen, in one of those effeminate vests of the manufacture of Miletum.

The very best code of sumptuary laws is that, which may be found in the common sense of an enlightened community. Nothing, that I have ever met with, upon this subject, appears more just, than the sentiments of Michael De Montaigne, vol. i. ch. 43—"The true way would be to beget in men a contempt of silks and gold, as vain and useless; whereas we add honor and value to them, which sure is a very improper way to create disgust. For to enact, that none but princes shall eat turbot, nor wear velvet or gold lace, and interdict these things to the people, what is it, but to bring them into greater esteem, and to set every one more agog to eat and wear them?"

No truth has been more amply demonstrated, than that a republic has more to fear from internal than from external causes—less from foreign foes, than from enemies of its own household.

To the ears of those, who have not reflected upon the subject, it may sound like the croaking note of some ill boding *ab ilice cornix*—but I look upon extravagant parade, and princely furniture of foreign manufacture, the introduction of courtly customs, transatlantic servants in livery, *et id genus omne nugarum*, as so many premonitory symptoms of national evil— as part and parcel of that luxury, which may justly be called the gangrene of a republic.

But does any one seriously fear, that an extravagant fandango, now and then, will lead to revolution, or produce a change in our political institutions? Probably not. But it will provoke a spirit of rivalry—of emulation, not unmingled with bitterness, and which will cost many an aspirant a great deal more, than he can afford. It will lead the community to turn their dwellings into baby houses, and to gather vast assemblies together, not for the rational purposes of social intercourse, but for the purpose of exhibiting their costly toys and imported baubles. It will tend to harden the heart; and render us more and more insensible to the cries of the poor; for whose keen occasions we cannot afford one dollar, having, just then, perhaps, invested a thousand, in some glittering absurdity. It will, ultimately, produce numerous examples of poverty, and fill the community with desperate men.

The line of distinction, between the liberality of a patrician and the flashy, offensive ostentation of a parvenu, at Rome, or at Athens, was as readily perceived, as the difference between the manners of a gentleman, and those of a clown.

Every rank of society, like the troubled sea, casts forth upon the strand, from year to year, its full proportion of wrecked adventurers—men, who have gone beyond their depth; lived beyond their means; and who cherish no care, *ne quid detrimenti Respublica caperet*; but, on the contrary, who are quite ready for oligarchy, or monarchy; and some of whom would prefer even anarchy, to their present condition of obscurity and poverty.

Law and order are of the first importance to every proprietor; for, on their preservation, the security of his property depends; but they are of no importance to those, who are thus, virtually, denationalized, through impoverishment, produced by a career of luxury. Such, if not already the component elements of Empire clubs, are always useless, and often dangerous men.

It was a well known saying of Jefferson's, that *great cities* were *great sores*. "In proportion," says Montesquieu, "to the populousness of towns, the inhabitants are filled with notions of vanity, and actuated by an ambition of distinguishing themselves, by trifles. If they are very numerous, and most of them strangers to one another, their vanity redoubles, because there are greater hopes of success." According to the apothegm of Franklin, it is the eyes of others, and not our own, that destroy us.

"Every body agrees," says Mandeville in his Fable of the Bees, i. 98, "that, as to apparel and manner of living, we ought to behave ourselves suitable to our conditions, and follow the example of the most sensible and prudent, among our equals in rank and fortune; yet how few, that are not either universally covetous, or else proud of singularity, have this discretion to boast of? We all look above ourselves, and, as fast as we can, strive to imitate those that, some way or other, are superior to us."

"The poorest laborer's wife in the parish, who scorns to wear a strong wholesome frize, will half starve herself and her husband, to purchase a second-hand gown and petticoat, that cannot do her half the service, because, forsooth, it is more genteel. The weaver, the shoemaker, the tailor, the barber, has the impudence, with the first money he gets, to dress himself like a tradesman of substance; the ordinary retailer, in the clothing of his wife, takes pattern from his neighbor, that deals in the same commodity by wholesale, and the reason he gives for it is, that, twelve years ago, the other had not a bigger shop than himself. The druggist, mercer, and draper, can find no difference, between themselves and merchants, and therefore dress and live like them. The merchant's lady, who cannot bear the assurance of those mechanics, flies for refuge to the other end of the town, and scorns to follow any fashion, but what she takes from thence. This haughtiness alarms the court—the women of quality are frightened to see merchants' wives and daughters dressed like themselves. This impudence of the city, they cry, is intolerable; mantua-makers are sent for; and the contrivance of fashions becomes all their study, that they may have always new modes ready to take up, as soon as those saucy cits shall begin to imitate those in being. The same emulation is contrived through the several degrees of quality, to an incredible expense; till, at last, the prince's great favorites, and those of the first rank, having nothing else left, to outstrip some of their inferiors, are forced to lay out vast estates in pompous equipages, magnificent furniture, sumptuous gardens, and princely palaces."

Like an accommodating almanac, the description of Mandeville is applicable to other meridians, than that, for which it was especially designed.

The history of all, that passes in the bosom of a proud man, unrestrained by fixed religious and moral principles, during his transition from affluence to poverty, must be a very edifying history. With such an individual the fear of God is but a pack-thread, against the unrelaxing, antagonist muscle of pride. The only *Hades*, of which he has any dread, is that abyss of obscurity and poverty, in which a man is condemned to abide, who falls from his high estate, among the upper ten thousand. What plans, what projects, what infernal stratagems occasionally bubble up, in the overheated crucible! Magnanimity, and honor, and humanity, and justice are unseen—unfelt. The dust of self-interest has blinded his eyes—the pride of life has hardened his heart.

If the energies of such men are not mischievously employed, they are, at best, utterly lost to the community.

No. LXXXIX

I noticed, in a late, English paper, a very civil apology from Sheriff Calcraft, for not hanging Sarah Thomas, at Bristol, as punctually as he ought, on account of a similar engagement, with another lady, at Norwich. The hanging business seems to be *looking up* with us, as the traders say of their cotton and molasses; though, in England, it has fallen off prodigiously. According to Stowe, seventy-two thousand persons were executed there, in one reign, that of Henry VIII. That, however, was a long reign, of thirty-eight years. Between 1820 and 1830, there were executed, in England alone, seven hundred and ninety-seven convicts. But we must remember, for what trifles men were formerly executed *there*, which *here* were at no time, capital offences. According to authentic records, the decrease of executions in London, since 1820, is very remarkable. Haydn, in his Dictionary of Universal Reference, p. 205, gives the ratio of nine years, as follows—1820, 43—1825, 17—1830, 6—1835, none—1836, none—1837, 2—1838, none—1839, 2—1840, 1. There is a solution for this riddle—a key to this *lock*, which many readers may find it rather difficult to pick, without assistance. Before the first year, named by Haydn, 1820, Sir Samuel Romilly, who fell, by his own hand, in a fit of temporary derangement, in 1818, occasioned by the death of his wife, had published—not long before—his admirable pamphlet, urging a revision of the criminal code, and a limitation of capital punishment. In consequence of his exertions, and of those of Sir James Mackintosh afterwards, and more recently of Sir Robert Peel and others, a great change had taken place, *in the mode of punishment. Crime had not diminished*, in London—it was *differently dealt with.* I advise the reader, who desires light, upon this highly important and interesting subject, to read, with care, the entire article, from which I transcribe the following short passage—

"*The enormous number of our transported convicts—five thousand annually, for many years past—accompanied, at the same time, with a large increase of crime in general, would seem, prima facie, to be no very conclusive argument, in favor of the efficiency of the present system.*" Ed. Rev., v. 86, p. 257, 1847. "What shall be done with our criminals?" Such is the caption of the able article, to which I refer. Lord Grey, and the most eminent statesmen of Great Britain have been terribly perplexed, by this awful interrogatory.—Well: *we* are a very great people.—Dr. Omnibus, Squire Farrago, and Mrs. Negoose have no difficulty upon this point; and there is some thought in our society, of sending out Mrs. Negoose, in the next steamer, to have a conference with Lord Brougham. Lord Grey's plan was, after a short penitentiary confinement, to distribute the malefactors, among their own colonies, and among such other nations, as might be willing to receive them. Sending them to Canada, therefore, would be sending them, pretty directly, to the States. Dr. Omnibus is greatly surprised, that Lord Grey has never thought of building prisons of sufficient capacity to hold them all, since there are no more than five thousand transported, per annum, in addition to those, who have become tenants of prisons, for crimes, which are yet capital, in England, and for crimes, whose penalty is less than transportation.

It seems to be the opinion of the writer in the Edinburgh Review, whom I last quoted, that, under the anti-capital punishment system, there has been *"a large increase of crime in general."* This he states *as a fact.* Facts are stubborn things—so are Mrs. Negoose—Dr. Omnibus—and Squire Farrago. They contend, that our habits of life and education, and the great difference of our political institutions entirely nullify the British example. They show, with great appearance of truth, that the perpetrators of murder, rape, and other crimes, in our own country, are more religiously brought up, than the perpetrators of similar crimes, in Great Britain. The statistics, on this point, are curious and interesting. They present an imposing array of educated laymen, physicians, lawyers, bishops, priests, deacons, ruling elders, professors, and candidates, in the United States, who have been tried, for various crimes, by civil or ecclesiastical courts; deposed, or acquitted, on purely technical grounds; or sentenced to imprisonment, for a shorter or longer term, or to the gallows, and duly executed. Now we contend, that the ignorant felon, and such he is apt to be, in all countries, where there is but little diffusion of knowledge, and especially of religious knowledge, when again let loose upon the community, whether by a full pardon, or by serving out his term, returns, commonly, to his evil courses, as surely as the dog to his vomit, or the sow to her wallowing in the mire. But we find, that men of talent and education, and particularly men, who have figured, as preachers, and professors of religion, who commit any crime, in the decalogue, or out of it, become objects of incalculably deeper and stronger interest, with a certain portion of the community—after they repent, of course—which they invariably do, in an inconceivably short space of time. Thus, when strong liquor, and lust, and prelatical arrogance turn bishops, priests, and deacons, into brutes, and prodigals, and sometimes into murderers, they, *invariably,* excite an interest, which they never could have excited, by preaching their very best, to the end of their lives.

I have sometimes thought, that, in the matter of temperance, for which I cherish a cordial respect, a lecturer, as the performer is called, though the thing is not precisely an abstract science, cannot do a better thing, for himself and the cause, when he finds, that he is wearing out his welcome with the public, than to get pretty notoriously drunk. Depend upon it, he will come forth, purified from the furnace. He will take a new departure, for his temperance voyage. His deep-wrought penitence will enlist a very large part of the army of cold-water men, in his favor. A small sizzle will be of no use; but the drunker he gets, the more marvellous the hand of God will appear, in his restoration.

From these considerations, our Anti-Punishment Society reason onward, to the following conclusions: that, whatever the penalty imposed may be, deposition, imprisonment, or death, it is all wrong, radically wrong. For, thereby, the community is deprived, for a time, or forever, of the services of a true penitent. They all become penitent, if a little time be allowed, or they are persecuted innocents, which is better still.

Besides, how audacious, for mere mortals to lessen the sum total of joy, among the immortals! As religious men, who, when *misguided*, commit rape or murder, invariably repent, if there is any prospect of pardon; hanging may be supposed, in many cases, to prevent that great joy, which exists in Heaven—rather more than ninety-nine per cent.—over one sinner that repenteth.

To be convicted of some highly disgraceful or atrocious crime, or to be acquitted, upon some technical ground, though logically convicted, in the impartial chancel of wise and good men's minds, is not such a terrible thing, after all, for a vivacious bishop, priest, or deacon; provided, in the former case, he can contrive to escape the penalty. Such an one is sometimes more sure of a parish, than a candidate, of superior talents, and unspotted reputation. It is manifest, therefore, that a serious injury is done to society, by shutting up, for any great length of time, these penitent, misguided murderers, ravishers, &c., and, especially, by hanging them by the neck, till they are dead.

This phrase, *hanging by the neck, till they are dead*, imports something more, than some readers are aware of. It was not uncommon, in former times, for culprits to come—*usque ad*—to the gallows, and be there pardoned, with the halter about their necks. Occasionally, also, criminals were actually hung, the halter having been so mercifully adjusted, as not to break their necks, and then cut down, and pardoned. Of thirty-two gentlemen, traitors, who were taken, in the reign of Henry VI., 1447, after Gloucester's death, five were drawn to Tyburn on a hurdle, hanged, cut down alive, marked with a knife for quartering, and then spared, upon the exhibition of a pardon. This matter is related, in Rymer's Fœdera, xi. 178; also by Stowe, and by Rapin, Lond. ed. 1757, iv. 441.

We are a cruel people. Our phraseology has become softened, but our practice is merciless, and our lawgivers are Dracos, to a man. When a poor fellow, urged by an impulse, which he cannot resist, seizes upon the wife or the daughter of some unlucky citizen, commits a rape upon her person, and then takes her life to save his own—and what can be more natural, for all that a man hath will he give for his life—with great propriety, we call this poor fellow a *misguided man*. This is as it should be. He certainly committed a mistake. No doubt of it. But are we not all liable to mistakes? We call him a *misguided man*, which is a more Christian phrase than to say, in the coarser language of the law, that he was *instigated by the devil*. But, nevertheless, we hang this *misguided* man by the neck, till he is dead. How absurd! How unjust!

A needy wanderer of the night breaks into the house of some rich, old gentleman; robs his dwelling; breaks his skull, *ex abundanti cautela*; and sets fire to the tenement; thus combining burglary, murder, and arson. He well knew, that ignorance was bliss; and that the neighborhood would be happier, in the belief, that accident was at the bottom of it all, than that such enormities had been committed, in their midst. Instead of calling this individual, by all the hard names in an indictment, we charitably style him an *unfortunate person*—provided he is caught and convicted—if not, he deems himself a *lucky fellow*, of course. Now, can anything be more barbarous, than to hang this *unfortunate person*, upon a gallows!

A desperate debtor rouses the indignation of a disappointed creditor, by selling to another, as unincumbered, the very property, which had been transferred, as collateral security, to himself. Irritated by the creditor's reproaches, and alarmed by his menaces of public exposure, the debtor decides to escape, from these compound embarrassments, by taking the life of his pursuer. He affects to be prepared for payment; and summons the creditor, to meet him, at a *convenient* place, where he is *quite at home*, and at a *convenient* hour, when he is *quite alone*—*bringing with him the evidences of the debt*. He kills this troublesome creditor. He is suspected—arrested—charged with murder—indicted—tried—defended, as ably as he can be, by honorable men, oppressed by the consciousness of their client's guilt—and finally convicted. He made no attempt, by inventing a tale of angry words and blows, to merge this murder, in a case of manslaughter: for, before his arrest, and when he fancied himself beyond the circle of suspicion, he had *framed the tale*, and reduced it to writing, in the form of a brief, portable memorandum, found upon his person. *He had paid the creditor, who hastily grasped the money and departed—returning to perform the unusual office of dashing out the debtor's name from a note delivered up, on payment, into the debtor's possession!* Thus he cut short all power to fabricate a case of manslaughter.

Why charge such a man with *malice prepense*? Why say, that he was *instigated by the devil*? Not so; he was an *unfortunate, misguided, unhappy* man. And yet the judges, with perfect unanimity, have sentenced this unhappy man to be hanged! The liberties of the people appear to be in danger; and it is deeply to be deplored, that those gentlemen of various crafts, who are sufficiently at leisure, to sit in judgment, upon the judges themselves, have not appellate jurisdiction, in these high matters, with power to invoke the assistance of the Widow's society, or some other male, or female, auxiliary *ne sutor ultra crepidam* society.

Footnotes:

[1] The palpable reluctance of Mr. Macaulay to deal in liberal construction, and to award the smallest praise, on such occasions, is not confined to Penn. A writer in Blackwood's Magazine, for October, 1849, page 509, after referring to the glorious defeat of the Dutch fleet, off Harwich, when the Duke of York, afterwards James II., commanded in person, remarks—"Mr. Macaulay, in his late published *History of England*, has not deigned even to notice this engagement—a remarkable omission, the reason of which omission it is foreign to our purpose to inquire. This much we may be allowed to say, that no historian, who intends to form an accurate estimate of the character of James II., or to compile a complete register of his deeds, can justly accomplish his task, without giving that unfortunate monarch the credit for his conduct and intrepidity, in one of the most important and successful naval actions, which stands recorded, in our annals."

Other English historians have related it. Hume, Oxford ed. 1826, vol. vii. page 355—Smollett, Lond. ed. 1759, vol. viii. page 31.—Rapin, Lond. ed. 1760,. vol. xi. page 272. "The Duke of York," says Smollett, "was in the hottest part of the battle, and behaved with great spirit and composure, even when the Earl of Falmouth, the Lord Muskerry, and Mr. Boyle, were killed at his side, by one cannon ball, which covered him with the blood and brains of these three gallant gentlemen."

[2] The editor of the New York Sun, *under date, Jan. 25, 1850*, says—"Yesterday, we were waited on, by the Rev. Lemuel Haynes, of this city, the person, who, convinced of the innocence of the condemned parties, aided in finding the man, supposed to be murdered."—The Sun must have been under a total eclipse. This very worthy man, the Rev. Lemuel Haynes, who figured, honorably for himself, in the affair of the Boorns, was born July 18, 1753, and died Sept. 28, 1833, at the age of 80—as the gentleman, who conducts the chariot of the Sun, will discover, by turning to Cooley's "Sketches of the life and character of the Rev. Lemuel Haynes, N. Y. 1839," p. 312. Some dark object must have passed before the editor's eye.